CHAPTER 1

1 NOVEMBER

The invitation reproached them from the mantelshelf.

'We'll have to go,' said Harriet with a mixture of gloom and shame, hand creeping out to the Turkish delight beside her.

The gloom was in anticipation of the inevitable ghastliness of it all; the shame that she was unable to look upon the whole issue more benignly. She was a woman whose personal failings cut deep. Hester, less given to self-flagellation, grunted in agreement as she consulted her knitting pattern. Harriet returned to her jigsaw, painstakingly sifting through the pieces, myopic eyes inches from the box. Further words were unnecessary. The subject had been discussed to death over the years—this would be the fifth—and no permanent solution was ever forthcoming. One year they had pleaded Hester's sprained ankle, but George had driven over to collect them. Another year the downstairs toilet had fortuitously blocked the night before; phoning to cry off so that they could await the emergency plumber, they thought they had the perfect excuse, only for George to appear within the hour armed with a plunger, a latter-day Galahad to the rescue. Just once—last year, when they had both succumbed to flu—George and Isabelle had failed to winkle them from their fastness; instead they had snuggled down in their hot, tangled beds, creeping downstairs intermittently for Bovril (Hester) and hot chocolate (Harriet). The sisters recalled that Christmas with unalloyed pleasure. Bliss.

'Oh God, little nasties and gluhwein,' said Harriet with a moue of disgust; they both shuddered. Last year Isabelle had surpassed herself with the little nasties: undercooked vol-au-vents with a grey gloop that might have been mushroom but—horribly—transpired to be shrimps, shrivelled and veiny. Hester, who adored cooking, was convinced her cousin's wife possessed a sort of perverse genius to be able to produce such monstrosities year after year. She wondered that Isabelle didn't question the huge quantities of leftover food each time. Perhaps she really believed George's hearty reassurances: 'They'll have had a big breakfast, my darling. And they won't want to spoil their appetites for Christmas dinner.' Isabelle seemed blithely unaware of the discarded food secreted in plant pots and behind Christmas cards by all but the hardiest of guests. Hester and Harriet, scraping barely nibbled canapés into the bin, would avoid catching one another's eyes. Both would think of the wafer-thin smoked salmon and chilled champagne nestling intimately alongside each other in the fridge, the kitchen fragrant with the aroma of Hester's seeded loaf, still warm from the oven. Each would, with some difficulty, suppress a groan. The horror that was Isabelle's Christmas dinner still lay ahead. 'Another gluhwein?' George would invariably offer, detritus bobbing in the murky jug.

Hester poured them both a Tío Pepe. Sipping hers appreciatively, Harriet said, 'You never know, perhaps it will snow.' Their cottage, The Laurels, lay at the end of an unmade road, badly potholed, where ice formed at the slightest provocation and driving in the depths of winter was often excitingly hazardous. Hester snorted, and threw the newspaper at her sister in response. It slithered off Harriet's lap to lie at her feet, the headline screaming UNSEASONABLY WARM CHRISTMAS IN STORE, SAY FORECASTERS.

They both knocked back their sherries.

Their apparent ingratitude was made all the worse, at least in Harriet's slightly kindlier eyes, by the fact that George and Isabelle were such *good* people. Good people, kind people. Salt of the earth. Do anything for you. George, a loss adjuster, had clearly missed his vocation as a vicar. Isabelle taught children with behavioural difficulties, volunteered for the Samaritans once a week, mentored recovering drug addicts and was chair of their parish council. They were assiduous in helping elderly neighbours, doing their shopping or ferrying them to hospital appointments; they mowed the verges that rightly were the responsibility of the council because 'it kept the village tidy'; they stepped up to every conceivable plate. The sisters had often mused that George and Isabelle might well be the blueprints for the Big Society, whatever that was. Generous and big-hearted, the couple were unfailingly solicitous of their widowed cousins; from the moment Hester and

Harriet had so unwisely bought a cottage in the next village, George and Isabelle had decided that they need never want for company. They assumed that two sisters in late middle age (or so they liked to think of themselves), both released from the constraints of childless marriages within a few months of each other, must of necessity be prey to loneliness and isolation. So, benevolently but relentlessly, they tried to incorporate the pair into their chaotic household, issuing frequent invitations to Sunday lunch, to drinks parties and, of course, their Christmas Day gathering. Lovely, kind, thoughtful people. And so crushingly, toe-curlingly boring.

'Why does everyone assume we need looking after?' grumbled Hester. 'All we need is a bit of peace and quiet.' She saw Harriet's hand hovering over the Turkish delight again, sighed inwardly, but for once forbore to comment.

'All we need,' muttered Harriet, easing the edge of a cloud into place in her jigsaw, 'is a miracle.'

CHAPTER 2

25 DECEMBER

Christmas Day dawns mockingly bright. The sisters call greetings along the corridor to each other, then return to their favourite activities, Hester back into the thriller she had so unwillingly put aside last night, Harriet sinking again into her pillow for a celebratory snooze. By half past eleven, unable any longer to put off the inevitable, they are showered and standing in front of the long mirror in the hall.

'How do I look?' says Harriet.

'Dowdy,' says Hester.

'Excellent,' says her sister. This year, they have decided to see if they can appear so shabby and unkempt that their hosts will finally decide that—duty notwithstanding—they ought not to expose their friends and neighbours to their indigent and faintly repellent relations any longer.

'You've a far worse cardigan than that,' says Hester. 'The one you do the gardening in?'

Harriet struggles into a mud-coloured cardigan belonging to her late husband, a garment now bereft of buttons and sporting a multitude of moth holes. The sisters regard it for some moments.

'Trying too hard,' says Hester, shaking her head.

Reluctantly, Harriet reverts to the bobbly cable knit. 'Slippers?' she suggests.

'We're going for eccentric, not doolally,' snaps Hester.

She marches into the kitchen and flings open the fridge to gaze longingly at the Serrano ham, the Roquefort, the pressed partridge terrine. Her mouth floods with saliva. Grimly, she closes the door.

Harriet places a hand on her shoulder. 'Five hours,' she says. 'We can last five hours, can't we?' This year, they have decided that in addition to the batty old women routine they will eschew any alcoholic fortification until the ordeal is over. 'Pleasure delayed . . .' says Harriet and reaches for the car keys. 'Come on, let's get it over with.'

The car rattles and jounces down the lane. 'Your hair looks a bit tidy,' says Hester, ruffling Harriet's grey helmet. Harriet returns the compliment and the car weaves drunkenly from side to side as the sisters shriek with mock alarm. They are beginning to enjoy themselves in spite of what lies ahead. Harriet is secretly relieved that Hester has not repeated last year's experiment: a sizeable glass—or two—of whisky before they set out. The stiffener coupled with the inescapable gluhwein on an empty stomach had exacerbated Hester's customary acerbity so that within ten minutes she was berating some inoffensive tax inspector on the iniquities of double fuel duty. George had led her quietly away and deposited her in the spare bedroom, where she had promptly fallen asleep, leaving Harriet to spend the next few hours apologising for her and wrestling unaided with a mountainous portion of leathery turkey. A few days later, Isabelle had stuffed a leaflet through their door—*Do You Have a Problem with Alcohol? We Can Help!!!*—and crept away. The sisters had been offended less by the leaflet's sentiments than by its use of multiple exclamation marks.

They turn on to the main road and start to make their way through Pellington village. The narrow street is bumper to bumper with parked cars on both sides, the numbers swelled by visitors and relations. The same thought strikes them: are these festively decorated houses filled with other mean-spirited, ungrateful people just like them, also dreading the enforced jollity, the badly-cooked food, the ill-chosen wines? The thoughts remain unvoiced. Instead, Harriet says, 'Let's hope Ben is through that phase of his.'

Hester nods. Interaction between them and the boy is virtually non-existent, given his tendency to hunch perpetually over his mobile, texting furiously, stopping only to refuel or complain about his parents' latest transgression. Neither will easily forget their nephew's (strictly their second cousin, they *know*) explosion of rage two years earlier when he was given the wrong Ex-Box or Wee-Wee or whatever it was called. The appalled silence that greeted his eruption was only broken when he threw the offending item to the floor and ran from the room, swearing. 'Another Celebration?' George had asked, holding out the box of sweets with a shaking hand, while Isabelle dabbed at her eyes. They don't want a repeat of *that*.

By the village shop, they are forced to back up and reverse into a perilously small gap to allow a huge four-by-four to squeeze by. Reversing is not Harriet's strong point and it takes her several attempts. The driver, grim-faced with holiday cheer, surges away without any acknowledgement. Harriet winds down the window and yells, 'Not at all! Our pleasure! You moron!', just as the verger hurries around the corner on his way to St Peter's. The sisters, conscious that it has been many months since they have set foot in church, give a hurried wave, mouth 'Happy Christmas' and, as Harriet accelerates away, dissolve into snorts of mirth.

They are forced to a halt again on the edge of the village as a car careers out of an imposing or pretentious (depending on your taste) gateway, engine gunning, and roars up the hill.

'Peace on earth at the Wilsons' as per,' says Hester, with a little frisson of excitement. She secretly finds Teddy Wilson strangely attractive, despite his rackety reputation. It affords Harriet no little private amusement that her otherwise rather forbidding sister should entertain such *tendresse* for so shameless a reprobate, especially as she herself is wholly immune to his louche charms. It has occurred to her before that the answer to the attraction may lie in Hester's marriage to such a dull old stick as Gordon. Good old Gordon. Solid (if not stolid), utterly dependable and—oh goodness—so predictable. Harriet had marvelled at his patience and relentless good humour over the years, especially when his wife was at her most prickly. And, true to form, Gordon had died as he had lived: quickly and quietly of a particularly aggressive but mercifully mostly pain-free cancer that had carried him off in five short weeks. If only her poor

Jim had been so lucky: his protracted battle with emphysema had been torture for him to endure and her to watch. Sitting opposite her as he fought for breath in those last few terrible days, Hester had said across his wasted body, pinioned by starchy hospital sheets, 'They put animals down,' and, hurt as Harriet had been by her sister's bluntness, in her heart she had felt the same. Her grief, when he finally succumbed and slipped away, had been tempered with huge, guilty relief.

She comes back to the present to find Hester twisting around in her seat as the Wilsons' house disappears from view, saying, 'She'll be at the Dubonnet before he's changed into second. Should we . . .?' She gestures vaguely back towards the house from where they almost imagine they can hear Molly Wilson sobbing.

'Best not interfere,' says Harriet, trying to find first gear, suspecting that Hester's apparent concern owes more to schadenfreude than genuine compassion. 'Don't you just love Christmas?'

The car jumps forward and judders onwards. Fifty yards or so outside the village, they pass the disused bus shelter. Hester glances into the gloom, in case old Finbar the tramp is in there. *We'll pop down with some mince pies when we get back*, she thinks. It's become a Christmas tradition that goes a tiny way to assuage their joint if faint shame at their lack of neighbourliness. Besides, Finbar is always so appreciative. *And a can or two, the old devil.*

But Finbar isn't in there. There's just a bundle of . . .

'For heaven's sake, Harry!' She is catapulted forward, the seatbelt biting into her bony shoulder.

The car stalls, shuddering. There is a faint scorched electrical smell.

'Sorry, sorry,' says Harriet irritably, turning the key and trying various gears. 'I think it slipped into second somehow.'

Not for the first time, Hester regrets not learning to drive. Surely it can't be that difficult? Harriet's driving, always slightly unreliable, seems to be deteriorating. The car coughs into life, just as a faint noise erupts beside her: a cross between a cry and a whine. A cat? She peers into the darkness of the shelter as Harriet grinds the gearstick forward and starts to pull away. The noise recurs.

'Hang on, Harriet,' cries Hester. 'Pull in a minute, would you?'

The car drifts to a halt. 'What now?'

Hester reaches for the door handle. 'I just thought I heard . . . there's something in the shelter. I'll nip back and—'

But—rather as Hester had hoped she would not—Harriet has thrown the car into reverse and is steering an erratic path back towards the bus stop. Two cars pass them, horns blaring. *Harriet really ought to try turning around or, at the very least, use her mirrors when she reverses*, Hester thinks. They draw level with the shelter; Hester clambers out and approaches the heap on the seat. It's not big or smelly enough to be Finbar. She is nearly upon it and about to give it a poke when she hears the odd sound again. She's certain now: it's a cat mewing, or a kitten. And then the heap suddenly moves. A pale hand emerges from what she now sees to be a thin blanket, and yanks it higher over what she surmises is a head.

'Hello?' she says.

The body jerks even further back, cowering in the corner.

By now Harriet has joined her, oblivious to the irate drivers weaving around the car, abandoned a good yard from the kerb. Hester holds out both hands in a gesture of bewilderment and looks to her sister for guidance. Harriet reaches past her and, before Hester can stop her, gives the bundle a shake. 'Hello? Everything all right?'

For a moment, nothing happens. The women stand irresolutely half in and half out of the shelter, staring at the heap. Then the hand creeps out again and this time slowly pulls down the blanket until two terrified eyes appear, then a trembling mouth. As the blanket slithers off the shoulders, another face, tiny and crumpled, emerges blinking into the chill December air.

'Please,' says the girl. 'No trouble.'

The baby's tongue peeps out cautiously.

'Trouble?' says Harriet, transfixed. 'No ... we thought ... are you all right?'

'All right, yes,' says the girl, holding the baby to her chest and cradling its head tenderly. 'Is permitted?' She sweeps her free hand around the shelter.

'What, to wait for a bus?' says Hester.

'Bus! Yes!' says the girl hurriedly. 'I wait for bus.'

'Right ...' says Hester doubtfully. 'But the actual bus stop is just up the hill.' She looks across to Harriet and raises an enquiring eyebrow. Harriet shrugs and shakes her head, then says.

'We could give you a lift to the next village.'

11

'No, I . . . thank you. Bus is better. Thank you.' The girl smiles weakly and looks away as if to signal there is no more to be said.

'Well, if you're sure . . .' Harriet retreats towards the car and, reluctantly, Hester follows. They are about to climb back in when the same thought strikes them. As one, they return to the shelter, this time a united front that will not be gainsaid.

'There are no buses on Christmas Day.'

The girl looks up at them, cornered, biting her lip; the baby picks up her anxiety and starts to grizzle feebly. There's talk of taxis, of a friend who might give her a lift, but they can tell it's all lies. She levers herself up and now they see how thin she is, how inadequate her clothing and the baby's. They're not leaving her here.

'We could take them with us.' Hester voices the possibility somewhat reluctantly. 'They'd be right up George and Isabelle's street.'

They look at the mother's huge, haunted eyes, the sallow skin, the baby's puzzled, muddled gaze and say in one voice: 'Or we could take them home.'

~~~

And so here they are. Back home. Bustling around the warm kitchen, slicing thick hunks of bread, laying out chutneys, cold meats, fat olives that bring a wan smile to the girl's face as she struggles to keep her eyes open. She reaches out a tentative hand to take the glass of rich red wine that Hester thrusts at her. The baby has fed on and off for the past half-hour while Hester has prepared the meal and Harriet has been busy making beds, fitting out a deep drawer as a cot. Now, sated, the baby sleeps on the girl's lap until Harriet gently lifts him up and carries him to his own little bed. Few words have been spoken, except for Hester's hurried apologetic phone call to George, in whose voice did she detect not only the expected concern but also the tiniest note of relief? Naturally he immediately offered to come over as soon as their guests have gone, but Hester is firm. *Spoil your Christmas, George? After all the trouble Isabelle has gone to? We wouldn't dream of it. No, no, we've plenty of food . . . So, sorry to be missing the party—and dinner . . . Yes, we've already found the number for Social Services, just in case; we'll ring them if needs be . . . Well then, we'll leave a message . . . Not to worry, we've plenty of room . . . You'd have done the same, wouldn't you? Of course you would! Bye!*

Harriet lays the tiny baby in the nest of blankets and tucks them carefully around him. He stirs and something—a memory? wind?—brings a smile to his lips and he flexes his starfish hands. Gingerly, she leans down and plants a kiss on his forehead, then creeps from the room, leaving only a sliver of light across the carpet from the hallway. Just in case he wakes.

CHAPTER 3

26 DECEMBER

It's one thing to take in waifs and strays on Christmas Day, full of the bonhomie of that most atypical of days; quite another to wake the following morning to realise that you have guests in the house; guests who need sustenance, looking after; guests whose clothes are drying in the utility room, who are sitting bundled up in clean but shabby and ill-fitting castoffs in your kitchen, feeding their offspring. More to the point, guests whose names you don't even yet know. Somehow it hadn't seemed necessary, would almost have felt intrusive yesterday. The sisters had installed the exhausted girl in the spare bedroom with the drawer-cot, left a tray outside the door at supper-time but had heard nothing save a few murmurs and the running of the bath mid-evening, while they were ensconced in the sitting room, deep into a fine merlot, Stilton and crackers and Morse on DVD.

Hester creeps downstairs to make the morning tea and discovers the girl quietly nursing the baby in the armchair beside the Aga. She makes as if to rise, but Hester waves her down.

'Sleep well?' she asks, unused to company this early, the words thick on her tongue.

The girl smiles cautiously. 'Yes, thank you. Bed is good. He does not wake you?'

The baby is suckling contentedly, little hands waving; Hester marvels at his tiny nails. She shakes her head. 'Not a peep. Once I'm out, I'm dead to the world . . .' Then, seeing the girl's confusion, 'I mean I sleep really deeply . . . Tea?'

A stricken look flashes across the girl's face; she turns involuntarily to glance at a mug beside her. 'I had thirst. I am sorry.'

'No, no,' says Hester, peering into the mug. 'Didn't you find the milk? In the fridge?'

A horrified expression. 'Milk?' says the girl, as though Hester has offered strychnine. 'Milk?!'

'Hester,' says Hester, offering her hand.

The girl's is rough, small, and very cold. 'Daria,' she says shyly. 'And this is—'

The kitchen door bursts open in a blast of arctic air and Harriet bustles in, two bulging bin liners preceding her.

'I thought you were in bed!' exclaims Hester. 'I was just about to take you up some tea.'

'Woke early, couldn't get back to sleep, had an idea,' gasps Harriet. 'Decided to strike while the iron et cetera. I'll have one now though. Hello!' This to the girl who is clutching the baby defensively and staring at the apparition in glasses, nightdress, boots and thick overcoat, topped with an ancient trilby.

15

'This is Daria,' says Hester, fishing a damp teabag out of the compost pot by the sink and dropping it into a mug for her sister. Hester rarely wastes a new teabag on Harriet, who likes her tea weak. Fortunately for Harriet the teabag is the only thing in the pot this early in the day. Shavings of vegetables are not uncommon accompaniments to her tea when Hester makes it. 'Daria, this is my sister Harriet. And this little fellow is . . .?'

'Milo,' says Daria, and all three gaze at the tiny pink face with that peculiar blend of covetousness and tenderness women reserve for babies.

Milo. *O'Shea*, thinks Hester. *Oh, I liked him: the twinkle in his eye and that lovely Irish accent—*

'*The Phantom Tollbooth*,' says Harriet with delight. She'd always longed to have a child to whom she could read it, snuggled up in bed, sleepy head on her shoulder, as the puns unwound page by page. Not a fantasy she would ever have shared, of course; she blushes to remember it. But the sisters smile at one another. Daria looks at them blankly.

'What on earth's in those?' says Hester, gesturing to the bin bags, which have been planted in the middle of the table.

Harriet takes the mug of tea and peers into its depths. She sips it cautiously.

'Supplies.' Harriet tears open the neck of one bag and pulls out a brown sheepskin coat, followed by three brightly coloured jumpers. She holds one up.

'You'll never get into that!' cries Hester.

'They're not for me,' retorts Harriet with scorn. 'They're for . . .' She gestures to Daria and Milo.

'Oh!' Daria looks astonished, then dismayed. 'But I have no—'

'And,' continues Harriet, delving into the other bag, 'that's not all. Just look at these!' And she holds aloft a jumble of items in a riot of colours, then drops them on the table. On the top of the pile is a minute Fair Isle cardigan with wooden buttons; underneath it are assorted vests and Babygros. Hester and Daria both look to Harriet for enlightenment.

'Brainwave!' she crows. 'I was lying there thinking that we need to get Daria'—she acknowledges the unfamiliar name—'and little Milo here some warm clothes. Then I thought: *I know, Oxfam!* I nipped over to Stote first thing and bingo! Some good Samaritan had dropped these off overnight.'

'Christmas night?' says Hester. 'Donating things to Oxfam on Christmas night? How extraordinary.'

'Not at all,' says Harriet. 'I read it somewhere. You'd be surprised how many bags there were. Plus a footbath and four dog baskets. Four! People don't know what to do with themselves—they've watched the Queen's speech, had their turkey, rowed with their rellies, so they storm off upstairs and start weeding out their wardrobes. Luckily for us. Although, when I saw that coat, I thought—'

'Oh God,' says Hester, realisation dawning as she examines it more closely. 'It does look familiar.'

''Fraid so,' says Harriet. 'Poor old Molly. Peggy says she chucks out all manner of things when she and Teddy have had a dingdong. Then he has to buy her a whole new wardrobe to make amends.'

'Poor old Molly!' scoffs Hester, siding automatically with Molly's errant husband. Unfaithful he may be—indeed undoubtedly is—but by all accounts Molly is a perfect cow and, by Hester's lights, deserves everything she gets. In this regard at least, Hester is far from sisterly. 'By the time he slinks home, there'll be nothing left in any of the wardrobes. Remember last Christmas?'

The sisters reflect on Molly's frenzied assault on Teddy's suits with the hedge trimmer the previous year, a variation on her usual response to his misdeeds, her frenzy exacerbated by (or so rumour, assiduously bruited far and wide by a gleeful Peggy Verndale, the village's arch tattletale, had it) a bottle and a half of Dubonnet. Molly's chosen tipple is a further reason for Hester's disdain.

They both notice Daria and Milo staring at them wide-eyed.

'Local gossip,' says Harriet, slightly ashamed. She holds up the tiny cardigan. 'For Milo?' If she is hoping for some sign of pleasure or delight, she is to be disappointed. Daria looks, frankly, terrified.

'No, thank you,' she says. 'You are kind but, please, I cannot pay.'

'Pay?' says Harriet. 'Oh, my dear, no, you're not paying for these. They are a gift.' She says quietly to Hester, 'I popped a twenty-pound note through the Oxfam letterbox.'

'Well, I did wonder . . . Strictly speaking, though, I think this counts as theft.'

'Stuff and nonsense. It was an *emergency*!'

'A . . . gift?' repeats Daria. Her eyes are swimming with tears.

'Hey, hey,' says Hester gruffly, 'no need for that. Let's sort ourselves some breakfast. I don't suppose you thought to get some nappies, Harriet, did you?'

Harriet snorts. 'What do you take me for? I stopped at the Shell garage by the motorway and bought some there. They're in the car.'

'Why didn't you use the place in the village? They're always open on Boxing Day.'

Harriet rolls her eyes.

'Oh, right,' says Hester, all at once remembering how impossible it is to keep anything private around here with Peggy Verndale within sniffing distance. Peggy has an unerring nose for anything out of the ordinary; as far as scandal is concerned, she is a bloodhound.

Hester makes for the fridge. It is only then that she notices the kitchen. It is tidy. And clean. Last night's dirty plates and crockery have been washed, dried and laid out neatly on the work surface, like exhibits in a museum. The cooker gleams. She looks down. The lino, though worn, now shows a faint impression of its original pattern. The mat by the back door is straight. She knows Harriet would no more have crept down in the night to effect this transformation than dance a jig. It is not that the sisters are slovenly exactly—they do have a woman in once every few months to try to impose some order on the chaos—but they are firmly old school. A peck of dirt before you die isn't going to kill you.

'Daria . . .' Hester begins.

The girl looks uncomfortable. 'I . . . is wrong? I want to help. To thank you.'

Hester shakes her head. 'No, no, it's just ... you really shouldn't. Not with the baby and ... well ...' She wants to say, *how thin you are and tired and altogether looking as though a puff of wind would blow you away.*

'Thank you very much, Daria,' cuts in Harriet. 'That's very kind. Very kind indeed. But you are our guest. No need to sing for your supper.'

'Sing?' says Daria with alarm, clearly fearing this must be some quaint English custom of which she is ignorant.

The sisters laugh. 'Not literally,' says Harriet. 'It's just an expression. What we mean is, we just want you to get your strength back so you can look after Milo before you ...' It seems impolite to be talking already of their departure, so she trails off. 'You leave the rest to us. Now where's that breakfast you were promising us, Hetty? I'm ravenous.'

~~~

They have not long finished eating but Hester is already busy in the kitchen, assembling something for their lunch. Harriet has gone through to the sitting room with Daria to spread a rug out in front of the hearth for Milo to lie on. The novelty of the situation has not yet worn off; they are in no hurry to see their guests leave.

The doorbell rings.

'I'll get it!' shouts Hester from the kitchen.

Harriet, who has been dangling a pompom cut from an old hat over Milo's uncoordinated hands, finds the baby suddenly snatched from under her as Daria hurtles out of the room and makes for the stairs.

She turns in the doorway. 'Please! Please . . . do not tell!' Her face is white with terror.

Harriet, disconcerted, nods and Daria sprints upstairs.

Harriet struggles up from the floor and, as Hester passes the doorway on her way down the hall, she grabs her sister's arm and puts a finger to her lips, jerking her head upwards. 'Not a word. I promised her.'

Hester's eyes widen, then she nods. Together, the sisters head for the door.

George is standing on the porch, armed with a carrier bag and an anxious expression.

'Hester! Harriet! Happy Christmas!' Without waiting for an invitation, George steps into the hall en route for the sitting room. 'I thought I ought to pop over and see that you were all right. After yesterday—' George glances at the rug on the floor, frowns, then continues. 'We missed you, of course. Isabelle sends her love. She would have come, but I'm afraid Ben is being . . . well, you know, these young people . . . anyway, I just wanted to check that everything was in order with the girl. You got her sorted?'

'Coffee?' says Harriet, before she can stop herself. Her natural hospitality has momentarily blinded her to the fact that they want to get their cousin out of the house as soon as possible, before Daria—or more likely Milo—makes their presence known. She suspects, indeed knows, that were George to be aware they were still here he would immediately take matters in hand.

Beside her, Hester inhales angrily and says, 'Oh, Harry, I thought we were going . . .?'

'Out! Yes,' says Harriet eagerly. 'Of course!' Inspiration strikes. 'The Wilsons. Drinkies,' she explains to George, fingers tightly crossed behind her back.

George's eyes fly to the clock on the mantelpiece. 'Isn't it a bit early?'

'Oh, you don't know the Wilsons!' exclaims Harriet gaily, hoping fervently that he doesn't. 'Old Molly is rather fond of a drop, I'm afraid. She likes to start bang on the dot of eleven on Boxing Day. It's a village tradition.' She starts to usher George out. 'So sorry, George ... Oh, hang on'—she extracts a bag from beside an armchair—'your presents. Just a little token. I'm afraid it's money for Ben. Again. A bit dreary but—'

'It's more than he deserves,' says George with uncharacteristic vehemence, then recovers himself. 'Forgive me. Thank you, Hester. Harriet.' He holds out his carrier. 'Yours are in here. And a little extra something from Isabelle.'

They complete that very British ritual of exchanging presents that none of them wants but each feels obliged to provide. There are smiles, diffident kisses and the sisters have almost succeeded in shepherding George out of the front door when he turns and asks, 'So what did you do with her? The girl? A hostel?'

Harriet and Hester freeze. A hostel? That sounds too dangerous; chances are, given George and Isabelle's local connections, they'll know every shelter and sanctuary within a fifty-mile radius. What if they check up?

'No,' says Hester swiftly. 'Turns out she had friends In London. We gave her a bite to eat and ran her to the station. With the baby. Obviously.'

George hesitates. 'Foreigner, did you say?'

Had she? 'Er . . . yes. From Eastern Europe, I think. Wouldn't you say?' She appeals to her sister.

'Oh, more than likely,' agrees Harriet.

Their cousin's frown deepens. 'Well, lucky she ran into you. Other people might not have been so charitable, giving up their Christmas Day for them. Missing our party and all the fun. Not to mention Christmas dinner. I hope she was grateful. Only, young people today . . .'

They sense he isn't thinking of their unexpected guest.

'Well,' he says with obvious reluctance when the sisters fail to pursue his theme, 'I suppose I'd better get off. See how things are back at the ranch.'

'And we must get going! Molly will be champing at the bit.' Harriet goes to the coat stand and takes down two rather disreputable raincoats.

George regards her quizzically. 'Are you off right away, then?'

'Yes indeed,' says Harriet enthusiastically. 'Not a moment to lose.'

'In your pyjamas?' says George.

CHAPTER 4

'That was close,' says Hester as George's car pulls away down the lane.

Harriet is still wiping her eyes, following their explosion of mirth in the aftermath of their cousin's departure. 'Poor old George. We are mean. He clearly wanted to talk. Oh well, best go and get dressed, I suppose. Let Daria know he's gone. And then, I think, we need to sit her down and have a bit of a chat. Find out what the big mystery is. Decide what to do with her. And the baby.'

'Absolutely. Give me a yell when the bathroom's free.' Hester goes off in the direction of the kitchen, calling over her shoulder, 'I'll get on with lunch; I thought I might rustle up a mousse with what's left of the smoked salmon.' Nothing settles Hester so much as a stint in the kitchen. 'Might bake some bread too.' She remembers George's carrier, doubles back to the sitting room and returns to her kingdom to discover at the bottom of the bag, neatly layered in a Tupperware box beneath two Christmas presents in festive paper, a dozen or so slices of grey, desiccated turkey, burnt at the edges. She drops them in the bin.

Harriet knocks on the door of the guest bedroom. As Daria's face, pinched and fearful, appears, Milo waves at her from his improvised cot. *If this is how little trouble babies are*, Harriet thinks, *I wish I'd got one years ago.* 'Coast's clear,' she says.

'Cost?'

'*Coast*. What I mean is, it's safe to come down. Downstairs. It was only our cousin, come to check up on us.'

'Check up?' Daria's face, if it were possible, looks even whiter, panic in her eyes.

'No, no,' says Harriet reassuringly. 'He wanted to check that we were okay. We didn't mention you. No-one knows you're here.'

Daria's face lights up with a hesitant smile. 'Thank you. Oh, thank you, Harriet.' She makes Harriet's name sound vaguely exotic. 'I am sorry to be . . .' She spreads her hands.

'You aren't. Really. Now, Hetty's in the kitchen and I'm off for a shower,' says Harriet. 'Then we'll sit down and have a chat.'

As she is heading to the bathroom, the doorbell rings once again.

'What the—'

'Harry!' shouts Hester. 'Can you get that? I'm—' The rest is lost.

Bloody men, thinks Harriet as she plods downstairs. *What does George want now?*

She opens the door to find it is a man, but it isn't George. Where George is tall and thin—not unlike Hester—the stranger is squat, weighty, feet planted firmly on the path, a combative look on his seamed face. A smoker's face, but one with a faintly weaselly look. His eyes peer past Harriet, searching the dark hall. He tips an imaginary hat.

'Morning. Sorry to bother you.' He doesn't look sorry. A smoker's voice, too, gravelly and full of phlegm. 'Christmas and that.'

Harriet looks past him to the lane. No car or van. A new neighbour?

'Good morning. What can I do for you?'

A shifty smile flits across his face, exposing uneven, yellowed teeth; the smile a mixture of embarrassment and suspicion. Harriet stiffens and grips the door's inner handle more tightly.

'Thing is, I'm rather hoping you can help me.' He moves a little closer, uncomfortably close.

'Oh?' Harriet folds her arms under her bosom, filling the doorway, all five foot four of her.

'Yes. See, I'm looking for someone.'

'Round here? Do you have an address?'

A laugh barks out.

He says almost to himself, as though Harriet has uttered a witticism, 'Do I have an address? If only.' Then his face goes hard, eyes like granite. 'I'm looking for a girl, see.'

'Girl?' says Harriet, a catch in her voice. Her heart thumps. Has she taken her blood pressure tablet this morning? 'What girl?'

'A runaway.'

'Goodness. Are you a policeman?' says Harriet, knowing the answer.

'Seen her, have you?'

He pulls a creased photograph from his pocket, holding it up in front of her so close that she has to pull back to see it clearly. It looks like a police mugshot (not that Harriet has ever seen one, except on TV) or a copy of a passport photo. Small, serious face, dark hair, smudged eyes. Unmistakably Daria.

'And who is this?'

A thin smile. 'You don't know her then?'

Harriet hates to lie; not only does she hate to lie, she is also hopeless at it.

She says firmly, 'I asked you who it was.'

'If you don't know her, her name won't mean anything to you, will it?'

Harriet shrugs as carelessly as she can, given the knot in her shoulders. 'I suppose not. I'm just curious. Seems an odd thing to be doing on Boxing Day, knocking on doors like this. This girl—is she your daughter or something?'

'Something.'

'And might I know your name?'

'Can't think why not, Mrs . . . er?'

'Pearson. Harriet Pearson.'

She waits. He smirks, then, after a sudden explosive cough, hawks. A gob of mucus glistens on the step in the pale winter sunshine. Harriet inflates her chest; she's not having this. The man's eyes drop away under her steely gaze; he rubs the spot with a mud-caked shoe, little flakes of dirt sprinkling the stone. He taps his chest.

'Beg pardon. Just can't shift it.'

'You always could try giving up smoking,' she snaps, emboldened by indignation.

27

This time he gives a genuine laugh. 'Touché.' He hands her a business card. Seeing the state of his nails, she takes it by the corner furthest from his hand. 'In case you do see her any time, there's my number. Be grateful for a call.' He starts to back down the path. 'Happy Christmas, Mrs Pearson. Take care now.'

She looks down at the grubby card.

Archie Dick
Lightfoot Intelligence
Private Investigations & Intelligence Services
Discreet * Efficient * Effective
07998 453212

Archie *Dick*? She gives an involuntary snort.

He turns back with an embarrassed smile, spreads his hands. 'I know. Bummer, eh?' He stops at the gate, as if he's just remembered something. Harriet isn't fooled.

'Oh, and there might be a kid. The girl, she might have a baby. Be about, what, three, four months? Maybe.' He shrugs as if it's of no significance, sketches a vague wave and shuts the gate behind him. 'Be seeing you.'

'Who are you working for, Mr Dick?' she calls after him. Even saying the name sounds risible.

In answer, he just waves again without turning and carries on up the lane towards the main road, stumbling once on the uneven surface. She waits a moment or two, heart still a little jumpy, until he disappears round the bend in the lane. She shivers, quietly closes the front door and, turning, sees Daria crouched on the half-landing, sleeve to her mouth, dark eyes unreadable. As Harriet goes to speak, she unfurls her body and runs into her room. Harriet goes down the hall into the kitchen.

'Who was that?' Hester is kneading dough; its yeasty richness perfumes the warm air.

Harriet sits heavily, picking idly at the crust of a quiche just out of the oven. Hester reaches across and slaps her hand lightly, leaving a dusting of flour on her skin.

'What's the matter?'

'Chap at the door,' Harriet says.

'Could you be more explicit?' says her sister acidly.

'Sorry. He was looking for Daria.'

'Oh dear.' Hester's hand flies to her mouth, smearing it with flour. 'Who was he? Father? Husband?'

'No, private detective.'

'Really?' Hester is astonished. 'Really and truly?'

Harriet hands her the business card. Hester pulls her glasses down from their perch in her hair and peers at it. 'Golly.' She peers again at the name. 'This is a joke, right?'

'I only wish it were,' says Harriet. 'I didn't like him one bit. Something about his . . . . I don't know. Bit frightening.'

'He frightened you?' Hester is surprised. It's a brave man who takes on her sister. 'What did he say?'

Harriet is thinking. 'Says she's a runaway. Daria. He had a picture. He mentioned a baby. "She might have a baby," he said.'

'Interesting. So he knew she was pregnant—'

'Or suspected. Which means she must have disappeared, done a bunk, whatever, before Milo was born. But how did he know that she was here?'

'You didn't tell him?! Harry, how could you?'

'No, of course I didn't tell him! Honestly!'

'Then how did he—'

'I don't know! But someone must've told him. Perhaps they saw us at the bus stop?'

Hester is rattled. 'I don't like the sound of this. What have we got ourselves into?'

The doorbell rings a third time and they both jump.

'Right,' says Hester, already dusting down her hands. 'I'll deal with it.'

Harriet gives her an old-fashioned look. 'I'm not scared of *bullies*,' she says sharply. 'I'm not in my dotage yet. I can manage!'

Nevertheless, Hester is drying her hands on a towel. 'Strength in numbers,' she says. She squints at the business card again. 'We'll sort out this Mr Dick between us. Besides, you're such a terrible liar. Come on.'

But when they fling open the front door, it is to find a more familiar face: nephew Ben, pimpled face aflame, and bloodshot eyes that look as though they have recently been dried. He slouches in the doorway, all lanky frame, shaggy fringe and attitude.

'Hi,' he says, with a feeble attempt at nonchalance, failing to master the emotion in his voice. 'I was out for a walk . . .'

Hester gives him a sceptical look—walking! He's at least five miles from home. 'Really? Your father's just left. I'm surprised you didn't see him.'

Ben shrugs. He won't meet their eyes.

Hester tilts her head quizzically. 'Is there . . .?' A thought strikes her and she looks down for a carrier bag: perhaps

Isabelle's dispatched him with reinforcements of turkey? But no, his hands are empty. He looks defeated, lost, tearful.

'Would you like to come in?' she says.

He nods, a picture of misery tinged with relief. 'Yeah. Been walking for, like, ages. I just wanna . . . you know.'

They don't know but the sisters step aside to let in the third stray dog in twenty-four hours.

As he shoulders his way past them, a pungent scent of testosterone and sweat invades the hall.

'Bath?' Harriet signals with one eyebrow. Hester nods. Wordlessly, she steers Ben towards the stairs, gently forcing him upwards.

'Oi! What you doing?'

'You, young man, are going to have a bath.' She eases him into the bathroom and hands him a towel from the airing cupboard.

'Bath? What the—? I never have a bath!'

'Evidently.'

'No, you cheeky—I have a *shower*, don't I?'

'Then have a shower. Either way, wash,' she says sternly. 'Clothes on the landing. I'll find you something to wear. And do your hair while you're at it.' Then she closes the door.

Five minutes later, she deposits a small pile of Gordon's clothes outside the bathroom door, then goes downstairs to find Harriet.

'That boy!'

'He's only fourteen.'

'Fifteen,' says Hester tartly. 'Remember? We sent him money for his birthday in July. Twenty pounds. Which he still hasn't thanked us for.'

Harriet fingers the two parcels on the dresser, peers at the labels. She goes to hand one to her sister. 'Here,' she says, then takes it back. 'Guess.'

It's a game they play every year: imagining the unimaginable, that George and Isabelle will have given them something unexpected for Christmas.

'Ooh, goodness, I can't think . . .' says Hester, screwing up her face in pretend thought. 'A book? Silk underwear? Or—I know!—toiletries!'

She tears off the wrapping: talc, soap and body cream. 'Just what I wanted.'

Harriet, with genuine excitement, laughs sympathetically and opens hers, delighted that her cousins are so predictable, anticipating the box of dark chocolate brazils she receives every year. 'Ta-dah! Just what *I* wanted.' Hester frowns: Harry's sweet tooth will be the death of her.

The gurgle of water from the shower reminds them of their more immediate concerns. Simultaneously, they glance up to the ceiling.

'What about the other two?'

'Neither hide nor hair. I assume Milo's asleep.'

'Well, that won't last. What do we tell Ben when he comes down?'

'That we're running a hostel for waifs and strays?'

⌣⌣⌣

Soup is warming on the stove. A pile of freshly-made sandwiches, a salmon mousse and a hefty slice of still-warm quiche sit in the middle of the table. Hester hands Harriet a bottle and she pours them each a glass of chablis.

'Bit early, aren't we?' says Harriet, knocking back a healthy swig. She can't help thinking how wickedly they traduced Molly Wilson earlier.

'Rules,' says Hester, raising her glass in salute, 'are only rules if they can be broken. Besides, I get the feeling that this is not going to be a normal Boxing Day, not by a long chalk.'

'We ought to phone George,' says Harriet, settling her broad bottom comfortably into the armchair. 'Let him know we have his errant son in safe custody.'

Hester slides onto one of the kitchen chairs at the table and makes herself similarly at ease. She slips her apron over her head. 'Of course we must,' she says. 'But let's hear Ben's side of the story first.'

'And Daria's.'

'And Daria's. Top up?'

⌣⌣⌣

'They're doing my head in.'

What is it, Hester wonders, *that makes today's youth so eager to be taken for the product of a deprived background? In my day, we strove incessantly to improve ourselves—and our diction—not to emulate guttersnipes.*

Ben is washed, sweet-smelling and clad in corduroys that fit him in the leg but are held up by a belt cinched tightly around his skinny waist. His dead uncle's Tattersall check shirt bags over his thighs. His wet hair is plastered to his head; and in the heat of the kitchen, little curls are starting to spring up. He looks sullen and vulnerable. But he has exchanged more words with his aunts in the last five minutes than in the whole of the preceding decade. He is on his fifth sandwich, the quiche and soup long since consumed.

'You might like to try tasting the food instead of just wolfing it down,' says Hester, as he reaches for further supplies.

'You what? Taste?' This sounds like a brand-new concept to him; given his parents' cuisine, Hester has some sympathy.

'Yes,' she says. 'Savour it. Experience it. It's not just fuel, food.'

'Yeah?' says Ben.

'Yeah,' echoes his aunt.

Harriet suppresses a smile and indicates the mousse. 'Have some of this. It's delicious.'

Ben frowns and draws back.

'Try it,' says Hester.

'What is it?'

'Salmon mousse.'

'Don't like fish.'

'Funny, you managed to force those tuna mayonnaise sandwiches down without too much trouble.'

'Oh yeah, well, *tuna* . . . That's not *fish* fish, is it?'

Harriet scoops a small portion of mousse onto a cracker. 'Here.'

'No, ta. Like I said—'

'Eat it.'

Ben gingerly takes the cracker, looks at it closely, sniffs it and finally shoves it swiftly into his mouth with a grimace. He might have been dosing himself with some noxious medicine. The sisters watch his reaction. A moment of incredulity, swiftly erased.

'There. Satisfied?'

'Scrumptious, wasn't it?' says Harriet.

Ben shrugs, truth fighting with bravado. 'It was all right. For fish.' He licks his finger. 'Why doesn't it, you know . . .'

'What?' says Hester.

'Collapse.'

'Chemistry,' says Hester.

Ben looks at her suspiciously. 'Chemistry?'

'That's right. That's what all cooking is: chemistry.'

'Yeah?' Ben frowns, then shrugs. 'Can I have a beer or something?'

No reply.

'Please.'

'A beer? Are you allowed to drink?' Ben gives Hester a contemptuous look that says, *I am fifteen!* Harriet reaches for the wine bottle, with a complicit glance at Hester. 'You can have a glass of wine, if you like.'

'Don't like wine.'

'Really?' says Harriet. 'There's a surprise.' She pours a small measure into a glass and pushes it across the table to him. 'Here you are.'

'You trying to poison me or what? First fish and now—'

Harriet indicates the glass with a purposeful nod and Ben wilts. He picks up the wine, lifts it to his lips and, mouth twisted with disgust, takes a tiny sip. A moment. He takes another, larger, sip. His eyes widen. He takes a mouthful.

'Not bad,' he says, holding out his glass for a refill. 'Don't taste like the stuff we have at home.'

'*Doesn't*,' says Harriet automatically.

'No, well, I should jolly well think not . . .' starts Hester, but Harriet swiftly interrupts. Best not get Hester going on her customary diatribe about George's appalling taste in wine. If she's not quick, the spectre of the gluhwein will be raised and then there'll be no going back.

'Right, time to spill the beans,' she says. 'What's all this about with your mum and dad?'

'Don't ask!' Ben bursts out.

'But I am asking, Ben,' she says firmly. 'We are going to ring your parents in a minute to let them know you're here—'

'No!'

'Don't interrupt. I'm sure they must be worried about you. But we thought we'd hear you out first. At the very least you owe us the courtesy of an explanation as to why you turn up out of the blue on our doorstep.'

'Yes,' chips in Hester. 'We might well ask: why our doorstep? We never see you from one year to the next and suddenly you pitch up here on Boxing Day and expect us to give you sanctuary. And while I think of it—'

Oh, never mind the birthday money! thinks Harriet irritably. She shoots Hester an exasperated look. 'You've never bothered much with us before, Ben, let's be honest.'

'Barely manage to be civil on the few occasions you deign to be in the same room as us,' mutters Hester.

'Look, Ben, we want to help, of course we do, but we need to know what the problem is. Besides, don't you have any friends you can talk to?'

Ben bridles, spots glowing. An uncomfortable expression flits across his face and is replaced with truculence. "Course I got friends! What d'you think I am, some saddo with no mates? I got loads of mates.'

Sullenly, he picks at the salmon mousse with a teaspoon. Some of it finds its way into his mouth.

'I'm sure you have,' says Harriet levelly, despite her growing frustration. 'We're just surprised to see you here, that's all. As we've said, we're only too happy to help. If we can.' She tries to catch Hester's eye but her sister appears mesmerised by the sight of their nephew now steadily demolishing the remainder of the salmon mousse.

Harriet ploughs on. 'Ben, look, you've clearly had a bit of a falling-out with your mum and dad—'

'Falling-out! Don't make me laugh! Laying down the law— *do this, do that.* I've had it with them. I mean it.'

'Now listen!' Hester has finally had enough. 'Once and for all, stop eating that mousse or at least cut a proper slice and tell us what the matter is before we pack you off back home right this minute!'

Ben slams the spoon down on the plate for all the world like a toddler having a tantrum.

'Sodding A-levels,' he snarls. 'I don't wanna do A-levels, do I. I wanna go to horticultural college.'

'Horticultural college?' Harriet is astounded. Of all the careers Ben might have chosen, this seems the least likely. She can't remember ever seeing evidence at George and Isabelle's house that anyone in residence has the slightest interest in matters arboreal or botanic.

'Yeah, like plants and that.'

'I know perfectly well what horticulture entails, Ben, I was simply expressing surprise.'

'Why not? I like biology. I don't mind getting my hands dirty.'

'I think there's rather more to it than that.'

'I know! I'm not an idiot!'

'Don't you need A-levels for that?' says Hester, ever practical.

'How should I know?' he almost shouts, reaching for the bottle of wine.

Harriet puts out a restraining hand. No need to waste a decent chablis on such an untutored palate.

Ben storms on. 'But I know what their game is. Bloody A-levels, university, all that crap. I'm not going. They started going off on one this morning: I need to work harder, do more homework, clean my room, wash my hair'—he glares at his aunts—'be more like some wanker son of one of their wanker friends. I've had it up to here. So I just lit out, started walking and ended up here. They're always going, *Ooh, why don't you talk to Aunt Harriet, she could advise you, used to be a teacher.* Yeah, right. Dunno why, but I thought you might understand. How wrong was I!'

Harriet, whose years of trying to educate generations of stroppy boys like Ben have inured her to such outbursts, nods sympathetically, but Hester, sterner and less forgiving, eyes her nephew critically. 'I'm beginning to think your parents may have a point, particularly if you behave like this at home.'

'Like what?' demands Ben hotly.

'Like a spoilt brat who can't get his own way. I'm sure George and Isabelle only want the best for you.'

'Oh, not you 'n all! That's what they always say! But what do they know? What does anyone know?' He pushes himself to his feet and towers over them. 'Don't know why I bothered. Nobody ever listens to what I want. You're all the same.'

'Oh, do sit down, Ben.' Harriet is finding it hard not to laugh. 'You're not going anywhere dressed like that.'

Ben looks down at what he is wearing and thumps back into his chair, arms crossed in revolt. 'Well, I never asked you to wash my clothes, did I?'

'D'you know, Harry, my respect for George and Isabelle is growing by the minute,' says Hester, regarding Ben sourly.

'I take your point.'

'What? What?' demands Ben, apparently suddenly realising that he is the subject of an unspoken conversation between his aunts. 'Don't you start taking their side too!'

'Then give us one good reason why we shouldn't,' says Harriet as Hester starts to clear the table, smoothly whisking the remaining sandwiches out of Ben's reach.

Ben, sensing an ally of sorts in Harriet, looks at her imploringly. 'I just wanna do something *I* wanna do—not what they tell me to do. Why can't I try it, yeah? Give it a go. They want me to do all this academic bollocks, but I'm not academic, am I? I really, really, really wanna do something practical— that's what I'm good at. You can't shove a round peg into a whatsit, can you? Eh?' And with that potent aphorism, he throws himself back in his chair, eyes suspiciously bright, and sniffs hard.

Hester, covering the leftovers with cling film, stops what she is doing. The sisters exchange a look and wordlessly reach an agreement, in Hester's case with considerable misgivings.

Harriet takes charge. 'Okay, Ben, now listen. You could do with a bit of breathing space by the sound of it—and so could your parents, I imagine. We're prepared to let you stay here for a few days—'

'Subject to conditions,' throws in Hester swiftly.

'—just until things blow over.'

'Stay? Here?' says Ben, frowning and looking around the kitchen as though it may be booby-trapped.

'Unless you'd rather go back and face the music. Or speak to one of your friends?'

'No, no,' he says, rather too quickly.

Aha, thinks Harriet, *something's up in that department.*

'Well, come along then, make your mind up; we haven't got all day,' says Hester.

Ben wrestles with his grievances, the weight of a hostile world, and finally says, 'Okay. But I'm not talking to him. Or her.'

Hester ignores this, determined to place her stamp on the arrangements. 'As I said, your stay here is subject to conditions. You do as you're told while you're here and no more whining. You eat what you're given and like it.'

She sweeps out, but not before he mutters, 'Whatever,' and then, just loud enough for them both to hear, 'Thanks.'

Harriet, getting up in search of the cake tin, squeezes his shoulder in passing; out of the corner of her eye, she sees him wipe his hand across his face.

Light footsteps on the stair. There is a brief muffled conversation in the hall that neither Ben nor Harriet can make out, until Hester says clearly, 'No, I promise you, there's no need to worry. In you go. It's only Ben. Our nephew.' And then Daria, with Milo in her arms, is standing on the threshold of the kitchen, warily eyeing the teenager as he reaches into the tin Harriet is holding.

'You're awake!' cries Harriet. 'Come in, don't be shy. This is Daria, Ben. And that's Milo. They aren't here.'

'Fair enough,' says Ben through a mouthful of Victoria sponge, as though invisible guests in the home of his eccentric aunts, one of whom is still in her pyjamas at midday, are commonplace. 'Hiya.'

Daria smiles and Harriet realises all of a sudden how pretty she is. Or could be, with a bit more flesh on her bones and a decent haircut. But for the present, she looks almost too frail to bear Milo's meagre weight.

'I am coming,' says Daria, 'for the . . .' She searches for the word. 'Nappy. Nappies. He is . . . Milo is . . .'

'Cool name,' says Ben.

Daria nods her thanks.

'They're in the car,' says Harriet. 'I'll get them. Come in and make yourself—'

Daria sways in the doorway and Harriet catches Milo just in time as the girl collapses into a chair.

'Here,' says Harriet, thrusting the bundle at her nephew. She expects him to recoil, but Ben confounds her. He stands up, enfolds the baby in his arms, hip slightly extended automatically, the head cradled in the crook of his elbow.

'Hello, mate,' he says, equal to equal, and Milo stirs briefly as though to acknowledge he's in safe hands. 'Fancy a bit of cake? It's well good.'

⌣⌣⌣

'Take him out for a walk. Ben! Are you listening?' Harriet marches across the room and switches off the television.

'Oi!' Ben hisses this softly so as not to wake the baby. Milo is lodged once more in Ben's embrace, bubbles of milk at his lips after his recent feed. His mother is upstairs, sleeping again. Harriet has squared Ben's temporary lodgings with George, after a long and painful conversation, during which she employed all her considerable powers of persuasion to convince him that he and his wayward son might both benefit from a little time apart.

'You gonna tell me, you know, what's going on? With, er . . .?' Ben nods down at Milo and jerks his head upwards to take in Daria.

'No,' says Harriet. 'Because we don't exactly know ourselves. But mum's the word, okay?'

'Fair enough,' says Ben equably.

'Right, you both need some fresh air,' says Harriet firmly. 'Do you the world of good. Before it gets dark. Come on.'

Ben gets carefully to his feet, scowling, ill temper at odds with his tenderness for Milo. 'Out? Of here? Where?' he mutters, as though the cottage were buried in an impenetrable forest.

'Trundle him round the common. Turn left up the lane, then take the little path off to the right. It's about a ten minute walk. You can take some stale bread for the ducks.'

'Ducks!' says Ben scornfully. 'How old do you think I am?'

'For the baby!' says Harriet.

'Milo? Like he's gonna be bothered with ducks!' retorts Ben, already a world-weary expert on child development. But he's on his way to the hall, lifting Milo's new cardigan off the peg and, with the baby across his knees at the bottom of the stairs, easing him into it as though he's done it a hundred times. He hands the bundled infant to Harriet without a word and shrugs his shoulders into his padded jacket. As he takes back his charge, his aunt slips a cashmere scarf (brown, reasonably manly) around his neck. He goes to protest, fingers the fabric, thinks better of it.

'Gloves?' says Harriet.

He gives her a withering look. 'Buggy?'

'Buggy?' says Harriet blankly.

'As in, thing I push Milo in?'

'We don't have a *buggy*!' says Harriet. 'For heaven's sake!'

'Well, I can't carry him—not all that way. Besides, it's not safe.'

The boy, Harriet has to admit reluctantly, has a point.

Milo, as though sensing the indecision, begins to stir.

Hester appears in the kitchen doorway. 'You two going out?' she says to Ben. 'Good idea. Get a bit of—'

'Fresh air, yeah,' finishes Ben dully. 'Yadda, yadda. Only we got no buggy.'

'*Have*,' chorus Hester and Harriet automatically.

Upstairs, footsteps cross the bedroom floor and make for the bathroom. The sisters exchange a glance. They want Milo— and Ben—out of the house before Daria comes down. It's time they found out exactly what sort of trouble their young guests are in. Harriet has already checked the lane: there's no sign of Archie Dick or any other undesirables.

'I know!' cries Hester. 'Wait there.' She darts into the sitting room to scoop up a cushion and a small rug and hurries through the kitchen to the back door.

'Am I going or what?' grumbles Ben. 'Only his nibs is waking up.'

And Milo is, tiny limbs stretching, one hand plucking ineffectually at the neck of his Babygro. Harriet finds her finger stretching out to stroke his cheek, to be rewarded by a fleeting smile. Probably just wind, but still.

Ben shifts his weight irritably. 'Why do I have to go out anyway? I wanted to watch the film.'

'Tough.'

There is a squeaking noise outside the front door. Harriet opens it to find Hester standing there in triumph, presenting her audience with a serviceable but battered bicycle, wheels laced with cobwebs, its front basket now a soft Milo-sized nest.

'There! Come on, pop him in. You can wheel him in this.'

Ben is speechless with incredulity. He looks at the bike, down at Milo, then up to Harriet, who is already braced with an encouraging smile in place. 'Perfect,' she says. 'Snug as a bug.'

'I'm not taking that pile of crap out. What if my mates see me?'

'Tell them your batty aunts made you. Besides, you're miles from home.' Hester reaches out for Milo and tucks him neatly into the basket until only his face is visible. His eyes seem to take them all in and another of his irresistible grins breaks out. 'See? He's happy as Larry.'

Harriet gently pushes Ben towards the contraption. 'Oh, hang on! Bread.' She hurries into the kitchen and throws the heel of a loaf into a plastic bag, then scoots back to the front of the house and ties the bag onto the handlebars. Hester looks smug.

Ben reaches into his pocket and pulls out a baseball cap, shoving it onto his head forcefully so the brim almost obscures his eyes. 'Christ!' he mutters under his breath. 'Christ almighty.' He starts to wheel the bike carefully down the path.

'Don't worry about the potholes,' calls Hester. 'Babies like being bounced about.'

'And just push it, Ben,' adds Harriet. 'Don't ride.'

Ben stops at the gate and turns the full glare of his outrage on them. 'What do you think I am? Stupid?'

'Hester!' hisses Harriet warningly before her sister can respond. She hurries down the path, whispering fiercely, 'Ben!' She checks up and down the lane. Deserted. Nevertheless she keeps her voice low. 'Don't talk to anyone you don't know. Ideally, don't talk to anyone. Do you understand?'

'If you say so,' says Ben. 'But I don't know anyone round here.'

'Even so, if anyone asks, Milo's your cousin, okay?'

'Okay.' Shaking his head, Ben starts pushing the bike up the lane.

Harriet retraces her steps to the front door where Hester is waiting.

'Notice anything odd about that boy?' Harriet asks.

Hester watches as the boy in question, plus bike and cargo, disappears from sight around the bend. 'Where do I start?'

'Seriously.'

'I am being serious. What?'

'He's been here a couple of hours already and not once has he got his phone out. It's usually welded to his hand.'

'Perhaps he's lost it. Or left it behind.'

'Left it behind! He's a *teenager*, Hetty. He'd no more forget his phone than forget to breathe.'

'I wouldn't put that past him.'

A withering look from Harriet.

'Maybe it needs charging.'

Harriet regards her sister pityingly. She really hasn't the first idea. 'Something's up, you mark my words.'

'Well, we know *that*!' says Hester snippily.

The sisters re-enter the house, Hester closing the front door firmly, just as Daria stumbles groggily down the stairs. They both watch her descend, eyes heavy, her blink slow like someone drugged. Drugged . . .

'Hetty,' whispers Harriet, 'you don't suppose . . .'

'No,' Hester whispers back, forcing a smile for the girl's benefit. 'She's just exhausted. And very, very frightened.'

CHAPTER 5

'So,' says Harriet, settling into her chair by the hearth and feeling a twinge in her back. She'll have to be more careful about lifting Milo in future. For such a tiny baby, he's surprisingly heavy. Or perhaps all babies are; she's hardly had much practice.

'So?' says Hester, eyes fixed on Daria, who is shrinking into the back of the battered Chesterfield, or as far as the lumpy springs will allow. 'Listen, my dear, we just want to help. But we can't do that unless—'

'Milo,' says Daria, wetting her lips, wringing her small hands in her lap. She resembles nothing so much as a tiny mammal cornered by predatory humans.

'Milo is fine,' says Harriet soothingly. 'As we said, he's gone out with Ben. For a walk, to get some fresh air. Perfectly safe.' *Please God*, she thinks, still coming to terms with her nephew's transformation, at least as far as the baby is concerned. 'Look, we want to help you, Daria, but if we don't know what's going on, it's hard for us to know what to do. You see?'

The girl nods, chewing her lower lip miserably.

Hester steps in. There are times when Harriet is *too* understanding. 'Now, listen, Daria: that man who came earlier—not our cousin, George; the other one—did you know him?'

Daria's eyes dart about the room. They can almost hear her thinking, deciding.

'No,' she says. 'I only hear his voice, but I don't know him. How he knows I am here?'

'It's all right. Don't panic. He doesn't actually know for sure. Not definitely. But Harriet'—she nods at her sister—'Harriet gave him to believe ... made him think ... that you weren't.'

Daria frowns, picking at her skirt—actually one of Hester's skirts, rolled over several times at the waist to accommodate the disparity in their heights; Harriet's, while a more sensible length, had simply slid straight over her hips. 'So, he goes, the man?'

'That's right,' says Hester emphatically. 'The man has gone.'

Harriet thinks her sister is being a mite optimistic. He might have gone for the moment, but . . .

'The thing is, we still don't really know who he is. Or why he was looking for you. We were wondering . . .' Harriet's not quite sure how to frame this without alarming Daria unnecessarily. 'I mean, it would seem that he's a detective—'

'A ... detective? Like policeman?' Daria blenches; a tic works over her left eye.

Harriet reaches out a hand to stop her leaping from the sofa. 'It's all right. Calm down. He's not a policeman. Well, I mean, he might once have been a policeman . . . they often are, these private investigators, or so I believe.'

'Harry! Do stick to the point! Listen, Daria, this man is obviously working for someone else. That's what they do, private detectives. They look for missing people. He said he was after a runaway. He had a picture of you.'

'Picture? What picture? Like, photograph?'

Hester looks to Harriet for confirmation.

'It was a photocopy. It looked to me like it was probably taken from a passport photo.'

Daria nods. For a moment she looks, bizarrely, almost relieved, her face brightening.

Hester stiffens. 'You do have a passport, Daria?'

There is an infinitesimal pause but they both register it.

'Yes,' says the girl, looking at her hands. 'Of course. Passport is necessary. Everybody has passport.'

Well, thinks Harriet, *that isn't strictly true. And I think you're only too aware of that, Daria, my dear.*

'So where is it then?'

Daria looks at Hester, then away.

'Your passport?'

'I have . . . I lose it.'

You are an even worse liar than my sister, thinks Hester. Aloud she says, 'You lost it?' She tries to mask her scepticism. She fails. 'Right.'

'Yes, yes,' says Daria desperately. 'My bag is stole at railway station . . . big boy, rough . . . I run after, but I am . . .' She gestures to her stomach. 'He get away.'

'I see,' says Hester dryly. 'So this . . . incident, the theft of your bag—and your passport—happened while you were still pregnant?'

'Pregnant, yes. With my baby, Milo.' Daria smiles winningly, but Hester forges ruthlessly on.

'So at least, what, two, three, four months ago? And, obviously, you reported this to the police?'

Daria pales. Her fingers knot again. 'No! I . . .' She looks down into her lap, as though surprised to find her hands there. She stills them. 'I do not tell police.'

'Why ever not?' There is no mistaking Hester's exasperation.

'*Hetty* . . .' Harriet almost groans. She's as anxious as her sister to get to the bottom of all this, but it's beginning to feel like an interrogation and Daria is visibly wilting under Hester's onslaught.

'What?' snaps Hester.

'Maybe we're being a little bit . . . heavy-handed?'

'I am simply trying to establish the facts,' says Hester very quietly, flushing. 'Madam here is spinning us a pack of porkies and all I'm trying—'

Harriet snorts. 'You sound like a TV cop. A bad one, at that.'

'I'm talking in *code*,' Hester says tersely. 'For obvious reasons. I think we're being spun a yarn and I don't like it.'

Harriet glances over at Daria, who is watching them both fearfully. 'And the suspect is terrified, can't you see?'

Hester gets to her feet and plants herself directly in front of Harriet, her back to Daria. She bends down to hiss in her sister's face, 'I think she's taking advantage of our good nature, that's what I think. She's presumably here illegally. She thinks we're a pair of nitwits. Well, you may be, but I'm certainly not.' And with that, she stomps out of the room. Seconds later, the kitchen door slams.

Harriet sighs, pushes herself out of her chair, crosses over to Daria and sits beside her on the Chesterfield, a spring poking her in the bottom. She takes the girl's hand; a tear splashes onto her wrist.

'Daria . . .'

'Sorry, sorry.' The girl's eyes swim with tears. 'I am so . . . I don't know what I must do. I am making trouble here.'

'Not at all,' says Harriet insincerely.

'Yes! For sure. Your sister is angry.'

'My sister is always angry. Never mind her. But, listen, Daria, you must trust us.'

'Trust?' The bitterness is palpable. 'You say trust, but ever since I come here to your country . . .'

'Yes? When was that?'

It is as if a shutter has been pulled down; Daria's face hardens, her eyes darken. She pulls her hand away.

'Please. I will go. When Milo is here, I go.' She gets up and moves over to the window, standing to one side to peer out from the shadow of the curtains.

'Where?' says Harriet patiently. 'Where are you intending to go exactly? Without a passport, in the middle of winter— you don't even have any decent warm clothing. Daria, don't be ridiculous. At the very least, think of Milo.'

The girl spins around. 'Milo? Of course I think of Milo! He is my son. He is everything I have in the world. Everything! What kind of mother you think I am?'

'Well,' says Harriet with growing asperity, 'I'm beginning to wonder. All we're trying to do is help, to give you both shelter and—well, forgive me, Daria—you are being totally obstructive. I mean, you refuse to tell us anything. Refuse to trust us. Why on earth do you imagine we brought you home with us if we didn't want to help?' She has become so frustrated that she has forgotten to temper her vocabulary but from the look on Daria's face, she appears to have picked up the gist of it.

'For whatever reason, someone is very anxious to find you. Now, I don't know why—and you seem extremely reluctant to explain—but, frankly, I don't take kindly to strange men like that creature earlier turning up out of the blue, forcing me to lie about you and Milo. Added to which—'

'Milo?' gasps Daria. She springs up, her hand to her mouth. 'He know about Milo! No!' She flings open the sitting-room door and stumbles out into the hall.

'No, wait—Daria!' Harriet scrambles to her feet in pursuit. 'He only said . . .'

But Daria has streaked up the stairs and into the bathroom. The door thuds shut.

Harriet curses.

'That went well, then,' says Hester from the kitchen doorway. 'I thought you were supposed to be the good cop?'

◡◡◡

'I'm not sure we're any the wiser,' says Harriet, sotto voce, in the kitchen. 'We still don't know who that man was or how he knew she was here, still don't know how she got here—'

'Or who Milo's father is,' says Hester, cutting thick slices of Dundee. 'We ought to get some full-cream milk.' Catching Harriet's incredulous expression, she says, 'Not for us! For her. She'll need it if she's breastfeeding.'

'Of course,' says Harriet, disappointed. Hester's had them

both on a low-fat diet for months and Harriet dearly misses the forbidden foods. She doesn't believe this changed regimen is having the slightest effect on their health or their weight and, as she said at the time, 'Hetty, if our arteries are furred up already, I can't see that the odd blob of double cream is going to make a ha'porth of difference.' But, as cook and chief food buyer, Hester had stood her ground, making an exception only for high days and holidays. Boxing Day, Harriet is relieved to note, is most definitely a high day, if the size of the cake portions is anything to go by. Personally, she thinks that if they are intent on extending their lives, a little less alcohol might be prudent, but she certainly has no intention of proposing that privation. *Besides*, she thinks, sinking her teeth into Hester's sublime Dundee, *who the hell wants to live forever?*

'That of course assumes she's staying,' she mumbles.

'Well, let's be realistic,' says Hester. 'We're not going to kick her out, are we? Not until we get to the bottom of this. They'll be here for another few days at least. And frankly, given the fact that we've lumbered ourselves with the boy as well, it hardly matters, does it? We might as well open up to all comers.'

'I quite like having a baby in the house. That's to say, I quite like having Milo in the house. You have to admit, he's very cute.'

'Hmmph,' says Hester. 'I hope you realise that if we'd just gritted our teeth and endured a few hours with George and Isabelle yesterday, we could be nice and cosy in front of the fire right now, with not a care in the world. Instead of which . . .'

The kitchen door inches open.

'Come in, Daria,' says Hester, not missing a beat.

The girl hovers.

'For pity's sake, close that door, will you? There's a terrible draught.'

Daria creeps in and Harriet pushes out a chair for her, noting the puffy eyes and red nose. Daria sits cautiously. The sisters wait.

'Please,' whispers Daria. 'I am sorry. I should not run away from you like that. I know you are good people. Very good. Only I am afraid.'

'Have some tea,' says Harriet. 'There's not a problem in the world that can't be solved with a nice cup of tea.' She pours a cup, while Hester cuts a mountainous slice of cake.

Daria looks aghast. 'All this . . . ?'

'You've got to eat. For the baby. Your milk.' Hester holds the jug over Daria's cup.

'No! No milk, please.' Again, that grimace, and Daria snatches the teacup away. A drop slops over the rim and onto her cake.

'Sorry. Sorry. No milk.'

'No, no,' says Hester, 'I meant *your* milk.' She gestures discreetly at Daria's breasts.

The girl starts and then laughs, transforming her face. 'Sorry. I thought . . . milk in my tea!'

Harriet laughs and even Hester smiles faintly.

'Black tea?' Harriet wrinkles her nose.

'Of course,' says Daria. 'Always black in my country.'

The women sniff an opportunity. 'Oh, I see,' says Harriet. 'So everyone drinks their tea black, do they, in . . . where was it?'

'Belarus,' says Daria automatically. 'Oh!' A cloud passes across her features.

Hester jumps in quickly. 'Belarus,' she says. 'Well, I never! I've heard it's a beautiful country.'

In truth, she has heard no such thing, has only the vaguest idea where Belarus is. Somewhere near Russia? But it's a start. She itches to get on to the computer and start googling.

'And you don't drink milk in Belarus?' says Harriet.

'Of course!' says Daria scornfully. 'But in tea—never!' Then, lest her hosts think her rude, 'Sorry.'

'No,' says Harriet. 'It's fascinating—what different people eat, I mean. We've never been to Belarus, have we, Hetty?'

Hester agrees they have not, thinking that Harriet is making it sound as though they are seasoned and adventurous travellers who just happen never to have quite made it to this corner of Eastern Europe, rather than a couple who return to the Scilly Isles year after year. She's racking her brains trying to recall if Belarus—wherever it is—is now part of the EU. Everything changes so quickly these days. Nothing for it: she needs to get on the internet. She's just pulling herself to her feet with that aim in mind when they hear footsteps coming around the side of the house. Hester darts over to the window and peers out into the darkening garden. Daria, she notices out of the corner of her eye, has vanished.

It's Ben, wheeling the bicycle with its precious load around to the back door.

Hester goes out to meet him. 'Everything all right?' she says, holding the bike steady as the boy gently lifts the sleeping baby from his nest.

He rolls his eyes but does not deign to reply. Instead he addresses all his remarks to Milo. 'We had a laugh, feeding the ducks, didn't we, mate? Stopped that swan muscling in.'

'Swan!' exclaims Harriet, remembering some scary encounters with the brutes along the Cam many moons ago. She is itching to take the baby from Hester, his temporary guardian as Ben divests himself of his outerwear. Hester doesn't look at all comfortable holding Milo; Harriet finds herself mildly gratified by her sister's apparent awkwardness.

'We didn't let the old bruiser get near us, did we, eh? Steered well clear, we did. Oh, great, cake—I'm starving.' Ben settles himself down at the kitchen table and holds out his arms for Milo. Hester, to her surprise and disappointment, finds herself handing him back. Ben tucks the baby in the crook of his elbow and sets to on the cake. 'Know what?' he says, spraying the table liberally with crumbs. 'Your cake don't taste nothing like Mum's.'

'*Doesn't*,' chorus the sisters, Hester thinking indignantly, *I should say not!*

'Did you see anyone while you were out? Any of your friends?' asks Harriet.

'No, thank Chr— . . . thank God. I mean, Milo's great, but he's not going to do much for my street cred, is he? They'll think I'm gay or whatever.'

'There's nothing wrong with being gay!' says Harriet, stout liberal that she is.

'I know that!' says Ben indignantly. 'One of my best friends is gay. But I ain't.'

This time the sisters forbear from correction. Harriet is just holding out her cup for a refill when Ben says casually, 'But there's a well dodgy bloke in a van halfway down the lane. Passed him going and coming back.'

The teapot stops its course and hovers over the cup. 'Doing what?'

'Nothing. Just sitting. Turned his head away when I went past.'

'Did he see you?' says Hester, trying to keep the anxiety out of her voice.

'I guess,' says Ben, reaching for a second slice of cake—carefully, so as not to wake Milo. 'I mean, I walked right by him.'

'Did he see Milo?'. Harriet flashes a worried look at Hester.

'Nah,' says Ben, 'shouldn't think. Just looked like a pile of old sweaters, didn't you, mate?'

As if on cue, Milo opens his eyes and stretches extravagantly, then, as the hall clock strikes five, with impeccable timing begins to cry.

'Hungry,' says Ben. 'Needs his mum, he does.' He strides over to the door into the hall and flings it open, only to discover Daria crouched against the wall. 'Hello? What's up? His nibs wants feeding.' He places Milo in his mother's outstretched hands and ambles back to the table. 'Any more tea?'

Daria is still hesitating in the hall; within a few short seconds Milo has transformed himself from an angelic bundle into a ball of infantile fury.

'Quick, quick,' says Harriet, hustling the girl into the kitchen as the crying increases in volume. 'Ben, shift yourself; Daria needs that chair. Hetty, turn the radio on.'

'The radio?' says a bemused Hester.

'Yes! Now. As loud as possible. Quick!'

The normally soothing tones of Radio 4's Carolyn Quinn shatter the calm of the house as, at deafening volume, she hollers news of the latest Middle East atrocity.

'Friggin' hell!' yells Ben. 'What the f—'

'Just a minute!' shouts Harriet, watching Daria closely as she slides into the chair Ben has vacated. She swiftly, and without embarrassment, offers Milo her breast. He stops crying instantly.

Harriet bustles across the kitchen and switches the radio off. Milo is now firmly latched on to his mother, his tantrum forgotten. There is a fragile feel in the air as though something has been broken or is waiting to break. The silence in the kitchen is faintly unnerving.

'Hetty,' says Harriet, 'you might like to draw the sitting-room curtains?' She is wondering how much Daria heard—and understood—when she was standing in the hall. The last thing she wants is to further frighten the girl.

Hester frowns in puzzlement, then her face clears. 'Good thinking,' she says, and pats her sister's shoulder as she passes.

'Good thinking?,' says Ben, bewildered. 'And what's with the radio?'

Daria is bending over her son, gently stroking his head. Harriet points at her and puts her fingers to her lips.

Like Hester, Ben first frowns, then nods. 'Right! Got you. *Pas devant les enfants*, eh?' His accent is execrable but Harriet is impressed that he has at least picked up a smattering of French. She must remember to tell George and Isabelle.

'Exactly,' she says. She and Ben exchange an understanding smile. Daria looks up at that very moment; she smiles too.

'Okay,' she says. 'Is okay.'

And Harriet, whose faith is a feeble and flickering thing at the best of times, prays that she is right.

CHAPTER 6

The evening passes uneventfully and, with Hester knitting furiously in the corner, Daria early to bed after supper (presumably to forestall another interrogation) and Ben buried in a peculiar comic book ('Manga,' he'd explained, astonished at her ignorance), Harriet reflects that things could be worse. She had sat beside Hester after supper as she surfed the internet and they have now satisfied their curiosity about Belarus for the moment, via Wikipedia, and have a reasonable handle on its location. Twice she'd crept out onto the dark landing to peer out at the lane, but everything was silent. She is struggling to her feet on her way to the kitchen to retrieve the wine bottle when a thought strikes her.

'Oh, damn and blast it!'

Hester's glasses are perched in her hair as she peers at her knitting pattern; she pulls them down into place and squints over at her sister. 'What now?'

Ben remains immersed in his comic, almost unconsciously turning his mobile over and over in his pocket. Every so often it vibrates: he retrieves it, replies at lightning speed using only his thumbs, and shoves it away again. Harriet can't help thinking that the human thumb was never designed to perform such acrobatics; she envisages a generation of arthritic adults with crippled hands in the years to come.

'What?' repeats Hester with a slight edge. Harriet is forever doing this: interrupting her and then going off into a little world of her own.

'Just remembered. We were going to pop some bits and bobs down to old Finbar, weren't we? We forgot yesterday.'

Hester glances at the clock. 'It's nearly nine. Besides, we've had about three glasses of merlot, the pair of us. I don't fancy you trying to negotiate the lane at this time of night, never mind getting breathalysed.'

'Fair point. But we don't both need to go. I suppose I could always take the bike.'

'Who's Finbar?' says Ben, without looking up.

'He's an old boy—a tramp, I suppose you'd call him—who lives in the bus shelter.'

'Except he wasn't there yesterday,' says Hester. 'He might have gone walkabout. He does that. Trundled off to Exeter a year or so back, remember? Was gone for weeks.'

'No, he's there all right,' says Ben. 'I saw him this afternoon when I was on my way here. Smelt him, I should say.'

Hester and Harriet laugh, both remembering their ill-advised offer of a bath for Finbar in their first few weeks in the village. It had taken days to clear the smell out of the bathroom, and the towels had never recovered. Still, they both retain a sneaking respect for him: a man who has survived on the streets for over fifteen years.

'I don't like to think of him out there in the cold tonight of all nights. Forget the bike, I'll just walk down with some beer and a bit of that quiche. I could do with stretching my legs,' says Harriet, then mouths to her sister, 'and I'll see about that van.' She goes through to the kitchen, listening out for Hester's footsteps: no-one has free rein in her kitchen. Sure enough, Harriet is just about to open the fridge when Hester appears and takes over. Soon a basket is filled with a generous slice of quiche, some smoked salmon rolls, a hunk of strong cheddar and three cans of the lager they buy especially for Finbar when it's on offer. Hester tears off a few sheets of kitchen roll and tucks them in too. Ben, who has wandered through in search of more food, looks surprised.

'Finbar,' explains Harriet, 'was a classics master many years ago. Appearances deceive. He may be a stranger to soap and water, but he still has standards.'

'Blimey,' says Ben, helping himself to some cheese. 'Classics master? What's he doing holed up in an old bus shelter, then?'

'He had some sort of breakdown, years ago. He was hospitalised at the time, it was that serious.'

'Yeah? Then why not a hostel or whatever?'

'He doesn't like the class of people there,' says Hester. 'He's very particular about his companions. He once struck a man for using a split infinitive.'

'A split what?'

'Another time,' says Harriet. She hefts the basket, testing its weight for manageability.

'Want me to carry that?' says Ben. A bit of exercise might take his mind off his troubles, he thinks—his best mate, Jez, in particular. Well, ex-best mate judging by the tone of his texts . . .

'Oh!' Harriet cannot get used to this new, helpful nephew. 'Well, yes, thank you, Ben. It would be nice to have some company.'

They go through to the hall to collect their coats and hats. This time, Harriet insists the boy wears gloves and he does not demur. As they step out into the chill night air, Hester hands her sister a torch.

Harriet says quietly, 'Lock the door after us.'

~~~

It's a clear, moonlit night, pleasantly cold on the face after the warmth of the house. Harriet sets off at a brisk pace, and Ben lengthens his stride to keep up with her. He follows her lead as she weaves confidently up the lane, avoiding the numerous potholes, navigating by moonlight. He points out where the van had been parked earlier but now the lane lies shadowy and deserted; occasional lights glimmer from the neighbouring houses set well back among the trees. When they reach the main road into Pellington village, Harriet switches on the torch to alert any motorists about to their presence. They trudge along in companionable silence for a few minutes, until Ben mumbles, 'Know what? You're all right, you two.'

Harriet feels inordinately pleased. 'Are we? Why's that?'

Ben considers. 'S'pose 'cos you don't keep going on at me.' The familiar aggrieved note has crept back into his voice.

She might have said, *That's because we don't have to live with you*. Instead she probes a little more: 'Ah. You mean like your poor parents?'

'Poor! You got no idea. Nag, nag, nag, all the time! *Clean your room, sit up straight, mow the lawn—*'

'In the middle of winter?'

''Course not!' retorts Ben. 'It was just an *example . . .*'

Harriet smiles in the darkness. 'Well, I'm sure they're only doing what they think is in your best interests.'

'Oh, not again! How do *they* know what's best for me?'

'Because they have experience. No, don't sneer. It counts for a lot. And they are your parents, Ben. Good people.'

'Who wants good people for their parents? They're just an embarrassment.'

'All parents embarrass their children at some time or another. It comes with the territory, I'm afraid. But you can be sure of one thing: they love you a great deal.'

Ben grunts. They walk on in silence. Light spills from the Glass & Cask, the windows steamed up, shouts of laughter punching the air. Passing the Wilsons' house, Harriet sees Teddy's car is back on the drive, parked haphazardly as though he was impatient to get back inside. She reflects how little one knows of other people's marriages: even now, she is prepared to wager, the warring couple will be entwined on the sofa, if not the bed, muttering tearful endearments to one another, their earlier altercation drowned in copious amounts of alcohol.

Ben breaks the silence. 'You know what Aunt Hester was saying—about cooking?'

'What about it?'

'What she said about it being all about chemistry. That true?'

Harriet thinks. 'Well, yes. Yes, it is, I suppose. Why?'

'Nothing.' A beat. 'I'm not bad at chemistry.'

The bus shelter lies dark and silent ahead of them. Harriet puts a hand on Ben's arm. 'He may be asleep,' she whispers. 'Let's not wake him. I'll just leave the basket inside and we can come back for it in the morning.' She gestures to Ben to stay put, relieves him of the basket and creeps forward until she is able to peer inside the shelter. There's no-one there, but the evidence of Finbar's occupation—his many carrier bags, his blankets, the wobbly faded tartan shopping trolley he drags around with him everywhere (decorated, heaven only knows why, with hundreds of torn and curling price stickers)—is strewn all around and there is no mistaking that pungent aroma. Harriet is just placing the basket carefully in among the rest of the detritus when a figure looms out of the darkness from the far side of the shelter, yelling furiously. Harriet drops her burden in alarm as Ben launches himself upon the assailant, rugby tackling him to the ground. There is a short scuffle, accompanied by a volley of swearing, until Ben staggers to his feet, armed with the stick he has wrested from the stranger, who lies winded on the ground. Harriet fumbles with the torch, then plays its beam over a furious Ben, stick raised aloft, and the ragged bundle at his feet.

'Finbar! For heaven's sake!' she hisses. 'Ben, put that weapon away. It's only Finbar.'

The old man, fighting to draw breath, looks up at her with rheumy eyes. 'Is that you, Harriet?'

'Of course it's me! Whatever were you thinking?'

'I thought you were after my chattels,' wheezes Finbar. 'A thousand apologies.' He manoeuvres himself upright on the side of the shelter and leans against it, making ineffectual efforts to brush his filthy clothes down. 'Dear lady, had I but realised it was you . . .'

'Yes, yes,' says Harriet impatiently. 'We came to bring you some food and to wish you a happy Christmas. Not that you deserve it. Honestly!'

Finbar sketches a mocking bow. 'Dear lady, you should have sent me word you were coming. I was simply answering a call of nature and returned to find what appeared to be an intruder. Another intruder,' he added bitterly.

'We came by yesterday,' says Harriet. 'You weren't here.'

'No!' says Finbar indignantly. 'I had been usurped. Can you believe it? Some chit of a girl had set up camp here. In my home!'

'Girl?' says Harriet.

'Yes! This is supposed to be a bus stop!' Finbar is incandescent with remembered rage.

Harriet, ignoring the absurdity of his complaint, presses on. 'What about this girl?'

'Tiny little creature. Waif-like, one might almost say, clutching a bundle to her chest. I thought at first it was some of my treasured possessions that she had purloined but I was mistaken; it proved to be an infant. Imagine! Clearly not from these parts; I could barely make myself understood. I essayed a phrase or two in Greek—modern, you understand—but she did not respond. I had merely moved my belongings out for a day or so to give my quarters an airing while I went into the city for a pre-Christmas rendezvous and I return to find a cuckoo in my nest! Things are at a pretty pass when an Englishman is evicted from his own little corner of God's kingdom—'

'Finbar—'

'She looked barely old enough to be out on her own. I gave her to understand that I expected to find her gone when I returned from a small libation at the public house. As indeed she was. Thanks to you and your dear sister.'

'What?'

'Oh, Harriet, my dear, do not be bashful.' Finbar wags a finger whose nail, Harriet can see even by the faint light of the moon, is gnarled and rimed with grime. 'You and your sister are both women of enormous charity. I would be the last'—he eyes the basket hungrily—'positively the last to criticise your tendency to offer succour to the needy. Still, she was not to know that, was she?'

'But how did you—'

'I saw you drive away as I rounded the bend on my way back from the inn. A child of such tender years getting into a car with two strangers! I'm not surprised her father came looking for her.'

'Her father?' chips in Ben.

'And you are?' says Finbar haughtily, looking the boy up and down while simultaneously delving into the depths of the basket.

'My nephew, Ben,' says Harriet. 'Well, strictly speaking, he's my second cousin, but never mind that now. You say the girl's father was looking for her? When was this?'

'This very morning. There was I, in the midst of my ablutions, when this van pulls up and a rather unsavoury character starts firing questions at me about a missing girl. He spoke surprisingly good English, now I come to think of it. Ah! This looks promising.' He sniffs the packages. 'Luckily, I was able to reassure him that his daughter had by happy accident been rescued by two ladies of irreproachable morals and point him in your direction—'

'Oh, Finbar! You didn't!'

'What? Did I do wrong? I thought she was a fugitive.'

'Well . . . she is, I suppose. But—'

'There you are then! Please refrain from barging in here and implying that I have somehow committed a faux pas. This quiche looks delicious—one of Hester's, I surmise? Are there no napkins?' Silently Harriet pulls a sheet of kitchen roll from the basket; Finbar tucks it into his collar.

'Finbar—about the girl. Look, we think she may be in a spot of bother. Should anyone else ask after her, would you mind awfully keeping schtum?'

Finbar squints at her for a moment from under his bristly eyebrows. 'Are we talking the police?'

'Good grief no! Hardly . . .'

'Well then, of course, dear lady. Your wish is ever my command. I hope the cheddar is good and strong. I recovered some from the bin outside the post office and frankly it was a disgrace, an insult to the palate. And someone had slathered it with Branston pickle! To disguise the taste, I imagine. Unsuccessfully.' Finbar is tucking into the contents of the basket with great gusto. Harriet hands him a lager.

'We'll be off, Finbar. Enjoy your feast.'

'Thank your esteemed sister for me, will you? I might perhaps drop by for a small potation one evening.'

'Oh,' says Harriet hurriedly, 'leave it for a few days, will you? We have guests.'

'Good Lord,' says Finbar through a mouthful, 'I shouldn't want to discommode you, dear lady. I shall double-check first. And as for you, young man'—he waves his can at Ben—'you should be more respectful of your elders.'

'Yeah,' says Ben, handing him his stick. 'I'll do that, mate.'

'Nice tackle, though,' says Finbar. He addresses himself to the smoked salmon and retreats into the shelter as though signalling the end of the audience. Harriet winks at Ben and aunt and nephew begin the journey home.

CHAPTER 7

27 DECEMBER

'We need a plan,' says Hester, taking Harriet her early-morning tea. She settles herself on the bed.

Harriet reluctantly puts aside the latest Susan Hill. 'For Ben or for Daria?'

'For both of them,' says Hester. 'Daria especially; I shouldn't be at all surprised if that Dick creature doesn't resurface. And Finbar's so unreliable once he's had a few drinks, Lord knows how many more people he might start gabbing to.'

'True enough. And they can't stay here indefinitely, who-ever's looking for her.'

'Them.'

'Quite. We probably ought to contact the police or some-body.' Harriet sighs. Good-hearted they may be, but they are also law-abiding. If Daria really is here illegally, as they both suspect, they will do what they must: they have no desire to be caught harbouring someone with no right to be in the country.

On the other hand, they do not want to jump to conclusions before they are absolutely sure of the facts. Who knows what has brought Daria to her current straits? They've both watched enough documentaries and read enough exposés to know that the system does not always safeguard the most vulnerable. And aside from Daria herself, frail and frightened, there's a helpless baby to consider . . .

'I just wish she'd tell us what the hell is going on,' says Hester crossly. 'I mean, God knows, we're only trying to help her.'

'I've been thinking,' says Harriet. 'When you were grilling her yesterday—'

'Oh, don't start all that nonsense again! I was not *grilling* her; I was simply trying to get to the bottom of—'

'I didn't mean that. Anyway, I didn't exactly keep my temper either, did I? And of course you were absolutely right; she was lying through her teeth. No, what occurred to me afterwards was this: what really upset her, the reason she went charging upstairs, was that Dick mentioned Milo. Well, not Milo by name, but a baby. Or rather, that there might be a baby.'

Hester purses her lips, thinking. 'So if this Dick fellow is working for the father, then Daria must have done a runner before Milo was born. When she was still pregnant.'

'Precisely,' says Harriet. 'So . . .'

'What?'

'Why is he so anxious to find her? I mean, she has no money, no possessions that we know of. And I can't imagine a private detective—even one like Dick—comes cheap. Which presumably means his client—the father, as we're assuming—is pretty wealthy.'

'Or desperate.' A thought. 'Or Daria's got something he wants or needs back.'

Harriet shakes her head. 'Everything keeps going round and round in my head. I was lying here staring at the ceiling half the night.'

Not quite true, thinks Hester. *You kept me awake for hours with your snoring.*

'But it's all guesswork,' Harriet concedes. 'Dick's client could be a debt collector, an immigration officer, anyone.'

'It's hopeless,' says Hester crossly. 'How on earth did we end up with two lost souls with such intractable problems under our roof? A destitute mother and baby on the run, and a recalcitrant teenager.'

'Well, as for Ben, that requires a lengthy conversation with George and Isabelle. But not today, if we can avoid it, eh? You know, I think we may have misjudged that boy. He's been positively falling over himself to be helpful.'

'I'm reserving judgement,' says Hester. 'For the moment, I think we're just the lesser of two evils.'

'You,' says Harriet, reaching for her book, 'are just an old cynic.'

'And you,' says Hester, making her way to the bedroom door, 'are a pushover.'

Snuggling down into her duvet for a few extra minutes with her novel, Harriet reflects that there are far worse things to be.

‿‿‿

Daria has swept through the ground floor like a whirlwind by the time Hester is dressed. Stacks of books that have not seen a duster for months now stand neatly aligned by their respective chairs. Receipts and old notes have been paper-clipped together. Mother's old china shepherdess with her irritating smirk is looking so perky that Hester can only surmise she has been given a proper bath instead of the desultory flick with a feather duster that one or other of the sisters occasionally affords her. She finds Daria in the utility room, mopping the floor. A pile of clean washing, expertly pressed, stands on the counter. She hasn't the heart to tell Daria that the iron normally only comes into service on extremely special occasions like weddings or funerals.

'Daria!' she says in a tone that hovers somewhere between admonishment and admiration, 'really, you don't have to do this. You mustn't.'

'No, please. I like to clean.'

'You *like* it?' This is beyond comprehension.

'Because'—the girl hesitates, her face confused—'how else I can . . . to thank you.'

'We don't want thanking,' says Hester gruffly. 'Come and have some tea.'

'No milk?' checks Daria.

'No milk, I promise. Where's Milo, by the way?'

'Here,' says Ben, materialising in the doorway in a pair of oversized borrowed pyjamas, the baby in his arms. 'He was having a bit of a snuffle, so I went in and rescued him.'

'Snuffle?' Daria frowns.

'Yeah, just making a bit of a fuss, weren't you, mate?'

The quartet make their way into the kitchen, where Hester starts assembling the ingredients for a fry-up. Low-fat diet notwithstanding, she's decided that their guests at least need building up—Daria because she's breastfeeding and looks half-starved anyway, and Ben because he's usually obliged to suffer his mother's unspeakable concoctions and, like all teenagers (or so she's been led to believe), has an apparently insatiable appetite. The air in the kitchen is soon fragrant with the delicious smell of grilled bacon and sizzling herby sausages. It drifts tantalisingly upstairs and it is not long before Harriet is lured down, Susan Hill temporarily abandoned in favour of a proper breakfast. With Hester busy at the stove frying eggs and patiently explaining to Ben the importance of the right temperature and using a teaspoon to trickle oil over the yolks, Harriet surreptitiously eases a rasher of exquisitely charred bacon, just this side of cremation, onto a thick slice of white bread and sinks her teeth into it gratefully.

'Harry!' exclaims Hester, glancing over as she slides the eggs onto a large plate that she hands to a waiting Ben. 'That isn't for you!'

Harriet chews furiously and takes another enormous bite. 'Oh dear, isn't it?' Then, in a bid to deflect her sister's irritation, she adds, 'You were going to cut my hair, remember?'

Ben, easing the eggs onto already-laden plates under Hester's careful scrutiny, snorts, 'You never heard of a hairdresser?'

'Your aunt Hester does a perfectly good job, thank you very much,' says Harriet tartly. 'No point wasting money unnecessarily.'

'This I gotta see!' Ben says with a snigger, spearing a fat sausage, and then another.

'Look and learn, young man,' says Hester, sitting down at the table and, like her sister, finding the remaining bacon too much of a temptation to resist. Harriet bites back a comment, but a gleam of triumph momentarily fills her eyes.

Daria, meanwhile, with Milo placidly sitting on her lap and watching all the kitchen activity wide-eyed, is steadily ploughing her way through the vast serving Ben has piled on her plate. Hester imagines she can almost see her filling out as she eats. She beams: there is nothing so satisfying as watching good food, lovingly prepared, being devoured.

'Any chance of another egg?' ventures Ben.

Hester starts to get up.

'Can I have a go?' Ben is already on his feet. He puts the frying pan back on the hob.

Harriet can see that Hester is struggling to remain seated; she really doesn't like any competition in her domain. 'Let him try,' she whispers.

A few minutes later, after detailed instructions have been imparted by a critical Hester from her chair, a rather ragged-edged fried egg with a wobbly yolk sits in front of a triumphant Ben. 'Nothing to it, this cooking lark.'

Hester bites back her criticism. He reaches over to filch two untouched sausages from Daria's plate and tucks in until finally he has managed to put away every last mouthful. He sits back, replete. There is that comfortable air of camaraderie engendered by a meal shared.

'Well,' says Harriet, 'this won't do, will it? I'll just go and shower and dress and then I suppose I ought to nip into town for milk and so forth. I imagine we need more nappies?' This last addressed to Daria.

The girl nods uncomfortably. 'Yes, please. But I should pay.' She flicks a glance at Ben.

Hester smiles. 'But you have already paid, my dear. You've paid in labour. All that cleaning and ironing.'

'No, but . . . that was nothing,' protests Daria.

'Not to us it wasn't. We normally pay someone to do it, so we'll pay you instead. Board and lodgings. How about that?' says Hester, glancing over at Harriet for support.

Her sister nods her agreement. No need for the girl to know that their cleaning bills are intermittent, and help is only summoned when the chaos threatens to overwhelm them.

Daria gives a timid smile. 'You are very kind, both . . . thank you.'

Harriet reaches over to the dresser for a pad and pencil. 'Right, so we need nappies—were the ones I bought the right size? It said nought to three months and Milo's quite small, isn't he?'

'Thank you,' says Daria awkwardly.

'And should I get some of those baby wipe things? And nappy cream? Or have you got all that?'

Daria is looking more and more uneasy. 'No, I . . . I did have, but I leave behind, because . . .'

'Because you left in a hurry?'

'Yes. Just Milo.'

Hester leans across the table, exasperated by the way everybody yet again seems to be dancing around the subject. 'But how can you possibly manage to survive with nothing? Even I know you need all manner of bits and bobs to look after a baby. You must have had all these things at some point.'

'I did! I did!' cries Daria.

'Then what the hell happened to it all?' Milo stirs fretfully in Daria's arms. 'I'm sorry, Daria, but this stonewalling isn't helping anyone! For goodness sake, make her see sense, Harry!'

'Oi, lay off her, will you?' Ben half shouts. 'You're upsetting the baby.'

And so she is, for Milo is now thrashing about in agitation.

Hester harrumphs and snatches up a couple of dirty plates and takes them over to the dishwasher. She shoves them in and kicks the door shut.

The awkward silence is broken only by Milo's whimpers and his mother's soothing murmurs as she tries to quiet him. Ben stares at Daria; he glances over at Harriet, colours, and shifts uncomfortably in his chair, inspecting his smeared plate intently.

'Daria?' says Harriet. 'We can't go on like this. I really think it's time you told us the truth.'

Alarm fills Daria's eyes. She looks down, seems to be struggling with something inside herself, and then shoots a look at Ben. A signal passes between them and he sits up straighter. Suddenly he seems bulkier, older. 'You want me to tell them?'

'Ben?' says Hester.

Her nephew doesn't answer. He keeps hold of Daria's gaze. 'Only if you say so,' he says, waiting.

The hall clock strikes the hour, ten long chimes. At length, eyes bright with tears, Daria nods.

'Ben, what's going on? What has she told you?'

'Listen,' says Ben, reddening, 'I just went in to see if Milo was okay, all right? Middle of the night. I could hear him

76

chuntering away. Probably your snoring what woke him.' He addresses this to Harriet.

'*That*,' she corrects him, affronted. 'It was my snoring *that* woke him. I have a deviated septum, as it happens.'

Hester, who has learnt to sleep through Harriet's cacophony on most nights, suppresses a smile.

'Worse than my dad, you are. And that's saying something.'

'I thought we were talking about Daria,' sniffs Harriet.

'Okay, okay, keep your hair on. *Anyway*, old Milo's fine, just a bit restless. So we have a bit of a chat.'

'You and Daria?' interjects Hester.

'Well, I wouldn't get much change from his nibs, would I?!' Hester's narrowed eyes tell him that he's overstepped the mark. 'Sorry . . .'

'Go on.' The atmosphere is growing increasingly frosty.

'So, like I say, we start chatting. And then she, Daria, ends up telling me everything.'

'Everything?' echoes Harriet.

He looks to Daria for permission to continue. There is an almost infinitesimal movement of her head.

'Look, you got to understand how hard this is for her.' He jerks his head towards the girl. 'Strange country, don't . . . doesn't speak much English, people take advantage . . .'

Daria's head is lowered. Harriet wonders if she is crying.

'You mean that man?' asks Hester.

'Well, yeah, but he's not the only one. Young girl, on her own—'

'How about starting from the beginning, Ben? That really would be most helpful.' Hester finds herself speaking rather more crossly than she intended, a crossness compounded by the fact that, despite their best efforts, she and Harriet have signally failed to get anything like a coherent story out of Daria, while their wretched nephew seems without the slightest difficulty to have the girl telling all. Unless this too turns out to be another fabrication.

'All right! I'm doing my best, but you keep interrupting . . . So. Daria comes from Belarus, yeah?'

'Yes, we know that.'

'I'm just telling you! From the beginning—'

'Sorry,' says Hester, with ill grace. 'We won't say a word.'

'Right. So she's from Belarus, okay?'

'Rakov,' whispers Daria.

'That's it, Rakov. Near Minsk. That's the capital.'

'Yes, we . . .' starts Harriet, then snaps her mouth shut at a glare from Hester.

'And there's been all these political protests, right? Against the government with, like, loads of people arrested and that. Including Daria's dad.'

'Your father?' says Harriet to Daria, startled. 'Your father's in prison?'

Daria nods. 'I do not know. Perhaps still. They arrest him. He is . . . he does not agree with government. He is . . .' She shakes her head, the right word eluding her. 'He is not criminal!' she clarifies quickly, lest there be any misunderstanding.

'A dissident? Is that what you mean?'

Daria looks to Ben for help.

'Is that what she means, Ben?'

'Yeah, I guess. I mean, he was banged up for protesting and that. Loads of people were. Or he wrote something they didn't like, I can't remember. Whatever. Which sucks, right? Plus they're dead worried they're gonna come after her eldest brother too—'

'Artem,' says Daria.

'Yeah. Right. Artem. So, it's getting, like, really dangerous, what with the army on the streets and the police and that spying on them, 'cos they're all under suspicion on account of the dad.'

'What about your mother, Daria?'

Grief sweeps across the girl's face; her eyes fill. 'Mama is dead.' She spreads her hand over her chest. 'Heart. Last year.'

'Oh, my dear! How awful.' Both sisters instantly reflect on the grandmother Milo will never see.

'Yeah, well,' says Ben, eager to continue. 'Artem—that's the brother—he says to Daria maybe she should get out of the country for a bit till things cool down, and seeing as there's this old friend of her dad's in London—'

'Stepney,' offers Daria, making three syllables of the name, the East End suddenly oddly exotic.

'Yeah, so anyway, somehow they manage to wangle a visa—'

'I have cousin . . .' starts Daria.

Harriet reflects that there's always a cousin, or a friend, with influence at an embassy . . . She tries to imagine living under a regime where everything is possible, for a price, with the right connections.

Daria adds quickly, 'And visa, proper visa.'

Ben continues. 'So she gets on the plane to London with just an address for this bloke. In Stepney. Only when she gets there, he's moved on and no-one knows where he is. And there she is, stuck in a strange city with nowhere to stay, and she tries to get hold of her brother and her dad, only she can't, so she doesn't know what's happening back home. Which is pretty scary.'

Daria nods vigorously. Hester and Harriet exchange a look, both waiting for the inevitable pick-up by a pimp posing as a fellow countryman at King's Cross. The papers are full of stories like this.

Ben forges on. 'Okay. So, fortunately, someone points her in the direction of this, like, advice centre and this family puts her up for the night—'

Oh, here we go, they think.

'And the next morning, they take her back to the centre—I mean, it's for people from Belarus and that, so it's all kosher— to see if there's anything they can do to help. You know, somewhere to stay, a job or whatever.'

'Without a work permit?' Hester cannot stop herself.

'What else is she supposed to do? Gotta live, 'nt she? Otherwise she'd be *sponging*.'

Harriet, watching Hester's reaction, sees that Ben has got his aunt's measure. She smiles inwardly.

'Is only temporary—just a week, two,' explains Daria apologetically. 'Just until I can . . .'

'Until she can get things sorted,' continues Ben. '*Anyway*,' he silences his aunts' potential interruptions with a look, 'there's this sort of job. It's just for a couple of weeks, helping out this woman with two new babies. You know, as a favour. It's not really a *job*. And Daria loves babies, don't you?' He smiles at the girl; she smiles back tremulously. 'I mean, this woman's English but she knows someone at this agency place or something. There's some connection anyway, I forget. Not important.' He pauses, throwing his mind back to the conversation, trying to remember all the details. 'Yeah. So it looks like it's going to be okay—'

The women's minds are racing. They look at Daria, so small and dark, at Milo, so pale and fair-haired ... *Oh Lord*, they both think.

'Except...' Ben lets the word settle into the expectant pause. *He's quite a raconteur*, thinks Hester.

'Except, one of the babies dies.'

'Oh, dear heaven!' exclaims Harriet. Whatever she had been expecting, it wasn't this.

'Cot death,' says Daria quietly, with an authority that speaks of much repetition. 'Marcus.'

'Yeah ... cot death. So they're, like, in bits, the couple. Well, you would be, wouldn't you? Wife goes to pieces, husband's worried sick about her. And he asks Daria to stay on, help them for a couple more weeks.'

'Only to help ... was wrong?' pleads Daria. 'They are crying all the day, all the night. Why I shouldn't help?'

'No, no,' Harriet reassures her, before Hester can reply. 'Of course it wasn't wrong.' *Well, not morally*, she thinks. She turns to Ben. 'What happened then?'

Ben glances again at Daria for permission. She gives it with a nod.

'All right. So Daria's living in the house, helping out with the baby and that, doing the shopping and the cleaning, cooking, whatever, just trying to keep things going. But the wife, well, she goes downhill fast, won't eat, won't get out of bed, can't be bothered with the other baby, little girl—'

'Mia.' Daria's face softens for a moment. 'She is such a good girl. Like she think, must not make trouble, must not cry. But the wife ... she is crying, crying, and no washing,' she says, nose wrinkling. 'Hair all ...' She pulls at her own, grimacing, to illustrate. 'Then the doctor ...'

'Yeah. That's it.' Ben picks up the thread. 'The husband calls the doctor and the doc says she needs to go to hospital. S'pose it was like a breakdown thing.'

'She is sick, very sick.' Daria gestures to her head. 'And the man, Peter, he comes home, it is night, he is so sad, so unhappy, I put my arms—so ...' She looks away out of the window as if reliving that time.

Harriet rolls her eyes at her sister. 'Oh dear, oh dear.'

'Outrageous,' says Hester, almost under her breath. But Daria hears. There is no mistaking the sudden tensing of her thin body; Harriet wants to comfort her, reassure her that Hester is not referring to Daria's behaviour but that of the man in whose house she has been offered refuge. But Daria is staring resolutely at the floor and will not meet her eye.

Ben coughs uncomfortably. 'Yeah. So. Later, much later, months later, Daria realises—'

'I am praying. On my knees, every day. I pray, please God. Please.'

And Hester, remembering a brief, ill-fated liaison with a tutor at university, about which she has never spoken to anyone, not even Harriet, recalls the nail-biting wait for that blessed spot of blood in the pan. Oh, the relief of it! The endless trade-offs promised to God if only he would bless her with the curse. She'd gone to the campus medical centre that same day and asked for a prescription for the pill. How far away those days seem now. Daria's soft voice calls her back to the present.

'But He does not hear me.' Still, she looks down with such love at the sleeping child in her lap that Hester is almost undone by regret.

'What a mess!' says Harriet. 'But I still don't understand . . .'

Ben holds up a silencing hand.

'I'm telling you! Right. So, she doesn't know what to do, does she? She gets through to her brother at last to tell him where she's living, but he says, no, don't come back yet, it's too dangerous. You're safer over there. Her dad's still in the slammer. And then, of course, she realises she's . . . well, she can't go home, not now. You know'—he leans towards his aunts as though to exclude Daria from the conversation—'unmarried mother and that. Plus she thinks her brother has enough on his plate, what with him trying to get his dad released and all that, without her telling him she's up the duff.'

But Daria has registered—and understood—the remark about her pregnancy. She turns her face away as a flush of shame colours her cheeks. Harriet's hand moves to envelop hers, but the girl gets up abruptly and crosses to the door, Milo clasped to her chest. 'He is needing clean nappy,' she manages and slips out into the hall.

The tension in the kitchen eases a little.

'But how did she end up here?' hisses Harriet.

Ben exhales heavily. 'Look, it wasn't her fault.'

'I'm not saying it was. I'm not blaming anyone. I mean, obviously she couldn't stay in that house.'

'No, that's just it. She did.'

'What?!'

'Where else was she supposed to go? This Peter bloke was all over the place, there's the baby to look after—I mean, he's not much use—and then the wife comes home, and she's better, a lot better, but she can't cope. And they beg her to stay. So does the wife's doctor. 'Course, he doesn't know about the visa and that. But apart from anything else, she's really fond of the baby. And they're in no fit state . . . Well, I mean, what else is she supposed to do?'

'So this . . . this *affair* . . . went on under the wife's nose?' Hester says, appalled.

''Course not!' says Ben indignantly. 'It was a one-off, heat-of-the-moment thing. The guy's really apologetic, terrified his wife will find out. And that's before Dar realises about the baby. I mean, she's well gone before the penny finally drops.'

'What do you mean?' says Harriet, stunned. 'She didn't know she was pregnant? How could she not know?'

'You're kidding, right? There's this girl at school, she never knew she was knocked up until she starts moaning and groaning about stomach pains. Starts wriggling around in maths and we all think she's taking the piss. Then they whip her into hospital and bingo! A sprog pops out. She was well surprised, I tell you.'

'Heavens above!'

'Yeah, I know! We all reckoned she was trying to get out of doing quadratic—'

'Ben!' says Hester severely. 'Could you possibly get back to the matter in hand?' She glares at Harriet to forestall any further interruptions.

'All right, all right! Give us a break!' Ben sighs heavily.

'So she's been there for, like, months and everything's hunky dory—well, not exactly, but ... anyway. And then the wife finds out Daria's up the duff and goes nuclear.'

'She knew it was her husband's?'

'Yeah, bastard fesses up almost straightaway 'cos he didn't know about the baby either.'

That poor girl, thinks Harriet, *nursing that secret all alone. How frightened she must have been!*

''Course, Daria's in a right hole. Her visa's expired, she's about six months gone, can't get home. They chuck her out, she'll be on the streets. Then the man comes over all noble—*it's my fault, blah blah blah, we must do the right thing.*'

'Well, that's a relief,' says Hester.

'Yeah, it sounds that way, but wait a minute. The wife—Daria says she thought she was going to kill her at first, till the bloke calms her down—well, she says to her husband, *I know what we'll do, we'll keep the baby. She can go back to Belarus and we'll bring it up.*'

'They said that? To Daria?'

'Not to her face, no. She overheard them.'

'Well,' says Hester, ever practical, 'I suppose you can see the sense in it.'

'Hetty!' says Harriet, outraged. 'How can you even think that? Taking advantage of a poor ignorant girl in the first place and then compounding it by trying to steal her baby. It's monstrous!'

'Yeah,' says Ben, equally incensed. 'It's her baby. They can't just nick it. Bastards. 'Course, she's wetting herself—a foreigner, no idea of the law. And this bloke's got dosh, you know? She's thinking lawyers, she's worried about her visa, the police and whatever. So the next morning she waits until this Peter bloke goes off to work, she feeds little Mia and then she legs it. Wife's upstairs in bed, so it's not like there's no-one with the baby. Trouble is, first day she got there, they took her passport for safekeeping—so called—so she's in a right state. Bloody thing's in a safe—literally—so no way can she get it back. And without a passport she's well f—. . . can't go home, can't go nowhere.' He corrects himself before they do. '*Anywhere.*'

'What on earth did she do?' says Harriet, picturing that frail figure scurrying along unfriendly London streets, hugging the shadows.

'Makes for that Belarus centre. Only place she knows. Then she thinks, no, can't go in there, they'll only tell the couple. So now she's in a right panic. Only there's this bloke outside; she sort of recognises him from before, or thinks she does.'

'Someone from the centre?'

'She's not sure. But, whatever, he's one of them. You know, from Belarus. Says he knows her dad's friend and that.' Hester and Harriet exchange knowing looks. 'So she tells him all about what's been going on. And he says he reckons he's got a good idea where the bloke is and he'll take her there.'

'Oh, the silly, silly girl!' cries Harriet. 'Whatever was she thinking? And with a baby coming!'

'She was desperate, wasn't she?' retorts Ben indignantly. 'Could have been worse. The guy could've been a . . . well, you know. Anyway, he says he's got to make a few phone calls and to come back later and meet him. She wanders around all day, sits in parks and things, until it's night. Off they go in his car, she's wiped out, falls asleep and then the bloke pulls up in this layby.'

Oh God, think Hester and Harriet simultaneously.

'There's a couple waiting in another car. Bloke gets out and has a quick chat with them, then he tells Daria this pair will look after her, take her to see her dad's mate and everything'll be okay.'

An image of Fred and Rosemary West springs into Harriet's mind. She feels sick.

'So she gets into the other car and off they go. The woman's chattering away, asking loads of questions, and then they pitch up at this place and all climb out.'

'What place?'

'A house. Next morning she finds out it's on a farm. 'Course she's expecting to see this family friend, but the couple say he's just moved on a couple of days before. *But don't you worry*, they say. *You can stay here for a bit.*'

Hester and Harriet go cold. What now?

'I know what you're thinking. But it turns out fine. They were okay, she says. The woman especially. Bloke's a bit iffy, especially when they see she's . . . but the woman talks him round. Tucks her up, gives her a room. She does a bit of cleaning and that—'

'How long does this go on for?'

'Dunno. Coupla months maybe.'

'A couple of months! And no problems about the baby?'

'Well, the woman was all right about it, at least. Didn't have none of her own, so she was dead nice to Daria. I mean, Dar told them what had happened in London and they were, like, really angry about it. Protective, you know? And guess what? Daria goes into labour and wifey only goes and delivers the baby. No sweat.'

'No!'

'Yeah, I know. Amazing. Still, s'pose she was used to it, the wife, being on a farm and that.'

'This is a baby, Ben, not a calf!'

'I know that! But it means no trouble with hospitals and that. Even though Dar was quite sick after Milo was born. Really weak, you know? But the woman looked after her and that.'

'And this all happened around here somewhere?'

Ben spreads his hands. 'That's the thing. She don't know.'

'*Doesn't.*' The sisterly chorus.

'Doesn't,' repeats Ben grumpily.

'Honestly, boy, don't they teach you grammar these days?' fumes Hester.

'You want me to finish or what?'

'Finish,' says Hester with a dangerous look in her eye. 'How can she not know? There must have been signposts, road signs—'

'Yeah, well, that's what I asked. But she, like, arrived at night. Pitch-black. Plus she's in a right state. She was just desperate to get away from the people in London. And once she gets to this farm place, well, the only thing she's worried about is the baby. Says she sort of—I dunno; the way she described it, sounds like she sort of went into hibernation.'

'Nesting,' says Harriet sagely, thinking of her old cat preparing to have kittens decades ago. She had chosen the most inaccessible place behind the immersion heater and resisted all

Jim's attempts to lure her out until her five offspring emerged. The airing cupboard had ever after smelt faintly of urine.

Hester ignores her sister's interjection. 'Let me get this straight. Daria runs away from this couple in London, fetches up in a farmhouse in a location she can't identify, gets taken in by two complete strangers who without demur offer her a job and somewhere to stay—'

'Without what?' says Ben.

'Demur,' murmurs Harriet.

Hester steams on. 'One of whom, it transpires, is able to deliver a baby. And they take her in, just like that, no questions asked? Who would do something like that?'

George and Isabelle, thinks Harriet immediately. *That's exactly the sort of thing they'd do.*

'How convenient is that? And then, presumably, she stays on after Milo is born, doing—what? A little light housework? And at no point does she ever find out where she is? Or try to get hold of her family, to let them know that she's still alive?'

'All right! Don't get on at me,' says Ben irritably. 'I'm just telling you what she told me, 'nt I? It was bloody difficult, I'm telling you, what with the accent and that. We were talking for like *hours*. Half the time I didn't get what she was on about.'

Knowing teenagers as she does, Harriet can see Ben is fast losing interest in the whole business, the novelty of being a storyteller wearing thin.

Hester, though, continues to worry away at the details.

'You're telling me she didn't have a mobile?' she says.

'Dunno, do I? She never said.'

'Oh, come on! Everybody has a mobile nowadays!' Hester says scornfully. 'Even your aunt and I have mobiles! I find it very hard to believe that she wouldn't.'

Ben's spots glow. 'Don't get at me! All I know is what she said. Maybe you should just ask her yourselves.'

'Oh, we will, you needn't worry about that!' growls Hester.

Ben pushes his chair back and gets to his feet. 'You try and help and this is the thanks you get. It's not my fault you've got landed with a runaway, is it?'

'*Two* runaways,' Hester corrects him tartly. 'And I'm not including Milo.'

'Oh, for frig's sake!' Ben yanks the kitchen door open.

'Don't storm off,' says Harriet in a conciliatory tone that earns her a glare from her sister. 'Ben dear, please: did she tell you at all how she ended up in Pellington?'

For a second or two, he looks as if he's not going to reply, but it's been Aunt Hester who's been a right pain, not Aunt Harriet.

'Oh . . . freakin' hell. I can't remember all of it, can I? Just there was some row or whatever on Christmas Eve, and next thing she knows, the woman's waking her up in the middle of the night, shoving her in the back of the van with fella-me-lad and dumping the pair of them by the side of the road.'

'At the bus stop?'

'I can't remember!'

'This woman,' presses Hester. 'Does she have a name?'

Ben lets out an exasperated sigh. 'I've told you what I know. Ask Daria, why don't you?'

And with that, he thunders up the stairs. The whole house shakes.

CHAPTER 8

The sisters face one another across the table, mulling over what they have just learnt. Faint murmurs reach them from upstairs as Ben presumably updates Daria.

'Well,' says Hester irritably, 'this is one unholy mess. I'm not sure we're any the wiser. Either Daria is one of those people who engender protective instincts in everyone they encounter—we being prime examples—or else she's a consummate liar.'

'That's not very kind.'

'Oh, come on, Harry! That farrago would do justice to *The Jeremy Cole Show*! Not that I've ever watched it.'

'Kyle. It's Jeremy *Kyle*,' says Harriet, adding quickly and untruthfully, 'not that I've watched it either. Obviously.'

Hester gives an exasperated sigh. 'I mean, the pair of us would be shouting at the television screen with a plot like this. It's got more holes than a slice of Emmental. And she seems to have Ben wrapped around her little finger.'

Harriet reflects that they, too, appear to be dancing to Daria's tune. 'You really think she's that manipulative?'

'When I look her in the eye, no. She just looks like a lost, frightened child. I was with her all the way through the London instalment, but, for goodness' sake, all that baloney about spending months in an unknown location? The farmer's wife playing midwife? Please!'

'Well, someone delivered Milo.'

'Patently,' snaps Hester.

'And, frankly, it's a blessing she did get away, by the sound of it. Maybe the man had designs on her. Wife gets wind of it and turfs her out.'

'How could she do that? At that time of night? And with a tiny baby? It's barbaric!' Hester suddenly recalls her reservations. 'Assuming it's true . . . any of it.' She considers for a moment. 'I mean, she's a sweet little thing, I grant you, but not exactly siren material, is she? Still, at least we now know for certain that she's not meant to be here. Even if she came into the country legally—and even that I'm beginning to doubt—she's certainly outstayed any visa she may have had.'

Harriet sighs. 'How long would it have lasted, do you think? Three months? Six?'

'Six max, I'd have thought. I could look it up online, I suppose.'

'Do that. I'd rather know exactly where we stand before we do anything we might later regret.'

'The thing is . . .'

'I know. Milo.'

'And, let's be honest, the poor kid has been through the mill already . . .'

'I didn't like the sound of that couple at the farm. Something not quite right there . . .'

'If it's true.'

Silence descends. Each wrestles with her conscience. What might appear quite straightforward and unarguably the right thing to do in principle is horribly muddied when real people— real people living under their roof—are involved. Harriet is struggling to recall the details of recent reports about the situation in Belarus in the paper (pretty disturbing, as she recalls); Hester, in her more pragmatic fashion, is thinking her way through the probable options and their own responsibilities as virtuous citizens. Foremost in both their minds is the image of a tiny, defenceless baby.

'So. Do we confront her again, Harry? Winkle the truth out of her?'

Harriet ponders a moment, then shakes her head. 'Not immediately. The last thing we want to do is frighten her into doing a bunk.'

'You think she would? Where on earth would she go?'

'I think she's so desperate to protect her child she would do anything. Anyway, it's Christmas: what's another couple of days?'

And Hester, concurring with apparent reluctance, finds herself secretly awash with relief.

'Incidentally,' adds Harriet, 'it's remarkable, isn't it, the way Ben got all that information out of Daria when we barely scratched the surface?'

Hester grunts.

'I told you,' says Harriet. 'There's more to that lad than meets the eye. Look how brilliant he is with Milo. And cooking his egg. Come on, admit it: you were wrong about him.'

Hester stiffens and says with some disdain, 'One egg— badly cooked at that—doesn't prove anything. Nor does it a chef make. I am reserving judgement, that's all. Unlike some people, I don't like jumping to conclusions.'

Harriet restrains herself with some difficulty from laughing aloud at this blatant falsehood. Having shared a house with Hester (not always totally harmoniously) for nearly six years, she finds her sister a bewildering and occasionally maddening amalgam of blinkered prejudices on one hand and breath-taking generosity and kindness on the other. She puts it down to Hester's advancing years. Now, mischievously and with studied seriousness, she says, 'Perhaps in that case we ought to phone his parents and send him packing.'

'Don't be absurd!' Hester fires back indignantly. 'We offered the boy sanctuary. We can't renege on that. What sort of an example would that set? Anyway, do you think we could possibly just forget all this for five minutes? I thought I was supposed to be cutting your hair?'

'You were. You are.'

'Well then. Before or after shopping?'

'Oh, before, I think. I look like a Bichon Frisé.'

⌣⌣⌣

The scissors lie on the table, Harriet already towelled and expectant, her hair wet from an unceremonious ducking under the kitchen tap. Hester flexes her slightly arthritic fingers and approaches the implements like a surgeon warming up before heart surgery. Harriet bends her head.

'What you doing?' Ben swipes the scissors from the table before Hester can lay hands on them. Neither of them had heard him return. His earlier ill humour seems to have evaporated.

Typical teenager, thinks Harriet. *From storm clouds to sunshine in the blink of an eye.*

'These are kitchen scissors!' he cries.

'I'm well aware of that, young man,' says Hester crisply, taking them back. 'They are perfectly adequate. We've been using them for years.' As if to demonstrate their efficacy, she grabs a hank of Harriet's hair and goes to snip it off.

'Don't!' yells Ben in outrage. He reaches across, relieves her of the scissors and holds them to his chest, daring her to challenge him. 'Well, that explains a lot. No wonder you both look like a pair of . . .' He thinks better of what he was about to say and finishes lamely, 'I don't believe you two.'

'I don't mind,' mutters Harriet, from her supplicant position. 'Just hurry up, will you? I'm getting a crick in my neck.'

'I *do* mind!' explodes Ben. 'Kitchen scissors, I ask you! Suppose someone sees me with you? They'll think you're nut jobs, the pair of you, wandering around looking like that.'

The sisters, remembering their recent ruse to avoid further visits to his parents, shift uncomfortably.

'I'm not going to a hairdresser and that's that,' says Harriet firmly, head still bent. 'Sitting around for hours, mindless chitchat about celebrities, lukewarm instant coffee and then an eye-watering bill. Not to mention the tip.'

'Wait there,' says Ben and charges up the stairs.

'More than meets the eye, eh?' says Hester darkly. 'In our own home!'

Ben descends the stairs swiftly and storms back into the kitchen.

'See?' he crows, waving an unfamiliar pair of long-bladed scissors under Hester's nose. 'These are what you should be using.'

Harriet looks up. 'Where on earth did you find them?'

'Back of the bathroom cabinet. Come on then. Do it properly.' He hands the scissors to Hester and stands back to watch, arms folded. Hester approaches Harriet's head once more. She repeats her earlier manoeuvre, only for Ben, with a theatrical sigh, to take the scissors from her for a third time and position himself behind the victim.

'Comb?'

'Comb?' says Hester blankly. 'You haven't cut it yet.'

'You have to comb it as you cut it,' explains Ben, as if to a halfwit. He holds his hand out and a fuming Hester digs a rather battered comb out of the kitchen drawer reserved for bits of string and other items of indeterminate but potentially valuable use.

Ben starts to cut Harriet's hair. Something in the way he handles and repositions her head, gently but firmly, reassures her that she is in safe hands. The worry with Hester's less disciplined approach is that ears will be caught up with the hair from time to time. It has happened. Now, Harriet finds it strangely soothing to sit back and let Ben control her head's movements. The comb, despite its missing teeth, slides effortlessly through her hair and she is lulled by the soft whisper of the closing blades, a sound sensation quite different from the crunch of the clumsy kitchen scissors.

'There,' says Ben eventually, an unmistakable note of satisfaction in his voice. He whips the towel away from Harriet's shoulders and guides her through to the mirror in the hallway, standing proudly behind her as she surveys his handiwork.

'Good heavens above!' says Harriet.

'Cool, eh?' says Ben, grinning.

Harriet hardly recognises herself. The unkempt grey thatch has been replaced by a slightly spiky layered look, which transforms her into an almost stylish older woman. She wishes now she had donned something other than her mustard-coloured roll-neck sweater. As if reading her mind, Ben says, 'Something brighter, that's what you need.' He flicks a silk scarf off one of the coat hooks and drapes it around her neck. 'See?'

Hester stands glowering in the doorway, watching all this with a mouth set to sulk.

'Hetty,' cries Harriet, 'you should let him do yours.'

For answer, Hester turns on her heels and stomps back to the kitchen. 'There's shopping to do,' she snaps. 'Come on.'

Harriet winks at Ben. 'She'll get over it. But where on earth did you learn how to cut hair?'

'YouTube, 'course. Where else? I done—*did*—Jez's girlfriend's for a bet. She was well impressed.'

They are both suddenly aware of being observed. Daria is peering through the banisters from the landing.

'Nice,' she says.

Harriet pats her head self-consciously, a deliciously unfamiliar feeling flooding through her. She recognises it as pleasure.

Daria runs lightly down the stairs. She stands at the bottom looking up at Ben, twisting a skein of her long hair. 'Please?' she says.

An unrecognisable Daria is testing the avocados, Ben alongside her with a sleepy Milo snuggled inside his coat. The girl's new gamine cut makes her look somehow older, more confident. There is nothing hesitant about her fruit assessment; she appraises and discards the unsuitable—the bruised or the overripe—with the speed of a seasoned shopper.

Hester, pushing the trolley around the enormous out-of-town hypermarket (on the Stote bypass, far enough from Pellington to avoid unwelcome encounters), is grudgingly admiring of Ben's abilities with the scissors as she inspects the expert styling of her sister's new hairdo; Harriet smiles to see her sister warring with herself in her attitude towards her nephew.

Having checked the lane for any sign of the hostile white van, Ben had marshalled them all into the car, fashioning the rear seatbelts into a haphazard but stout mesh to secure the baby safely, albeit illegally, in his bike-basket carrier. Daria's initial reservations about leaving the house had been overruled by Hester; words between the sisters were unnecessary as neither was prepared to leave the girl behind. Now the sisters, having trudged to a distant corner of the vast emporium following the directions of a young, overworked but very obliging shelf stacker, are inspecting the display of car seats surreptitiously, knowing that Daria will raise objections if she discovers their intentions. Spending money on haircuts is one thing; ensuring the safe carriage of their tiny guest quite another. Somewhat to Harriet's surprise, it had been Hester who mooted the idea of acquiring a proper seat; Harriet is not altogether convinced it is wholly on account of the illegality of their current arrangements.

'After all,' Hester had said, avoiding her sister's eye, 'one never knows when something like that will come in handy.'

'Indeed,' Harriet had replied neutrally.

'I mean, someone might visit—'

'With a small baby—'

'Exactly.'

They had skated over the likelihood of someone arriving, child in tow, on foot and suddenly being in need of vehicular transport. Nor did they dwell long on the identity of such visitors, the vast majority of their friends and family being long past childbearing or rearing. Only too aware of the shakiness of their reasoning, Hester had hurried on. 'I mean, it's conceivable that one day even Ben might start a family. Think how handy it would be to have a car seat then.'

Harriet had reflected that by the time Ben was a parent, it was highly improbable he would be in need of an ancient car seat, which would no doubt be mouldering somewhere in one of their sheds, already repositories of years of accumulated tat and rubbish, some of it transported from their previous homes—broken sun loungers, faulty toasters, three chairs missing their full complement of legs, a grotesque birdbath incapable of holding water since a huge chunk had sheared off one particularly icy winter . . .

They gaze, bewildered, at row upon row of boxes ranging in price from the suspiciously cheap to the breathtakingly expensive.

'It might seem a bit of an extravagance . . .' starts Hester hesitantly, unwilling, like Harriet, to voice the obvious: *Why are we doing this if Daria and Milo will soon be leaving?*

'No, no,' says Harriet heartily. 'Milo must have a proper seat.'

'Of course he must.'

'I mean, it would highly irresponsible of us not to—'

'Of course it would. Otherwise how on earth can we take him out?'

'We don't want the poor child permanently confined to barracks.'

'We certainly don't! And I'm sure we'll get a decent amount of use out of it. After all, whatever happens, you know, with Daria and Milo, these things take time. In the meantime, they've got to live somewhere . . .'

Good grief, thinks Harriet, *I think you're coming round, you old grouch.* She stifles a grin.

They really aren't that much trouble, thinks Hester. *And it's quite nice to have a baby in the house. It's not as if it's a permanent arrangement . . .*

'So what about this one?'

'It's a bit pink . . .'

Harriet, instinctively opposed to gender-specific colour choices, struggles to remember if that in fact makes this a good option for a boy. Hester, sighing irritably, decides not to engage right now in yet another lengthy feminist argument with her sister. She moves along the shelves.

'Oh, I say, this one's a serious bit of kit! But how on earth does that buckle work?'

'Look, this one has a five-point safety harness with one pull adjustment: nine to eighteen kilos.'

'Is that good?'

'God knows. How heavy do you think he is?'

Hester considers Milo's weight in her arms. 'About five bags of sugar? Ten pounds or thereabouts?'

'Really? I'd have said more than that.'

'Well, he's not *nine* bags of sugar, is he? For heaven's sake, Harry!'

Within a few minutes, they are both tetchy and ready to admit defeat. They sidle up to a couple engaged in the same errand, who are delighted to offer advice to two bemused ladies, who are then obliged to endure a lengthy lecture—*worse than George*, thinks Hester—on the relative merits of each brand and model. Finally, with effusive if insincere thanks, they make their choice—'You won't regret it,' says the man, 'that's in the *Which?* top ten!'—and escape, hurrying to the checkout before Daria can get wind of their purchase. 'Nip out to the car and fit it,' says Harriet (all things motoring except the actual driving being Hester's province), 'and I'll go back and pay for the rest of the shopping.' Hester disappears towards the car park as quickly as the bulky box will allow.

Harriet spies Ben and Daria in the dairy section, heads bent over a tub of yogurt. She stops and observes them for a moment. Daria is laughingly trying to decipher the list of ingredients; for the first time since they found her, she looks genuinely happy. Relaxed. Perhaps it's the security of her changed appearance. Perhaps it's Ben's friendship and protectiveness towards her and Milo. They might almost, thinks Harriet, be a young married couple (well, *very* young, given Ben's age) going about their daily lives. *Oh dear*, she admonishes herself, *I must stop this. I'm getting horribly sentimental.* She bustles up to them, ordered, sensible. She checks the shopping list off against the contents of the trolley and they make for the tills. As the alarmingly big load is placed on the conveyor belt, she chases the youngsters out to join Hester, anticipating with secret glee their reaction when they see the new seat for Milo.

Except that when she finally wheels the trolley out to the car, it is to find Hester and Ben still struggling to install the seat in the back, the atmosphere laced with frustration and hostility, Daria standing awkwardly in the background, nervously scanning the car park.

'If you would just leave me to—'

'But it doesn't go like that! Read the bloody instructions!'

'How dare you speak to me like that, Ben!' Hester is scarlet with rage. Milo starts crying in sympathy.

'See!' yells Ben. 'Now you've upset Milo.'

Curious heads are turning in their direction, eager to witness a public spat. One woman even pulls out her mobile phone to take a picture. Harriet hurries over.

'For goodness' sake, you're making a spectacle of yourselves,' she hisses. 'How difficult can it be?'

She soon finds out. Ten minutes later all three of them are crouched in the back of the car, wrestling with the incomprehensible instructions and repeating again and again the same errors.

'Not there! How can it go there? It's the wrong shape!'

'This bit's far too short.'

'You need to lengthen the strap.'

'I have lengthened it. You watched me do it!'

There is a tap on the fogged-up window. Daria, now sitting quietly in the front passenger seat feeding Milo, gives a little cry of alarm.

'Excuse me.' A man's head pokes into the car. 'Can I help?'

It's the husband of the helpful couple.

'Couldn't help noticing you were having a spot of bother with the car seat. Thing is—may I?' He jiggles the seat into a different position while Hester, Harriet and Ben all try to squeeze back to allow him access. 'Thing is, this is definitely the best buy on reliability and safety, but it's a bugger to fit. Let's have a butcher's at the instructions.'

Ben holds them up for him to read.

'Okay, so that threads through there and this little fella clips in ... there! In goes baby, straps over his shoulders, this one between his legs and bingo! Safe as houses.' He nods with satisfaction and then extracts himself from the car, like a potholer retreating from a particularly tight cave mouth, still expounding the manifest merits of this particular model of seat.

Harriet and Hester thank him fulsomely, while Ben mutters, 'I could have done that!' and moodily presses himself into the corner of the back seat. Soon Milo is safely anchored in his new seat, sandwiched between Ben and Daria, while Hester, tight-lipped, sits seething in the passenger seat. Harriet throws the car into gear and screeches out of the car park.

'Harry!' says Hester crossly. 'We have a baby on board.'

Harriet slows to a more seemly pace and is just about to turn off on to the road home when Ben leans forward and asks if they could call in at his place.

'About time, too,' says Hester. 'Your parents must be worried sick about you.'

'I'm not going home!' exclaims Ben. 'I just want to pick up my phone charger and some clothes.'

'Well, really!'

'You said I could stay.' Ben pleadingly catches Harriet's eye in the driving mirror. 'You said I could stay a couple of days.'

'We did, Hetty,' agrees Harriet. 'He only arrived yesterday.'

'Is that all?' snaps Hester. 'It feels much longer.'

'Incidentally, Daria,' offers Harriet, ashamed they had not mentioned it earlier, 'we thought you might want to ring home, see how things are over there.'

'Oh, please!' Daria's face lights up, then clouds as a thought— Milo, presumably—strikes her.

'Just to see if there's any news of your father and, well, to speak to your brother . . .'

'Artem. Yes. Thank you.'

'No need to mention . . .' Harriet glances at Milo in the rear-view mirror.

'No. But is Christmas. Special time . . .'

'Of course.'

'For families.' She falters.

'Of course. Well, as soon as we get home then.'

Daria buries her face in Milo's hair.

Minutes later, they pull up outside George and Isabelle's house. Ben, much to Hester's ire, refuses to get out of the car ('They'll only start on at me again!') and it is left to Harriet to ring the bell and confront Isabelle, George being, fortuitously, around the corner helping an elderly neighbour with a recalcitrant sink.

'Oh! Harriet!' says Isabelle. 'Your hair! I hardly recognised you!'

'Oh, yes,' Harriet says, preening. 'Ben cut it for me.'

'Ben?!' Isabelle gazes forlornly out towards the car and her son's averted profile. 'You mean our Ben?' She is rendered momentarily speechless. But only momentarily. 'I don't know what we've done wrong, Harriet, really I don't. All we want—'

'I know,' says Harriet.

'I mean, we've always tried to do our best—'

'I know.'

'We're beside ourselves—'

'I think he just needs a little breather, just a few days to think things through.'

'But imposing on you! At your age!'

Harriet bridles. 'I think we're quite capable of looking after a teenager for a few days. We're both still hale and hearty, thank you, Isabelle.'

Isabelle looks stricken. 'Oh, Lordy, I didn't mean . . .' She leans forward, squinting. 'Is there someone else in the car?'

'Oh, just a neighbour from the village. We're giving her a lift.'

'You are good. Oh, listen to me, wittering on while you're standing on the doorstep. Won't you come in?'

'No, no,' says Harriet hurriedly, eager to forestall any further questions. 'Just some underwear and a change of clothes? He says not his Disney T-shirt.' She knows if she crosses the threshold, she'll be in there for hours, with the danger that George will return.

Isabelle scurries upstairs to Ben's bedroom while Harriet paces the path, praying that the neighbour's sink is well and truly blocked. A few minutes later, Isabelle re-emerges with a bulging rucksack and hands it over to Harriet. She is just saying her farewells when Isabelle, lip trembling, cries, 'Wait!' and rushes away again, emerging a minute or so later with a parcel wrapped in tinfoil. 'I'll just give him this. It's his favourite. I only made it last night.' With which, her eyes filling with tears, she goes to slip past Harriet, just as the phone rings in the hall. She hesitates, torn between her desperate desire to see her son and the impossibility of ignoring the insistent ringing. 'Oh dear . . .'

'Let me,' says Harriet, taking the parcel. 'You'd better get that, hadn't you? Sorry, Isabelle, we must dash.' She charges down the path, leaps into the driving seat, throwing the rucksack in Hester's lap, and, after the usual tussle with gears, screeches off down the road, like an inept getaway driver. 'Here,' she says, tossing the tinfoil package over her shoulder.

'A token from your mother, you ungrateful boy. She's absolutely heartbroken, you know.'

'Oh God,' says Ben, 'don't tell me. She's made a cake.' He opens the foil.

'What is *that*?' gasps a horrified Daria, poking at the contents.

'Told you,' grunts Ben. 'See?' He thrusts it through the gap between the front seats. Both women recoil.

'Dear Lord,' says Hester, inspecting the solid grey block. 'What in the world is it?'

'Chocolate fudge cake. So-called.'

'Chocolate . . .' Words desert her. She shakes her head in wonderment. 'How is it even possible? She expects you to eat that?'

'Now you see why I had to get away!' cries Ben and Hester's tough old heart instantly melts with pity.

'You poor boy. I'll make you a proper cake when we get back.'

'Yeah? Can I help? I'd really like to know how.'

'Well,' says Hester, flattered, 'that's most commendable. Too few people these days know how to bake a decent cake. All right. Provided you do as you're told and wash up afterwards.'

Harriet catches the eye of a smug Ben in the rear-view mirror. 'Later,' she says, firmly, 'when we get back, we are going to have a chat about you and school. And you are going to phone your parents. You will speak to your mother and you will thank her for the cake. Nicely. And that's not negotiable.'

Ben sinks down in his seat with a mulish expression. Milo's flailing hand manages to snag a hank of his hair; crowing triumphantly, he tries to bring his prize to his mouth. Daria bursts out laughing, Hester, twisting around in her seat, joins in, and Milo squeals with joy. Ben, fighting to stay grumpy, growls, 'But I don't have to eat it, do I?' and the whole car erupts with laughter as Harriet fights to stay on her side of the road. The laughter redoubles when Ben opens his window, unwraps the cake and tosses it over a hedge with exaggerated effort.

They are still fizzing with merriment as Harriet swings into the drive beside the cottage. She is just opening her door when Finbar pops up from behind a hedge.

'Oh, damn it,' she whispers to Hester. 'He can't be after a drink this early in the day. It's not even noon.'

But this is not a social call. Finbar beckons Harriet over.

'Forgive the intrusion, dear lady. But I felt it incumbent upon me to give you warning that there is possibly more trouble on the horizon.' He looks across to the car as Daria lifts Milo out, and Harriet's heart skips a beat. She quickly unlocks the front door, gestures to Hester to join them, and indicates to Ben that he should start unpacking the groceries. Mother and baby disappear into the house, watched by a curious Finbar.

'Trouble,' says Harriet quietly to Hester, who looks to their visitor.

'Lovely quiche, by the way,' he says absentmindedly, peering past them into the house to watch the girl.

'Thank you,' says Hester distractedly. 'Is this about Daria?'

'Daria, is it? Unusual name. And her little one! I was unaware . . . I am not, I feel no shame in admitting it, fond of babies. They are both noisy and noisome. But even I would not accommodate a child of such tender years at a bus stop.'

'Never mind all that. Just tell us—he's been back, has he? That horrible man?'

'No, no, my dear, not he. I'm afraid I have had another visitor today. It seems that yesterday's caller is not the only one in pursuit of the wee lassie.'

'What?!'

'Indeed. She would appear to be much sought after. It all calls to mind the ancients: a beautiful temptress or siren luring men—'

'Finbar! We don't want a classics lesson, thank you very much! Come on!: who was it?'

'The classics have much to teach—'

Hester's eyes narrow; her nostrils flare. Finbar draws back, wisely in Harriet's view.

'All right, all right, dear lady, I have no desire to ignite your famously short fuse—'

'My . . .?!'

'Finbar!' Harriet cuts in. 'Please. This . . . person. Who was it?'

The old man spreads his hands. 'I wish I knew, my dear. The fellow made a laughable attempt to persuade me he was her father.'

'Her father!'

'Quite so. I longed to ask him how he would explain his supposed daughter's impenetrable foreign accent—'

'But you didn't?' Harriet knows only too well how hard Finbar finds it to resist scoring points.

He gives her a withering look. 'I did exactly as instructed. I pleaded ignorance of any girl—or indeed any accompanying baby, once he had mentioned same—as was your desire and sent him on his way.'

'So, yet another man, then . . .'

'My choice of pronoun would suggest that, yes.'

'Finbar!' hisses Hester.

'Apologies, dear lady. The lowest form of wit, I agree. Yes, a male personage whom I attempted to bamboozle but, in truth, I am not confident he was convinced by my mendacity.'

'But how did he find you? And why you?'

Finbar rolls his eyes. 'Dear lady, I live, as it were, *en plein air*. It is hardly an Herculean task to spot me, as indeed this fellow did as I was en route for some refreshment. I am plagued by lost souls seeking directions, morning, noon and night. As if I were an outpost of the tourist information centre! Were there any justice in this benighted world, I ought to be recompensed for my services, not harassed by officialdom.'

'Never mind all that,' interrupts Hester, in a bid to stem Finbar's customary plaint. 'What did he look like, this man?'

Finbar raises his eyes theatrically to heaven, to reflect. 'Medium height, medium build, almost stocky—might, come to think of it, have been a tidy rugby player upon a once—stubble, rather greasy mousy brown hair, I noticed.'

You've got a cheek, thinks Harriet, observing his own lank locks, strangers to shampoo.

'Not the cheeriest of demeanours,' Finbar concluded. 'Indeed, I would go so far as to say he was possessed of a peculiarly dour mien.'

'How old?' presses Hester.

'My dear Hester, I have many talents, but divining a stranger's age—'

'Finbar!'

'Forty? Forty-five?'

'Thank you! And you'd never seen him before? Not local? What was he driving?'

'To answer your questions seriatim: no, I don't think so, and some tatty old van spattered in mud. I'm not awfully good on vehicles, I'm afraid.'

'Thanks, Finbar,' says Harriet quickly. 'And you're sure you didn't—'

'Of course not!' says the old man indignantly, with a haughty adjustment of his clothes that releases a powerful waft of his singular aroma. Harriet doughtily holds her ground while Hester finds a sudden need to check the interior of the car for any stray purchases that might have escaped the carriers. She takes a deep breath of uncontaminated air before resurfacing.

'Did I not give my word that no reference to your house guests would pass my lips?' demands Finbar.

'You did, Finbar, you did,' says Harriet humbly. 'Honestly, I didn't mean to suggest—'

'I'm relieved to hear it. One does not like to be thought unreliable. One's word is, after all, one's bond.'

Unless you've been drinking, Harriet thinks, nodding frantically in appeasement.

Finbar, having made his point, then adds casually, 'Incidentally, my mystery caller was furnished with a photograph, if that's of any interest.'

'A photo?'

'Of your house guest. *Guests*, I should say. Mother and child. On his mobile phone, if you can believe it. Extraordinary

111

devices, are they not? Although she looks a little different today without her luxuriant locks. No less alluring, though. Of course, I swore blind, photograph or no photograph, that I had never seen either of them.'

'I don't suppose he gave you a name, this man?' says Hester.

'He neither offered one, nor did I seek same. I felt that might raise some unnecessary suspicions. Besides'—this with a touch of his previous hauteur—'it is hardly my place to monitor all the visitors to our little Eden.'

'No, quite,' says Hester.

'I did, however, suggest he might consider informing the police if he was so worried about his missing daughter and grandchild.'

'The police? Oh, Finbar!' Harriet almost wails.

Finbar's eyes narrow. 'I am not without a little native cunning, Harriet! It was perfectly clear to me this chap was not exactly *comme il faut*. I simply wanted to observe his reaction.'

'Which was?'

'Shifty in the extreme. *No, no*, says he, *no need for that just yet*. He then intimated that his daughter had a history of mental health problems and he was anxious to avoid any involvement of the authorities. *She'll come back, I'm sure*, he says. *Thanks all the same*. Couldn't escape fast enough.'

'Thank you, Finbar,' says Harriet, weak with relief. 'That was most sensible—and clever—of you.' Beside her she hears Hester harrumph.

'I flatter myself I have one or two neurons still firing. Anyway, once I was confident he had departed, I toddled up here as fast as my ageing legs would allow. The ladies, I thought to myself, must be apprised of these events with all speed. I made myself inconspicuous though, just in case any more miscreants of whatever stripe should be in the vicinity. Hence my emergence from your bushes just now.'

He regards the sisters with a mixture of curiosity and hope, until Hester, realising that the quickest way to get rid of him is to supply his bodily needs, hurries to the kitchen to assemble a makeshift picnic. Harriet, meanwhile, deflects any possibility of an incursion into the house by asking Finbar about his Christmas rendezvous with his fellow mendicants, upon which he is happy to expatiate.

As Hester returns and hands the food to the old man, who deftly secretes it in innumerable pockets about his person, Ben comes out to collect the last two carrier bags from the boot. Finbar, eyeing the largesse hungrily, makes his farewells. He stops beside Ben.

'How very fortunate it is that you are in temporary residence, young man. Your aunts, redoubtable though they be, may have need of a protector. I trust you will fulfil that office.'

'Yeah?' says Ben, somewhat bemused. Then comprehension dawns. 'Yeah, right.'

Finbar scuttles off down the lane, patting the booty in his pockets to reassure himself as to its security, as Ben turns to his aunts, smirking.

'Well, you heard what he said. Have to stay now, won't I?'

CHAPTER 9

It takes a degree of ingenuity to destroy a simple larder system, but Ben has managed it. In the few short minutes Hester and Harriet spent waving Finbar off and discussing tactics for their next conversation with Daria, Ben has put away all the shopping in an attempt to be helpful and to persuade his still-unconvinced Aunt Hester of his bona fides, while at the same time disrupting her unique food storage system, a method so esoteric that none but she can fathom it. Of course, she does not know this yet; nor is Harriet minded as yet to make her aware of the fact.

Entering the kitchen while Hester goes into the cloakroom, and watching him shove a tin of prunes in with the sweet corn, Harriet thinks that the boy deserves credit, not censure, for his endeavours. Hester, her sister ruefully acknowledges, is firmly of the school that holds all visitors to be like fish: after three days they stink. On this occasion, Hester appears to be working to an even shorter timetable. Harriet, who is never anything less than fair, concedes that she is generally of a similar mind, but the alarums—not to mention the excursions—of the past few days have introduced something she hadn't realised was missing from their lives: adventure. True, their unexpected visitors have thrown their usual routines into total disarray, but she can't help thinking that that is no bad thing. *We don't want to get stuck in a rut. Of course, with Hester, it's an age thing, I suppose*, she muses, complacent in her sixty-three years. So she watches Ben with unaccustomed fondness as he shoves the shopping bags (she wincing inwardly because Hester, at odds with her usual untidiness, likes them folded) in a drawer. He looks up with a faint air of self-satisfaction, as if to say, *See? I'm worth having around, aren't I?*

'Old codger buggered off, has he?'

'Finbar has gone, yes,' says Harriet as coolly as she can. It won't do to give Ben too much rope. She wasn't a teacher for nearly four decades without learning how far and how quickly young people will push the boundaries if they think you are a soft touch.

'He's a laugh, in't he?'

'A character, I think we could say. Tell me, how much did you hear of what he was telling us?'

'What you saying? I was earwigging, or something?' Ben is suddenly all affronted dignity. His pimples flame.

'If you mean eavesdropping, no, I simply meant, did you catch anything?' *Goodness me, how quick these young folk are to take offence!*

Ben relents a little. 'That's all right, then. Only, I don't like it, people getting at me, making accusations and that.'

By *people* Harriet takes him to mean Isabelle and George. This face-off with his parents is becoming increasingly tiresome, especially after her earlier painful encounter with Isabelle.

'Ben, you really must learn not to be so touchy. No-one's getting at you. I know at your age it seems like the whole world's against you, but it isn't. We aren't, certainly.' Realising how disloyal that sounds to her cousin and his wife, she hurries to make amends. 'And while we're on the subject, I think it's about time you gave some thought to the toll your leaving home is taking on your parents. Your poor mother is beside herself. Your father too, I have no doubt. This evening you will give them a ring. And no argument.'

Ben, scowling, scuffs his feet on the kitchen floor, looking for a moment with his bottom lip sticking out more like a sulky toddler than a teenager. It is as much as his aunt can do not to laugh. Instead she says severely, 'And I don't want to hear that it's not fair. While you stay with us, you behave in a civilised fashion and take criticism where it's warranted.'

'I put all the frigging shopping away, didn't I!' cries Ben.

'Nor,' says Harriet, a laugh bubbling in her throat, 'do we swear in this house, thank you. And if the rules do not suit, you have one simple solution.'

'Oh no! Please!' For a second, Ben looks heartbreakingly young and desperate, like an orphan about to be banished to a workhouse. 'Don't send me home. Not yet. You promised. You promised!'

Harriet fights the urge to take this lanky child by the arms and give him a good shake. If not a cuddle. 'Well, just you mind your manners, then, young man,' she says and then, treacherously deflecting responsibility, 'Your Aunt Hester won't stand for any nonsense.'

Hester chooses that moment to reappear. All she sees on entering the kitchen are, to her surprise, bare surfaces and Ben hurrying over to the kettle. 'Shall I make some tea?' he says eagerly, disarming both aunts in an instant.

'Where's all the shopping?' says Hester suspiciously. She has never known Harriet to put it away. It's one of their many unspoken rules, like her car maintenance and lawn mowing. Harriet's responsibilities extend mainly to financial management and the occasional bit of light dusting.

'Away,' says Harriet. 'Ben did it.' She beams at him. Then, to pre-empt Hester's automatic move towards the cupboards to check the grocery disposition, she adds quickly, 'We were just talking about what Finbar was telling us.'

'Who d'you reckon he was then, this bloke?' says Ben, confirming Harriet's suspicions that he'd caught the gist of the conversation. Before she can reply, however, Hester jumps in.

'Well, I can only think of two possibilities. Either it's this Peter character in London—Milo's father—or it's the man from the farmhouse. If it's the chap from London, it means that Dick creature has put two and two together since his visit and given him the heads-up—'

'Then why not come straight here?' says Harriet. 'He knows where we live.'

'Dick? Who's Dick?' says Ben, reminding the sisters that he's a little behind them in the knowledge stakes. After a nod of consent from Hester, Harriet quickly explains.

'A private detective?' says Ben admiringly. 'Wow! But his name: that's a joke, right? This is getting really—'

'Quite,' says Hester quickly, conscious Daria might reappear at any second, having gone straight to her bedroom to feed and change Milo on their return from the supermarket. 'So we agree it's most likely to be the man from the farmhouse, then? Because you're right, Harry: Peter thingy would have surely come straight here. He'd know exactly where to come, thanks to Dick.'

'That really his name?' Ben laughs. 'That's classic.'

'If only it were,' says Hester.

Ben pours the boiling water into the teapot, but, caught up in the current conundrum, neither sister, both firm teabag-in-the-mug tea-makers, thinks to query where he has found the pot, last given an outing when the vicar called around soon after they moved in. Hester reaches up automatically to retrieve the biscuit barrel from the shelf.

'Ben, I don't suppose Daria ever'—she jerks the tightly-fitting top off the barrel and dips her hand in—'described this fellow to you?' Her hand swirls round the depths of the barrel and emerges biscuitless. She peers into the barrel, mystified. 'Where on earth—'

'Who?' says Ben quickly, pouring milk into the mugs. 'You mean the bloke—'

'Where the hell have the biscuits gone?' demands Hester. 'I only made them yesterday. And add the milk to the tea, Ben, not the tea to the milk.'

'I had one this morning,' confesses Harriet, fearing that she knows the answer to the mystery. She looks over to where Ben stands at the counter, back resolutely turned on them. Hester, eyes narrowed behind her glasses, glares across the kitchen and then, very, very quietly, with a deadly calm that her subordinates at the town hall had learnt over the years to fear more than any raised voice, says, 'Might you have any ideas, Ben, by any chance? About the whereabouts of an entire batch of biscuits? Mmm?'

A moment of silence as Ben weighs his options. He decides finally and wisely, given Hester's unerring nose for prevarication, to come clean. He is unable, however, to match his aunt's self-control, plumping instead for the impassioned defence.

'Well, I was hungry, wasn't I? I'm always hungry! I can't help it, can I?'

Hester is just drawing herself up for a full-throated flaying when Ben, to Harriet's enormous relief and not inconsiderable admiration, plays his masterstroke.

'And they were, like, so delicious, I couldn't help myself, could I!'

Harriet could clap. Her sister's face clears like the sun emerging after a storm; nothing is more guaranteed to win her approbation and induce immediate pleasure than praising her cooking—especially as, had Ben but known it, her stem ginger biscuits are famed far and wide for their irresistibility.

'Delicious, were they?' she says in a voice that to the uninitiated might sound gruff, but that to Harriet's experienced and Ben's fast-learning ears is tending more towards the softer end of Hester's vocal scale.

Ben, sensing victory, turns slowly around and, with a bashful raising of his dark eyelashes (*He's going to be quite a looker once that skin clears*, thinks Harriet with surprise), looks into his older aunt's eyes with an unashamed plea for mercy and forgiveness. Time hovers accommodatingly in the kitchen as Hester considers her response.

'Well,' she says casually, as though the precipice on which their entire relationship had so recently teetered had never existed, 'We shall just have to make some more, shan't we? Assuming I've got the necessary ingredients.' And she starts to move towards the cupboards to check.

Harriet, knowing how fragile the current ceasefire probably is and desperate to postpone the moment Hester discovers her reordered provisions, interjects swiftly. 'Hetty, hang on a minute. What about that man?'

This stops Hester in her tracks.

'Oh yes! At the farmhouse.' Glancing up, she keeps her voice low; Daria's hearing is keen and it is clear she understands English rather better than her halting speech might suggest. 'Ben, did she ever describe him to you?'

Ben, carrying two mugs of tea over to the kitchen table, shakes his head. 'Don't think so. Why would she?' His face brightens. 'Tell you what, though. She's got a little stash of photos in her room. Family and that. On the dressing-table. Might have one of this bloke. Worth an ask.'

Harriet frowns. 'A bit unlikely, isn't it? Besides, we don't want to alarm her. I mean, she knows nothing about this latest development.'

'Well, I could nip in and have a look while she's downstairs,' says Ben. 'You call her down and I'll—'

'Ben!' cries Harriet. 'That would be an invasion of privacy!'

'Oh, for heaven's sake, Harry!' There are times when Harriet's liberal tendencies infuriate her sister. 'We're trying to protect the girl, not breach her human rights! If Ben can find out what we need to know without putting the wind up Daria, that's got to be better than charging in with all guns blazing.'

'There's no need to snap my head off,' retorts Harriet huffily. 'I still don't see how that helps. Supposing there is a picture, we'd still have to ask Daria if it's him.'

'Not necessarily,' says Hester. 'We could simply . . . borrow the photo—well, any that show a middle-aged man—and nip down to show them to Finbar.'

'I know!' said Ben. 'There's a much easier way to find out. Ask Finbar what sort of accent he had, today's bloke.'

Both sisters frown in puzzlement. Ben looks at them pityingly. 'Posh, he's what's-his-face from London. Obviously.'

'Why obviously?' asks Harriet.

''Cos he's some big shot, n'he, according to Dar? Big house, big earner. Bound to speak posh. Whereas some dude on a farm—'

'Might be just as posh himself. Really, Ben, you must learn not to stereotype people—'

'Harry! This isn't the time! I think Ben may have a point. It's worth a try anyway.'

'Yeah,' says Ben smugly as Harriet fumes. His face lights up again as a thought strikes him. 'Plus, I bet I'm right 'cos Dar said they both spoke funny, the pair at the farm. And I said, funny how? And she said, English funny. And eventually I worked out she meant they had funny accents.' He catches the look on Harriet's face and adds quickly, 'I mean funny to her. As a foreigner.'

'Excellent, Ben. Well done,' says Hester, feeling a tiny bit ashamed after her spat with Harriet and relieved that a painless solution is on offer.

'Want me to go and ask him, then? Yeah?' Ben seems eager to atone for the biscuit gobbling. 'Take me ten minutes tops.' He's already on his way out to the hall to find his jacket. Harriet, never one to nurse a grudge for long, softens, put in mind of a puppy desperately angling for affection. Ben calls out, 'Don't start making them biscuits till I get back!' The front door bangs shut.

A slightly awkward hiatus. Then Harriet remembers the shopping and the devastation in the larder.

'He's trying his best, Hetty.'

'Is he.' Hester may have partially defrosted but there are still a few slivers of ice in her heart as far as Ben is concerned. 'There was almost a full barrel there. Unless you've been helping yourself again in the middle of the night. Honestly, Harry, you'll never lose weight at this rate.'

Harriet, not wanting to reopen the earlier argument and in truth not bothered about the tightness of her waistbands, murmurs something inconsequential and sips her tea. The silence is not quite as companionable as usual. She decides on a different tack.

'You were going to look up visas from Belarus on the computer.'

'I was.' Hester is on her feet, mug in hand, beside the fridge. 'Oh! Is this right?'

'What?' Harriet looks over to where Hester is studying the calendar.

'What day is it?' Hester asks.

'Tuesday.'

'Oh no,' says Hester, peering at the page. 'You know what we've forgotten? Bridge.'

'Oh, hell!' says Harriet. 'Of course. Peggy and Cynthia. Where is it?'

Hester turns with a dismayed expression. 'Here. In an hour.'

'Oh my Lord.'

The sisters ponder the problems: Ben, Daria, Milo. And Peggy Verndale, the nosiest woman in the village, whose curiosity will be thoroughly piqued by the visitors, who will want to know—and will undoubtedly succeed in extracting—their life stories in five minutes flat.

'We could phone and cancel,' Hester suggests.

'After the fuss you made about playing last week?' says Harriet. 'I think not. She'd want to know why.'

Hester frowns. 'Tell her we're ill. Food poisoning or something.'

'You know what she's like. She'll be round with soup and sympathy in a trice.'

'Damn,' says Hester, wondering why they are so plagued with good Samaritans. 'How about we ask if we can play at her house? We could pretend our heating was on the blink. Except of course'—scuppering her own plotting—'we've got the fire.'

'Look,' says Harriet. 'Let's be sensible. Milo's almost certain to be asleep—he always goes off after a feed in the afternoon for a good two hours. We can explain to Daria that we've got guests and maybe she and Ben could go for a walk.'

'For two hours? In the middle of winter?'

'Well, okay. They could stay upstairs and use the computer. We'll tell Peggy our nephew's with us for a few days and that he's in his room. Worst case, we make him come down and say hello. Cynthia won't be any trouble.'

'No,' agrees Hester, ''course she won't. Cynthia will just want to play cards.' She glances up at the clock. 'Goodness, I'd better get cracking. Peggy'll definitely smell a rat if there are no biscuits on offer. I've just about got time to bung some in the oven.'

'No, hang on, Hetty. Why not offer them Dundee? It *is* Christmas.' Harriet has visions of further upsets as Hester discovers the ruin of her arcane but meticulous storage system.

Thankfully, Hester is persuaded and the sisters go through to the sitting room to erect the bridge table and lay out cards and score pads. They have just finished their preparations when Ben returns.

'Well?' hisses Hester, pulling him unceremoniously into the kitchen, conscious that noises from above suggest Daria is just about to come down. 'What did he say?'

'Nothing. He wasn't there.' Ben unwinds his late uncle's scarf.

'Damn it. We should have told you to look in the pub,' says Hester.

'Yeah, but he didn't ought to leave his stuff lying around,' says Ben. 'Anyone might nick it. And them books. All over the place. I stacked them in the corner. What time's lunch? Or we going to make biscuits first?'

CHAPTER 10

'I'm exhausted,' says Peggy, taking another large bite of Dundee cake. 'Three days with my grandchildren and I'm fit for nothing. I mean, don't misunderstand me, I adore them, of course I do. They're the dearest little darlings—and so bright! Ethan's form teacher says she's never known a boy with such energy and curiosity. But, my goodness, they're demanding. I was minded to phone and cry off this afternoon and then I thought how disappointed you'd both be. Oh, and you too, Cynthia, naturally. Besides, I felt a change of scene would do me good. I don't suppose you could squeeze a drop more tea out of that pot?'

Cynthia, universally known as Silent But Deadly among the bridge fraternity (or, more accurately in this case, sorority), is swiftly shuffling one pack and placing it ready beside her, having refused cake and drunk her tea in double-quick time. She's here to play cards, not take refreshments. A thin, nervous woman who favours muted, heathery tweeds and sensible shoes, with a neck that always reminds Harriet of a giraffe, topped with a granite face and untrimmed curly eyebrows, Cynthia is almost pathologically single-minded where bridge is concerned. She plays to win with religious fervour. Flexing her extraordinary neck, she shoots frequent glances at Peggy, assessing the number of bites left on her plate, and taps the table with ill-concealed impatience as Hester—who should be dealing—reaches across to top up Peggy's cup.

The visitors are already one rubber up and a game ahead in the second, in large part due to Cynthia's ruthless play, but also because the sisters have eschewed their usually more adept bidding in favour of getting their opponents out of the house as soon as possible. To their surprise, the mention of a nephew lurking above sparked little interest in Peggy, who was too busy regaling them all between and during hands (to Cynthia's intense annoyance) with tales first of Ethan's extraordinary academic prowess and then of being woken repeatedly during the night by the latest addition to her extended family—'I told her to feed him at ten o'clock. It's the only way. But will she listen? Of course not!'—and the damage wrought on her pristine home by sticky fingers, horseplay and felt-tipped pens. Harriet can't help feeling faintly smug that *their* baby is such a little angel. Hester, for her part, is thanking Providence that Milo is months away from wreaking similar havoc and will be long gone before he is any position to do so.

'Lord knows I'm not an interfering mother-in-law—no-one could accuse me of that!—but I have brought up three children of my own,' continues Peggy, diamond rings flashing as she sorts her cards, which Hester has finally dealt.

Harriet can sense Cynthia tensing beside her, whether from the contents of her hand, or her longing for her partner to concentrate not on her apparently fraught Christmas but on closing the rubber.

'I mean, I don't want you to get the wrong end of the stick, I adore Kelly—*adore* her—but there are some aspects of child-care that frankly are beyond her. I tried to raise a couple of things tactfully with Adrian, but he practically bit my head off. But that's sons for you. Always side with their wives. Thank heavens for daughters, that's what I say.'

'And how are the girls, Peggy? asks Harriet, as she dutifully asks every time. Beside her, Cynthia sighs impatiently.

'Viola is very well, but Ella has just finished yet another round of IVF without success, I'm afraid.'

'Oh dear, Peggy, I am sorry.' Even Cynthia manages to look sympathetic for a few seconds; everyone in the neighbourhood knows of Ella's lengthy battle with infertility, thanks to her mother's frequent bulletins about the state of her womb.

'Yes, well, she's not getting any younger, is she? And with these cutbacks in the health service . . .'

'And they wouldn't consider adoption?'

'Oh, don't get me started on that!'

Cynthia's face, usually so inscrutable, briefly lights up at Peggy's apparent intent to drop the topic. But once again she is to be disappointed.

'The hoops you have to go through! Tests! Interviews! And the rules change every five minutes. I said to her only the other day, it would be easier to go out and buy a baby, it really would! I mean, look at Madonna and that Jolie woman. Still, there you are. Are you bidding, Hetty?'

Hetty is not; with a bare twelve points she might under normal circumstances and with a sense of mischief risk one club, her longest suit, or even at a pinch a weak no trump, but she is conscious that time is ticking away. The sisters glance at the clock on the mantelshelf, exchange a look and then address themselves once more to their hands. Both sets of ears strain for any sound of infantile waking above. There is none.

'One . . .' Peggy as usual hesitates after an apparently confident start, '. . . no trump?' She says it in a way that suggests this might be a bit of a long shot. At the bridge club, she would not dare to commit such a breach of protocol, but she feels safe enough among friends. Nevertheless, Cynthia, a stickler for the rules, raises a critical and bushy eyebrow. In the nearly two hours she has been in the house, aside from the initial pleasantries and her bids, she has barely spoken.

Harriet passes.

'Four clubs,' says Cynthia unhesitatingly, throwing her partner into a blind panic.

'Four clubs?' Peggy repeats the bid with a mixture of excitement and terror, aware that the stakes have been suddenly and dramatically raised. Cynthia nods curtly.

There follows a feverish performance opposite consisting of frequent skyward looks, fumbled counting of cards and fingers, and a very wobbly reply. Finally, after this palaver has been repeated a second time, they settle on six hearts, which Cynthia, to her secret delight and Peggy's intense relief, is to play. Hester studies her hand, deciding how best to open the defence.

'Oh my God!' shrieks Peggy, startling them all. 'I completely forgot! Have you heard the latest about Molly and Teddy?' Clutching her cards to her chest, she leans forward in an attitude of bubbling excitement that generally presages a salacious revelation. A cloud of heady, heated L'Air du Temps wafts from her formidable cleavage over the listeners. Harriet, closest to the source, recoils a fraction.

Hester, in the throes of laying down her ace of clubs, stops. No need to ask which Molly and Teddy: everyone knows the Wilsons. 'What about them?'

'Are we playing?' says Cynthia tersely. 'Your lead, Hester.'

'You haven't heard!' cries Peggy with delight, oblivious to her partner's displeasure. 'I can't believe it! Where have you been? He's only been having an affair! I thought it was all round the village—'

'An affair?' scoffs Hester. 'Teddy's always having affairs.'

'I know, but you're never going to believe who it is this time,' says Peggy slyly, pursing her lips as though she's reconsidered her decision to share her treasure. 'You'll never guess.'

'Go on,' urges Harriet, unable to resist. 'Who?'

'For crying out loud!' Cynthia explodes. 'Can't this wait until we've finished?' She is almost salivating at the thought of a small slam.

'Mrs Vicar!' says Peggy triumphantly. Having delivered her bombshell, she throws her considerable bulk back in her chair to enjoy the fallout, oblivious to an ominous crack from the perilously dry walnut frame.

Harriet and Hester are dumbstruck, Hester's card frozen in mid-air above the table. 'Mrs Vicar as in . . .?'

'Yes!'

'Oh, Peggy, you aren't serious?' says Harriet. 'Really? With Teddy? Are you sure?'

'Card, Hester, please,' hisses Cynthia.

Hester, still regarding Peggy with open-mouthed incredulity, waves her card tantalisingly over the table. Cynthia is finally provoked into breaching all etiquette; she snatches the card out of Hester's hand and slaps it down on the table. As she sees what it is an exultant gleam, swiftly extinguished, lights her eyes.

Hester, momentarily drawn back into the game by this incursion, looks back at her now empty hand with some confusion, then squints at the card on the table. 'Is that my ace?'

'Lay them down, Peggy,' says Cynthia, only the slight wobble in her voice betraying her inner turmoil. But Peggy has further juicy gossip to impart that a game of bridge—albeit one involving a high-stakes bid—cannot come close to trumping. She ignores her partner's interjection and, with a self-satisfied tightening of lips, reveals, 'Not only that, but it's been going on for two years! Can you imagine? Two years! No wonder Molly's been consoling herself with Dubonnet.'

Good Lord, thinks Harriet, *who'd have thought it? Two years! Mind you, the vicar is a bit of a dry old stick, and she always looks so fed up. Who wouldn't be—all those parish meetings and cups of tea and flower arrangers making up to your husband...*

Well, well, well, thinks Hester. *I'm not surprised. Poor old Teddy, putting up with Molly all those years. I won't say I approve exactly, but who could blame him for seeking a bit of comfort elsewhere? Not that I can believe Teddy has truly confined himself to just one dalliance for two whole years...*

Cynthia has waited beyond the endurance of any reasonable bridge player. She reaches across the table, whips Peggy's cards out of her unresisting hand and lays them down in four neat vertical rows, swiftly rearranges two rag spades into proper descending order and in an instant maps out her campaign. Extracting the three of clubs, she lays it on Hester's ace, then turns to Harriet expectantly, only to find her still lost in wonderment at Cynthia's revelation.

'Club,' snaps Cynthia. Harriet, with barely a glance at her hand or the trick on the table, absent-mindedly places her king on the pile. Cynthia, the queen in dummy, is almost beside herself as she slams the two of hearts on top to trump Hester's ace and take the trick. She looks around for some reaction—admiration from her partner perhaps, dismay from her opponents, who surely will be hopping mad to discover she has a void in clubs in hand and that they have wasted their two masters—only to find no-one paying her or the cards the slightest attention and Peggy poised across the table, ready to unleash her next thunderbolt. With murder in her heart, Cynthia places the ace of hearts in the middle of the table with flamboyant deliberation. And waits.

'I got it all from Jenny this morning, while we were walking the dogs,' continues Peggy, revelling in the role of raconteur. 'Apparently Molly turned up at hers in a state of utter hysteria and very much the worse for drink just as she was about to dish up Christmas dinner. It only turns out he's leaving her! For good this time.'

'Oh, Peggy, honestly, he's said that before,' points out a sceptical and somewhat deflated Hester. 'Dozens of times.'

Harriet nods in agreement. 'He was going to leave her years ago for Susie Pitherwood, remember? And that all fizzled out.'

'What about that fling he had with that blonde hairdresser from Old Stote? Rumour had it she left her husband for him and then he dumped her at King's Cross.'

'Oh, and Robert Byng's cousin: remember her? She was loaded apparently.'

'But not as loaded as Molly.'

'I know, I know all that,' retorts Peggy, unperturbed. 'But this time it's different. This time, he's bought a little flat in town'—she licks her lips salaciously—'a love nest, if you will, and Mrs Vicar is already installed there. What do you think of that!'

'No!' cries Harriet. 'He's actually bought somewhere for her?'

Triumphant nodding from Peggy.

'And she's already moved in?!'

Peggy's head bobs even more vigorously.

'Then it must be serious. Mrs Vicar!' None of them can actually remember Mrs Vicar's first name: she's such a mousy little creature, creeping around the edges of church activities in faded frocks and droopy cardigans. To think that Teddy—Teddy of all people!—has fallen in love with her. 'Are you absolutely sure, Peggy?'

Peggy is affronted. 'Are you accusing me of *gossiping*?'

'Not at all,' says Harriet swiftly. 'But the vicar, poor man—what about him?'

'Oh,' says Peggy, unmoved, having promptly lost interest in the Wilsons' dirty linen and the catastrophic impact of Teddy's philandering on a sleepy rural parish now she has exhausted her arsenal. 'I've no idea. Still, he's never been very popular, has he? Not since all that unpleasantness with the pews. Anyway, let's not waste any more time. I thought you were playing six hearts, Cyn?'

The visitors are in the hall, donning their winter coats. Hester and Harriet have belatedly congratulated a still-ruffled Cynthia on her triumph (she'd made a grand slam in the end, thanks to Harriet's inattention in the first trick) and are anxiously trying to ease their visitors on their way when Peggy says grumpily, 'Oh, I suppose you've heard what that wretched farmer is threatening to do now? Only put up a gigantic fence in the field at the bottom of our garden!'

Peggy lives in a delightful Georgian rectory on the far side of the village. When she had first moved in some thirty years before, the fields beyond the garden had been uncultivated, and had so remained, but for infrequent grazing, giving the illusion that Handfast House still sat amid a vast estate. Unluckily for Peggy and her spouse, the owner of the farm had sold it to Teddy Wilson some seven years ago. Teddy—a man with myriad business interests, not all of them snowy white according to local scuttlebutt—had promptly secured planning permission (by dint, said the less kindly disposed, of brown envelopes dropped into the eager hands of several members of the planning committee) to develop some derelict barns at the top of the hill. Rumours sped around the village, fanned primarily by an outraged Peggy. When Hester had jokingly suggested it might be the site of a stud farm or even a vineyard, despite the absence of any evidence in the way of vines, it was common knowledge within a day. 'Absurd!' Peggy had exclaimed loudly in the post office to the world at large. 'Coachloads of inebriated wine buffs clogging up the village!' She remained unplacated when someone pointed out that the approach road was on the far side of the farm, near the motorway, and any traffic was extremely unlikely to venture anywhere near their village.

In the event it proved to be a complex of luxury holiday apartments. This intelligence did nothing to allay Teddy's reluctant neighbour's concerns. 'Kids screaming all day long, cars bumper to bumper, rowdy parties every night!' When Harriet had said mischievously, 'I dare say he'll put in a swimming pool and playground,' Peggy's fury had known no bounds. The mythical swimming pool remained undug, the playground unconstructed. In truth, the development was some considerable distance from her house but, given its location at the top of the hill, nosy holidaymakers would have had an unhindered view of Peggy's lovingly tended gardens and the large terrace where she was wont to enjoy her pre-prandial G&T. Or so Peggy raged.

But her worries proved unfounded. Perhaps the complex was too isolated. Perhaps the apartments were insufficiently luxurious to satisfy an increasingly demanding clientele. Perhaps the whole scheme was, as was widely believed, merely yet another of Teddy's tax dodges. Whatever the reason, the complex remained unoccupied and, as the years passed,

Peggy's complaints became less about the distant blot on what she considered her demesne and more about the lack of maintenance and the general untidiness of the development. Personally, neither Hester nor Harriet, short-sighted as they are, can understand what all the fuss is about; on their occasional afternoons and evenings on Peggy's terrace, they have barely been able to make out the features of what Peggy still refers to as 'that monstrosity'. Her glee at the Wilsons' current marital shenanigans owes more than a little to her enduring resentment over the whole affair.

'Farmer?' says Hester. 'I thought Teddy owned that land.'

'Oh, I think he's leased it or something. He ruins our view, then he leaves the place to go to rack and ruin. Then this new creature takes over and—hey presto!—this horrible great fence is in the offing. The next thing we know there'll be rows of those God-awful poly-tunnels blighting the landscape.'

'Well,' offers Harriet, trying to herd Peggy and Cynthia towards the door, 'you won't be able to see them, will you? Not if there's a fence in the way. Anyway, cultivating the land again would be no bad thing. We could do with growing more crops: food security is very important. We import far too much as it is.'

Harriet clearly makes a very poor sheepdog, for while Cynthia is now hovering beside the front door, Peggy is rooted immovably in the hall. Her lips purse. 'That's all very well for you to say, Harriet. Of course we need to grow more food. But you wouldn't want some industrial-scale agricultural development at the bottom of your garden, would you? Even if we can't see it, thanks to the fence, we'll certainly hear and smell it.'

'Well, what are they planting?'

'Nothing yet, as far as I can see. Occasionally, when the wind's in our direction, we get a most unpleasant smell, and from time to time I've spotted some activity over there—'

'How? With a telescope?' says Hester. 'It's miles away!'

Peggy fixes her with a disdainful look. 'We're not all as blind as you, Hester. I can see perfectly well without enhancement. I'm telling you, there have been people up there on and off. Lights at all hours. When they open those big gates, you can just about see in.'

The sisters' interest is piqued in spite of themselves.

'Maybe they're doing up the apartments. Or letting them again.'

'In this climate? I hardly think so. Besides, they must be in the most frightful state by now. Haven't been looked after at all. No, I'll tell you what I think. Before we know it, they'll be moving in hordes of those dreadful foreigners to pick sprouts and leeks and whatnot.'

Harriet can feel her blood pressure rising; once she and Peggy stray from the relatively safe territory of bridge, their diametrically opposed politics and world views bring them into swift and vitriolic conflict.

'I thought you said they hadn't planted anything?'

'Not yet, as far as I can see, but it's only a matter of time. Bound to be some ridiculous EU subsidy they can claim. And I'll tell you another thing: it wouldn't surprise me in the least if Teddy Wilson was involved in some way. Show me any skulduggery around here and I'll be prepared to bet that man's fingerprints will be all over it. You may frown, Hester, but I wouldn't trust him as far as I could throw him.'

'Peggy . . .' calls Cynthia from the end of the hall, her hand on the latch. 'I really do need to—'

'Mark my words, they'll ship them over here and be cramming them in as tight as they can. They won't care what state those places are in. People like that will live anywhere.'

Hester shoots Harriet an imploring look that says quite unequivocally: *Not now! Leave it!* But Harriet, incensed by Peggy's casual xenophobia, chooses to ignore her.

'People like what, exactly, Peggy?'

Had Peggy a less rhinocerotic hide, she might have been more attuned to the *froideur* in Harriet's voice. But whether from insensitivity or intent, Peggy ploughs on. 'Don't be obtuse, Harriet.'

Hester freezes. Her sister is usually slow to anger (well, slower than she is, anyway, which, Hester would be the first to concur, sets the bar pretty low) but Peggy has an uncanny knack for lighting upon those topics guaranteed to rouse her. And then to accuse Harriet—Harriet of all people!—of obtuseness . . .

Peggy is in full flood. 'You know perfectly well who I'm talking about. These blessed East Europeans, of course. All well and good for lefties like you. You don't have to live side by side with them, do you? Flooding over here, clogging up our hospitals and taking our jobs.'

'What jobs? Like picking sprouts?' says Harriet. Hester jabs her sharply in the back.

'Sprouts, cauliflowers, Lord knows what. And just look at the unemployment rates in this country!'

Hester jabs her again, but Harriet can't help herself. 'You aren't seriously suggesting that anyone else would do such a filthy job? Backbreaking work from first light—'

'Of course they would!' snorts Peggy. 'People want jobs, any jobs! These foreigners will just undercut them, price them out of the market. You only have to follow the news to know that.'

'Oh right,' says Harriet, her dander well and truly up. 'So your precious Simon would take a job like that, would he, if only he weren't being frozen out by some freeloading East Europeans?'

Peggy bridles and draws herself up to her full height, bosom aquiver. 'Precious' is not a word to use lightly, certainly not in relation to poor dear Simon; the barb is unambiguous. She is well aware of Harriet's politics: she's seen her buying her morning paper. 'Now you're just being silly, Harriet. You know perfectly well that Simon has a degree. Of course he wouldn't pick sprouts.'

'A job, any job?' parrots Harriet, still outraged at Peggy's selective invective. They all—with the exception of his doting aunt, and she surely is being wilfully blind—know that Simon is a work-shy sponger whose only real talent lies in avoiding effort of any sort, physical or mental. He'd scraped through his degree course with an *aegrotat*, having fortuitously come down with glandular fever as his exams loomed. 'So what exactly would poor dear Simon be prepared to do?'

Harriet glares at Peggy; Peggy glares back.

In the hot, crowded hall, they are all suddenly wondering how their pleasant afternoon of bridge has degenerated into such rancour so quickly, when the unmistakable cry of a baby pierces the uncomfortable silence. Milo has awoken.

CHAPTER 11

During her quietly competent ascent of the local government ladder, Hester had learnt one important lesson—or, rather, she had learnt to apply her father's dictum: *never haver, never dither.* Major Ernest Ribbleswell was a soldier of the old school, firmly of the belief that more battles had been lost by vacillation than any military historian was prepared to admit. 'If there's a job to be done, do it,' he would say, if ever his wife and daughters hesitated over reaching a decision. 'In hindsight, any decision can be justified. Any decision is better than none. So just make one. Get stuck in there before some other bugger does.'

Hester applies this axiom now. As Cynthia, hand still clamped around the front door handle, and Peggy, red-faced from her tiff with Harriet, gaze upwards in amazement, Hester takes charge. She has to move quickly; Harriet is as quick-witted as she, and she dare not risk the collision of two opposing solutions, so she exclaims with exasperation, 'Oh, that boy!'

As three pairs of eyes swivel in her direction, she hurries to the foot of the stairs and calls up irritably, 'I told you before, Ben! If you must play that wretched game, at least turn the volume down.' As Milo's fretful cries escalate, there is the thunder of footsteps across the landing, and then a sudden, disconcerting silence. Only Hester and Harriet know that this is due to Daria's attentions, fulfilling her son's basic but urgent need to be fed. Cynthia and Peggy, foreheads creased with almost comical befuddlement, look quizzically at their hostesses.

'These computer games!' huffs Hester. 'Can you believe it? Some fool program from school that involves looking after a baby. Supposed to teach them social responsibility. I ask you! You know the sort of thing: it gets harder and harder the better you get at it. The ghastly thing pings when it's time for a feed and you've got to do the necessary to shut it up. Only Ben will leave it running, so I'm having to bawl him out every five minutes when the blessed thing goes off. It's driving us mad, isn't it, Harry?'

Straight-faced, Harriet agrees that it is.

For a moment, doubt and distrust flit across Peggy's face. Then she says in an injured tone directed mainly at her political adversary, 'Well, I'm glad to see some people show a modicum of concern for others. We could do with more social responsibility, if you ask me. I'm all for it. What's it called, anyway, this game? I might get it for the grandchildren.'

'Ah,' says Hester, her wits, now the crisis has apparently been averted, temporarily deserting her.

'*Managing Milo*,' chips in Harriet. 'I'll check with Ben, but I think that's right. Made by . . . oh, let me see . . . the people who make *Grand Theft Auto*, I think. I'll find out and let you know.' To the naive observer, she seems to be offering Peggy an olive branch after their altercation.

'And are we to meet this nephew?' says Peggy grandly, not quite ready to accept the overture yet, but still wishing to appear gracious, despite the injury done to her.

'Oh no, Peggy dear,' says Hester, 'we gave him the strictest instructions he was not to show his face and interrupt play.'

'Quite right,' mutters Cynthia, whose meagre store of affection is reserved for her labradors and her husband (in that order) and certainly does not extend to children of any complexion. Now, easing the front door open to admit a sharp blast of cold air, she says, 'Peggy, I don't want to rush you but I really do need to get back to the dogs . . .'

'Yes, yes,' says Peggy impatiently, as though Cynthia's labs are constantly discommoding her. 'Well, my two'll be desperate for walkies too. Let's get going. Thank you for the game, ladies.'

The atmosphere is still a little frosty, but the sisters know that in a day or two the fracture will mend. Peggy, for all her other faults, is not one to nurse a grievance. Harriet and Hester wave their visitors off and close the door, knees weak with relief.

'*Grand Theft Auto*? *Grand Theft Auto*?!' splutters Hester.

'Some of us like to keep abreast of modern life, Hetty. Besides, it did the trick.'

'*Managing Milo*? Where did that come from? She'll be surfing the internet the minute she gets home.'

'Peggy?' scoffs Harriet, still rankling slightly from their recent run-in. 'She'll have forgotten all about it already. Besides, she thinks computers are the devil's spawn. Remember what a fuss she made when they installed them in the library?'

Ben's head appears at the top of the stairs. 'That was close,' he hisses. 'Is it safe to come down?'

'Close?' says Hester. 'That is putting it mildly. I need a drink.'

Ben scoots down the stairs, hardly bothering with the treads. 'I'll pour it,' he says. 'Can I have one too?'

'I thought you didn't like wine,' says Hester, following him into the kitchen.

'Yeah, well, it's part of my education, innit? Who plays *Grand Theft Auto*?'

⌣⌣⌣

Seven o'clock. Harriet had waited a few minutes after Peggy and Cynthia's departure and then driven down to the bus shelter, to find no trace of Finbar or his trolley, but his books still stacked where Ben had left them. *Must have gone off on a jaunt*, thinks Harriet, *or more likely down the pub. He was probably answering a call of nature when Ben went looking for him.*

The four adults (*Well*, thinks Hester, *I suppose Ben just about qualifies as such*) are seated around the kitchen table, the remains of a lasagne just about to be scooped out of the dish by Ben, whose appetite both delights and appals Hester. He had watched intently as she put the dish together, even being entrusted with the responsibility of stirring the béchamel sauce and managing not to let it catch. A second wine bottle has been opened and in the warmth and comfort of the kitchen it is hard to remember how stressful the past few days have been. A sort of torpor has descended on them all; Milo sleeps in his mother's arms; the air is heavy with contentment. The only sound is the repeated scrape of the serving spoon against the large Pyrex dish as Ben digs out every last morsel of pasta.

Harriet, although sleepy with good food and several glasses of Chianti, doesn't miss Hester's pleasure at his patent enjoyment of her cooking. She rouses herself reluctantly. 'Sorry to spoil the party, but I think it's about time we made some decisions.'

Ben stops, spoon halfway to his mouth. 'Oh, please, Aunt Harriet, not my frigging parents *again*.'

'Language,' says Harriet automatically. 'No, not your … parents. Or not just them. We have staggered, in my view, from crisis to crisis over the past few days and we need to take control of events.'

'Absolutely,' says Hester, refilling her glass. 'It's time we got off the back foot.'

'Back foot?' says Daria. Since her enforced banishment of the afternoon and the near disaster of Milo's crying, she has been on edge, displaying too much of her earlier nerviness for the sisters' liking. They are both aware that she has been watching them apprehensively, probably anticipating further uncomfortable questions.

Ben mutters something to her that the sisters do not catch, but it seems to satisfy her and she relaxes. *Odd how easily the pair of them seem to communicate*, thinks Hester, *in spite of the language differences*. Milo twitches in his sleep, eyelids fluttering for a moment, then he snuggles even deeper into Daria's embrace.

Harriet reflects, with some surprise, on how normal this all seems. Even Ben, with whom Hester appears to have reached some kind of rapprochement, feels almost part of the fabric of the cottage now. Harriet reaches for a pad and pen.

'Right, first things first. Once Milo is in bed, Daria, you must try to get hold of your brother. And you, young man, are going to phone your parents once we've cleared the dishes.'

Ben scowls. Harriet writes *Daria: Phone home* and *Ben: Phone home* and underlines them both.

'You're sending me back, are you?' he demands, bottom lip on its way out.

'Oh no,' cries Daria, laying her hand on his arm. 'Ben, do not go.' She turns to Harriet. 'I go. Not Ben. I am trouble. Not Ben.'

'That's a matter of opinion,' says Hester, touched by the girl's obvious affection for the boy.

'Oi—' starts Ben, but his aunt cuts across him.

'Daria, my dear, you are going nowhere for the moment.' Hester is firm, her voice reassuring. 'You are staying here, where you and Milo are warm and safe, until we get things sorted. Ben, on the other hand, has a home of his own.'

'But I don't want—'

'Just at the moment, Ben, your needs are secondary. I won't say your presence hasn't been helpful at times—'

'Well then!'

'—but we made a promise to your parents to offer you a temporary cooling-off period, and now you've cooled off, I think it's time you went home and had a good long talk with them. This nonsense has gone on long enough.'

'Yeah, but . . . but . . .' Ben is desperately trying to fashion a persuasive argument. Suddenly he finds what he thinks is the clincher. 'What about Finbar then? Eh?'

'What about him?' asks Hester, moved, despite herself, by her nephew's dismay and not a little impressed by his spirited defence.

'What he said, I mean. About you needing me here. For protection.' Ben puffs out his chest with pride. 'That's what he said, didn't he?'

'Well, yes . . .' Harriet, ever fair, concedes. 'Be fair. He did, Hetty.'

Hester waves an impatient hand. 'For heaven's sake, Finbar's an old woman. Frightened of his own shadow.'

'Yeah, but you're old women too, in't you?' says Ben, caught up in his argument. Too late, he realises what he has said.

'I beg your pardon?' says Hester. The temperature in the kitchen plummets. Ice forms in the crevices of her face.

'I meant . . . no, what I was saying . . . I didn't mean . . . oh, frigging hell.' Ben, defeated by his inarticulacy and conscious that he may very well have sealed his fate, slumps back in his seat.

'I'm surprised we can manage to feed ourselves, aren't you, Harry?' says Hester with asperity. 'And as for you getting behind the wheel of a car—at your age!—it shouldn't be allowed.' At the back of her mind, there is a lightning reflection that there may be more than a grain of truth in that observation. 'Perhaps we should just sit by the fire and knit.'

'Yeah, but you do knit!' bursts out Ben. 'I seen you!'

Hester's eyes narrow still further. Daria shrinks down in her seat, arms protectively shielding Milo from the arctic currents eddying round the kitchen. It doesn't take a great command of English to work out that there is trouble not just brewing, but well and truly brewed.

'If I were you, Ben, I would stop digging,' says Harriet quietly. 'Hetty . . .'

Hester sniffs loudly and subsides, pointedly moving the wine bottle over to her side of the table.

'Now,' says Harriet, 'can we return to the matter in hand?'

'So that's it, then? Can't you say you need me here? I can do jobs. I can help with Milo. What if there's more trouble?' pleads Ben.

At the word *trouble*, Daria inhales sharply, and Milo twitches in her arms as though absorbing her distress.

Ben, sensing advantage, hurries on. 'Make anyone think twice, wouldn't it, though, if there's a bloke in the house? I mean, three women on their own . . .'

Perhaps not the wisest gambit, given Hester and Harriet's natures and feistiness, but they can both see some sense in his argument. After all, if they were both to go out, it would leave Daria alone in the house and, for all that she has filled out a little, she's still no match for a man, however aged or small. And as for Finbar's most recent caller . . .

'We'll come back to this later,' decides Harriet, before Ben's future threatens to monopolise the entire conversation. 'Let's talk about Daria. No, no, my dear,' she says reassuringly as Daria flinches, 'no need to be alarmed. We just want to work out what's best.'

'Best?' whispers Daria fearfully.

'Daria, listen—this is England, a free country. You have no need to cower in the shadows.'

Daria seems to catch her drift and nods uncertainly, but whole body is still tensed.

'That man—the man who came to the house—however much he might have frightened you, he and whoever is employing him have no power over you.'

'No?'

'Absolutely not. However, while it is a free country, there are controls, rules, laws—'

'Laws?'

'Yes. About entering the UK,' says Harriet gently.

'But I had visa!'

Harriet does not wish to enquire too closely into the circumstances under which Daria, given her family's political affiliations, had managed to acquire the visa.

'I am sure you did, my dear. But it has expired, hasn't it?'

Daria shrugs sulkily. 'Is not my fault,' she mutters.

Harriet, sensing that Hester is growing increasingly irritated beside her, swiftly continues. 'Daria, whatever the rights and wrongs of the situation, and regardless of the troubles you've encountered, the fact remains that you have no visa to remain in the UK. Add to that the loss of your passport, and you're basically here illegally.'

'Illegal?' Terror sweeps across Daria's face.

'Yes, I'm afraid so. You must have entered on a general visitor visa—Hester was checking online before supper—and I'm sorry, but you've well overstayed the time you're allowed to remain.'

Hester, who has reached the limits of her patience and is tired of her sister's kid-glove approach, steps in. 'Basically, Daria, we think you ought to speak to the authorities and tell them everything.'

'Everything? No! No!'

'Hang on!' cries Ben.

'You must go and explain what's happened and . . .' She wants to say *give yourself up* but that sounds ridiculously melodramatic.

'Explain? How I can explain? I get people in trouble when they have been so kind—'

'Kind? Dumping you and your baby by the side of the road?'

'Well . . . yes . . . no . . .' Daria looks bewildered. 'She is my friend, Tina. She help me.'

'Tina? She's the woman at the farmhouse?'

Daria, cornered, nods miserably. 'I promise her . . . I promise . . .'

'What? What did you promise?'

'Not to tell.'

Harriet and Hester exchange a mystified look.

'I am trouble. They look after me. Protect me.'

'Protect you! They kept you a virtual prisoner by the sound of it.'

'No, no . . . I don't think. It was to keep me safe. That is why they take my phone. Tina say police can find me from my phone. Tina is good woman.'

'And her husband?'

A cloud passes over Daria's face. She looks away, chewing the inside of her cheek.

'Daria?'

'He is not so nice, Scott.'

Scott. At least they have a name now. Two names.

Daria looks down at her sleeping son. 'He does not like baby crying. Milo is not bad boy but he cry. All babies cry, yes? And

Scott say, silly girl, too young for baby, you should give away. Start again.'

'Give away . . .?' murmurs Harriet, aghast.

Hardheaded Hester, on the other hand, has to stop herself from nodding in sympathy with Scott's views.

'He say, lots of nice people want baby. No problem. Nice home, good life. Better life than you can give. Then you can work.'

Hester and Harriet immediately think of Peggy's daughter and the thousands she's spent on IVF, all to no avail.

'But Tina was on your side? Is that why she drove you away?'

'I don't know! I think perhaps . . . yes, maybe.' Daria looks uncertain, bereft, frightened.

For the first time, Hester doubts her own suspicions. The girl is so desperate, so obviously conscious of her story's lack of credibility, that Hester's conviction that they have been fed a pack of lies begins to waver. She glances over at her sister and sees her own confusion reflected in Harriet's face.

Daria sits forward and grasps Hester's wrist. 'You think I lie. I see this. You tell me this story and I will say, no, is not possible. But it happen. To me. And to Milo. How I can make you believe? And if you do not believe, you who save me, protect me, then man in big office, man who does not care, how will he believe, huh?' Her passion is mingled with rage, seemingly at her power-lessness, at her inability to keep her son safe. But this is a new Daria, stronger, more determined. 'You think I want to hide always? Not to walk in the sunshine with my baby?' For a split second something, a memory perhaps, snags her. 'To feel my heart *bang bang* every time someone knock at the door?'

'Daria . . .'

'I am not wanting to be trouble to you. Not to Tina. To anyone! But I cannot go home. I am prisoner here.'

There's some truth in that, reflects Harriet, as Hester remains silent. *And we, in a sense, are your gaolers. We hold your future in our hands.*

'Look,' she says, as Daria releases Hester and finally breaks her gaze. 'We want to help you, you know that. But it seems to us that, whether you meant to or not, you *have* broken the law.'

'How has she?'

'Ben—'

'No, look, all she's trying to do is keep Milo safe.'

'Yes, but—'

'That bastard sends a private detective after her, they threaten to take her baby—'

'BEN!' Hester has had enough.

Milo, unsettled by the raised voices, wakes and starts fighting in Daria's grip, but for once she seems oblivious to her son's distress. Ben reaches across without a word and takes the baby from her; he puts Milo over his shoulder and gets to his feet to start walking him around the kitchen.

Hester draws a deep breath and addresses her remarks to Daria. 'Listen, my dear, we need to sort this out. You have no passport, no visa, and you have been working while in the UK.'

'No, I—'

Hester holds up her hand. 'Let me finish. Please. It doesn't matter whether you were helping out this couple in London, it doesn't matter whether you were paid or not, as I understand it, that still qualifies as working—'

'Well, that's not fair for a start!' hisses Ben, to be rewarded with one of Hester's coldest looks. He retreats.

'—which is not permitted under the terms of your visa. A visa that has, in any event, expired. Now, I know things are difficult in Belarus, or so Harriet tells me. She's more acquainted with foreign affairs than I am. But this is what I suggest: Harriet and I will get your things back, including your passport, and then—'

'But my passport—'

'We know. It's in London. However, that man Peter has no right to take it from you or keep it. We will get it back—there's no need for you to see him or his wife—and then we will go with you to the authorities, the police or whoever—'

'The police!'

'Daria, this is England. You can trust our police.'

'*Trust* them?!'

'She has a point, Hetty,' says Harriet. 'After all, think of Plebgate, the Stephen Lawrence inquiry and—'

'Harry, please! You are not helping. Never mind all that, Daria. Ignore her. As I say, you will have to go and explain how you came to overstay your visa, but with your passport, it should be much quicker and easier for you to return home.' She doesn't add, although she is pretty sure she is correct, *They will deport you anyway.*

'Home?'

'Yes. Back to your family. And then everything will be sorted. You'll be back safe with Artem and—'

'Safe? How I am safe? I tell you already! My father, he is in prison!'

'Yes, but . . .'

'He is not criminal, not bad man, he is . . . only against the government. That is all. And my brother, he is in danger—'

'I know, I know . . . I am so sorry, my dear, but what are we to do?' Hester has reached the end of her planning. Further than facilitating the return of the passport and getting Daria back into legitimate circulation, she has nothing more to offer. From here on in, if they are entering the murky waters of Belarusian politics, she will hand over to Harriet.

'I cannot go home!'

'But, Daria—'

'Never! Never.' And, ashen-faced, she looks over to where Ben is holding a now settled and peacefully sleeping Milo.

'Oh, come, come,' says Harriet, as understanding dawns. 'You silly girl. Your brother and father may be a bit upset, of course they may, but once you explain everything, I'm sure they'll understand. In time. For goodness' sake, you won't be the first girl who . . .' She trails off as she sees Daria shaking her head and staring imploringly at Ben.

'Thing is,' he says, very quietly so as not to wake his charge, 'she didn't quite tell you everything earlier. Or me. And when she did this afternoon, I didn't tell you 'cos she asked me not to. Thought you might turn her in. See, it's not just her dad and brother who are in trouble; she's on some sort of list too—in Belarus. She got caught up in some student protest. That's really why she left. She goes home, chances are she'll be arrested at the airport and then what happens to matey here?'

CHAPTER 12

'She's exaggerating, surely?' says Hester a few minutes later, once she and Harriet have retreated to the sitting room. They've instructed Ben to phone his parents and Daria has disappeared to put Milo to bed. 'I think she's being a touch overemotional. You know these Russian types. Just look at Chekhov.'

Harriet absent-mindedly considers a piece of her jigsaw. 'She's from Belarus, Hetty. Anyway, how would we know? All sorts of terrible things go on around the world that would be unthinkable here in the West. Just think of *los Desaparecidos*.'

'What?'

'Argentina. The disappeared.'

'Oh. Right.' A thought. 'Was that true, about her phone? That she could be traced through it?'

'I wouldn't be at all surprised. We're all under surveillance— pretty much constant surveillance—one way or another most of the time. Just read the papers. Phone taps, email interceptions, CCTV on every corner . . .'

'All right! Spare me! You are such a conspiracy theorist—
you swallow everything that paints the government in a
sinister light.' As Harriet goes to protest, Hester heads her off.
'Anyway, true or not, it was a damned cunning way of keeping
her isolated. Poor kid must be beside herself. And her family,
come to that. Who knows what's happened over in Belarus
in the past few months? Let's hope we find out more once she
spoken to her brother.'

⌣⌣⌣

But they don't find out more, because when Daria rings her
brother's mobile, she discovers the number is unobtainable.
Next she tries to contact her friend Polina, but the call goes
straight to voicemail. She leaves a message but her disappointment and anxiety are plain to see in her pallor and the
nervous working of her lips. The haircut that earlier in the day
had looked so chic and sophisticated, now, with the increased
anxiety and the shadows under her eyes, makes her look shorn,
defenceless. A victim.

The sisters sit in thought for a few minutes. This lack of
communication with Rakov makes everything seem even
more complex.

Harriet slides a piece of tree into place. 'The thing is,' she
says, 'we've been proceeding so far on the basis that we were
trying to get Daria back to Belarus. Or at least, I have.'

'And me,' says Hester with a sigh. 'I mean, insofar as I had
thought it through, I was imagining we'd sort out this passport
business and hand her over and the authorities would pop her

on a plane. After all, they're bound to send her back—either for outstaying her visa or for working here illegally—aren't they?'

There is a tentative knock on the door. Ben's head pokes round. He looks the picture of despair. 'I've done it. I've spoken to Dad. He's coming around.'

'What, now?' chorus the sisters,.

This is all getting a bit much, thinks Harriet.

'He said an hour. Mum's out.' Ben's gangly frame fills the doorway, his face forlorn. 'Can't you say you need me or something? Just for a few more days? He'll be on at me non-stop till I go back to school, I know he will.' His voice wobbles; for a moment, Harriet thinks he might be about to cry.

Then Hester says matter-of-factly, 'Well, as it happens, your aunt and I need to go up to London tomorrow.'

'Do we?' says Harriet.

Hester looks exasperated. 'Harry, how else are we going—'

'What, so I can, like, stay a bit longer?' Their nephew looks from one to the other cautiously, the faint flicker of hope transforming his expression. 'You know, make sure Dar and Milo are okay?'

'A *little* longer,' says Hester firmly. 'Just to keep an eye on things while we're away.'

'As long as that's all right with your father,' chimes in Harriet.

'Cool,' says Ben, his mouth stretching in a grin which he quickly suppresses. 'Yeah, well, ta an' all that.'

'As long as your father has no objection,' repeats Hester.

'I'll just tell him Dar needs a hand with … oh yeah …' says Ben, realising the implications of his parent's imminent arrival. 'Best I get up there and tell her to lay low, eh?'

155

'Lie,' say the aunts in unison.

'Seriously? To Dad?'

'No!' Hester exclaims. 'It's *lie* low, not lay!'

'Whatever,' says Ben. And he's gone.

'The pity of it is,' says Harriet, putting into words what they are both thinking, 'George is precisely the sort of person who'd know where Daria stands. Or if he doesn't, he'll know someone who does.'

'I know,' says Hester soberly. 'And we both know exactly what he'd advise us to do.'

'As we would advise someone else in the same circumstances.'

'Precisely. Except . . .'

'Yes.' Each is thinking how the sands shift once matters become personal. At a remove, there would be no doubt as to the correct course of action. Now, however, those certainties have been shaken by events and, of greater significance, by their growing attachment to Daria and Milo. But, they reason, surely mother and son are safer here in the interim, while they try to clarify matters? A solution that, in addition, is not costing the state a penny! They console themselves with this sophistry, but separately, and secretly, both recognise a deeper and more uncomfortable truth: they are almost enjoying all this excitement.

Harriet, suppressing the thought for the moment, says, 'And what specifically are we going to do in London?'

∽∽

George is wearing an expression every bit as miserable as his son's after their brief telephone conversation. The two days Ben has been absent from home have clearly exacted a heavy price. Harriet understands this; he must be feeling that he has failed somehow in his patriarchal duties if his son can so cavalierly quit the family roof. She wants to reassure him from her long experience of teenagers of both genders that these sorts of histrionic fallings-out are an almost unavoidable rite of passage. It was the ones who meekly followed every familial diktat who tended to go off the rails later. But she says none of these things, only too aware how patronising she would sound. She's been at the receiving end of too much parental resentment in the past: 'What the hell do you know about it? You don't have any kids!' She had so often been tempted to retort: 'No, but I've spent a darn sight longer in your child's company than you probably have. I bet I know more about their hopes and fears than you do.' But of course she never had; she had bitten her lip and kept her counsel. As she does now.

'Harriet, I cannot tell you how sorry Isabelle and I are that you and Hester have been put to all this trouble,' George is saying, surreptitiously trying to find a spring-free section of the Chesterfield. 'We know only too well how difficult Ben can be.'

Harriet finds herself in a slightly cleft stick, Hester having hurried off in search of wine and glasses. Say, 'He's been no trouble at all,' and you risk offending the parent, who assumes you are criticising his child-rearing prowess. Agree with George and he has the perfect excuse to remove the source of all this inconvenience. She settles for a neutral, 'Not at all,' which can be read either way.

Hester returns with three glasses of claret on a tray and ruins Harriet's carefully calibrated reply by saying, 'Has Harry told you how helpful Ben has been?'

'Ben?' stammers George, in an echo of his wife's earlier response, with an intonation that suggests they must surely be talking about another boy who just happens to share a name with their son. 'Helpful?'

'Yes, indeed,' says Hester, blithely unaware that she is undermining her sister's cunning stratagem.

Harriet coughs, tries to signal silently to Hester while George's face is buried in his glass, and says quickly, 'Well, I think he was trying to get in our good books, that's all. Isn't it always the way with children? Little monsters at home and perfect angels when they're out.'

'Angels?' splutters George into his glass. He is looking thoroughly nonplussed.

'Hmm,' says Hester darkly, thinking that Harry has rather over-egged this particular pudding. 'Anyway, we were wondering if it would be all right if he stayed another night or two. Just to finish a couple of jobs we had lined up. That is, if you and Isabelle don't mind.'

'Sorry?' George manages to swallow his mouthful. 'Jobs? Ben? Really?'

'We thought it would be good for him to earn a bit of cash,' says Harriet. 'Learn the value of work, et cetera.'

'We did?' exclaims Hester, immediately thinking of the mountains of food—not to mention the glasses of their good wine—that Ben has consumed. And now Harriet wants to *pay* him?

'No, no, no,' says George. 'You mustn't pay him! Good Lord above, after you've been so kind! But'—he frowns—'what kind of jobs are we talking about? Is he really up to it? I mean, I'm all for encouraging a bit of responsibility, but I don't want him mucking things up for you. As I've said I don't know how many times, if there's anything that needs doing—'

Hester and Harriet see immediately the trap they have laid for themselves and Harriet leaps in. 'It's just things we've not got around to, George, honestly. Nothing difficult. Nothing that requires an *expert*. Clearing out the shed, that sort of thing.'

'Cutting back the hedge,' offers Hester. Luckily George is no gardener and so is unlikely to comment on the inadvisability of pruning privet in December.

'I see ...' George struggles to come to terms with this new, obliging son. He frowns, trying to picture, or so they imagine, what shape this unfamiliar boy takes. 'What exactly has he been doing, as a matter of interest?'

'Oh, you know, running errands,' says Hester vaguely.

'Of a charitable nature,' adds Harriet, thinking of Finbar.

George gulps another mouthful of wine and croaks, 'Charitable? Ben?'

'Yes, indeed,' Harriet hurries on. 'Delivering food parcels to the homeless, that sort of thing.' George stares at her, mute with astonishment. For a moment, she imagines he is about to drop his glass; instead he places it on the table beside him with a trembling hand. 'You know the old boy who lives in the bus shelter?' George does, everybody does. 'We often drop in the odd morsel, especially at Christmas—a bit of cheese, quiche and what have you. And Ben volunteered to deliver it.'

'Really?' Incredulity props George's mouth open.

'And he's been extremely handy in the kitchen, hasn't he, Hetty?' Harriet can't resist a mischievous dig.

Hester's eyes narrow almost imperceptibly. She decides to play along.

'The kitchen? Yes. Absolutely. Very interested in cooking, of course. As you would know, George.'

George is floundering, punch-drunk after so many mind-boggling revelations. 'I would? Yes! Of course. Cooking . . . and Ben. Well, I have to say, I . . . I . . . I leave most of that . . . food and whatnot . . . to Isabelle, as you know only too well.' Oh they do, they do. 'The kitchen, that is her bailiwick, as it were. Her little kingdom.' He registers Harriet's sudden inhalation from the chair opposite, as does an amused Hester. *That'll teach you to take the mickey!* George, bewildered as he is, recognises his blunder, and seeks to smooth Harriet's ruffled feminist feathers, feathers he has inadvertently ruffled on more than one occasion in the past, to his cost. 'From choice, I hasten to add.' A nervous laugh. 'I mean, horses for courses. If Isabelle were less able . . . or, rather, were I more able . . . in that department, I should be only too thrilled to lend a hand. I mean, rather than just washing up and so forth. Although of course we do have a dishwasher . . .' A sudden face-saving thought. 'After all, not all women cook, do they? Correct me if I am wrong, but I believe you, Harriet, leave all culinary affairs in Hester's more than capable hands, don't you?' *Touché*, thinks Hester, as Harriet, momentarily wrong-footed, admits that indeed she does. But George's thoughts return once more to his son. 'I must confess, though, I was unaware that Ben had the slightest interest in . . . you mean, preparing food? Actually cooking something that someone might *eat*?'

'Yes, fried eggs, lasagne—'

'Lasagne?!'

'Well, to be fair, he and I did it together, but . . .' Hester can't quite bring herself to tell an outright lie, 'he was in charge of the béchamel sauce.'

'Béchamel sauce?' breathes George, as if this were a feat beyond the capabilities of any but the most illustrious of chefs. Harriet doubts he has the first idea what béchamel sauce is.

'Well'—he essays a sort of half-laugh—'I suppose I should be pleased . . . well, thrilled even. Where is he, by the way?'

'He's just waiting for us to call him down,' says Harriet, feeling more than a little guilty at the way they are duping poor old George. 'We said we wanted to speak to you first. I hope you don't mind.'

She gets up and goes over to the door. Ben is poised on the fourth step of the stairs, as far as he could retreat before the door opened. He's grinning. His antipathy to eavesdropping seems to have evaporated. Pointedly, Harriet looks past him and calls softly up the stairs, 'Ben! Would you come down, please? Your father would like a word.' She narrows her eyes at him as she firmly closes the sitting-room door. A judicious five or six seconds later, Ben knocks politely.

'Ben! How are you, son?' George is on his feet, trying to sound distant and austere, but failing miserably. He looks at his progeny with undisguised love, tempered with anxiety, as the truant ambles into the room, face now wiped clean of its earlier look of glee.

My, thinks Harriet, *the little tinker can act too.*

'Dad,' says Ben, with just the right blend of trepidation and relief. He bites his bottom lip.

Don't overdo it, sonny, thinks Hester.

'We've missed you, son,' croaks George, features fighting a losing battle with his emotions. 'Your mother baked a cake.' Fortunately, he's wiping his eye and misses the involuntary twitch of Ben's lips.

'Yeah,' manages Ben. 'I know.'

Hester and Harriet assiduously avoid one another's eyes, thinking of that leaden lump sailing over the hedgerow.

'We hoped you'd want to come home and ... break bread with us once more,' says George pitifully.

Ben can't quite suppress a look of scorn at his father's vocabulary. Harriet's heart goes out to George but Hester's does not. Break bread indeed! Shop-bought rubbish: no wonder the boy ran away!

George stumbles on. 'But I understand your aunts need you here for a little while longer. In view of their kindness, I think it's the least you can do. And I'm not here to talk about your future, not today. I simply wanted to reassure myself—and your mother, of course—that you are all right. And behaving yourself. Which I gather you are. I'm delighted to hear how helpful you've been. I'll explain things to your mother. I'm sure she'll understand.'

And the two women, knowing Isabelle's fond and foolish heart, are sure she will.

'We'll just leave you two to have a chat, then,' says Hester, leading Harriet to the door and ignoring Ben's beseeching look. It's all very well being understanding, but she's not going to let the boy get off scot-free. George deserves a few minutes alone with his errant son. She pauses in the doorway. 'Can I get you a top-up, George dear?' she says.

'A top-up?' says Ben, eager to show off his new-found interest. 'What is it? A burgundy?'

George gives Ben a look of pure disbelief. 'A burgundy?'

'It's a claret, actually,' says Hester. *Careful, sonny, your father's not a complete idiot.*

'Oh, right,' says Ben. 'I don't mind. Can I have—'

'Ben!' warns Harriet from the hall.

'A Coke,' stammers Ben. 'That is, please may I have a Coke?'

⌣⌣⌣

George drives away, refusing any more wine and eager to report back to Isabelle. Ben had walked out with him to the car, father and son looking more relaxed in each other's company than Harriet could remember seeing them for years. She calls Hester back from the kitchen, and her sister emerges with a tray of bread, cheese and homemade chutney.

Ben reappears instantly, eyes lighting up at the sight of supper. 'I'll get Dar down, shall I?'

The girl joins them. Hester and Harriet have decided not to pursue the issue of her return to her home country just for the moment. Instead they will concentrate on the practicalities of retrieving her passport and any belongings. As anticipated, the colour drains from Daria's face when they explain their plan.

'Go to their house?'

'Well, we can't think how else to get your things back.'

Daria shakes her head violently. 'I do not want ... no, please ...'

'Daria,' says Hester with her customary sharpness, 'we don't have a choice. Without your passport, you can't do anything. We must get it back for you before we can decide what's best for you and Milo.'

'We go, we go,' cries Daria.

'Don't be daft,' growls Ben, through a huge wedge of bread and cheese. 'Where the frig you going to go? And in this weather?'

Daria shrugs miserably. 'That man ... that woman ...' Her voice is weighed down with misery.

'The woman is ill,' says Harriet. 'You said so yourself. I'm sure she means you no harm.'

'And the man,' says Hester, 'is just a man. For goodness' sake! Let us have the address and we'll sort this out once and for all.'

Eventually Daria nods, gets to her feet and disappears upstairs. No-one speaks, but Ben slices off another hunk of cheese and, when he thinks his aunts are not watching, pours himself a small measure of wine. The fire crackles in the hearth, the flames leaping as the door opens again and cooler air swirls in from the hall. Daria hands Hester a piece of paper bearing a London address, and sits down, hugging herself. Hester glances at the address, puts the paper to one side and picks up her knitting.

'Right,' she says, shoving her glasses to the top of her head and reaching for the pattern, 'Peter and Elizabeth Sampson. I'm glad that's all sorted. We're starting to get things under control. Like that claret, do you, Ben?'

CHAPTER 13

28 DECEMBER

'Keep a close eye on her, won't you?'

Harriet is whispering to Ben in the hall as Daria sits at the table in the kitchen feeding Milo. Ben seems totally unembarrassed by the sight of her breastfeeding. *How different from our generation at that age*, thinks Harriet. *We wouldn't even have dared use the word 'breast'. And as for getting one out for all the world to see . . . Our mother would have had conniptions.*

Ben, still half asleep, grunts. He looks at his aunt properly for the first time that morning. 'Blimey, you off to the palace or something?' Harriet, in the suit she last wore for another, older nephew's wedding some five or six years before, is gratified. Yes, she thinks she looks pretty smart too, and there's something surprisingly pleasing about getting dressed up once in a while. She is waiting in the hall because Hester is upstairs, grumpily changing from the old trousers and cardigan she had come down in earlier.

'I'm not going to London with you looking like that!' Harriet had exclaimed, while Hester eyed her suit with suspicion.

'Since when did you get so picky?' she had snapped.

'There are standards,' responded Harriet with an asperity that would have done their mother proud.

Hester had stamped back up the stairs but not before peering aghast at Harriet's face. 'Is that *makeup* you're wearing?'

Harriet had merely raised her eyebrows and then, when Hester's bottom rounded the newel post at the top of the stairs, had admired herself and her new hairstyle in the hall mirror. She remembers how much Jim had liked it when she put on her glad rags, as he called them. She wonders now why she hadn't done it more often, when it gave him so much pleasure. Dear, kind Jim. She had been lucky.

''Kay,' says Ben and wanders off towards the kitchen and breakfast.

Harriet calls him back quietly. 'And if she tells you anything else while we're away . . .'

'You wanna know about it.'

'Obviously. Ring us on our mobiles.'

'Only if she gives me the okay.'

'Ben!'

'Only if she gives me the okay. I ain't—*I'm not*—shopping her. End of.'

And with that proviso Harriet has to be content.

༼ ༽

They drive to the station, passing Teddy Wilson on the High Street, spick and span in a pinstriped suit, climbing into a brand-new Jaguar with its personalised numberplate, W11S0N, which each privately thinks is a bit naff. They both wonder where he's off to. And where he's been.

'Where did Peggy say this supposed flat was?' Harriet asks.

'I don't think she did say, did she?'

'Might be that one with the "Let" sign over the fish-and-chip shop.'

'You're meant to be watching the road, Harry! Anyway that's hardly Teddy's style, is it? The smell of chip fat?'

'Who knows? Besides, if love is blind, perhaps it's also anosmatic.'

'Very funny. Watch out! You're supposed to give pedestrians priority at a zebra crossing.'

Harriet stamps on the brakes and, as they wait for an elderly couple to inch their way across the road, glances down at her sister's feet in the foot well. They are still shod in scruffy brown lace-ups. She has gone so far as to put on a respectable tweed skirt and cashmere jumper under her bulky winter coat, but would not budge on the shoes. 'I'm not tramping up and down the streets of London in heels,' she'd growled, glaring at Harriet's neat courts. 'Not with my feet.' Harriet had decided that she'd done as much as she could. If people stare at them, they might—with luck—assume they are just friends, not sisters, whose consanguinity somehow always carries a shared culpability in matters sartorial.

It being that no-man's-land between Christmas and New Year, the station car park in Stote is sparsely populated and they have no trouble finding a space some distance from other cars, which, given Harriet's skill (or lack thereof) in manoeuvring, is a blessing for the other motorists. They abandon the car at a jaunty angle and set off for the booking office, Senior Railcards at the ready.

Two places down in the queue, resplendent in a bright purple coat with fur-trimmed hat and leather boots, stands Peggy. She squeals with delight, all unpleasantness from the previous afternoon forgotten. The poor traveller sandwiched between the trio of women is forced to endure their conversation—Peggy's mainly—around both sides of him, leaning back and forth to accommodate the speakers. Eventually, tired of performing this inelegant dance, he gallantly motions Hester and Harriet forward to take his place.

'Where are the pair of you off to, then? The sales? I have priority notification from Liberty's, of course.'

'The sales?' says Hester, horrified. 'Good grief, no. We're going to see—'

'Our solicitor,' says Harriet quickly. She beams at her sister, who nods.

'Oh? Nothing troublesome, I trust,' says Peggy delicately, clearly hoping the exact opposite. 'Lawyers are so devilishly expensive, aren't they? I remember when we had all that trouble with the wretched farmer, solicitors' letters flying back and forth . . .' Then, mercifully, a clerk becomes free and she is forced to a trailing halt as she steps forward to buy her ticket.

'See you on the train,' she calls out, her purchase completed, as the sisters approach another counter. 'Must pick up a *Telegraph*.'

They won't of course see her on the train: Peggy will undoubtedly be travelling first class. They are not. And nothing on earth would persuade Peggy to invest in a Railcard, however much she might save. Fancy advertising your advanced age to all and sundry.

Just as they are making their way down the platform, their train approaching, they see Teddy Wilson appear in some haste and hurry up to the far end, where Peggy is waiting to board in all her purple splendour. There is no way of avoiding her; Teddy raises a hand in greeting and, to Hester and Harriet's amusement, follows Peggy into her carriage.

'Bless him,' says Harriet as they bag adjacent seats facing forward. 'She'll grill him all the way from here to London. Pound to a penny she finds out where Mrs Vicar is closeted.'

The train pulls away from the station, rattling over the bridge and steadily gathering speed, soon leaving behind the factories and warehouses that line the route out of town. Mist hovers over fields still rimed with frost; birds dart through the chill winter air, alighting on skeletal trees silhouetted against a cold blue sky. Heat blasts their ankles from the vents in the dilapidated carriage.

'I thought they were upgrading this line,' grumbles Hester.

Harriet, watching a man throwing a stick for a dog on a deserted common, says thoughtfully, 'Hetty, I'm just wondering if it mightn't be a good idea to go and see old Henry.' Henry Walters is their solicitor—or, rather, he acted for Gordon, Hester's husband, for over thirty years. From habit and inertia, both sisters have continued to use him in widowhood. 'We could ask his advice.' She doesn't spell out what advice they might need; you never know who could be listening.

'What, after we've been to see . . .?'

'Or before. Assuming we get to see . . . our chap. He might be away sunning himself in the Bahamas. Or skiing.'

Hester shakes her head. 'It's Christmas. Henry won't be in the office. Anyway, it's not his area of expertise, is it?'

'Worth a try,' says Harriet. 'I bet he'll know someone who knows. I've got his number in my diary.'

She pulls her mobile from her bag and dials. The response is immediate. A brief conversation with the receptionist and Harriet finishes the call with quiet satisfaction. 'Eleven o'clock, for half an hour. We caught him on the one day he's in this week.'

'Someone must be on our side,' says Hester.

They complete the rest of the journey in silence.

⌣⌣⌣

'Confidential? Of course it's confidential! Client privilege, my dear.'

Henry Walters, rotund in his three-piece suit, was born to be a lawyer, if not a solicitor. Pedantic, ponderous, he fills any room with an air of benign competence. He sits opposite the sisters, black eyes observing them closely from under straggly eyebrows.

'Not my bag, frankly, immigration; I won't lie. But I can find out. Or suggest some other johnny who might know the ropes. Still, as I say, my gut instinct is to go to the authorities.' He holds up his hand as Hester starts to protest. 'I know, I know, my dear, you don't want to right away. I'm just advising you. As your lawyer.'

Harriet leans forward. 'It's not just the girl, you see, Henry.'

'Good Lord, how many more of them are there?'

'She has a child.'

Henry frowns. 'Dear, oh dear.'

'A baby, actually,' says Hester. 'Milo.' She turns to Harriet. 'What is he, three, four months old?'

'I was at school with a Milo,' says Henry. 'Right little bastard.'

'Ah, well,' says Harriet, 'funnily enough, so is ours. I mean, he's a gorgeous baby, but she's not married to the father. And he's English.'

'The father? Well, well, well, that complicates things, potentially. Or simplifies them—I'm not altogether sure. Does he acknowledge the child?'

The sisters exchange a glance. 'We don't know,' says Hester. 'We're going to try to see him after this.'

⌣⌣⌣

Twenty minutes later, the picture seems a little clearer. In Henry's view, the fact that Milo was born in the UK of a British father (provided he can be induced to acknowledge the child) makes him British, with a right to stay permanently. He is cautiously optimistic about the prospect of regularising Daria's status, but given the complication of her visa violation, he undertakes to check things out and report back as soon as possible. So it is with lighter—much lighter—hearts that Hester and Harriet set off for Chiswick and their encounter with Mr Peter Sampson, and possibly Elizabeth, his wife.

They walk across the common and up leafy Duke's Avenue, discussing tactics. 'I think you should start,' says Hester. 'No beating about the bush. Establish our credentials and then ask for her passport and things. We won't go in, just in case he turns nasty. On no account tell them our address.'

'He's probably got that already, Hetty, if he's the one who hired Dick.'

'*If* he is—let's not take that as read until he confirms it one way or the other.'

'And if he won't oblige?'

'Then I'll chip in and we'll play it by ear.'

'Our good cop, bad cop routine, you mean.' Harriet laughs.

'This isn't a game, Harry,' says Hester grimly.

Turning into a quieter, tree-lined side street, their footsteps slow. Hester checks the paper again. 'There it is.' She points at a house across the road, well-tended, with a bright-red front door. Two bay trees in pots stand either side of the porch. The lights are on. 'Looks like we're in luck.'

They both straighten their shoulders and make for the house. Harriet is feeling rather queasy. She's not looking forward to this. A picture of Daria and Milo swims into her mind, strengthening her resolve.

A rather twee *ding-dong!* greets her press of the bell. Distantly, a dog barks. They haven't factored in the danger of any canine reinforcements. Both pray silently it is not a Rottweiler.

It isn't. It's a cute little Pomeranian, nestling in its owner's arms and, on seeing the visitors, eager to lick them. The man, casually dressed in jeans and a sweater, holds the dog to his chest. 'Quiet, Mitzi! Quiet!' His wire-framed glasses give him a faintly professorial air. The sisters are glad to see he is no beefy rugby player; unless Finbar was exaggerating (a not unlikely scenario), he is probably not the second stranger. Tennis seems more this chap's game. Or bridge.

'Hello?'

The disparity between their imaginings and this reality makes Harriet nervous. 'We're here about Daria,' she blurts out with an aggressive tone she had not intended.

'Sorry?'

'Listen,' she says, hardening her voice, 'don't make this more unpleasant than it needs to be.' He frowns, and his attempt to play dumb inflames her anger. 'We know all about you. Just give us her passport and the rest of her things and we'll be off.'

'Passport?' repeats the man.

'Or we'll call the police,' says Hester, stepping forward.

'The police?' He looks disconcerted. It fires Harriet's courage and outrage.

'Oh yes, you don't like that, do you? All very well to threaten a poor defenceless girl, take advantage of someone young and vulnerable, but mention the police and the boot's on the other foot, isn't it?'

Hester weighs in. 'You ought to be ashamed of yourself! We're sorry you had such a terrible time losing your baby like that, but to seduce someone hardly more than a girl under your own roof and then plan to abduct her unborn child—'

The man's face has been growing steadily darker under this onslaught. 'Baby? Child? Girl? What the fuck are you on about?' he yells as another figure materialises at the end of the hall and moves towards them. It's gloomy in the hallway, difficult to see clearly.

'Ha!' says Hester. 'Let's just see what your wife has to say about it all!'

'My *wife*?' The man falls back in disbelief, oblivious of Mitzi furiously exercising her tongue on his face, as another man arrives on the doorstep and puts his arm around the first man's shoulders.

'Anything wrong, love?'

The two women stare back at the men as the penny drops with a resounding clang.

Harriet wets her lips. 'Hester,' she whispers, 'could I have another look at that address?'

Hester hands the paper to her without a word, eyes still glued to the men's faces. 'You're not Peter Sampson, then?' she croaks at the man holding Mitzi.

'Seventeen Barrowgate Terrace?' says Harriet in a tiny voice.

For answer, the man, puce with fury, points theatrically at a tasteful slate on the exterior wall of the house that reads *Seven*. He glares back at the sisters. 'Try wearing your glasses next time, you . . . you . . . you stupid old bags!' he spits, before stepping back, his partner's arm still around his shoulders, and slamming the door.

Hester and Harriet creep back down the path, mortified. *Stupid* stings. It stings a great deal.

CHAPTER 14

Peter Sampson isn't lying on a beach in the Caribbean or swooping down the slopes at Val d'Isère. He's standing in the doorway of 17 Barrowgate Terrace, face grey with shock.

'Daria?' he says for the second time. 'Then you know where she is? Oh, thank God. Thank God.'

Whatever the chastened sisters have been expecting, having unleashed their bombshell on the real Peter Sampson, it isn't this mixture of astonishment and . . . well, relief. He looks over their shoulders into the empty street, searching the parked cars for occupants.

'We came on the train,' says Harriet, wondering why she feels the need to share the information with this bewildered man. 'Alone.'

Beside her, Hester tuts. 'Daria is many miles away,' she growls. 'Far from your clutches. She's safe.'

'Oh, I can't tell you . . . my God,' mutters Sampson, holding the doorframe as though uncertain of his balance. Then, 'Clutches? Whatever do you mean?'

'Oh, come on,' Hester says curtly, 'don't try to pull the wool over our eyes. We may be getting on a bit, but we're not *stupid*.' There's an added savagery to the adjective, still needling both women after their recent faux pas. Despite the fact that much of what they suspect is conjecture, she ploughs straight in. 'Sending people snooping around the village. Terrorising elderly gentlemen. *Indigent* elderly gentlemen,' she adds, for good measure. 'Don't try to deny it.'

'I'm sorry? What are you talking about?' Either he's a good actor or he's genuinely confused. Increasingly, as she observes his reactions and his pallor, Harriet is tending towards the latter.

Hester snorts. 'Don't deny it. And I'm still not altogether persuaded it wasn't you nosing around in'—she catches herself just in time—'in our neighbourhood yesterday. Luckily Finbar is a good friend and came straight round to warn us.'

Sampson looks from Hester to Harriet, shaking his head. 'Finbar? What? I'm sorry, but I have absolutely no idea what you are talking about.' As if suddenly remembering his manners and the temperature outside, he says, 'Perhaps you should come in. The street is hardly the place for a conversation like this.'

He steps aside and Harriet goes to enter; Hester grabs her arm. 'Remember what we agreed?' she hisses, jerking her head in Sampson's direction. 'Remember what Finbar said?'

'Hetty,' returns Harriet in a low tone, 'just look at the man.'

She is right: one glance, if one were not possessed of a mistrustful mind like Hester's, would confirm that he offers no threat, indeed, looks totally confounded by their accusations. Harriet shrugs off her sister's restraining arm and marches past Sampson into the house, making for what appears to be the living room. 'In here?'

Sampson nods and then, closing the front door, eels past her—'Allow me'—to precede them into the room. The reason for his haste is apparent when they enter. Sitting on the sofa, hugging a cushion, is a thin, limp-haired woman wearing a blank expression that does not change even when she turns her head slowly to look at the strangers.

'My wife, Elizabeth,' says Sampson, sitting beside her and taking an unresponsive hand. 'Please . . .'

He gestures to two armchairs and Hester and Harriet cautiously sit, Hester shrugging off her heavy coat. Harriet won't deny it's good to get the weight off her feet; the unaccustomed court shoes are beginning to pinch. Not that she'll tell Hester *that*.

'Lizzie,' says Sampson gently, 'these two ladies have come with some news. About Daria.'

At the name, the woman flinches, blinks and sits up straighter. 'Daria?' The cushion falls to the floor. Her hands dance with a tremor as she pleats and re-pleats the fabric of her skirt. 'I . . . where is she? Is she here?'

Sampson stills her fretting hands with one of his. 'No need to upset yourself, darling. She's not here. But these two ladies know where she is.'

'And the—?'

'I don't know. Let's just see what they have to say, eh?'

Elizabeth stares at the sisters fearfully, then, as though trying to impose some normality on the situation and her own behaviour, gathers herself. 'Sorry. Tea?'

Sampson leaps up. 'I'll do it.'

'No. No!' she cries, pulling him down violently and pushing herself upright, eyes blazing. 'I can do it! I can make a bloody pot of tea!' She stumbles out of the room, steadying herself on the doorjamb. The door bangs shut.

The air sings with discomfort. Hester flicks a glance at Harriet, who gestures silence. After a few awkward seconds, Sampson rises and leaves the room. They look around the comfortable, colourful room with its thick rugs and modern paintings. There's money here. Everything speaks of effortless good taste. Distantly, they hear voices, the rattle of cups in the kitchen and the surge of an electric kettle coming to the boil. Suddenly, Harriet inhales sharply. She reaches over to pick up a photograph on the table beside her; Hester hurries to her side.

'Goodness me!'

'That's remarkable. I always think all babies look alike,' whispers Hester, 'but the likeness is uncanny—'

Two blond babies stare at them from the photo. The slightly larger of the two is Milo's doppelganger.

'Well, there's no mistaking who Milo's father is . . .'

Footsteps approach; Harriet quickly replaces the photo as Hester resumes her seat.

'I'm sorry about that,' murmurs Sampson. 'I just wanted to check . . .' He gestures vaguely in the direction of the kitchen and Harriet utters some noncommittal noises meant to minimise his distress and embarrassment. 'She's not really . . . she doesn't mean to be . . .'

'No, no,' says Harriet. 'Of course.'

'She has good days and bad. This is one of the latter.' Sampson bites his lip. 'This is all rather . . . perhaps we should introduce ourselves? I'm Peter Sampson, as I gather you know. And my wife is Elizabeth.' He looks enquiringly across the coffee table, mainly at Hester, whom he has clearly already decided is the main protagonist. Harriet sits and waits. And waits.

Finally . . .

'Hester. That's all I'm prepared to tell you at this stage. And my sister, Harriet.'

Harriet gives a brief nod; her tentative smile is answered with one similar. Hester stares at Sampson implacably.

'All right,' says Sampson, struggling to get a foothold in this unfamiliar territory. 'And . . . can I ask? Is Daria all right? Is she still in England?'

'She could hardly leave, could she?' snaps Hester. 'Without a passport.'

Oh, Hester, thinks Harriet, *do give the man a chance. Tell him what he wants to know, for goodness' sake.* 'She had a boy,' she says aloud.

Hester glares.

A smile starts across his face. 'A boy? Yeah?' The smile spreads, deepens. Hester looks away.

'He's beautiful,' says Harriet. 'A little darling.'

Now the man's face has relaxed, she can see the resemblance even more. The shape of the chin, the broad forehead. And his hair, a dark blond, mirrors Milo's baby fluff.

'What's his name?' says Sampson, a break in his voice.

Hester jumps in. 'You don't need to know that right now. First we want some answers.'

The light dies in his eyes, his whole body deflates, then he nods and says, 'Look, I don't know what you imagine has been going on but we were in Paris yesterday.'

'Paris?' Hester manages to sound both incredulous and offensive at the same time.

'We were there over Christmas. I thought . . . well, not one of my better ideas . . .' He gives a wan smile then rallies. 'Listen, I don't know where you've come from, or where you live, but wherever it is, I wasn't there yesterday. Ask my wife.'

'And why should we believe her?' says Hester aggressively.

'Hetty, please!'

'Well, we've only got his word for it, haven't we? After what Daria told us—'

'What? What did she tell you?'

'In a minute. First, do you deny you sent a man called'—she can hardly bring herself to say it—'*Dick* to our house on Boxing Day?'

Sampson's face hardens.

Don't try to flannel us, thinks Hester.

We mustn't underestimate him, thinks Harriet, *however upset he may be.*

'I don't deny employing a man of that name, no. He's been working on my behalf for several months, trying to establish Daria's whereabouts.'

'Why?'

'I was worried about her! Why do you think? I felt responsible for her. For obvious reasons.'

Hester raises a sceptical eyebrow, mouth pursed.

'All right, all right! I suppose she's told you what happened?'

Hester inclines her head a fraction.

'I can see how it looks. But you weren't here—you've no idea what it was like! I was beside myself. Lizzie was just starting to come through things after . . . Marcus, and then it all came out . . . what happened between Daria and me.' He catches Hester's implacable stare. 'All right, what do you want me to say? I know it was wrong. Unforgivable. But then Daria just vanished.'

Hester and Harriet are silent.

Sampson sighs with apparent frustration; it's clear he is unused to his word being doubted. 'Look, I tried to find out where she might have gone but no-one was prepared to talk to me. I'm not saying I blame them, but that's why I hired Dick. I had no idea that he was planning to do anything over Christmas, though. He rang me the day before we left for Paris—on the twenty-third—to say he had a lead and would be following it up. He didn't say when.'

'What lead? How did he find out where we lived?' Hester presses him.

'I don't know! He just said he was keeping me in the loop and that he'd let me know how things worked out. I was in a meeting. We didn't talk long. Now please . . .' His tone becomes importunate, his body tense, eyebrows knitted with anxiety. 'Please tell me about Daria. We've been worried sick. When she left, we didn't know where—'

'She didn't leave—she ran away,' interrupts Hester. 'To escape from you and your wife.'

'Escape? Why on earth would she want to do that?' To Harriet's ear, his bafflement sounds genuine.

'Oh, come on!' scoffs Hester. 'You threaten to steal her baby and you wonder why she—'

'Steal her baby!' The door swings open and Elizabeth, tray in hand, stands there, trembling. 'Are you out of your minds?' The contents of the tray rattle alarmingly as she slams it down on the coffee table. Milk slops from a jug and spreads out in a white pool.

'Hey, hey!' Sampson is on his feet, arms around his wife.

For a moment, it looks as though she is about to fight him off, then her resistance dies and she lets herself be led back to the sofa. Tenderly, he eases her down, crouching beside her, cradling her head in his hands, murmuring reassurance, endearments. When she looks up, her face is wet with tears.

This is unbearable, thinks Harriet. She clears her throat. 'Look, Mr Sampson. Mrs Sampson. I think it's only fair we tell you what we know and then you can tell us your side of the story. No, Hester, let me. We have to get to the bottom of this, if only for Daria's sake. And Milo's. That's his name: Milo. He's a bonny, adorable baby. And Daria is a wonderful mother, really wonderful. She's had a terrible time of it over the last few months. All we want to do is help them, nothing more. But first, might I have a cup of tea?'

Sampson mops up the milk and pours the tea as Harriet talks. She introduces herself and Hester properly this time, without revealing their surnames or where they live, and sets out their version of events, or rather Daria's.

When Elizabeth goes to interject, Sampson stops her. 'In a minute, darling. Let her finish.'

Harriet tells them all they know of Daria's journey to eventual sanctuary in their house, including her account of what happened in the Sampsons' home. Several times more Sampson has to restrain his wife from cutting in. A kaleidoscope of emotions flits across his face as the narrative unfolds; Elizabeth's betrays surprise, anger and pity in turn. Finally Harriet tells them about their visit to Henry Walters and the advice they were given. Her quiet voice fills the room for a good ten minutes, the only interruption the occasional passing traffic. Finally, the tale told, she falls silent. Hester gives a brief nod of approval.

Elizabeth shakily replaces her cup and saucer on the table. She is for the moment calm, certainly calmer than she has been since their arrival. As her husband goes to speak, she lays a hand on his arm to silence him. 'Harriet, Hester, I think there has been the most terrible misunderstanding.' Her voice is low and, despite her apparent composure, still shaky with emotion.

Poor woman, thinks Harriet, *she's been in a very dark place.*

'Everything Daria told you about me is true. About Marcus, our son, and what happened ... about me being so ill. I was ill, for a long time. A long, long time.' She says it almost to herself, almost as if she is talking about someone else. She laces her fingers, her knuckles whitening under the pressure. 'And Daria was a marvel, our saviour, caring for Mia when I couldn't and keeping things together all through those terrible weeks.'

'Months, darling,' says Sampson quietly.

'Yes, I suppose so. Months then. I trusted her. And Mia loved her. I couldn't bear to hold Mia, you see. I expect you think that I'm a monster, but I just couldn't—everything about her reminded me of Marcus. But I knew somewhere deep inside—don't ask me how—that she was safe with Daria. I couldn't have articulated it, though, not then. Everything was blurred, the whole world skewed and out of alignment. I thought everyone was against me. I suppose I was a little bit mad.

'And when I found out about her and Peter . . . I wanted to lash out. I don't blame him. Not now. Or her. But I did then. I wasn't thinking straight. Everything was crowding in on me. To me, it suddenly seemed she was a malign spirit, the cause of everything terrible that had happened: Marcus's death, seducing my husband, getting pregnant. I thought . . . no, I don't know what I thought—it was like being in a dark, dark tunnel with no way out. Things happen when you're in a bad way and they overwhelm you. But stealing her baby! No, never. All I can think is she must have overheard us talking and misinterpreted what we were saying. Perhaps I did say we could adopt her baby—it was Peter's, after all—I don't remember. But I didn't mean it! Not like that.'

Husband and wife look at one another as though there is no-one else in the room. He squeezes her hand and the ghost of a memory passes over her face. She turns back to the sisters. 'I know Peter was desperate to find her. But I was angry. She had betrayed me with Peter and then she abandoned Mia. How could she do that?'

'I think her only thought was—' starts Harriet.

'Yes, I see that now! For her baby. Don't you think I understand that?!' Elizabeth gulps, swallowing her incipient

hysteria. 'I'm sorry.' She gathers herself and continues more calmly. 'But back then I was glad she had gone from our lives. I just wanted to forget her. Forget all about . . . Peter, I'm so—'
A sob escapes her.

Her husband pulls her towards him. 'Don't, my love. You've nothing to reproach yourself with. This is all my fault.'

Absolutely, thinks Hester.

Oh dear, oh dear. What a tangle, thinks Harriet.

Elizabeth shakes her head and sits back. She takes a deep breath and turns to Hester and Harriet.

'And I swear to you that Peter was with me in Paris yesterday. We only got back this morning. We couldn't bear the thought of Christmas at home this year. My mother offered to take Mia for us—we're due to collect her this afternoon. I can show you the Eurostar ticket, the receipt from our hotel in Montmartre . . .'

'No, no,' says Hester, discomfited by Elizabeth's evident sincerity. *I've misjudged her*, she thinks. *Too hasty by half. When will I learn?*

Harriet's mobile rings. Cursing the interruption, she quickly silences it. If it's Henry, she'll call him back later.

Sampson has watched his wife unflinchingly throughout; looking away at last, he wrestles to find his own words. 'I behaved badly, I can't deny it. Appallingly. I can't explain it or excuse it. When Lizzie needed me most, I let her down. I let Daria down too, I know that. But we never meant Daria any harm, you must believe us. As for her passport—I suggested she put it in the safe, that's all. It wasn't part of some master plan. We'd had a spate of burglaries in the area just before she arrived, and stolen passports are big business. I'll go and get it now.' He gets to his feet and slips from the room.

Elizabeth says in a low voice, 'He's a good man, you know.' And for the first time since their arrival, they see the faintest glimmer of a smile. A sad smile, signalling the long way she still has to travel, but a smile nonetheless.

Hester, to Harriet's considerable surprise, gets up and goes to sit beside Elizabeth. She takes her hand. 'We're very sorry for your loss, my dear. To lose a child . . .' The unspoken words echo around the room. She hesitates, then continues. 'You must forgive us for being so . . . well, for me being so fierce when we arrived . . . Harriet will tell you what a battleaxe I can be.'

Harriet, across the room, nods—rather too eagerly for Hester's liking—and as she and Elizabeth exchange a rueful look, a little of the sadness in the room dissipates.

'I don't suppose . . .' Elizabeth's voice is low. They hear a drawer being opened upstairs. 'Do you think, perhaps, we might see Daria and . . . Milo?' As Hester's face hardens, she adds quickly, 'I don't mean immediately, but one day?'

Hester purses her lips. 'Not right away.'

'No, no . . .'

'Daria's very fragile at the moment.'

'Of course. But'—Sampson is descending the stairs—'in a little while? I mean, Peter is the father.' Harriet can see how much it costs her to say the words.

Sampson reappears, passport in one hand, a small bag in the other. He holds them both out. 'She left some things.' Hester takes them. 'I was wondering . . . do you think there's any chance—'

'I've already asked.'

'Oh.'

'Of course. In time. But, you'll understand, not immediately.' Sampson's face falls. 'There's a lot we need to sort out. For Daria. Her status for a start . . .'

'I understand. But, look, if there's anything we can do—I mean, money, a lawyer, testimonials—you have only to ask . . .'

'Mr Sampson . . .' says Hester hesitantly.

'Peter.'

'You do realise that you might be in trouble yourselves? You know, employing someone without the correct papers.'

Sampson shrugs. 'Believe me, that's the last thing on our minds right now. And, anyway, we weren't exactly employing Daria. It was a casual arrangement, just for a week or so and then . . .' He spreads his hands. All of the ensuing months of misery and despair are encapsulated in that little gesture.

'Before we go,' says Hester, 'would you do something for us? Get hold of Dick and ask him who gave him the information about Daria's whereabouts. And also, tell him you've found her. We'd rather not have another visit, if you don't mind.'

'Of course, of course. I'll do it now.' He pulls his mobile out of his pocket and quickly flicks down his contacts, then jabs the keypad.

They wait in silence, listening to the faint ringing tone. To their disappointment, it goes through to voicemail and Sampson leaves a brief but urgent message. 'Sorry. That's really annoying. I'll be in touch as soon as I get hold of him. And don't worry, he won't trouble you again, I promise.'

Hester and Harriet get to their feet. Harriet helps her sister into her coat and then tucks her scarf into the neck of her suit.

They both pull on their leather gloves. Sampson holds out his hand.

'We can't thank you enough for coming. You've no idea what it means to me—to us—to know what happened. To know about . . . Milo.' He tries out the unfamiliar name. His son.

Harriet fleetingly wonders if she ought to remark on Milo's astonishing resemblance to his half-brother. She does not. That's something for the future, for a happier occasion when Milo meets his father and he—and Elizabeth, when she is stronger—can see for themselves.

'We thought, you see, Lizzie and me, as time went by and we heard nothing, that we'd never see Daria again.'

'We'll be in touch,' says Hester, face softening.

Harriet shakes his hand, then his wife's. 'It will get easier,' she whispers, and finds herself wanting to hug this frail and grieving stranger.

As they set off down the street, Sampson and Elizabeth huddle in the doorway, his arms tight around her.

'Please,' he calls after them, 'please tell Daria we're sorry.'

⌣⌣⌣

'So,' says Hester, as they retrace their steps to the Underground, carrying the holdall, Daria's passport safe in Harriet's handbag, 'it has to be this Scott chap who was badgering Finbar yesterday, hasn't it? We know it wasn't Peter Sampson, or Dick. Blast Finbar for disappearing like that! And what is it about that girl that attracts these ne'er-do-wells? She hardly knows more than a handful of people in the country and yet every man and his dog seems to want to find her.'

Harriet is struggling to keep up as she fiddles with her phone, trying to check missed calls. 'I was wondering just the same thing. Who else could it be? You know, we really are going to have to put some pressure on Daria when we get back. She's definitely keeping things from us.'

'Well, we know that!'

'Where on earth do I find the call log on this thing? Hang on!'

Hester stops abruptly, almost colliding with a jogger who had been about to overtake her. He hisses a stream of invective as he veers around her, skidding on a sodden discarded sandwich wrapper and almost losing his footing. He swears even louder. Harriet seizes the opportunity to sit on a nearby bench and catch her breath. Hester, she notes, is not even out of breath, despite the cracking pace she set. Even through her thick skirt, Harriet feels the chill of the cold metal. Her shoes, her seldom-worn almost box-new shoes, are horribly tight now; on her little toe, a corn throbs. She glances longingly at Hester's sensible footwear. 'Ah, here we are! Oh, it's home. Ben must have been trying to get hold of us.' She checks her texts. Nothing.

Panic hits them simultaneously. 'Oh no,' cries Hester. 'Please God, nothing's happened. Quickly, ring him back.'

Which Harriet does. But their home phone rings and rings and eventually goes through to the answerphone. On hearing her own voice, Harriet terminates the call. Her palms are clammy.

'Try his mobile,' urges Hester.

But Harriet doesn't have his number.

'Ring George, he'll have it.'

'Won't he wonder why Ben isn't busily getting on with those jobs we wanted him for?'

'Just tell him . . . I don't know—tell him we sent Ben out on some errands while we were gone and we forgot something.'

'What?'

'What does it matter? Milk, bread, cheese—just ring him, will you!'

But George and Isabelle are presumably out doing good works or otherwise saving the world because their number too rings unanswered.

The sisters hurry on towards the station, Harriet's feet screaming in protest, her soles on fire. To distract herself from both her pain and her wild imaginings about possible disasters back home, she starts reviewing their encounter with the Sampsons until Hester snaps at her to stop. So it is in a sombre mood that they descend the escalator in silence, each of them lost in private nightmares of shadowy figures and dead babies.

CHAPTER 15

They both fall asleep on the train home. While neither would admit it to the other, they are exhausted. As Harriet slides unstoppably into oblivion, her last thought is: *We're a bit long in the tooth for all this excitement*. She won't use the word *old*. Her feet ache, her bones ache. She eases her back into the uncomfortable seat and lets the steady beat of the wheels on the rails lull her into an uneasy dream, where Peter Sampson steals into a darkened bedroom and lifts Milo out of his cot-drawer while Daria sleeps on, oblivious. Then Sampson's face morphs into Dick's unsavoury features on their doorstep on Boxing Day, ferrety expression, stained teeth and that repellent phlegmy cough. Harriet shivers and wills herself to wake.

Beside her, Hester is similarly troubled, her head falling ever further onto her chest as the train rattles along. Behind her lids race a potpourri of images: Elizabeth wringing her hands, those sorrowful eyes, the weight of loss heavy in the room; Ben cradling Milo, with Daria's frightened face swimming eerily in the background as though underwater. She is calling for something but Hester can't make out the words. All she can feel—almost touch—is the fear.

Harriet forces her eyes open. Her mouth feels dry, tongue coated with something unpleasantly musty. They haven't eaten since late morning, when Henry's secretary had brought in a plate of indifferent biscuits with the coffee. She fumbles in her bag for her phone, tries to ring home again. No answer. The seed of worry reignited by her dream stirs again in her stomach. Her heart races uncomfortably. She wants nothing more than to be sitting by the fire, jigsaw on a tray in her lap, one of Hetty's cheese and homemade chutney sandwiches in hand, a cup of tea on the side. And no-one else to disturb her save her sister reading in the armchair opposite. She nudges Hester awake. 'Nearly there.'

The familiar shape of the town's football ground heaves into view, its floodlights streaming out into the darkness.

Hester moans softly. 'Gosh, I'm stiff.'

They pull their collars around them, anticipating the chill of the night air, and get unsteadily to their feet, holding on tightly as the train negotiates the kinked line that runs into the platform. It seems a long step down from the carriage. Harriet flexes her sore feet, yearning to get home and kick off her shoes. Trying not to limp, she totters after Hester, who has set off for the exit at her usual uncompromising pace.

'Well, this is a pleasant surprise! Evening, Harriet,' says a familiar voice, and Teddy Wilson is smiling down at her, the citrus tang of his aftershave sharp in the night air. He looks handsome, yes, as usual, his clothes impeccable, but there's a tightness to his skin she hasn't noticed before, his complexion dulled, almost grey. 'If I'd known we were on the same train, we could have sat together.'

'Hester, hang on a tick!' calls Harriet. Then, smiling back at Teddy, she says, 'Not unless you were prepared to slum it with the plebs. We saw you this morning getting in the first-class carriage. With Peggy Verndale.'

His face clouds briefly, before he rearranges his features into his habitual smooth smile. 'Ah, yes. Dear Peggy. Quite a chatterbox.' He raises his eyebrows and they share a conspiratorial look. 'Been to the sales too, have you?'

Harriet suppresses her reflex annoyance: why do men always assume women are only interested in one thing? 'No. We were visiting friends in West London.' Then she adds mischievously, 'But how did you get on? Did you pick up some bargains?'

'I wasn't at the sales! I meant Peggy!' says Teddy sharply, then seeing Harriet's overly-innocent look, 'Oh.' He acknowledges the point has hit home with a thin smile.

Harriet raises an enquiring eyebrow.

'Oh, you know, few bits of business.' This is evidently a strictly masculine pursuit because he does not elaborate and Harriet is reminded why she remains so resolutely immune to his charms. But her antipathy is tempered slightly with concern: he does look weighed down with worries. Juggling too many balls, presumably, both business and personal.

Hester has stopped at the station exit and is waiting impatiently for them to catch up with her. She greets Teddy less warmly than she ordinarily would; they could do without this delay.

Teddy, by contrast, seems in no hurry to part. 'Can I offer you a lift?' he says. The sisters demur—'We've got the car, thanks'—but Teddy, instead of bidding them farewell and setting off to retrieve his own, lingers. His face looks yellow under the station lights, and Harriet wonders whether she's imagining those shadows under his eyes. Is he ill? No, she decides, he's simply worn out. Strung out.

'Everything all right, Teddy?' She instantly regrets the words: he'll think she's fishing, wanting to quiz him about the latest rumours of his love life. Bad enough that he had to travel to London in Peggy's company; she'll have interrogated him mercilessly and the last thing Harriet wants is to be bracketed with the village nosey parker. Hester is giving her a filthy look, jerking her head towards the car park. Harriet, weary, embarrassed, blurts out before Teddy has a chance to reply, 'I mean, did you have a nice Christmas?' Oh hell, what made her say that! She can imagine exactly what kind of Christmas he had. Cursing her ineptitude, she unzips her handbag and starts ferreting for her keys.

'So-so,' says Teddy. Commuters edge irritably around the trio as they stand in the entrance. 'Not my favourite time of the year, to be frank. Never is.'

'Nor me,' says Hester, starting to move away. If only Harriet would shift herself, they could escape. Get home and find out where the hell Ben has got to ... 'Well, Harry, I suppose we ought to ...'

'How about you?' says Teddy unexpectedly. 'What did you two get up to?'

'Oh ...' says Harriet, finally locating the keys amid the crumpled tissues, till receipts and assorted clutter. 'You know. Family, few drinks—'

'Peggy was saying you've got house guests.'

'House—? Oh! Ben, yes, our nephew; he's just staying for a few days,' Hester improvises quickly, putting her hand on Harriet's arm. 'We really should get back.'

'Right,' says Teddy. 'I thought she meant you had a houseful.'

As the two women start moving off, he falls into step beside them. 'I didn't know you had a nephew.'

Why would you? thinks Hester, irritated by Teddy's persistence, her anxiety growing with the delay. *Must be dreading going home, I suppose. But who is he dreading going back to? Molly or Mrs Vicar?*

They reach their car and Harriet stabs the remote to unlock it, Teddy hovering beside them. Hester has to work around him to get into the passenger seat. He gallantly holds the door for her, then suddenly looks over her shoulder and stiffens. In the same instant, Hester's heart plummets.

'Good Lord—a baby seat,' says Teddy. 'What on earth are you doing with that?'

Cursing their sloppiness, Hester lets out a rather wobbly laugh. It's meant to be carefree but it's definitely wobbly. 'Oh that! We . . . er . . .'

'We volunteer for the hospital car scheme,' says Harriet smartly. 'Mostly it's just old folks but once in a while there's a baby we have to . . . transport.'

'Right,' says Teddy, his tone suggesting it is anything but. 'I thought that was scrapped last year. I remember seeing something in the paper.'

Hester scrabbles to recover. 'Yes, the *official* scheme was . . . but we belong to a sort of . . . well, how would you describe it, Harry?'

'Unofficial . . .?'

'Yes, unofficial scheme.' She thinks herself into George and Isabelle's shoes. 'Our cousin organises it. George. And his wife. Great champions of the . . . what's it called, Harry?'

'The needy poor?'

'No! The Big Society. That's it. Very public-spirited, both of them. Saints, really.'

Steady, thinks Harriet.

An awkward silence falls. Then Teddy gently eases the passenger door shut.

'Well, lovely to see you. Love to . . . er . . . bye.' Hester sketches a wave through the window as Harriet hurriedly buckles her belt and starts the engine.

Teddy knocks on the passenger window. Hester jumps. He points at the dashboard and mouths, 'Petrol'. Sure enough, the red warning light is winking.

Harriet rolls her eyes at him and raises her hand in thanks, then bangs the steering wheel in frustration. 'Damn, I meant to fill up the other day.' For someone otherwise so uncon-cerned about the car, Harriet is obsessive about ensuring they never run too low. The appearance of the warning light always occasions a sense of panic, ever since she ignored it once many years ago and they ended up stranded for hours on Bodmin Moor until a supercilious AA man came to their rescue.

Teddy raps on the window again. Hester lowers it. 'You should go to the Texaco station on the bypass—it's the cheapest for miles,' he says.

'Thanks, Teddy. We'll do that,' says Hester, then stares brightly ahead through the windscreen, teeth clenched, aware of a dampness around her neck. 'Goodbye.'

Teddy does not move. After a few false starts, Harriet finds reverse and swings out of the space, driving over to the pay station, so Hester can climb out and feed in the ticket. In her rear-view mirror, Harriet can see Teddy still motionless, still watching them, mobile clamped to his ear. 'Come on, come on,' she mutters, pulse racing as Hester peers short-sightedly at the payment instructions. He starts to walk towards them, still talking. Hester at last extracts the ticket from the machine, clambers back into her seat and Harriet zooms up to the barrier before she has the chance to refasten her belt. She glances in the mirror. Teddy is closing in on them. She shoves the ticket into the exit machine and the barrier slowly rises. As the car lurches through, in her wing mirror she sees Teddy reach the pay station and get out his own ticket. Her heart skips a beat. *You idiotic old fool,* she chides herself. *What is the matter with you?*

'Are you okay?' says Hester, shoving the seatbelt into its housing just in time and grabbing the door handle as Harriet takes a corner too fast. 'Steady on! Anyone would think the police are after us!'

'That bloody baby seat!'

'Harry!'

'Sorry. Why on earth didn't we think to take it out? Imagine if someone like Peggy had spotted it? There's no way she'd have bought that load of nonsense. And Teddy. Didn't you think he was a bit peculiar?'

'I thought you were a bit peculiar! What on earth possessed you to start talking about Christmas? Poor fellow. That's all he needed.'

Harriet bridles. 'That's not what I meant. I meant, when have you ever known Teddy to take the slightest interest in what we're up to?'

'He's always charm personified,' says Hester. Her soft spot for Teddy, sorely tried at the station, has now returned.

'I'm not saying he isn't,' Harriet lies, swerving around a learner driver.

Hester closes her eyes, simultaneously stamping on an imaginary brake.

'It's just that what he normally says—charming as it is— never really amounts to much. Nine times out of ten all he talks about is himself.'

'Harry,' says Hester, legs braced as the traffic lights ahead turn amber, 'he's clearly—oh God!' as Harriet shoots the lights. 'I do wish you wouldn't. He's clearly cut up about all his marital shenanigans and wanted a bit of a chat, not to be subjected to the third degree. He'll have had that from Peggy this morning, God help him. Will you slow down!'

Harriet applies the brakes none too gently and proceeds to crawl along at an infuriatingly slow pace, until an enraged driver behind her blasts his horn repeatedly and she resumes an acceptable, but legal, speed. Teddy speeds past them in his Jag, but doesn't wave.

They drive the next couple of miles in grumpy silence. Arguments, reflects Hester, should never be conducted on empty stomachs. As the village lights twinkle in the distance, she says, 'You've got enough petrol to get us home, haven't you? Once we've checked that everything's okay, I'll get cracking on supper, while you fill up the car.'

They pull up outside the house, both heads swivelling around to see, to their immense relief, lights blazing.

'Thank heavens for that,' grunts Hester, climbing out. 'Hang on. I'll find out what's been going on. Oh.' She looks across at Harriet. 'Pick up another couple of pints of milk at the garage, will you? Full cream.' She hurries up the path and inserts her key in the lock, calling out as the door swings open, 'Ben? Daria?'

'Hello? Hester?' comes a voice from upstairs.

Hester turns back towards the car and puts her thumb up to Harriet, then steps inside.

◡◡◡

Full cream, thinks Harriet gleefully as she zooms back down the lane, heady with relief, enjoying jouncing over the potholes; she always drives even more cavalierly when she's alone. *Good old Daria.* The car's springs protest as it thumps over the uneven surface: Harriet finds her spirits reviving. Her stomach growls. Supper can't come soon enough. While she's filling up the car, she might just pick up a Curly Wurly—they're so thin they can't contain that many calories, surely—to tide her over until they eat. Then back home for a nice reviving glass of wine, ideally before they talk to Daria and tell her about the Sampsons. She almost laughs now at the dire scenarios they had entertained earlier when they couldn't get hold of Ben. *Chasing shadows*, she thinks. *Been reading too many thrillers.*

She ignores Teddy's advice about the Texaco station and makes for her usual garage, which is much closer; she can't be bothered to go all that way to save a few pennies. There's quite a queue at the pumps, giving Harriet time to look around at her fellow motorists, all of them wearing that resigned look of people longing to be anywhere but waiting on an oily forecourt for the privilege of paying a king's ransom for a drop of petrol. A few sorry bunches of chrysanthemums wilt in a bucket beside the paper stand, a suited chap picking over them disconsolately. Finally, he lifts one dripping bunch out of the display and, holding it at arm's length with a look of distaste on his face, enters the shop. Harriet sees him hesitate by the sweets; he reaches for a large box of Ferrero Rocher. *Gosh,* thinks Harriet, *he must really be in the doghouse.*

A horn sounds behind her and the shaven-headed driver in the Astra points angrily at the pump from which the car in front has just moved off. Harriet edges forward then gets out and starts to fill the tank, studiously avoiding looking at the occupant of the car behind. Honestly, people are so rude these days. She glances across the forecourt at a mousy woman in a quilted jacket staring into space as she fills her battered Land Rover. A gust of wind catches the hair straggling over her face and blows it up in the air, revealing for a second or two an angry swelling over her right eye, its brow puffy, the lid swollen. Her hand goes up to catch the hair and pull it down, curtaining her face again. Harriet looks away, embarrassed, as the woman hurries past on her way to the shop.

A minute or so later, she follows her in, to find the woman apparently completing her purchase. Just as she seems about to leave, though, she stops and, scrabbling in her bag to extract a piece of paper, shows it to the cashier and begins whispering urgently over the counter.

The man waiting in front of Harriet exhales noisily with irritation, shifting impatiently from foot to foot. He turns and catches Harriet's eye. 'Some of us have homes to go to.' He misreads her brief non-committal smile as encouragement. 'Oi, mate,' he shouts to the cashier, stepping out of line, 'couldn't you open another till or something? We haven't got all day.'

The cashier, young, inexperienced, looks around for assistance. None is forthcoming. Cheeks hectic with colour, he abruptly pushes the woman's piece of paper back at her and pointedly looks over her shoulder at the next in line. 'Which pump?'

As the customer steps up to the counter, the woman snatches at her paper; in her hurry it flutters to the floor. The man in front of Harriet, somewhat placated by the success of his complaint, bends down to retrieve it. It's not a scrap of paper after all; it's a photograph. Harriet takes a surreptitious look as he hands it back: a family snap, mother and baby, from the look of it, although his thumb is over the mother's face. Then, in the split second of the handover, the whole picture is exposed. Harriet starts. There, smiling tentatively at the camera, cradling a tiny Milo in her arms, is Daria.

In a shop, if one suddenly needs to leave, it is easy enough to stuff the items back on a shelf or simply abandon them. But buying petrol is another matter. One has no option but to wait and pay, however long that takes, given the consequences if one does not. As the woman slips swiftly out into the night and hurries over to her waiting car, Harriet is trapped. All she can do is crane her neck to see which way the woman turns onto the road. She edges forward in an agony of frustration as the testy man in front finally reaches the counter, thrusts

201

his credit card into the machine and punches in his number. Then it is her turn. As quickly as the procedure allows, she completes her payment and runs out to her car, to find Astra thug glaring at her. She ignores him. Pulling away from the forecourt, swerving around a Clio parked beside the hole-in-the-wall, she hears him gunning his engine as he draws up to the pump. Numbskull.

Her little car will be no match for a Land Rover but she zooms off in pursuit anyway, hoping against hope that the woman is a law-abiding citizen who obeys speed limits. The road is dark, no tail-lights in sight. Quickly, she runs through the road ahead in her mind. There is one turning in the next two miles, on the left, leading only to an isolated industrial unit. Next is their village, with several roads on both sides, and then a T-junction, leading to the main road towards Stote in one direction and the motorway in the other. If she fails to catch up with the woman before she enters Pellington, she stands little chance of ever finding her. Harriet presses down on the accelerator, adrenalin pumping, watching the speed-ometer climb ... 40 ... 50 ... 60 ... Breasting the hill above the village, she is momentarily blinded by a lorry grinding towards her. He dips his headlights as she hurtles past and down the approach road, past Handfast House, the row of council houses, the war memorial, the village hall, the pub, the bus shelter. She stamps hard on the brakes, which scream in protest, and wrenching the wheel over towards the kerb, comes to a jolting halt with a scrape of rubber. She turns off her lights. Waiting a few moments to allow her pulse to slow to something approaching normal, she levers herself out of the car and limps stealthily back to the bus shelter, beside which the Land Rover, engine off but lights blazing, is parked.

The woman is inside the shelter, cautiously lifting up assorted garments, plastic bags, newspapers and blankets, the detritus of Finbar's life. Of the old man there is no sign, but his unmistakable and pungent aroma is very much in evidence. Harriet is guessing he is tucked up in a corner of his favourite pub, nursing a pint and hoping some gullible soul will buy him a refill.

'Can I help you?'

The woman jumps, spinning around guiltily, hand raised instinctively to conceal her injured eye. As Harriet takes a step closer, she cowers as though expecting an assault. Something in her defensive posture, dark eyes darting about like a trapped animal seeking an escape route, reminds Harriet of Daria on Christmas morning; the woman is plainly terrified. Harriet repeats the question more gently.

The woman shakes her head. 'No, no, I was just . . .' She is edging towards her car; in the beam of the headlights, Harriet sees that she is trembling. If she makes a run for it, Harriet hasn't a hope of stopping her. Not only is the woman as thin as a whippet and probably just as nifty, the corn on Harriet's little toe is excruciating, pressing into her tender flesh like a needle. She transfers the weight to her other foot for some temporary relief.

'I saw you at the petrol station. You were showing the lad serving a photo?' The woman freezes. 'I couldn't help noticing how upset you were.'

Fear then hope flares in the woman's eyes. She snatches a ragged breath. 'You know where she is?'

Harriet ducks the question. 'You're looking for someone, are you? Who is it?'

'My daughter,' says the woman quickly, too quickly. Her face relaxes for a second or two into an unconvincing smile. 'She's ... well, she's not been well. You know.' She taps her head. 'It happens apparently sometimes ... after a birth ... hormones flying about.'

'She's got a baby?'

'Yes, a little boy. We're worried sick about him. About her. Her mental state, you know?' She fixes Harriet with a searching look. 'So ... you've seen her?'

'Let me see the picture again,' says Harriet, stalling. 'May I?'

Without taking her eyes off Harriet's face, the woman pulls the photo from her bag.

Harriet whips off her glasses to get a better look. Definitely Daria, definitely Milo. She tries to spot any clues in the background, but the photo could have been taken anywhere—anywhere indoors, anyway, the artificial light falling harshly on mother and child. 'Sweet,' she says, shaking her head.

The woman, thank heavens, reads this as a denial. Hope dies in her eyes; she looks desperate once more, lips bloodless.

Harriet presses home her advantage. 'What made you look here?'

The woman hesitates; Harriet watches her concocting an explanation. 'When I ... I mean, someone thought they'd seen a girl around the neighbourhood. In the last couple of days.'

'Well,' says Harriet heartily, 'no-one would be mad enough to hang around this shelter—an old tramp sleeps here most of the time, as you can probably tell by the smell. He doesn't like people poking about in here. Understandably.' She gestures at Finbar's possessions.

The woman looks shamefaced, then blurts out, 'Look, I really do need to find her! My husband is . . . beside himself. I mean, it's urgent.' Once more her hand flies to her damaged face and, for a moment, Harriet thinks she's going to cry. The woman begins edging out of the shelter towards her car. Harriet needs to stop her, to keep her talking . . .

'That's a nasty bump you've got there. Looks painful.'

The woman barks out a harsh, unexpected laugh. 'This? Christ, this is the least of my worries.' And slipping past Harriet, she slides into the Land Rover, slams the door shut and in seconds is roaring up the road. Harriet watches her disappear into the distance and then slowly hobbles back to her own car, thoughts churning.

∾

Her mobile rings just as she turns into the lane for home. It'll be Hetty, she knows, remembering something else she wants getting for supper. *Too bad*, thinks Harriet. *We've more important things than our stomachs to worry about.* She lets it ring.

But it's not Hester. It's Ben, whom she sees standing in the doorway of the cottage, phone clamped to his ear. The second he sees Harriet's car, he runs onto the drive, shouting, although Harriet can't make out a word. She screeches to a halt as Ben leaps back to avoid being crushed against the garage door and then flings her door open.

'Quick! Quick!' he yells. 'It's Aunt Hester.'

Harriet struggles out of the car, Ben pulling on her arm, and the pair of them stumble like drunks into the hallway. At the end of the hall, on the threshold of the kitchen, she can see Daria kneeling on the floor and, beside her, a pair of legs. She hurries towards them, breathless and fearful. 'What on earth—'

'Will you all stop fussing!'

Oh, the blessed relief of Hester's indignant voice. Harriet steps around Daria and leans over her sister. Hester is red in the face, looking more furious than hurt.

'Hetty?'

'Help me up,' snaps Hester. 'I'm just winded, that's all.'

'No, no,' cries Ben. 'Don't move her. She might have a head injury.'

'A head injury?' says Harriet, aghast. She flicks the hall light on, sees Hester's glasses lying on the floor, picks them up.

'Yeah, a boy at school, he knocked his head playing rugby. Got up right as rain: ten minutes later he was dead.'

'I have not got a head injury!' barks Hester. 'I fell, that's all. Now help me up!'

'Wait a minute!' cries Harriet. 'Ben's right. We can't be too careful. How long have you been unconscious?'

'I haven't been unconscious!' shouts Hester. 'Give me strength!'

Harriet presses on. 'But I've been gone a good ten, fifteen minutes—'

Hester struggles to a sitting position, straddling the doorway. 'Hell's bells! I yelled up to Daria when I got in. She couldn't hear me—'

'In bathroom,' says Daria. 'With Milo.'

'Right. I went down the hall, peered into the kitchen, just as the wretched phone rang. It was Peggy, rabbiting on about next week's bridge and the bargains she'd picked up in the sales. Finally got rid of her, went back towards the kitchen and bam! I fell. I've been down here about five seconds. Well, about five *minutes* now after you've all given me the third degree. Satisfied?'

They lift her to her feet, lead her still grumbling into the kitchen and Daria guides her over to a chair at the table. Only now does Harriet notice the devastation. All the surfaces seem to be covered in a thick layer of flour. Sugar grinds under the soles of her shoes, which, she realises, are sticky with a mess of yellow and something translucent that she surmises can only be broken eggs. A smashed bowl lies on the tiles.

'What's happened here?'

'You might well ask,' mutters Hester, rubbing her arm. 'Have we been burgled? Where are my glasses?'

Harriet hands them to her. With glasses in place she looks more like the Hester of old, formidable if a little dishevelled.

'We were cooking,' says Ben. Daria, behind him, is wearing an expression somewhere between guilt and fear.

'Cooking?!' Hester's astonishment is unbounded.

'Yeah, why not?' says Ben, in an truculent tone.

Dearie me, thinks Harriet, *when will this boy get the measure of his aunt?* She wills him to stop, but thought transference clearly does not figure among her many abilities. Ben ploughs on.

'Wanted to get supper ready for you, didn't we? I tried to ring you to check but you didn't answer. Went out to do a bit of shopping this afternoon, give Milo a blow'—ah, so that's why no-one answered the phone—'was gonna do a pie or something.'

'A pie?' Hester is scorn incarnate. 'A *pie*?'

'Yeah!'

Ben, Ben, Ben, for goodness' sake! Less belligerence, more contrition, thinks Harriet.

'With pastry, I suppose?'

''Course with pastry. How else you gonna make a pie?'

His aunt clings on to her temper. Just. 'Have you the first idea how to make pastry?'

'Looked online, didn't I?'

Hester's eyebrows shoot up; Harriet swallows a smile and, catching Daria's eye, sees her do likewise.

'Figured it couldn't be that difficult. Yeah, and had a butcher's at your books.'

'You looked in my recipe books?'

'Yeah . . .' The swagger has diminished. Finally, Ben seems to be catching on to the danger he's in.

There are many things in life that Hester regards with indifference—clothes, accessories, furniture, to name but a few—but books are not among them. Books are special, precious and none more so than her considerable collection of cookery books, built up over the years, whose stains and blemishes bear witness to their utility and their history. Four heads swing around to the dresser, where—oh, blessed relief—the books sit neatly in their accustomed places.

'I put them back, didn't I?'

Hester, temporarily appeased, sweeps her hand around the ruins of her kitchen. 'And this?'

Ben has the grace, or wit, to look a little sheepish. 'Yeah, well . . .' He shuffles his feet awkwardly, succeeding only in stirring the mess upon the tiles into a grey glue.

Daria says in a tiny voice, 'We play.'

'Play?' The edge in Hester's voice would cut parmesan. Daria, running a nervous hand through her hair, nods. 'With Milo. Flour . . . like snow. Make him laugh.'

Harriet could imagine, but Hester in her present mood is not to be mollified by the image of a baby entranced by a flour storm.

'And?'

Ben takes over. 'It got a bit silly.'

'Evidently.'

'Yeah. So then I knock the bowl off the counter, and as I go, like, to catch it, my elbow hits the eggs and they smash, so then I have to go to get some more. So Daria goes up to clean up Milo in the bath while I nip down to the shop before they close, and when I get back ready to clear up the mess, you're sprawled all over the floor . . . and I thought you was a goner, so I rung Aunt Harriet—'

'Rang,' says Hester.

'Yeah, and that's that.'

'That is most certainly not that! You will clean this mess up immediately.'

At once Daria is in the utility room in search of cloths and mops.

Hester pulls herself upright with Harriet's help and stands shakily. 'Your aunt and I will go through to the sitting room. You will bring us both a cup of tea. And when order is restored, I will make us all omelettes.'

Hester turns and makes a little groggily for the door, where, hanging on to the doorjamb, she heels off her shoes. 'These will need cleaning too.'

'Er . . . Aunt Hester?'

'What now?'

'Your skirt . . .'

Hester twists around to look at the large egg stain on the seat of her skirt. Even Harriet pulls back fearfully in expectation of an eruption.

'Apron,' says Hester in a voice of thunder. Ben hands her one from behind the door.

'Was it okay? London and that?'

Daria reappears in the kitchen as Ben asks the question.

'Later,' barks Hester, wrapping the apron around her bottom to cover the stain and stomping out of the kitchen. Harriet, having at last released her throbbing feet from the confines of her shoes, follows in her wake.

In the sitting room, Hester settles herself in her armchair; suddenly she looks utterly drained, beyond words. Harriet sits forward in the chair opposite, her sister's wellbeing for the moment displacing her recent encounter at the bus shelter in importance.

'You sure you're all right?'

Hester nods. Something is troubling her, something much more important than a messy kitchen and an overexcited nephew. She has half a mind to keep it to herself for the moment, but Harriet's frown of concern persuades her otherwise.

'Hetty?' says Harriet, watching her sister closely. 'Tell me what happened. Did you bang your head? Ben's right, you shouldn't take any chances.'

Hester, conscious of a swelling lump on her temple, mercifully hidden by her hair, doesn't want to add to Harriet's alarm. 'I whacked my arm on the doorframe as I fell, that's all.'

'Show me.'

Hester pushes up her sleeve; a livid red stripe presages a large bruise. 'It's nothing.'

'We ought to get it looked at.'

'Bit of arnica's all it needs. Be fine in the morning. Which is more than I can say for my kitchen, judging by the state of it.'

'They're only kids,' says Harriet, wondering why Hetty has taken their high spirits so hard. 'But come on. Tell me exactly what happened.'

'It must have been the wind. The door just slammed into me.'

'The kitchen door into the hall?'

Hester frowns, nodding. 'A draught, I suppose.'

'Where from, though? I saw you shut the front door as I drove away. Was the back door open, then?'

'No.'

Hester recalls her surprise at finding the front door ajar on her return, the distant splash of water from the bathroom, bright lights from the kitchen sketching a path along the unlit hall. She distinctly remembers pushing the front door shut, can see herself, hand on newel-post, calling up to Daria, hear the insistent ring of the telephone, interrupting her passage into the kitchen. She relives her extended conversation with Peggy, then walking towards the kitchen, her progress halted abruptly as the door smashed into her . . .

'The thing is, I don't think I fell, Harry. Or slipped. I think someone slammed the door in my face.'

CHAPTER 16

Harriet stares at her sister, anxiety flooding back. She looks—well, frankly, she looks *cowed*. And that is a condition Harriet cannot ever remember associating with her sister, no-nonsense Hetty who disposes of spiders in the bath and threatening situations with equal aplomb, who as a child would climb the highest trees without a qualm and unhesitatingly stand up to bullies in the playground. Even in her marriage, Hetty had been the leader, the self-effacing but accommodating Gordon trailing admiringly in her wake. But now she is sitting opposite, grey of face, in obvious discomfort, if not pain, thoroughly deflated, as though the air has been knocked out of her entirely. Diminished.

On the other side of the hearth, Hester struggles to remember the sequence of events on her homecoming, to retrace her steps from the moment she pushed the key into the lock only to find it already open and entered the hall. That in itself had stirred some distant alarm. Something about the atmosphere in the house felt wrong: it had had not the customary welcoming warmth, but an edge, a chill that subconsciously she supposed was due to the fact that the front door had not been shut tight. And yet . . . that smudge of something on the hall carpet, illuminated by the light spilling from the kitchen. That oddly sharp tang that caught the nostrils, like a . . . like a . . . No, try as she might, she can't get a handle on it. Her mind feels woolly, her reactions dampened. She looks across at Harriet, brow furrowed with apprehension.

She tries a mocking laugh; it comes out all wrong. 'Probably just my imagination, a trick of the light or something. You know what things can be like if you're tired. Let's face it, we're both on our knees, after the day we've had.'

Harriet shakes her head. 'No. Come on. From the beginning.' She knows only too well when her sister is trying to play something down, how she likes to appear unruffled at all times. Hester hates to feel out of control, at the mercy of outside events.

'I don't know why I even said that. It just came into my head, out of nowhere. Forget it. I must be going doolally or something.' Despite the attempted levity, there's a note of finality in her voice, an attempt to close the subject down. But Harriet is not to be deflected.

'Hetty, come on! Was the kitchen door open or closed when you came through the front door? Could you see into the kitchen? Think.'

Hester tries again, willing her brain to paint her a credible picture. But the images remain stubbornly vague; they aren't really images at all, just impressions, shadows, fragments on the edge of her consciousness. It all happened so quickly.

'I don't know . . . open, I think. Yes, I could see the kitchen light was on. Not fully open though . . .'

'What? As though someone was hiding behind it?'

The same thought has just occurred to Hester. *No, really,* she thinks almost simultaneously, *we're both getting carried away here. Perhaps with the hall in darkness, I just walked into the door myself. I was in a tizzy after the phone call, and not really looking where I was going. Never mind my occasional dizzy spells . . .* If Harriet finds out about those, she knows, she'll never hear the end of it. Conscious of Harriet's continuing scrutiny, she bats the idea away with an unintentional dismissiveness. 'Honestly, Harry, I think you're adding two and two and making five. I'm sure it was nothing, just my own stupid fault—'

The sitting room door swings slowly open and Ben advances across the carpet, carefully balancing a tray bearing two mugs and a plate of buttered crackers. 'Thought you might want something to keep you going while me and Daria get supper,' he says. 'And clear up the kitchen and that.'

Harriet reaches gratefully for her tea, forbearing to point out that these cheap, thick mugs are the ones they reserve for gardening or the lubrication of visiting tradesmen. 'Thank you, Ben. That's very thoughtful of you.' She eyes her sister surreptitiously: she's covering something up, she's sure of it.

Hester, accepting her tea with brusque thanks, says, 'What do you mean while you and Daria get supper? I'll be through in a minute to make the omelettes—assuming the replacement eggs are still intact.'

'No, no,' says Ben firmly, ignoring the dig. 'You sit tight and relax. You've had a shock. You didn't ought to be rushing about. We'll sort it.' And he's out of the door before Hester can demur.

'Oh God,' she groans.

If Harriet didn't know her sister so well, she might think she was in pain. 'Whatever it is, we'll have to eat it.'

'Can't I plead invalid status?'

'Hetty, you ingrate!' Secretly, Harriet is heartened by Hester's return to form. 'Give the boy a chance, will you? He's trying very hard.'

'Is he?'

'Look, never mind about him for the moment. Hetty, I know something's up. Just tell me, for heavens' sake! What happened? Ben wasn't here, and Daria was upstairs with Milo . . .'

'Exactly,' says Hester, with an involuntary shiver. 'So if there was an intruder—*if*, although I think the idea's bonkers, personally—then it was a good job you dropped me off when you did. And I still think it was an accident.'

'Okay.' Harriet allows herself to be mollified, desperate now to tell Hester about the woman in the Land Rover. 'Hetty, listen.'

Hester has sunk into her chair, eyes closed. 'What?' she says faintly. Her skin looks papery, ashen, all her vitality drained away.

After supper, thinks Harriet, *it'll wait*.

'What?' repeats Hester with some of her customary impatience.

Above their heads, a baby starts to grizzle; footsteps thunder up the stairs seconds later. Ben to the rescue. Hester opens her eyes and they both glance towards the ceiling.

'Something happened—at the petrol station,' starts Harriet as Hester's eyes drift shut again. 'There was this woman, thin little thing, looking as if a feather would knock her over. She had a black eye. It looked as though someone had beaten her up.'

Harriet recounts their encounter. When she mentions the photo, Hester's eyes spring open and remain trained on her sister's face. Harriet feels her anxiety levels climbing as she sees again the swollen cheek and forehead, hears that desperate voice, smells the woman's fear. By the time she finishes her tale, her stomach is clenched tight. She looks across to Hester, who is digesting this further complication.

'English, then?'

'Definitely.'

'So you think this is the woman who took Daria in?'

'Tina. Yes, probably. Well, almost certainly. Who else would have a photo of Daria? She hasn't been anywhere.'

'Assuming she's telling the truth.'

Harriet lets this pass. 'And she was scared, Hetty; I mean, really scared. Like her life depended on it. No, don't look at me like that. I mean it.'

'But she threw Daria out in the first place. Why is she now trying to find her? It doesn't make sense.'

They sit wrapped in their own thoughts for a moment or two, the air in the room heavy with worry and confusion. Hester mutters, as if to herself, 'That poor girl is probably beside herself out there, wondering what happened down in London. We ought to go through and put her out of her misery, oughtn't we?'

'You know very well, Hetty, what we ought to do,' says Harriet quietly. 'Go to the police.'

There, she's said it. Relief trickles through her; the tension across her shoulders dissipates a fraction. She sips her tea and nibbles on a cracker, heedless of the crumbs peppering her skirt, as she waits for her sister's response.

Hester reaches automatically for her knitting, smoothing the soft mohair over her lap. Her hands move rhythmically over the surface, as though there's comfort to be gained from such a mindless activity; she always thinks best when she's caught up in some mechanical task. Harriet leans over to offer the plate to Hester, who takes a cracker but does not eat it. Instead, after considerable thought, she says with great firmness, 'No.'

Harriet is nonplussed. 'Hetty! We're out of our—'

'Listen to me a minute. I think we should wait for Henry to check things out first.'

'Yes, but—'

'He promised to get back to us. Better we know exactly where we and Daria stand before we do anything we might regret. And what difference will another day or two make, in the long run?'

'But, Hetty . . .'

'In any event, I'm not even sure it is the police, is it, that we need to notify? I ought to have checked it out—I think it might be the Border Agency or whatever they're called these days. And we both know what that would entail.'

Harriet has a sudden image of detention centres, barred windows, guards, dogs. Are they really prepared to be responsible for that fragile girl and her defenceless baby being locked up somewhere like Yarl's Wood? She shudders.

Hester sits forward determinedly, her earlier lassitude gone. 'Look, suppose we do go to the police,' she says, 'what would we tell them exactly? That Milo's father employed someone to find Daria, that Dick pitched up on our doorstep on Boxing Day. So what? He may have been unpleasant, but he didn't threaten us or anything—well, not in a way that the police would understand or be interested in. Employing a private detective isn't illegal. As far as I can see, at the moment the only thing that's likely to happen is that we drop Daria in it for being an illegal immigrant, which is the one thing we are trying to avoid. And possibly we'd be dropping ourselves in it for harbouring her. Besides which, ought we not in all conscience to warn Sampson before we reveal his involvement in all this, after all that poor couple have been through?'

Hester's sudden impassioned defence of two people that not six hours earlier she had been lambasting is thoroughly disconcerting. Harriet finds herself unexpectedly on the other side of the argument. 'So we do nothing? Seriously? We can't! What about the other man pestering Finbar? Never mind whoever might have broken in here and assaulted you—who might or might not be the same man! And there's the woman I saw at the petrol station. All these different people after a missing girl. Who isn't missing, but is living here, without a visa or work permit, with her illegitimate baby. Hester, I'm sorry, but I am well outside my comfort zone.'

Hester slaps her uneaten cracker down on the side table in a spray of crumbs; they speckle the mohair in her lap. 'Don't be so melodramatic! I told you. I'm not sure what happened earlier—it was probably all my imagination. Where's the proof? I'd look a complete idiot if they can't find anything. And it'll be all round the village before we know it. The last thing we want right now is to draw attention to ourselves and Daria.'

Harriet is unable to deny it. Police cars and flashing lights down their little lane and Peggy will be on the scent in minutes. Then a thought strikes her. She stands, her corn reawakening with a vicious stab. 'Well,' she says, breathing heavily, whether from their disagreement or the effort, 'I think you're wrong. We do have some proof!' She hurries out to the kitchen. Daria and Ben look over, startled, as she bursts into a kitchen restored— indeed, more than restored—to order. The footprints she was hoping to find clearly visible in the flour and egg-encrusted floor are long gone, erased by Daria's deftly wielded mop. Surfaces gleam, the table is neatly laid and the air is fragrant with herbs and the earthy aroma of root vegetables.

'What?' says Ben, as if to an intruder. ''S'not ready yet. Give us a chance, will you?'

A thwarted Harriet returns to the sitting room. Hester, mid-stitch, looks up and raises a questioning eyebrow, but Harriet ignores her and snatches up another cracker before resuming her chair. She takes her time chewing and swallowing.

'All right,' she says at last, testily, 'suppose you tell me what you propose we do next. Just sit here, do we, waiting for the next bombshell? Is that what you're suggesting?'

'No,' says Hester, setting her knitting aside and getting a little rockily to her feet. 'First things first. Never make a decision on an empty stomach. I suggest we go through and see if this famous meal is ready. Then we sit Daria down and we find out once and for all what the hell is going on.'

The girl is at the hob, busy stirring something in a saucepan. 'Oh! Hester, you are okay now? Your . . . hitting?' She gestures to her head.

'Yes, thank you, my dear, much better. Just a bump.'

'And your journey . . . London . . .' She has obviously been waiting with trepidation for the opportunity to ask. 'It was . . . okay?'

Ben cuts in, 'Can we get this lot sorted first and then you can tell us all about it?'

Whose kitchen is this? thinks Hester with a flash of anger, joining Daria at the stove. The saucepan bubbles with a thick ruby-red liquid. 'Everything is fine, Daria,' she murmurs. 'You don't need to worry. We'll tell you later.'

Relief floods across the girl's face. For a moment, Hester thinks Daria might hug her, but instead she indicates the saucepan's contents with her spoon. 'Not ready quite. Ten minutes.'

Hester peers in and sniffs appreciatively. 'Borscht?'

Daria beams. '*Tak!* Borscht! You like?'

'We do. Don't we, Harry?'

Harriet, still bruised by their contretemps, nods half-heartedly from the doorway.

'You are sure?' says Daria anxiously. 'You do not have to . . . I will make other . . .'

'Not at all,' says Hester. 'Harriet loves it. Really.' She gives her sister a stern look: *For goodness' sake, snap out of it.*

Daria holds up a pot of cream. 'I am putting in lemon to make . . .'

'Soured cream.'

'Yes. Is okay?'

'Fine,' says Hester, glad to see the preparations are in capable hands; hands, that is, other than Ben's. 'Why don't I get . . .' She moves over to the bread bin.

'No, please!' cries Daria. 'All is . . .'

'Under control,' says Ben, heating some oil in a frying pan. 'You go and sit down.'

'You sure you know what you're doing?' says Hester to her nephew, the doubt plain in her voice.

Ben flicks a withering look in her direction and mutters, '*Jesus!*' under his breath, ostentatiously turning his full attention to his preparations.

'Please,' whispers Daria. 'You permit us . . .?'

Defeated, Hester retreats, but not before sweeping half a bottle of claret off the counter and grabbing a couple of glasses.

Harriet is already back in the sitting room by the fire, massaging her feet. Hester pours the wine and they both take a grateful gulp.

'Head all right?' says Harriet. 'I'm not really sure you should be drinking.'

'Stop fussing, my head is fine. Now, let's get things into perspective. There is nothing to be gained by going to the police right at this moment. Agreed?'

Harriet nods slowly. 'I suppose not.'

From the kitchen comes the whine of the liquidiser.

'Good. We'll fill Daria in about the Sampsons—I'm sure that'll be a weight off the child's mind at least—and give her

221

back her passport and her things, and you can ask her about your mystery woman. And this time, we don't take any nonsense. If she continues to string us along, that's it. We turn them in. We'll have done our best and it's over to the authorities to sort out the mess.'

'What, a detention centre? You'd see them both in one of those places?'

'Now who's changing their tune?! Harry, if she won't trust us and let us help her, what choice do we have? I don't know about you, but right now I could do without any more excitement.' She tips back her glass and reaches for a refill.

CHAPTER 17

The borscht is delicious, so too the dark rye bread that Daria — with, Ben is quick to point out, his help—has baked to go with it. The food, as good food always does, restores the house's equilibrium and the spirits of its occupants. Hester and Harriet can feel the tensions of the day leaching away as they eat. The soup finished, Ben goes over to the oven and takes out a platter of little pancakes, plump and nicely browned, which he proudly places on the table, before retrieving a plate of thinly sliced cold roast beef from the fridge. Hester examines the pancakes closely.

'These look good.' She looks over to Daria for enlightenment, but the girl gestures to Ben.

'He is making.' She smiles at the boy, proud as any mother of her son. '*Draniki*. I am giving him . . .'

'Recipe.' Ben grins. 'With a bit of help from Google.'

'Yes! But he is making. You know *draniki*?'

'No,' admits Hester, easing one on to her plate and cutting into it. A little puff of steam rises up as she applies her fork. 'Potato? Onion?'

Daria nods happily, then watches anxiously as Hester lifts a forkful to her mouth. 'Is okay?'

'Goodness!' exclaims Hester. 'Absolutely gorgeous. Harry, do try one.'

Ben and Daria cannot contain their glee. They clink their wine glasses in celebration.

'Well,' says Hester, beaming, 'I think this calls for a toast!' She and Harriet reach for their glasses.

The phone rings. Harriet rises to answer it.

It's Peter Sampson. 'Did you get home safely? Good, good. Listen, I spoke to Dick, asked him how he knew where Daria was. Apparently he got his lead from a chap who approached him outside the advice centre. He'd obviously seen him asking questions and offered to sell him some information.'

'Sell?'

There is an edge of embarrassment and impatience in Sampson's voice. 'Yes, Harriet, sell. It's how these things work. Money talks. Or gets people to talk.'

'Right. Sorry. So this man told him what?'

'That he'd driven Daria down to your neck of the woods at night and handed her over to a couple who took her away. That's all he was prepared to say. Dick said he offered him more money but the guy wouldn't play. He got the impression he was protecting someone. Either that or he was hoping for a better offer. So Dick came down your way to see what he could find out and then he stumbled over some tramp who pointed him in your direction.'

'Okay,' says Harriet, heartened that Dick's story corroborates Daria's account. 'Thanks. Thanks very much.'

'I've told him the case is now closed.' A beat as Harriet absorbs that pleasing news. 'And, before you go, how *is* Daria?' says Sampson quickly when it's clear their conversation is about to end. 'And . . . Milo. Have you told her yet?' His anxiety is palpable.

'We're just about to,' Harriet reassures him gently. 'We'll be in touch.'

'Please,' he says desperately. 'Please tell her—'

'We will, I promise. Bye.'

Harriet replaces the phone in its cradle and turns back to three enquiring faces. 'Peter Sampson.'

'Oh!' Daria's hand flies to her chest.

'It's all right, my dear. You've no need to worry any more about him or his wife. We were just about to tell you—'

The phone rings for a second time.

'It's Piccadilly Circus in here tonight!' says Harriet, reaching for it again. Then, 'Teddy!' she exclaims, eyes flashing across the kitchen at Hester. 'Is something wrong?' In all the years they have known the Wilsons, they have never had a call from either of them. She listens for a minute or so.

'Oh . . . no, I don't think so. Hang on, I'll just ask Hester.' She covers the mouthpiece. 'It's Teddy. He says he found a purse in the car park after we left. Wonders if it belongs to either of us?'

Daria slides out of her chair and passes both women their bags wordlessly. They check them quickly. Two purses.

'No, no, not ours, Teddy. And there's no identification in it? No credit cards? Oh I see, just cash. Oh, poor woman, whoever she is. Better hand it in, I suppose. Thanks anyway for asking.

What? No, we're fine, just having supper ... Yes, we're both fine ... yes ... And you. Bye.'

She frowns as she once again replaces the phone in its cradle. 'Where were we?'

'Toasting the cooks,' says Ben, with a suspicion of a smirk.

                                          ⌣⌣⌣

With the washing-up done, Milo tucked up in his cot-drawer for the night and Hester upstairs changing into some clean clothes, Harriet is waiting in the sitting room for Daria and Hester to join her when the phone rings for a third time.

'I do hope this isn't an inopportune moment to call,' says George. 'We just wanted a word with Ben.' He sounds burdened with embarrassment and unhappiness.

Harriet is riven with regret for being party to his distress. They ought to have insisted Ben went home by now. They've been far too lax. Poor old George. Poor Isabelle.

'Not at all, dear. I'll just call him.'

'Before you do, Harriet, Isabelle and I had a thought. We wondered, seeing that you missed our Christmas do, whether you might like to come over on New Year's Eve. We usually have a few neighbours round.'

Harriet thinks fast. The delectable food and wine she has just consumed reminds her only too vividly of the likely offerings chez George. But the one thing she cannot do in all conscience, given the events of the past few days, is turn them down. So she says, with a sudden flash of inspiration, 'That would be delightful, George, we'd love to, but with one proviso—you must allow us to bring the food. No, please'—as George, predictably, protests—'I must insist. And so will Hester. You did all that work for Christmas Day; the least we can do is reciprocate. You know how Hester loves to cook. She's even teaching Ben a trick or two.'

'Ben?!'

'You'd be surprised, George; he's got quite a talent in that regard.'

'Ben? Talent?'

'He's just made us some little pancake things. Very tasty.'

'Good Lord,' says George faintly.

Harriet can hear a hovering Isabelle in the background, whispering, 'What? What did she say?'

'So why don't we sort the food at this end and then we'll all come over with Ben and bring it with us. He can help. How does that sound?' She tries a little humour. 'Sort of return of the prodigal!'

Privately, she is simultaneously planning the wine they will take with them: she knows Hester has a couple of bottles of 2000 Barolo she has been saving and there is a very palatable non-vintage champagne in the wine cupboard. Their sacrifice on a few probably uneducated palates is a small price to pay. Whether from natural exuberance or her years of geeing up recalcitrant pupils, when Harriet is in persuasion mode she is hard to gainsay. People find themselves swept along with her enthusiasm—*bulldozed*, Hester has been known to observe acerbically. As so it proves now. George, shell-shocked by these further astonishing revelations about his son, puts up only minimal resistance, which Harriet deals with in no time. With smug satisfaction, she puts down the phone to summon Ben and advise Hester of her victory, before they settle down to tackle Daria.

⌣⌣⌣

Hester listens in silence as Harriet relates their adventures in London, the one omission being their encounter with the Sampsons' neighbours: the memory remains a raw and humiliating one. It will be some time before they will feel able to turn the episode into a self-mocking anecdote. Once or twice, Daria has looked as if she might interject, but has restrained herself, partly because it has been clear that Harriet will brook no interruption. Watching her from across the room, Hester has a sense of her sister's quiet authority in the classroom; no wonder so many pupils remain in touch. Harriet still treasures a cutting from the local paper from years back, when a former pupil who had gone on to great success had thanked her 'inspirational teacher Mrs Pearson' for instilling her with confidence and self-belief. Hester had found the cutting carefully folded in her sister's bedside cabinet when she was looking for the luggage straps one year before their annual holiday. She has never told Harriet.

Daria sits in her customary pose, hands tightly clenched in her lap, her whole body tensed, her face displaying a wide range of emotions—anger, consternation, puzzlement, shame—as the account unfolds.

Finally, Harriet looks over at Hester. 'Have I forgotten anything?'

'Not that I can recall.'

Harriet digs in her handbag. She pulls out the dark-blue passport and hands it to Daria, who clutches it to her breast, index finger stroking the embossed crest on the front. Hester wonders what it must feel like to be stateless, however fleetingly, to lose one's place in the world, all the old certainties overturned and one's very identity in doubt.

'Thank you,' breathes the girl, turning to the page that shows her long-haired self staring neutrally to camera. She's lived a lifetime and a half since that picture was taken.

The sisters wait; time stretches in the silent room as Daria marshals her thoughts. Her voice, when it comes, is tiny. 'So. He is wanting to see Milo, Peter Sampson?' She looks at Harriet, then Hester. They both nod.

'Daria,' says Harriet gently, 'he *is* Milo's father.'

'*Tak, tak* . . .' Daria bites her bottom lip, fighting for control. 'Of course. I see this. But he cannot take . . . he cannot take Milo? I am mother, yes? I am . . . most important?' She looks cornered but fierce, a vixen protecting her cub.

This is rocky ground, because neither Harriet nor Hester is certain of the facts. 'We need to check things out, Daria. Harriet and I will get on to it first thing tomorrow, but we don't think there's any danger of that—no.'

Daria's face remains taut with worry.

'Listen, my dear, you mustn't imagine the worst. Of course you're Milo's mother, no-one disputes that, but Peter Sampson has rights too. That's the way things work in England.'

'England, yes,' says Daria eagerly. 'In England, law is fair, yes? No secret police, no spies—no people disappearing—no . . .?'

'Well, not as a rule,' starts Harriet, ever honest.

Oh, Harry, thinks Hester crossly, *this is not the time to get on to your wretched* Guardian *high horse. We'll be on to Tony Blair, the Iraq war and detention without trial before we know where we are.* She jumps in to quell the incipient exploration of human rights and excessive state interference in the lives of its citizens. 'No-one is going to take Milo away from you. We'll make sure of that.' She studiously avoids looking at Harriet, whom she knows will consider such a blanket reassurance irresponsible.

Daria lets out a long, slow sigh of relief. Her eyes fill. 'You are so kind. Hester. Harriet. Like . . . mother—you are both like mother to me. To me and Milo. Thank you. Thank you.' She grabs Hester's hand and, to her hostess's intense embarrassment, kisses it. 'I am believing man, Peter, he is no good, but I see I am wrong.'

She still has hold of Hester's hand. The older woman is eager to withdraw it but doesn't want to appear to be rejecting Daria's overture.

'You teach me. Make me see. Because you are wise. And Elizabeth. You see her too. She is not bad woman, no. Just sick, yes?'

Hester has opted for inertia: her hand lies like a dead fish in Daria's grasp. Then the girl reaches across and takes Harriet's nearest hand and kisses that too, the three women linked into an unlikely and—as far as the sisters are concerned—very discomfiting daisy chain. The release engendered by Harriet's narrative seems to have untied Daria's tongue.

'How can I ever . . . You give me home, shelter. Warm house. Clothes. Good food. Safe place for baby—'

'Really,' says Hester, trying gently to extricate her hand (apart from anything else, Daria has taken hold of her bad arm; the muscles are beginning very quietly to protest), 'you don't need to thank—'

It is as if she hasn't spoken. 'I am wanting so much to tell my brother! Yes! And Tata. One day you come to my country— meet them. So I can say: see, good women from England. Angels. My friends!' She squeezes their hands in gratitude. Hester winces. 'And later, when Milo is boy, is man, he will remember kind *babulki*. I will tell him: they put you in little wooden box—'

'Drawer,' corrects Harriet, easing her hand away under the pretext of picking up her tea. Hester, on Daria's other side, curses, wishing she had thought of that. To worsen matters, Daria now angles herself around and clasps Hester's hand in both of hers. At least it relieves the pressure on her arm a little.

'In little drawer,' repeats Daria, barely stopping for breath. 'Little baby sleeping in drawer. Like a story, no? Like Jesus. We will remember. Always.' Her face lights up with pleasure. 'And one day, yes, for sure, you come to Belarus. Meet Artem— you will love him, yes. So kind, so funny. Like a bear, my father say.'

'Goodness me,' says Harriet. 'Do you have bears in Belarus?' She catches Hester's desperate eye. 'How about a drop more wine?'

Hester throws up her hands in what Harriet feels is an unnecessarily stagey gesture, but it does the trick. 'Excellent idea,' she cries, clamping her now freed hands on the arms of her chair. 'I'll go!'

'No, no,' says Daria, already on her feet. 'You are . . .' She gestures to Hester's head. 'Must rest. I go. I am getting bottle now.'

As the sitting-room door closes behind her, the sisters sink back in their chairs with a joint sigh of relief. They find young people today so *emotional*. The soaps have a lot to answer for, in their view, their protagonists perpetually in states of fury or lust or murderous intent, forever shouting the odds and threatening one another and hatching farfetched schemes. And as for reality shows . . .! They abhor the increasing tendency to broadcast one's innermost thoughts at every opportunity to a salacious world. Privately, both sisters found the hysterical convulsions following Diana's death in 1997 wholly repellent. They reserve their own histrionics for occasional bouts of shouting at the radio, particularly when John Humphrys is hogging the conversation and won't allow his victim to get a word in. They both yell at the television if ever Jeremy Clarkson inadvertently appears.

In the aftermath of Daria's outburst, Hester examines her knitting pattern with exaggerated care, while Harriet picks up the newspaper; it is several seconds before she realises that her glasses, without which she cannot read, are nestled in her hair. She abruptly pulls them down, hoping Hester hasn't noticed.

'Well, that went as well as could be expected,' she whispers. 'Now to tell her about today's little encounter with the lovely Tina.'

'Assuming it *was* Tina,' Hester whispers back. 'But remember: no prisoners.'

The door swings open as Daria returns with a tray, an opened bottle of wine and glasses. She is smiling to herself, looking so uncharacteristically carefree, so relaxed, relieved of so much heartache, that for a moment both sisters almost lose their nerve; can't they leave the interrogation until tomorrow, enjoy the momentary lull in the storm? Then Hester's innate commonsense reasserts itself: they need to sort this whole mess out here and now, for everyone's sake. There has been too much delay and indecision already. Daria is beginning to pour the wine; Hester readies herself for the showdown. 'Daria, my dear . . .'

Ben clatters down the stairs and pokes his head around the door.

'Ben! Do you mind?'

'Sorry to interrupt, Aunt Hester, but I just been in to Milo. He's still wide awake and he needs changing, Dar, I reckon.'

'Oh!' says Daria, looking up from pouring the third glass. 'I only give him clean nappy a little while before.'

'He's well niffy now, I tell you.'

'Niffy?'

'Yeah.' Ben pinches his nose and wafts his other hand in front of his face. Daria laughs.

'Couldn't you change him, Ben?' says Hester. 'Only we want to—'

'Me?' Ben's face is a picture of disgust.

'It can't be that difficult!' Hester says scornfully—she who has never changed a nappy in her life.

'But it's gross,' says Ben, grimacing. 'I mean, what? Cleaning up all that—'

Daria hands each sister a glass. 'No, no, I do it. Not a job for a man, doing baby bottoms.'

No? thinks Harriet. *Why on earth not?*

Daria runs lightly upstairs.

'Dad told me about New Year and that,' says Ben, throwing himself on the sofa, a glass somehow in his hand. How had he managed that? 'So I been going through your recipe books for ideas.'

Hester stiffens, momentarily distracted from her frustration at Daria's absence. Her face sets in an ominous frown. Looking at her recipe books indeed!

Ben holds his glass up to the light. 'What's this then?'

'Have a guess,' says Harriet, quickly stepping in, given Hester's reception of her nephew's temerity.

Ben sniffs the wine, rolls it around the glass, as he is learning to do. He takes a cautious sip. 'Dry,' he says. 'Bit appley?'

'Good,' says his aunt. 'New world or old?'

'French, defo.'

'Why?'

This flummoxes Ben. 'Dunno, just tastes French.'

'Well done,' beams Harriet, thinking: *What an astonishing difference a few days has made to this boy! Oh, I do miss young people's company. Young minds, so receptive . . .*

Hester, for her part, is eyeing Ben sceptically, having seen, as Harriet has not, that the bottle label is turned in his direction. If that young man is daring to make fun of her sister . . .! Aware of her beady inspection, Ben turns on her his practised look of innocence, then, deflecting his threatened unmasking, says, 'Like I say, I been thinking about New Year. About food.'

'Have you really?' says Hester with more than a hint of acid. 'And what precisely have you been thinking?'

'About the menu and that. Dad said you'd offered to cook.'

'Well, strictly speaking, I think you'll find that it was your Aunt Harriet who offered—which means that I will be in charge of the preparations. Your aunt, despite many other admirable qualities, is not really in her element in matters culinary.'

Harriet nods in wry agreement.

'Yeah, I know. Whatever. So I was, like, thinking maybe I could help.'

'Help?'

'Yeah, with some of the dishes and that. I mean, like, cook some of them.'

Hester suppresses a guffaw of derision. She supposes he might just—under tight supervision—be entrusted with vegetable peeling and general clearing up. Given the boy's parentage, the idea of him actually taking charge of any part of the menu is risible: Isabelle's ineptitude in the kitchen is so monumental, she doubts that Ben even knows what most cooking implements are for. She is trying to think how to let the lad down gently when she finds a piece of paper being waved under her nose.

'Some ideas,' says Ben, with apparent sangfroid. Hester regards the paper with all the distaste she would afford a top-shelf magazine and recoils. Harriet, anxious to avert any unpleasantness and keen to spare Ben humiliation, leans across, takes the paper and begins to scrutinise it, more as a way of buying some time than with any real interest.

'Oh!' she says, caught up despite herself. 'Mini salmon en croute. That sounds nice. Mushroom tartlets . . .'

'Yeah,' says Ben. 'One of the books had, like, suggested party menus. I picked the ones I liked the sound of and wrote them down. With the page numbers, see?'

'Give it here!' Hester, bruised arm forgotten, snatches the list. She swiftly runs her eyes down it. Bacon and quails' eggs tartlets, smoked salmon pinwheels, Parma ham parcels, cream cheese and chive flutes, Roquefort toasts . . . Her mouth waters just reading the menu. She looks at Ben in astonishment. He is grinning.

'What d'you reckon, then? Classy or what?'

~~~

Harriet creeps into Hester's bedroom. Next door, they can hear the muffled sound of music playing on Ben's iPod, and on the other side of the hallway, the soft murmur of Daria's voice as she gives Milo his midnight feed. He had been unsettled all evening, so much so that Daria had eventually brought him downstairs after a fruitless hour trying to get him to settle. As babies do, he had instantly perked up, especially when Ben started playing peek-a-boo. Finally he had fallen asleep in his mother's arms, whereupon she had crept upstairs and not emerged since. Reluctantly, but with a certain secret relief, the sisters had decided to wait until the following morning to quiz her about the woman they supposed to be Tina.

'How's the arm?'

Hester lays aside the new Ian Rankin. 'Stop mithering.'

'You're not still miffed with Ben?'

'I am not miffed!' retorts Hester a mite too forcefully. 'Surprised, I'm just surprised. I didn't have him down for a Jamie Oliver, that's all. We'll have to see if all his fine talk translates into anything halfway edible.' The atmosphere in the sitting room had started to thaw after Hester's initial shock as she went over the proposed menu with her nephew; he had flown to the kitchen and returned with a stack of recipe books, over which the pair of them had pored for the next hour. Ben appeared to have done his homework; almost every misgiving of Hester's was answered; her amendments accepted with good grace. Harriet, ostensibly completing her crossword, had listened with considerable amusement as Ben wormed his way deeper and deeper into Hester's affections using the one weapon against which she is powerless: food.

'Anyway,' says Harriet, 'never mind about that now. I was just lying in bed trying to finish the last clue—infuriating, I can't see it at all—and I had a thought about Finbar's second visitor. You don't suppose it might have been the chap Daria was originally supposed to stay with in London? Her father's friend?'

Hester frowns, thinking, then shakes her head. 'No. Surely Finbar would have mentioned it if he thought the man was a foreigner. And how would the father's friend know that Daria was down here? Anyway, didn't she say no-one knew where he'd gone? That's why she took the job with the Sampsons and—'

'Yes, I know that,' interrupts Harriet, 'but the people who put her up that first night, they knew him, didn't they?'

Hester isn't sure. They only know what Ben told them after his initial heart-to-heart with Daria. And who knew what was lost in translation? Perhaps they can check this out with her too tomorrow morning . . .

Harriet picks at a pulled thread on Hester's blanket, to which she clings stubbornly despite duvets and central heating. It's a shabby old thing, now faded to dull smudges of colour, which lay for thirty years or more on the marital bed; perhaps that's why she keeps it. Funny how sentimental the most apparently hard-headed folk can be. The sisters rarely talk about their dead husbands and when they do it's in a distant, rational tone, like discussing vague acquaintances they once knew. *I wonder if Hester ever feels lonely*, thinks Harriet. *Like I do.* It takes you unawares, she has found, comes at you out of the blue, that sudden desire for a hug, for arms around your waist. That's why babies are such a blessing: all that unconditional love, the excuse to hold another human being close.

She gets up stiffly from the bed. 'Oh well, another theory bites the dust. We're missing something, I know we are.'

'Bed,' says Hester. 'Try to get a good night's sleep. We'll talk about it tomorrow.' She snuggles down in the bed, her hand feeling for her book.

Harriet heads for the door, then stops.

'What now?' Hester asks.

'Finbar.'

'What about him?'

Harriet stands in the shadowy doorway, hugging herself in her dressing gown. 'I can't help worrying. His books.'

'Pub,' says Hester unhesitatingly. 'He'll have been in the pub. Perhaps he decided he's past dragging all those books around with him everywhere.'

'Then why were they strewn all over the ground? He loves those books!'

'Perhaps he was interrupted. Perhaps he was having a sort out?'

'Finbar?!'

'Well, what's he supposed to do when he goes out? He can't exactly lock his front door, can he? And anyway, no-one's going to want any of his old rubbish, are they?'

'That's not the point! Besides, he cleared all his stuff out before his pre-Christmas jaunt. The barman lets him store his bags in one of his sheds on the q.t. when he's on his travels.'

'Yes, but he was away a couple of days then.'

Harriet is silent.

'Come on, what is it? There's something else bothering you.'

'It couldn't have been more than a few minutes after he left us yesterday when Ben went to find him. And he'd already gone.'

'So?'

'We'd just given him some food.'

'And?'

'When have you ever known him not to sit down and eat whatever we give him the minute he gets it?'

CHAPTER 18

29 DECEMBER

Ben emerges from the bushes, scratched and ill-tempered. He's trodden in something squashy and unpleasant at the back of the bus shelter and is now trying to scrape it off on the kerbside. Harriet walks to the other side of the shelter and peers into the foliage. It's a cold, raw morning, still not fully light; the chill fingers its way down her neck and she pulls her scarf closer.

'Almost new, these trainers are,' complains Ben. 'Now look at them! Cost me fifty quid, these did.'

'More fool you,' says Harriet sharply, annoyed that thus far their visit has proved entirely unproductive. All they have established is that Finbar is not in residence and his tartan trolley is nowhere to be seen. The detritus strewn around the shelter looks untouched since her encounter with the woman from the petrol station the night before. Harriet had steeled herself and felt the mound of blankets for any residual warmth;

they had felt cold, even slightly damp. She can't wait to get home and wash her hands.

'Is that metal I can see in there?' she asks.

'It's probably where he does his frigging business. Stinks like it.'

Harriet ignores his grouse. 'Just push through here, will you? I'm sure I can see something.'

'There's nothing there! How many more times do I have to tell you? Yanking me out of bed in the middle of the night—I haven't even had any breakfast yet!'

Aunt and nephew face up to each other, Ben towering over Harriet. A car pulls up, threads of morning mist pirouetting in the headlights. Down goes the window and a head pokes out.

'Morning, Harriet. You're up early.' He looks Ben up and down suspiciously. 'Everything all right?'

'Teddy! Gosh, you startled me! Yes, yes, fine, everything's fine. I see you're up with the lark too.'

Teddy continues to regard Ben with mistrust. 'This lad's not giving you any trouble, I hope?'

'No!' says Ben angrily. 'What d'you mean?'

'This is my nephew, Ben. He's staying with us for a few days.'

'Ah! The famous nephew.'

Ben scowls.

Teddy stares at the pair on the pavement as though expecting further elucidation. When none is forthcoming, he says, 'Bit early for the bus, aren't you? I could give you a lift into town if you need one.'

'No, ta,' says Ben ungraciously. 'We're just trying to—'

Harriet cuts in. 'We were out for our morning walk.'

'At this hour?' says Teddy.

'Oh, it's part of my new exercise regime,' says Harriet hurriedly. 'Thirty minutes' brisk walking before breakfast.' She rolls her eyes theatrically. 'Hester's idea, needless to say. She's forever trying to get me to shift a few pounds. Anyway, Ben kindly offered to accompany me this morning, didn't you, Ben?'

'What? Oh, yeah.'

'We were just trotting along having a nice chat and then we thought we saw something in the hedge.'

Teddy looks enquiringly from Harriet to the bushes and back.

She stumbles on. 'Heard something, I should say. Thought it might be a trapped animal or something.'

Ben chimes in, 'Sent me in there to look, she did. Couldn't see nothing.' An exasperated look at Harriet. '*Anything*.'

'Ah,' says Teddy. He reaches for the gearstick, his hand resting on the knob but not engaging gear. Harriet and Ben wait. Teddy peers past them into the shelter. 'It's true, is it, that somebody actually lives in there?'

'Oh, Teddy, come on! You must know Finbar. Everyone knows Finbar.'

'Can't say I've had the pleasure . . . I don't often catch the bus, as it happens.' He lovingly taps the heel of his hand on the steering wheel.

'You surprise me,' says Harriet wryly. 'I take it this is your latest acquisition? Very nice.'

'Isn't it, though?' Smugness doesn't come close to describing his expression. 'XKR-S coupé—top of the range. Bit of an extravagance, but have to keep up appearances, after all.'

'I'm sure you do.' Something about the way the light falls on his face, accentuating the cheekbones and the hooded eyes, brings into sudden and vivid relief another face in another life. Of course! No wonder Hetty has this inexplicable fondness for this man: he has a very faint but, she sees now, indisputable likeness to Gordon. How could she have missed it all these years? Does Hetty herself realise that it's a memory of her dead husband, not the man himself, that draws her to Teddy?

He is looking at her quizzically. 'Sure I can't tempt you with a lift? Five-litre V8 supercharged engine. No? Shame. Anyway, where is he then, this famous tramp?'

'Oh, out for his constitutional too, I dare say. Must get going ourselves, I suppose. But nice to see you. Again.' Harriet smiles, then adds mischievously, 'Regards to Molly.'

Teddy's features tighten. He forces a smile. 'Thanks. Yes. I'll tell her. And mine to Hester. She's okay, is she?'

'Oh, still tucked up in bed.'

'Bully for her,' mutters Ben. 'Wish I was.'

'Not ill, I hope?' says Teddy. Gosh, he looks tired. Must be exhausting, shuttling between two homes. Two beds. Assuming the rumours are true.

'Good Lord, no. Just likes her sleep, does Hester.'

'And me,' moans Ben.

'And you're all right, are you, Teddy? Not overdoing it?'

'What do you mean?'

'Well, yesterday, at the station, we both thought you looked—'

'What?' Has she hit a nerve?

'A tiny bit . . . weary. You've not had this nasty virus that's doing the rounds?'

Teddy's face is tight, lips tighter. 'What? No. Lot on my plate, that's all.'

'Oh. Any joy with that purse?'

'Purse?'

'The one you—'

'Oh yes . . . I'm going to drop it in to the station booking office this morning. Take care now.'

He crunches the gears and accelerates away from the kerb, spitting gravel.

Ben watches him speeding up the road and out of sight. 'Nice car. Must be loaded if he can afford a Jag. Top of the range, too. Blimey. Shame he's such a tosser.'

'Don't be so rude. He's an old friend,' says Harriet indignantly.

'Didn't like the way he looked at me.'

'Well, you were hardly civil, were you?'

Ben scuffs his trainers on the asphalt, still staring up the road. 'Shouldn't jump to conclusions, then, should he? Anyway'—he rounds on Harriet—'what was all that cobblers about trapped animals? Wondered what you were on about at first. All very well for you to get mardy with me, but you was glad enough to see the back of him too, you ask me.'

'*Were*,' says Harriet automatically, her eye caught by something a little further up the hill. 'Isn't that . . .? Ben, I'm sure that's . . . Go and look, will you?'

⌣⌣

Ben and Harriet hurry back home, chilled and hungry. But at least they've located the missing trolley, although Harriet's not sure whether she should be pleased or alarmed. Amid much carping on Ben's part, they had extracted it from the hedgerow and wheeled it back to the shelter, installing it in the darkest corner and shrouding it in a pile of carriers and blankets.

'Should've brought the car,' complains Ben, eyes drawn inexorably to the unsightly stain on one of his trainers. He can't wear these out with his mates in this state: they'll think he's a charity case. Worse, after all that's happened at home, he can't see his dad shelling out for a new pair. He decides to approach his mother instead; she'll be so pleased to have him home, she's sure to succumb to a little impassioned blackmail.

'Hester!' calls Harriet loudly from the front door. 'No sign of him—but you'll never guess who pitched up. Where are you?' She scurries down the hall to the kitchen to find it empty. The door to the sitting room is open. She looks up the stairs. 'Hester?'

Her sister's head appears over the banister. 'Oh, thank heavens you're back. I was about to ring you.'

'What now?'

'Milo's not well.'

'Not well?' Ben takes the stairs two at a time. 'What's wrong?'

Harriet, hurrying after him to join Hester on the landing, catches a fretful grizzle coming from Daria's room.

Ben rushes in, bending over mother and child like an anxious father. 'What's up, mate?' he murmurs, resting his hand lightly on Milo's head.

Hester whispers to Harriet, 'He's awfully hot. Daria says he had a disturbed night, wouldn't settle. She's tried to feed him this morning, but he's not interested. I've never seen him like this: he's so listless. We just sponged him with cool water but he's burning up.'

The two women, inexperienced and helpless in the face of the terrors of child-rearing, dither in the hall.

'Could he be teething?' says Harriet.

'I've no idea. How can you tell?'

'Oh . . . I think you feel along the gums. I'm sure I read that somewhere. We could Google it, I suppose.'

But Hester is already on her way into the bedroom, where she puts the suggestion to Daria. Harriet, following her in, is shocked to see how flushed the baby is, his hair damp against his forehead, a blue vein pulsating at his temple. The crusted remains of some sticky discharge clog his lashes. How can he have become so sick so quickly?

Daria gently inserts her finger into the baby's mouth and rubs it back and forth along the gum line. She shakes her head. 'Is no tooth, I think.'

'Babies get dehydrated very quickly,' says Harriet softly into Hester's ear, not wanting to alarm Daria further. 'We ought to take him to the doctor's.'

But Daria, missing nothing, raises her head immediately and says, 'Yes, please. Doctor. Please.' She lifts Milo's body away from her lap slightly as though offering him to the women, her eyes shadowed with worry but trusting them to help. The image of Elizabeth Sampson's dead child cannot be far from her thoughts.

'I'll get the car,' says Harriet.

Hester has phoned their doctor and discovered, to her over-whelming relief, that there is a surgery that morning. Given the season, however, the doctor is seeing emergency cases only. Hester assures the receptionist this is an emergency, and the minute she mentions a sick baby, the voice on the other end of the phone changes from that of a gatekeeper guarding her employer from malingerers to one of supreme efficiency. No-one these days takes any chances with ailing infants. 'Bring him straight in. Doctor will see you immediately.'

Daria and Ben are sitting in the back of the car on either side of Milo, who is strapped into his seat. Occasional whimpers punctuate the silence as Harriet drives with extreme caution to the other side of the village.

It is only as they are pulling into the surgery car park that a thought strikes Hester and she says to Harriet under her breath, 'Oh God. I suppose they will treat him, will they? I mean, as non-residents?'

Harriet pulls up beside the entrance with a jerk. 'He's ill, Hetty! Of course they'll treat him!' she hisses. It is inconceiv-able to her that anything would prevent succour being offered automatically to someone in distress. Hester, on the other hand, after years negotiating the labyrinthine ways of local government, is never surprised to find some absurd regulation that flies in the face of reason or common humanity. She prays that on this occasion Harriet's instincts are right.

And so it proves. God or fate is on their side. The minute the five of them appear in the doorway, the lone receptionist abandons her post and hurries across the waiting room. 'Poor little lamb,' she says tenderly, looking down at the limp baby in Daria's arms. 'We'll get you sorted.' She glances around the group, settling on the only male. 'Are you the father?'

Ben, appalled, mutters a denial. In spite of the urgency of the situation, or perhaps because of it, Hester barks a laugh.

'Please,' Daria implores Harriet in a small, tearful voice, 'you will come?' Harriet nods.

Without any apology to the three other patients in the waiting room, the receptionist shepherds the two women down a short corridor towards a door from which an elderly man, accompanied by an equally elderly lady, has just emerged. 'It's that baby, Doctor,' cries the receptionist with barely veiled excitement, pushing the door wide open.

The doctor rises and comes to greet them. 'Well, well, little fellow, now what seems to be the matter? Let's have a look at you.' And Daria hands Milo over into those safe and reassuring hands.

⌣⌣⌣

Back in the waiting room, Hester is distractedly answering the receptionist's questions, half her thoughts down the corridor in the consulting room, the other half trying to negotiate a believable path through the rules governing non-registered patients.

'They're just visiting you, you say,' presses the woman. 'But they live abroad?' Her fingers hover over the keyboard. 'Here for Christmas, are they?'

'That's right,' says Hester, adding quickly, 'But the father's English.'

The receptionist gives her a curious look that Hester chooses to ignore.

'It's just we have to code them.'

'Of course.'

'So I can put your address down as their temporary residence?'

'You can.'

The receptionist's fingers tap the keys briefly as she cuts and pastes their details.

'And the baby's name is Milo? Milo what?'

Hester looks aghast. She has absolutely no idea what Daria's surname or patronymic or whatever they call it in Belarus is.

'His surname?'

Ben looks up from his plastic chair. 'Yushkevich.'

Hester stares at Ben. The receptionist leans across the counter. 'What's that, dear?'

Ben repeats it. 'Yushkevich.'

'Can you spell that?'

He can. Hester regards her nephew with something edging towards admiration. She answers a few more questions about Milo's age, his mother's first name, and then sits down beside Ben, eyebrows raised in query.

'I asked her, didn't I?' says Ben.

⌣⌣⌣

The doctor gently wipes Milo's eyes clean with cotton wool and gestures to Daria that she can put his Babygro back on. He's taken Milo's temperature with a thermometer in the armpit, tested his heart and respiratory rates. 'How long has he been in the country?'

'He was born here,' says Harriet.

'And he's not been out of the country?'

'No.'

'So it's nothing he's picked up abroad, then.' The doctor sits back at his desk and writes out a prescription. 'Liquid paracetamol, that's what we'll give him. Ask the receptionist which chemist is on duty today.'

He addresses his remarks mainly to Harriet, while Daria busies herself dressing Milo. He's not their usual doctor, for which Harriet is profoundly grateful: she's never been that convinced about patient confidentiality in a small community like theirs.

'Looks like our old friend, the upper respiratory tract infection. They go downhill so quickly at this age. Just try to keep him cool and give him sips of boiled water. Does he take a bottle?'

'I don't know,' says Harriet. 'Daria breastfeeds him.'

'Try one, smallest teat you can find. He may not like it, but persevere. Some babies will manage with water off a spoon but he's maybe a wee bit young for that. Keep a close eye on him. If he doesn't seem to be picking up pretty quickly or you're worried in any way, don't hesitate to ring. If the surgery's closed, it'll go through to the out-of-hours service. Mum's okay, is she?'

He looks over to the couch where Daria is buttoning Milo's clothes and cooing softly to him. 'She's very young,' says the doctor. 'Is she looking after herself?'

'Don't worry,' says Harriet. 'My sister's a very good cook. If anyone can tempt the tastebuds, it's Hester. We're building her up.'

They smile like conspirators. 'She's a lucky young lady to have such caring relatives.'

⌣⌣⌣

'We are turning into a pair of alkies,' says Hester, gulping a large slug of wine. 'We never used to drink every day. Certainly not mid-afternoon.'

'It's after five. And it's winter,' retorts Harriet. 'Gets dark earlier. Anyway, after the day we've had . . .'

They reflect on the dash to the doctor, the long wait at the only pharmacy open in the vicinity, where every coughing, hawking and sneezing resident for miles around appears to have congregated, the battle to get Milo to accept the bottle hurriedly purchased at the supermarket, the relief when, after his dose of medicine, they could tuck him back into his little cot and finally persuade Daria to doze beside him for a couple of hours. Lunch somehow passed them by. Hester's arm is throbbing gently, while Harriet's back has set up its periodic complaint. They are both feeling their age. And not liking it one jot.

'Anyway,' says Hester. 'Finbar's trolley. In the hedge. You're sure he hadn't just hidden it there for safekeeping?'

'It wasn't hidden! It looked like it had been thrown there. It's his most treasured possession—well, after his books, at any rate. If he was intent on leaving it behind—which, incidentally, he never does—he'd have put it somewhere secure, wouldn't he? He wouldn't just heave it into the bushes. Besides, he'd never have had the strength.'

'I suppose it definitely was *his* trolley?'

'Hetty, don't be ridiculous! There is no other shopping trolley in the world quite like Finbar's. All those ridiculous stickers. It was his, beyond a shadow of a doubt.'

'Hmm.'

'He's an old man, vulnerable . . .'

'And you think something's happened to him.' Hester finally puts into words what both of them have avoided saying.

Harriet sighs. 'I know. I know it sounds ridiculous and melodramatic, but . . . something's not right. I mean, you know Finbar: he's a creature of habit. If he goes anywhere at all, that wretched trolley goes with him. You can hear him a mile off, the way those wheels squeak.'

'Well . . . maybe he's been taken ill. He might be in hospital for all we know. He might even—God forbid—be dead.'

'Hetty!'

'Well, he might. He's no spring chicken.'

'Then let's call the hospital and check. I'll ring the pub, too. See if they know anything.'

'All right, let's do that. But I'm prepared to bet if anything untoward had happened, the news would be all round the village. Peggy, for one, would be sure to know. She's always moaning about the bus shelter—Lord alone knows why, as I doubt she's ever been on a bus in her life—and Finbar can barely draw breath without her commenting. I know he can be a bit of a pain, but people do look out for him, Harry.'

'Yes, yes, I'm sure you're right.' Harriet so wants to believe this.

'Chances are there's some perfectly rational explanation. The old rogue has probably toddled off on a jolly—'

Harriet shakes her head vehemently. 'On a jolly? Not without his trolley, Hetty. Not without his trolley.'

Police. The word is lodged in both their minds. And with the word, the accompanying concerns about the many unplugged holes in Daria's story.

Four days ago, thinks Hester, *we were two law-abiding women minding our own business in a cottage in the country. Now we're harbouring an illegal immigrant and hiding from some nefarious person or persons who seem to want to do her— and possibly us—harm.* A shadow, a fragment of memory, floats just out of reach.

She gets to her feet. She's off to do the one thing that always calms her and helps her get things into perspective. She's going to cook.

'Hetty—'

'Ring the pub and then the hospital. Then come and talk to me in the kitchen. And the minute that girl wakes, we have to ask her about your mystery woman.'

As Harriet reaches for the phone book, Hester grabs the wine bottle and makes for the kitchen, to find Ben chopping vegetables by the sink. 'Soup,' he says, gesturing to the mound of onions and carrots. A withered parsnip and half a pepper await his attentions.

'Since when did you decide the menus in this house?' says Hester frostily. 'Do you have the first idea how to make soup, young man?'

'Got a recipe, n'I?' retorts Ben smartly, pointing to the book lying open on the counter at his side.

Hester inspects it suspiciously, annoyed to discovered that it is one of her old stalwarts. Not that she would require a recipe to make a decent vegetable soup. Grudgingly, she says, 'There's some stock in the fridge.'

'Yeah, I know.' He nods at a jug standing beside him.

Hester gathers the tatters of her irritation around her, then concedes defeat with a reluctant, 'Thank you.' She opens the bread bin. 'We'll finish up this loaf.'

'Nah. Just made some rolls.'

Hester, hand hovering over the heel of her own one-day-old loaf, is speechless; Ben allows himself a self-satisfied grin but is careful to direct it at the chopping board. 'Not that difficult, once you get the hang of it. I watched this bloke on YouTube.'

His aunt goes over to the oven and peers in. A tray of neat rolls are browning nicely. Hester straightens up, outrage warring with respect. Respect wins. 'They look very good,' she admits, but cannot resist adding, 'If you wanted them to be crusty, you should have put a little bowl of water in with them.'

'Yeah?' says Ben, impressed. 'Didn't know that. Wasn't on YouTube.'

'Well, there's a surprise. It just goes to show: your precious internet doesn't have all the answers.'

'Can I lob one in now?'

'Not at this stage. Just remember the next time.'

Ben notes the 'next time' and risks a smile.

'Well, I suppose I might as well go back to the other room and sit down again, since I'm clearly surplus to requirements here,' says Hester, looking around her domain, searching in vain for something to restore her sense of ownership.

Ben addresses himself to his vegetables once more, humming loudly and tunelessly. Hester, admitting temporary defeat, turns on her heels and retreats to the hall. She is about to return to the sitting room when it occurs to her that she hasn't yet thought to check her emails.

A few minutes later she is upstairs in the study, opening a brief message from Henry. *In haste (late for my train—again!): good news. Your girl should qualify for leave to remain in light of paternity, provided the father confirms it. Will fill you in with more details tomorrow. Regards, H.*

'Oh, thank God!' In an instant all the worries that had seemed so enormous diminish. Leaping to her feet, she hurries down the hall. She is about to knock on Daria's door when she remembers the poor girl is having a much-needed nap. Let her sleep: what difference will an hour or so make? At least she can tell Harry and Ben. Light of heart, she hastens downstairs.

Harriet is finishing a call in the sitting room. 'No, thanks very much, I was just a bit worried about him . . . Yes . . . Yes . . . No, I'm sure you're right. But if he does pop in for a pint, would you be good enough to call me back? That is so kind. I'll give you my number . . .'

Hester waits impatiently for her sister to hang up.

'Fantastic news, Harry! Henry's just emailed to say Daria will almost certainly be granted permission to stay.'

'Oh, Hetty! Oh, that *is* wonderful!' Both faces are wreathed in ecstatic smiles. 'Have you told her?'

'I was going to, but I didn't want to wake her.' Hester crosses to her chair and retrieves her knitting, bubbling with happiness. Then she remembers Finbar with a jolt. 'No joy at the pub, I gather?'

Harriet shakes her head. 'They haven't seen him for a couple of days.' Her face falls, crumpled with renewed worry. 'I'll try the hospital now . . .' She goes to dial; stops. 'I've just realised something. So silly. I've no idea what his surname is. Have you?'

Hester's needles cease clicking. 'Oh!' She blinks, thinking hard. 'D'you know, I don't. I'm not sure I ever have. Finbar . . . Finbar . . . God, no, I haven't a clue.'

'Damn.'

Upstairs a floorboard creaks. Daria must have awoken. Hester immediately shoves her knitting to one side and gets up. 'I'll go and break the good news.' She stops halfway to the door, forestalling Harriet. 'You get on and ring the hospital. Just ask if they've had an old reprobate in over the last day or two.'

'Oh . . . okay.' Harriet is disappointed: she wants to see Daria's reaction too. 'I bet they won't know, though,' she says. 'I mean, on the switchboard. Think how many people they admit every day. Still, it's a very uncommon name. I'll give it a go.'

But before either of them can move, the phone rings.

Hester pauses in the doorway as, with some trepidation, Harriet answers it. Her greeting is met with a torrent of unintelligible words.

'I'm sorry, I . . .' She pulls a face at Hester, indicating incomprehension.

Another avalanche of words, but this time she thinks she hears the name 'Daria'.

'Hang on! Did you say Daria? Is it Daria you want?' She signals to Hester to fetch their guest.

Hester hurries into the hallway to call up the stairs urgently, 'Quick! Daria, quick! You're wanted on the phone.'

Seconds later, a tousled head appears over the banister. 'For me?' Excitement is mixed with alarm. 'Telephone?'

'Yes, yes, quickly.'

Daria flies down the stairs and runs into the sitting room. Harriet hands her the phone.

'I think it's for you. I can't understand—'

'Tata? Artem?' cries the girl, cradling the phone as if it were a missal, eyes alight with joy.

CHAPTER 19

Everyone freezes and looks over as Daria slowly enters the kitchen: Ben in the throes of extracting the tray of rolls from the oven, Harriet ferreting around in the cutlery drawer for soup spoons, Hester peering critically into the saucepan. The girl's face is white. She holds on to the doorjamb for support.

'What is it?' says Hester, crossing the room and putting a hand on Daria's arm to lead her to the table. She can feel the bones through her sleeve. 'Your brother?'

'No. Is not . . . is my friend, Polina. From Rakov. The girl I—'

'Left a message for, yes, I remember,' cuts in Harriet, suddenly apprehensive. 'Is everything all right?' She dumps the spoons on the table with a clatter.

Daria sits heavily. 'So much is happening . . .'

'You sit tight.' Hester takes control, gesturing silently to Ben to get busy. He tries to ease the rolls out of the bun tin with the aid of a palette knife. He swears softly. *I bet he didn't oil*

258

it first, Hester thinks instantly. 'We could all do with something to eat. We'll dish up supper and then you can tell us all about it. Nothing's ever quite so bad once you've got some food inside you.'

⌣⌣⌣

'. . . So I say, Polina, what is news? My father? Artem?'

'Eat, Daria, come on now,' urges Harriet gently. They have all tucked into the soup—a brief thumbs-up from her to Ben and a curt nod of approval from Hester, the old misery—with the exception of Daria. Harriet leans across and breaks open a roll for her. Then she tops up their glasses, noticing that one has magically appeared beside her nephew.

'She knows them, does she?'

'Polina? Of course. Old friend since . . .' Daria indicates a toddler with her hand. 'And she is working with Artem. At the university.'

'He's a student?'

'Student? No. He is teacher. English. He teach English. Very good.'

Hester and Harriet's eyebrows rise in unison. Harriet is mortified to realise she has been nursing an inexcusably clichéd picture of Belarus, where hardy peasants in bright ethnic garb and stout boots cultivate the unforgiving soil, possibly singing snatches of gloomy folk songs while roasting the occasional goat.

'He is telling Polina, we worry. No news from Daria—'

'Well, at least she can reassure him now. And your father,' says Hester.

Daria shakes her head violently. 'No, this is before! This is October, I think.'

'Eat, Daria. Your soup is getting—'

'Since October, she is not seeing him.'

The sisters' hearts sink.

'Dar, eat,' says Ben, nudging her bowl towards her. 'You gotta eat.'

Obediently she sips a spoonful of soup, then takes the piece of buttered roll he holds out to her. From upstairs comes a faint cry.

'I've got it.' Ben's up and off before anyone else can respond.

The spoon pauses on the way to Daria's mouth. 'He is losing job. Because of Tata. It is how it goes in my country. His . . . the other teachers, they try to help . . . but it is dangerous. Polina say Artem tell them, no, please, be careful. Don't make trouble for you. I think perhaps also it is my fault.'

'Your fault? How?' says Hester.

'Because I . . . because I am making protest. Police. Spies . . .'

'What about the police?' says Ben, returning with a flushed Milo and just catching the tail end of the conversation.

'In Belarus,' snaps Hester. 'Not in England. Don't interrupt.'

'Here,' says Ben, gently placing the baby in his mother's arms. 'Looks a bit better, doesn't he?'

Marginally, thinks Harriet, noting Milo's flushed cheeks.

Wishful thinking, reflects Hester, with one look at the baby's heavy eyes.

Daria pushes her soup aside and opens her blouse. Milo thrashes about feebly for a few seconds then latches on to the nipple. Silence descends on the kitchen, broken only by the scrape of Ben's spoon as he finishes his soup, simultaneously edging Daria's bowl back in front of her. Beside him, his phone buzzes; abandoning his food, he checks it and starts texting at lightning speed.

'Do your parents allow you to use that thing at the table?' says Hester crossly, noticing with relief that Daria has taken another bite of bread.

'You what?' Ben looks up, thumbs hovering over the keypad.

'We are eating, Ben!'

'Yeah?'

'Can't that wait?'

'Wait?' queries Ben as though the suggestion is beyond comprehension.

'It's called good manners. I am sick and tired of seeing that damned phone glued to your hand or clamped to your ear!'

'Hetty . . .'

Hester ignores her sister. 'Buzzing and beeping every five minutes. I'd be grateful for a bit of peace!'

Harriet is well aware what has caused Hester's latest flare-up: it's worry. It's the piling on of yet more complications and disasters in Daria's already complex life. Ben just happens to find himself in the firing line. It might equally well have been her.

He, of course, does not know this. All he sees is yet another adult on his case, making his life a misery.

'All right! Jeez . . . no need to go off on one! I'll put it on vibrate if that'll shut you up!'

Oh, Ben . . . thinks Harriet, as Hester's mouth opens in outrage. But before she can find the words, Daria hisses angrily, 'Rude. Rude boy! You say sorry to Hester.'

Ben looks as though he has been slapped. An ugly blush suffuses his face; his pimpled skin flares. He gapes almost comically for a second or two then grabs his phone, shoves his chair back and storms towards the hall. Turning back in the doorway, he seems ready to explode; instead, as his eyes light on Milo, still feeding, he spits, 'I'm sorry, all right? Satisfied? I'm going to my room.' The stairs shudder in protest as he thuds up them.

Hester flashes a look at Harriet that says, *There, what did I tell you?*

Harriet instinctively wants to leap to Ben's defence, to explain to her sister that he's at the mercy of his hormones, that the wiring in his brain is still developing, that he won't have meant it. But she doesn't. There are times when it's worth taking Hester on. This isn't one of them.

'Daria, there's something we need to tell you,' she cuts in. 'Well, two things actually. But first, the good news.'

'Good news?' repeats the girl doubtfully.

'Yes, really good,' says Hester, aggrieved that Harriet has stolen her thunder and also that yet again she seems to be cast in the role of villain. Surely Harriet can see how ungrateful and boorish the boy is? It's high time he was sent packing. 'You know we went to see a solicitor when we were in London?'

'A . . .?'

'A lawyer,' explains Harriet.

'Yes?' Mistrust flits across Daria's face.

Harriet guesses that in Belarus any connection with the law is viewed with suspicion, so she adds quickly, 'He's a family friend.'

'Okay . . .' Daria is still frowning.

'We asked him to look into your status.' Daria freezes. 'About your right to remain here in the UK. Now, because Milo has an English father, it looks as though you will be allowed to stay—'

'Forever?' Daria's eyes are bright now, not with tears but with hope.

The sisters exchange a look, weighing the desire to offer Daria a cast-iron assurance against the need to be absolutely sure of their facts. The last thing they want after all she has endured is to give the girl false hope.

'Probably,' they say together.

'Oh, thank you! Thank you, God!' Daria's free hand flies to her breast, her eyes upwards. 'My heart is . . . my heart . . .'

'Yes,' says Harriet tearfully, 'we know. We feel just the same, don't we, Hetty?'

Hester, struggling to retain her composure, manages a nod. Then, in a rather thick voice, 'You didn't finish telling us about the phone call.'

Daria, disbelief and joy battling as she gazes down at her now sleeping son, comes back to the moment with a shake of her head. 'Oh yes, I forget. Polina, she say she does not know about my father. So I ask her to please give Artem your number if she see him. Is okay?'

'Of course.'

'Because . . .' Daria's eyes suddenly swim with tears as the emotion she has been trying so hard to contain bursts through her fragile defences. 'Because how he will know I am all right? I am safe?'

Hmm, thinks Hester, *safe is perhaps pushing it a bit, in spite of Henry's news. Still, at least you've a roof over your head, I suppose.*

'Did you tell Polina about Milo?' says Harriet, laying her hand over Daria's. The girl blinks back fresh tears, turning her hand over to squeeze Harriet's in gratitude.

'No . . . I do not. I think perhaps it will be big shock—not so much for Polina, she is woman, she is friend—but for Artem and Tata, without I can explain. Without I am telling them—'

'No, absolutely,' says Hester firmly. 'I think you made the right decision there.'

Daria's smile is full of such relief that both women, only too conscious of their own good fortune and security, have to swallow hard once more.

'Now then,' says Hester, with the tiniest quiver in her voice, 'you hand me that young man, my dear, and finish your soup. And that roll.'

'Quite,' says Harriet, robbed of the chance of a cuddle by Hester's uncustomary gesture. 'We'd hate for all Ben's hard work to go to waste, wouldn't we, Hetty?'

Before Hester can fashion a riposte, the phone rings again. With a sigh, Harriet levers herself up. 'I'll take it in the sitting room.'

∽∽∽

'Mrs Greene?'

'No, this is Harriet Pearson. If you could just hold—'

'No, no, please!' The caller's voice sounds a shade desperate.

'You'll do just fine, Mrs Pearson. I've been trying to get hold of one or the other of you.'

'Who is this?'

'I'm phoning from the district hospital. About your brother.'

'My . . . brother?' Harriet thinks, *How many more so-called relatives are going to crawl out of the woodwork?*

'Now, Mrs Pearson, there's no need to be alarmed. He's absolutely fine.'

'No, no, I'm afraid you've made a mistake. I don't have a brother.'

There is a snort down the line, whether of amusement or exasperation Harriet isn't sure. 'Yes, he said you'd say that.'

'Who did?'

'Your br—. . . the gentleman currently occupying a bed on Primrose Ward, awaiting discharge. Mr Barr.' There is the sound of papers being shuffled. 'Francis Ignatius—not sure I've said that quite right—Nathaniel Barr. He warned us there was a bit of history between himself and his sisters. The thing is, Mrs Pearson, much as we sympathise—and believe me, we understand only too well—we do need the bed and, as I say, he is ready for discharge. More than ready, in fact. Could you possibly see your way clear to letting bygones be bygones and collect him first thing tomorrow morning? Say, nine o'clock? As early as you like, really. If not earlier.'

CHAPTER 20

The Laurels lies dark and silent, its chimneys silhouetted against a sky streaked with cloud and lit by a watery moon. An owl skims low over the hedge that bounds the lane and swoops on an unlucky shrew, talons extended in a merciless embrace. A brief skirmish, a flurry of leaves and wings, then silence falls again.

Milo dreams the formless dreams of a baby, safe and warm in the cocoon of his blankets, a thread of dribble collecting in his neck, snuggled against the hand that hangs over the edge of his mother's bed above him. She is drowning in memories, strands of the past woven together in a bewildering tapestry: her father's smile, the crease of his brow, the texture of Artem's hand in hers, his huge, guffawing laugh. Flitting in and out of her dreams are more disturbing memories: the cold night air, the rattle of a van bouncing over uneven ground, the whimper of a tiny child.

Hester, fragmentary thoughts scudding through her mind, distorted images swimming in and out of focus, tosses in her hot sheets, deaf to the rattle of Harriet's snores next door after so many years. Once or twice, she almost rises to the surface of consciousness until exhaustion pulls her under again.

A volcanic snore rouses Harriet from a deep sleep; she opens her eyes to pitch-black, curtains tightly drawn against the slightest chink of light, annoyed to find herself the author of her own abrupt wakefulness. She lies for a few moments, blinking in the darkness, weighing up the need for a trip to the bathroom against the warmth of her bed. The bathroom wins. Struggling into her dressing gown, she pads down the hallway, the click of the pull switch sounding like a shot in the silent house. A few minutes later, water thunders through the pipes, followed by another report as she pulls the cord again and creeps back towards her room. At the far end of the corridor, light bleeds under Ben's door. She squints at the luminous numbers on her watch: just before midnight. He should be asleep. She hovers outside her room, ears straining for the click-click of his phone's keypad or the hiss leaking from his headphones. Nothing. Perhaps he's fallen asleep with the light on: she'd heard him creep downstairs earlier in the evening, presumably to raid the larder while she and Hester were talking to Daria and finally— finally!—establishing that the woman at the petrol station was indubitably Tina. Daria, ecstatic at the news from Henry and feeling much more secure now she was once more in possession of her passport, had needed little persuasion to confirm that, yes, it must have been Tina and yes, she had taken a photograph of Daria and Milo a few weeks after his birth.

'Perhaps she want to check I am okay?' Daria had said hopefully. 'Because I do not think she really want me to leave— Scott, yes, maybe—but not my friend Tina.'

Harriet had mumbled something reassuring, she and Hester having decided in a swiftly exchanged look that they would not share with the girl their concern about Tina's motives and her husband's possibly more sinister involvement in the hunt for her and Milo.

Harriet hesitates on the threshold of her bedroom. She is loath to leave Ben sleeping with his light on. It's less to do with thriftiness than a hangover from her childhood where her father had religiously switched off every light (and electrical appliance) before retiring.

She creeps to the end of the corridor and places one ear to Ben's door. The room, indeed the entire house, seems blanketed in silence. The door gives with a tiny creak. 'Ben?' she whispers, pushing the door open a little way. A fug of boy and sweat assails her. She nudges the door again until the bed comes into view. The empty bed.

Harriet steps into the room and peers around. No recalcitrant teenager to be seen. She bites back a profanity and hurries in bare feet downstairs, stopping to check the hooks in the hall. No sign of Ben's jacket. Seconds later she discovers the back door unlocked—how could he be so *stupid* with all that's been going on?—and his shoes, which she remembers seeing beside the mat during supper, missing.

It takes Harriet all of three seconds to decide not to alert Hester to Ben's flight. Presumably, when she had heard him coming downstairs earlier he had been not in search of sustenance but was on his way out. And that must have been at least an hour ago. He must have decided to return home after their ill-tempered exchange in the kitchen earlier. *Idiot!* And close on the heels of that thought: *Whatever will George and Isabelle think?* Entrusting, albeit extremely reluctantly, their son to his aunts' care, how will they react when they learn he is walking the streets at dead of night to escape them?

It takes her only another second or two to decide she has to go after him. For one thing, she feels a huge responsibility for his safety and is sick with worry at the thought of him tramping the unlit lanes in the pitch-dark. Second, she cannot bear to allow Hester the satisfaction of seeing all her misgivings about their nephew proved right.

Fleetingly, she considers going upstairs to dress, but discounts the idea almost immediately lest she wake the others. Besides, she doesn't know how fast Ben's walking: he might be almost home. Better she nips out, finds him, brings him back, tucks him up in bed after a good talking-to and no-one need be any the wiser. Goodness knows there's quite enough on their plates without Ben and his problems muddying the waters any further. She shoves her feet into a pair of orange Crocs (bought in a fit of madness at a garden centre sale a few years back and worn only in extremis, generally when putting out the bins), grabs an old duffel coat, a woolly hat and her keys, and slides quietly out of the back door, locking it soundlessly behind her.

Releasing the handbrake, she lets the car roll down the drive into the lane before starting the engine, selecting first gear with meticulous care so as to minimise any chances of Hester's Pavlovian response to her sister's usual driving technique. Only when she reaches the first bend in the lane does she turn on the lights and accelerate away in her habitual cavalier manner, careering into the main road at the junction rather faster than the village speed limit allows. Suppose Ben has jogged home? Suppose he's already there, spilling the details of his awful sojourn at The Laurels into his parents' appalled ears? Suppose in his rage he reveals the subterfuges she and Hester have employed over the past few days to keep George and Isabelle at bay? She cringes to imagine her cousins' pain and hurt when they learn how they have been bamboozled and hoodwinked. Harriet stamps on the accelerator.

She flashes past the village shop, breasts the hill by the church so fast that for a moment she fears she may leave the road, races past the dark, unoccupied bus shelter, swerves around a row of parked vehicles opposite the almost empty pub car park—and slams on the brakes. With her trademark zigzag reversing, engine screaming, she accelerates back to the Glass & Cask and screeches to a halt. Leaping from the car as quickly as her inelegant and lumpish footwear will allow, she stumbles across the car park's tarmac and with an outraged yell, throws herself on a thug assaulting her nephew, who is curled up on the ground.

The speed and ferocity of her attack take the assailant by surprise, a surprise compounded by the sight of a diminutive woman of mature years in a mishmash of shabby clothing and sling-back resin clogs of a repellent hue taking him on. Not unreasonably perhaps, given the hour and location, he takes the newcomer for an inebriate. He staggers back from the body on the ground, hands held up defensively.

Harriet, a ball of fury, flings her contempt at him—'You filthy coward! Hitting a man when he's down!'—while rushing to Ben's side, placing herself between him and the other man.

She checks Ben quickly for any obvious injuries or blood; seeing none, she draws herself up to her full height and is just about to chase the aggressor from the field when another young man emerges from the pub and runs towards them.

'Ah! Thank God. Would you ring the police, please? This man has just attacked my nephew.'

He ignores her completely, grabbing the other youngster by the upper arm and hissing into his face, 'I warned you! Didn't I warn you? The boss is spitting tacks in there. Now get out of here before I lose it. And take this so-called friend of yours with you. And this pissed old bag!' Then he's gone, back into the pub, slamming the door behind him.

A long, long moment passes in which the three figures, two upright, one prone, remain frozen. Then Ben groans, tries to sit up and vomits copiously.

~~~

'Get in,' says Harriet tersely, slamming the front seat forward so Jez can crawl into the back. He folds himself almost in half and squeezes his bony knees either side of her seat.

'Do your belt up.'

Jez doesn't argue.

Ben, standing alongside the car, gulps in lungfuls of cold night air. He's none too sure he doesn't want to throw up again and Aunt Harriet, already in a snit of mega proportions, will go ballistic if he bokes in her car.

'Ben!'

He risks it.

⌣⌣⌣

Harriet is boiling with rage. To be spoken to like that! To be mistaken for a . . . for a . . . she can't bring herself to even *think* the word. To discover that Ben wasn't being attacked at all; that he and his best friend Jez had been thrown out of the pub by the barman, who, it transpires, is Jez's cousin and has turned a blind eye to them being under-age. Except that now the landlord has found out and the cousin is in grave danger of losing his job . . .

'I hope you're both very proud of yourselves!' Her fury demands a release. The air crackles with ire. She is going to take Ben home right this minute and damn the consequences.

'Aunt Harriet . . .'

'Don't even try to apologise!'

'No, Aunt Harriet . . .!'

'Lord alone knows what your parents—'

'Please. Stop.'

'Stop?! I haven't even started!'

'No, the car.'

'I think he wants to be sick,' says Jez in her ear, treating her to a blast of stale beer.

She slews to the kerb, Ben throws open the door and manages to hold on just long enough for most of his remaining stomach contents to land outside the car. The acrid stench of vomit fills the car's interior; Ben continues retching.

'How much has he had to drink?' She glares at Jez in the rear-view mirror.

He grimaces. 'Three or four pints.'

'He's fifteen!'

'Yeah, well . . .' mutters Jez miserably. 'He was pretty pissed when he arrived.'

'How could he—' starts Harriet, then stops abruptly. Of course: wine with dinner. And perhaps before dinner for all she knows. And who introduced him to that particular delight? Oh Lord . . .

Ben wipes his mouth and sits back in his seat, pulling the door shut. 'Be all right now.'

At a more seemly pace, Harriet sets off for George's house, via Jez's, driving as smoothly as she can manage. She pulls up some distance from Jez's house at his request—'Don't want my old man catching me coming home. Ta for the lift and that'— and waits until she sees him disappear through the imposing entrance. Ben climbs back in and re-buckles his seatbelt, mumbling something she doesn't catch.

'What?'

'I said, can I come back with you?'

'Can you . . .? You've got a nerve, young man! You creep out without a word, you leave the back door unlocked, you go drinking when you're far too young (you do realise the publican could lose his licence because of you?), you humiliate me—not to mention how unforgivably rude you were to your poor Aunt Hester—and then you have the colossal cheek to ask if you can continue to stay under our roof!'

Impassioned, and with more than a hint of tears, Ben ploughs on. 'Yeah, but can I? Only if I go home now, smelling like this, with all this crud on my gear, the 'rents'll never let me go anywhere ever again. Yeah, yeah, I know I've behaved like a proper little shit but I'm really, really sorry and I promise on my life I'll never ever do anything like it again.'

Harriet is not a vindictive woman. She is firm, as past pupils would attest, but she is also fair (they would grant that too) and, luckily for Ben, extremely susceptible to expressions of remorse from errant youths. Furthermore, she has been tying herself in knots for the past fifteen minutes trying to concoct a plausible story for George and Isabelle to explain why she is returning their son, well past midnight, smelling like an alcoholic, with smears of vomit down his jacket.

Maintaining her look of flint lest Ben think she is a complete sucker, she turns the car around and heads for home.

CHAPTER 21

30 DECEMBER

'Harriet!' says Peggy Verndale, pulling her dogs swiftly to one side as Harriet barrels out of the village shop with two pints of milk in each hand. 'You're up early.'

'Oh!' *Damn, of all the people . . .* 'Morning, Peggy. Morning, dogs. Yes, woke first thing and we were out of milk . . .' Harriet elects not to mention she's been up since six checking the state of Ben's jacket, which she'd sponged down last night, not wanting to risk the washing machine at that hour (it has the most horrendous rattle on the spin cycle). They had crept like thieves into their rooms and silently closed their respective doors after them. 'Do not,' Harriet had hissed, 'even think of using your phone.' The jacket looks fairly clean now and seems relatively odour-free. Luckily, Milo hadn't woken at his usual ungodly hour, so she hadn't had to contend with Daria and any questions from that quarter this morning. She thinks they might just have got away with it.

'That's a lot of milk,' says Peggy suspiciously. The woman has the instincts of a bloodhound.

'Oh, Ben, you know, our nephew,' says Harriet gaily. 'You must remember what teenagers are like: eat you out of house and home. Never seen such a boy for guzzling milk. Well, I'd better . . .' She starts to move away towards her car, only to be confronted by her sister, hair awry and clearly still in her pyjamas under an ancient Barbour.

'Harry! Here you are! I thought you must have gone to collect—oh, Peggy! Good morning. Quite a little gathering. I've just popped down to pick up some—oh! Right.' She recoils as Harriet waggles the two bottles of milk under her nose. 'Good.' She shoots a quizzical look at her sister: *What's going on?*

Harriet shakes her head infinitesimally, not wanting to give any ammunition to Peggy, who is still holding her position and frowning distrustfully. A car streaks past, distracting them all.

'Wasn't that . . .?' says Hester, squinting. The morning light falling across her lenses reveals them to be in dire need of a good clean.

Peggy sniffs and hoists her sizeable bosom aloft. 'Teddy Wilson, yes. Showing off in that new car of his. He's been back and forth through the village for days like a . . . dog with a bone.'

'A dog with two tails?' offers Harriet.

'Whatever the expression is,' says Peggy dismissively, annoyed she's given Harriet the opportunity to score. 'Anyway, the other day on the train, I had it out with him.'

'Had what out with him?' asks Hester, blindsided by Peggy's

276

change of topic. 'About Mrs Vicar?' Surely even Peggy wouldn't go that far!

'Not Mrs Vicar!' hisses Peggy, looking around automatically for eavesdroppers. 'What do you take me for? That would be gossiping, and I'm sure no-one would accuse me of *that*!'

Both sisters inspect the pavement.

'No, what we were talking about at bridge: the land behind our house. I mean, I'm as anxious as the next person not to upset my neighbours—'

'Teddy's not exactly a neighbour of yours, Peggy; he lives a good mile from your place,' Hester points out.

'I'm not talking about where he lives,' says Peggy crossly. 'As I just said, I'm talking about the land at the back of our garden. The place he's leased out. God alone knows what the tenant is growing there. The smell is revolting if the wind is in the right direction. Wrong direction, I mean. Absolutely ghastly.'

'That's the price you pay for living in the country, I'm afraid,' says Harriet. 'The smell of manure and slurry and whatnot.' She's never been altogether sure what slurry consists of exactly but it sounds pretty vile.

'I know all about living in the country!' retorts Peggy. 'If it were simply manure, I wouldn't complain. I was brought up in the country, I'll have you know.' Both sisters recognise the subtext: *unlike you two townies*. 'Manure I can deal with, but—'

'What does Ron say?' Harriet can see Peggy is working herself up into a full-scale whingeing session; they'll be there for hours if they can't divert her onto another subject.

'Oh, Ronald!' (Peggy doesn't like her husband's name shortened—even though he always introduces himself thus—feeling that it diminishes him and, by association, her. She seems to have no such reservations about her own diminutive; indeed, has never been known to use her full name.) 'Don't talk to me about Ronald. He says I'm imagining it, which is rich, given the fact he has absolutely no sense of smell whatsoever since he was thrown at the Boxing Day Meet in 1996.'

'Thrown? Was he?' says Hester with pretended surprise, having heard the story at least twice before. On each occasion, the details have become more and more dramatic: she's wondering how far Peggy will go this time. At least it distracts her from her original gripe.

'Oh, Hester! Surely you've heard about it! He was almost killed!'

'Killed?' says Hester, mouth wide with horror, careful not to catch Harriet's eye. 'Killed? Really?' The last iteration of the tale had had Ron mildly concussed.

'Out cold,' says Peggy, shaking her head at the terrible memory of the accident. 'They thought he'd been caught by a flying hoof in the mêlée.'

'No! How awful.'

'It was. Touch and go. I mean, head injuries . . .'

'Absolutely.'

'Can't be too careful.'

'Of course not.'

'Hetty . . .' says Harriet. There are times when Hester doesn't know when to stop.

Hester ignores her. 'So, he had to have neurosurgery, then, did he?' Anyone but Harriet would think Hester is entirely caught up in the gruesome details. 'How horrible! I always think they look like cauliflowers, brains.'

Peggy shudders. 'No. Fortunately, that wasn't necessary.'

'Phew,' says Hester. 'What a relief. Still, you must have been worried sick.'

'I was. Oh, yes, I was. Anyway'—Peggy is clearly eager to move on—'the only lasting damage is the loss of his sense of smell. He's had no end of tests, but they say there's nothing they can do. It's called anosmia, you know.'

'Is it really?' says Hester, wearing her serious face.

Harriet grabs her by the arm. 'Hetty, I'm on a double yellow!'

Hester allows herself to be led away.

〜〜〜

'I went to make the tea and found we were out of milk. Is it me or is there a rather nasty niff in this car? You haven't got something on your shoe, have you? Anyway, I suppose that wretched boy was up to his usual tricks last night, raiding the fridge.'

You don't know the half of it, thinks Harriet, as her heart skips a beat. She opens her window a crack to try to dispel the slight but lingering note of vomit.

'Then I saw the car had gone and I thought, surely she's not gone to get Finbar already? Or should I say Francis Barr?'

'Extraordinary, isn't it?' says Harriet, pulling on the handbrake outside the house, grateful for the change of topic. 'All these years and he's never let on. Why Finbar, I wonder? I mean, apart from his initials.'

They climb out of the car and make their way up the path.

'I think it's an Irish name,' says Hester, 'so I suppose we ought to have smelt a rat. Talking of smells—'

Harriet cuts swiftly across her. 'You were very naughty with Peggy, you know.'

'Was I?' says Hester innocently. 'I was just showing an interest.'

Harriet snorts. 'As Ben would say, yeah, right.'

They are both laughing as they bid Daria and Milo good morning.

~~~

'We should have woken him.'

'Ben? Hetty, it's only half past eight now! Hardly late.' Hester having thrown on some clothes after a swift breakfast, they are now en route to the hospital.

'Still, I know what these youngsters are like; they'd lounge about in bed all day given half a chance.'

Harriet refrains from entering into a discussion—one that she anticipates will quickly regress into an argument—about young people's sleep patterns. *Honestly, what she knows about teenagers could be inscribed on a pin head!* Anyway, Ben is a subject best avoided at the moment lest she inadvertently alert Hester to last night's dramas, what with her sister still itching for an excuse to send him packing after yesterday's unfortunate contretemps. Harriet also knows from her brief visit to Ben's bedroom while Hester was dressing that he is nursing a ferocious hangover; and while on the one hand she feels such suffering is both a salutary lesson and only what he deserves, on the other she feels he's best kept out of circulation until he looks a little less green about the gills.

'Do we know which ward he's on?' asks Hester as they turn into the hospital car park.

'Primrose.'

'What ghastly names they choose,' sniffs Hester. 'So twee.'

'Infantilising,' says Harriet. So at least they're agreed on something.

They find a mercifully generous parking spot that requires a mere four attempts for Harriet to fill it. Hester struggles out from the passenger seat without comment; at least Harriet has plenty of room on her side.

'Ticket,' says Harriet.

'Ticket?'

'You have to pay. Look, Pay and Display, see?'

'We have to pay? To pick up a patient?' Hester is horrified. 'You're joking!'

Harriet sighs. After such a disturbed night and far too little sleep, she's not in the mood for one of Hester's rants. 'I'll get it.'

⌣⌣⌣

'We're here to collect Mr Barr,' says Harriet into the intercom outside Primrose Ward.

'You're rather early—oh! Mr Barr did you say? Of course! Come in.' With a buzz, the door gives and they push through. A plump middle-aged woman in uniform comes out from behind the nursing station at the end of a corridor to greet them. 'Thank you for coming so—yes, he's extremely eager to get away, your brother. This way.'

She walks off, clearly expecting them to follow, saying over her shoulder, 'We're just awaiting transport to take him to the Departure Lounge.'

Harriet thinks instantly of an undertaker's waiting room.

'I'll let the discharge coordinator know you're here.'

She leads them around the corner to another corridor, off which there is a series of four-bedded bays. At the third, she stops and gestures over to the far corner by the window. Hester and Harriet peer short-sightedly at the figure seated beside the bed, a rather patrician-looking elderly gentleman with snowy-white shoulder-length hair and a luxuriant beard, a folded newspaper held inches from his nose. Two of the other beds are occupied by patients who appear to be asleep. Or, shudders Harriet inwardly, comatose. She loathes hospitals.

'There must be some mistake, nurse,' whispers Hester. 'That's not Fin—our brother.' They had agreed on the journey over that they would play along with the fiction for the moment.

'Sister,' corrects the nurse sternly, then raising her voice with practised modulation that avoids waking the others, calls, 'Mr Barr?'

The old man looks over immediately. His eyes light up. 'Ah, Hester, Harriet! At last! Now perhaps'—this to the sister—'you'd be good enough to release me from this purgatory, Sister Brice.'

Her lips thin. 'It will be my pleasure entirely, Mr Barr, I assure you. As soon as we can, we'll get you downstairs, your medication sorted and then you can be on your way.'

As she sweeps off, Hester and Harriet advance towards the figure seated by the window.

'Finbar?'

'Yes?'

'Is it really . . .? What on earth . . .?' Dumbstruck, they take in the bushy beard, the silky hair curling on his shoulders, the faded but clean checked shirt, the polyester trousers. He looks up at them anxiously.

'I have to know . . . my trolley? My books?'

'Safe and sound. But, Finbar!

'I know, my dears. I am beyond mortification.' He plucks distastefully at the fabric of his trousers.

'You are beyond recognition, Finbar.'

'You will not believe the indignities to which I have been subjected. Stripped, forced into a bath, my apparel destroyed . . . mere chits of girls addressing me as though I lacked capacity— and as for Sister Brice . . .!'

'What about Sister Brice?' demands said lady, returning in a cloud of barely contained animosity.

Finbar, recognising he has more than met his match, deflates.

She cocks an eyebrow. 'Well?'

'Dear lady . . .'

'Do not *dear lady* me or attempt to worm your way around me with your nonsense. We've all had quite enough of that. My sympathies are entirely with your sisters.'

Finbar bridles. 'The truth of the matter is, I'm lucky to be getting out of here alive.'

'In more ways than one,' murmurs Sister Brice, almost but not quite under her breath.

'I heard that!' says Finbar indignantly. 'Whatever happened to angels of mercy?'

'They saw you coming and flew away,' she retorts without missing a beat.

Finbar can only glare.

Hester takes the opportunity of the momentary hiatus to ask, 'But what on earth happened, Finbar?'

'Finbar?' echoes Sister Brice with incredulity.

'Oh!' Hester recovers immediately. 'A family nickname . . .'

Finbar affects a pained but self-satisfied expression. 'They thought I had had a heart attack.' This is clearly a matter of some pride.

'It was heartburn,' mutters Sister Brice sourly. 'All that fuss, moaning and groaning, ECGs—'

'*Acute* reflux oesophagitis,' intones Finbar, narrowing his eyes at her, 'that's what I had.'

'Exactly. Heartburn. As I said.' She whispers to Hester out of the side of her mouth, 'Too much Special Brew.'

'Special Brew?' hisses Finbar, his hearing as sharp as ever. Involuntarily, they all glance over at the two other patients, who remain inert. 'I do not drink Special Brew! Only down-and-outs drink that. What do you take me for?'

Sister Brice's nostrils flare. 'Oh, please, Mr Barr, don't tempt me. A porter will be along in five minutes. Good day. Goodbye.' Harriet can sense the effort it is costing Sister Brice not to add 'good riddance' too.

～～～

'We signed our lives away for you in there, Finbar,' complains Hester, when they finally escape the attentions of the discharge coordinator, who demands repeated assurances that Mr Barr can be safely released to his sisters' tender care. The medicines, which Finbar keeps protesting he has no intention of taking anyway, take ages to materialise, forcing Harriet out to the car twice to pay for additional parking; she decides not to share with Hester the astronomical cost. Finbar resolutely refuses to discuss either his subterfuge or the circumstances surrounding his admission until freed from the hospital's clutches.

'Remember Publilius Syrus,' he murmurs conspiratorially, sweeping a look around the mass of humanity resigned to hours on uncomfortable plastic chairs watching mindless daytime TV with the sound turned down.

'Who? Oh, never mind! What did he say?' Hester is desperate for a strong coffee and is therefore extremely short-tempered.

'*Qui omnes insidias—*'

'In English, Finbar!'

'Hester, my dear, I thought you studied Latin.'

'Yes, Finbar, I did—about fifty years ago!'

'I had no idea your memory was—' One look at Hester's face and he retreats. 'What he said was, he who fears every ambush falls into none.'

Hester stares at him disbelievingly. 'And you think someone in here is going to ambush you?'

Finbar taps the side of his nose; Harriet notices even his fingernails are clean. 'Trust no-one. I've already been ambushed once. I'm not going to risk it a second time.' Whereupon he falls silent and nothing will induce him to reveal more.

⁓

Harriet pulls away from the hospital and then at Hester's insistence stops at the first run of shops they pass, which blessedly boasts a cafe.

Hester leaps from the car, leaving Harriet to release Finbar from the rear. There is a minor altercation on the pavement as she tries to persuade him into the old anorak they keep in the boot in case of emergencies. 'It's the middle of winter, Finbar! Don't be difficult.' She finally prevails, but not without much griping on his part about a man of his sensitivities being forced into women's apparel.

By the time they enter the cafe, Hester is seated in front of a large cafetière, three mugs and two generous slices of flapjack. 'Aren't you having one, Hetty?' says Harriet, reaching for a slice gratefully.

Hester holds up a knife. 'I thought we could share.' She looks at Harriet as if daring her to argue.

Coffee poured, milked and sugared to individual taste, bites of flapjack ('Not bad,' says Hester) taken, the sisters can contain their curiosity no longer.

'Okay, Finbar—now tell all,' Hester orders.

CHAPTER 22

'It was the same man. Back rootling through my possessions, if you please. I didn't see him at first. I was too distracted by your victuals, Hester, if truth be told—which, incidentally, they stole at the hospital and I never saw again. I've a mind to lodge an official complaint . . .'

'Finbar!'

'Well, if you'd seen what I was expected to eat in there! And I'll have you know they destroyed my clothes—I'd had that coat for years!'

'Never mind all that. Just get on with it.'

Finbar looks aggrieved. For a moment he seems ready to protest but Hester's expression is so flinty that instead he adopts a look of wounded forbearance.

'I don't suppose there's a spot more coffee?'

Harriet obliges.

'So, as I say, I came upon the miscreant: I think we both had rather a fright. I challenged him, naturally, demanding to know what he thought he was doing invading my domain. Do you know what he had the temerity to say? *It's a bloody bus stop, mate*—excuse the crudeness, but I am reporting verbatim. *I got*—most ungrammatical—*as much right as anyone to come in here.*

True, thinks Harriet. *In so far as it's public property, I suppose . . . or was.*

'But not, I rejoined, to interfere with my possessions. He had strewn everything—including my books, mark you—all over the floor. My books!'

'It's all right,' she reassures him. 'Ben retrieved them and stacked them on the seat.'

'Did he indeed?' says Finbar wonderingly. 'That is excellent news. There is a distinct possibility I may have misjudged that young man.'

Hester snorts into her coffee.

'But to proceed with my narration: I asked him to leave forthwith, quite reasonably. But no. He was intransigent. *You know where she is, don't you?* says he, with, I might add, an unwarranted boorishness. Again, I professed total ignorance. I may have sworn at him.' He looks at the sisters with a mixture of truculence and guilt. 'I felt *besieged*. And then he started to threaten me, push me, jabbing his finger in my chest. Calling me all manner of names. I'm afraid I snapped.'

'Oh dear,' says Harriet quietly.

'As you say, Harriet, oh dear. I should not have allowed him to rile me. As you both well know, I am normally the most placid and mellow of fellows. But there it is. I reacted. I grabbed my trusty trolley and tried to repel his advances. In my defence, I would say I did not altogether fancy my chances against a man of his stature and, frankly, age. And initially my tactic was successful. I caught him squarely on the shin and he leapt backwards, howling. But far from causing him to flee, it simply enraged him further. He grabbed hold of the other side of the trolley and we engaged in a very unseemly tug of war until he gained possession and hurled it over the hedge. My trolley! I was, as you may imagine, incandescent. And that's when it happened.' He pauses dramatically and takes a huge bite of flapjack.

Hester and Harriet sit forward.

Finbar chews slowly, swallows and slaps himself theatrically on the chest. 'The pain, my dears! I have never felt anything like it. It radiated across here.' He demonstrates with a gesture down his sternum. 'I thought I was being consumed by fire! Truly. One begins to appreciate—if only slightly—the agonies endured by the Tudor martyrs. I fell like a stone to the pavement and could only wait helplessly for the coup de grâce. But I was spared—who knows why? One minute the villain is roaring at me, the next he is running for his van and I hear the screech of tyres as he flees. Perhaps he thought I was in my death throes. It certainly felt like it. Perhaps he felt a modicum of responsibility. Seconds later, a good Samaritan is bending over me and summoning assistance in the form of an ambulance. I am whisked into hospital and then subjected, as previously advised, to the most monstrously intrusive procedures.' He shudders at the memory.

'But it was only heartburn, as it turned out,' says Hester disdainfully.

Finbar bristles at the casual dismissal of his ordeal. He tugs the collar of the despised anorak tighter around his neck and gives Hester a look of deep reproach.

'Yes, indeed, *as it transpired.* When the pain subsided—eventually—I feebly protested that I required no further assistance, but it was as if I had never spoken. All my expostulations were ignored. Needles were inserted, wires attached, all sorts of other violations were visited upon my poor defenceless body.'

He leans forward confidentially. Hester thinks she catches a hint of his habitual odour, reinhabiting his body.

He whispers across the table. 'In my opinion, they were using me for demonstration purposes. Experimentation, even. There were positively *hordes* of people preying on me. And then came the final outrage—'

Hester and Harriet compose their expressions. As one, they raise their coffee mugs.

'Denuded of my apparel—entirely!—and forcibly lowered into a bath while people—women!—watched.'

'They *were* nurses,' says Harriet, lips twitching. 'It's just a job to them. You won't be the first man they've seen—'

Finbar's expression would have done justice to the finest tragedian. 'The sensibilities of other men are not my concern. What is a man without his carapace? A poor, bare, forked animal, as the Bard has it.' He has never looked so noble, or so nakedly vulnerable.

Harriet, stricken, reaches out a hand. 'It must have been horrible for you, Finbar.'

He nods, overcome.

The three of them contemplate the frailties of ageing flesh and the insecurities that accompany it. It is, predictably, Hester who breaks the silence and changes the subject.

'Finbar, Harriet and I were only too glad to come and collect you—we've been extremely worried about you, I'll have you know. But why this cock-and-bull story about being our brother? We'd have come, no matter what, surely you knew that. So I don't quite understand—'

Finbar holds up a finger to stop her, then inserts it into the luxuriance of his beard for a good scratch. He looks decidedly shifty. When he speaks, he avoids looking at them.

'Ladies, I beg you to forgive the deception. I know how you both abhor untruths. But I really had no choice. Not if I wished to preserve my privacy and my independence. At every turn I was being pestered for names, addresses, contacts, and I could see only too clearly which way the wind was blowing. One hint of my—let us say—less-than-conventional living arrangements, and I would find myself saddled forever with a social worker or some other busybody determined to make me conform to what society believes is the appropriate conduct for someone like myself. Since I chose this way of life—and be in no doubt, I did choose it, it was not thrust upon me—I have had countless close shaves with so-called authorities. I was already in a state of some vulnerability, not to say distress, as I have described, and I deemed an insignificant canard a price worth paying to ensure I could return unhindered to the place I call home.' Now he does look at them. 'And I knew beyond a shadow of a doubt that you would both rise to the occasion and respect my right to determine my own fate. I am truly, eternally, grateful. *Is est amicus qui in re dubia re juvat, ubi re est opus.'*

'Finbar . . .' says Hester severely.

'Oh . . . really!' He searches for the translation. *'He's a friend indeed who proves himself a friend in need.* Plautus. Or of course, in your case, *she,'* he adds swiftly, catching Harriet's eye.

'Be that as it may,' presses Harriet, 'there remains the small matter of your name.'

'Ah . . .' he says, shifting uncomfortably. 'I can explain.'

'Oh, do. Please do. We are agog.'

And so it all emerges. How he elected to shed his old identity when he went on the road, wanting to cut all ties with his former life. How he had always hated the name Francis. How he saw a ready alternative in his initials and had always had a fondness for all things Irish and found in Saint Finbarr an affinity for solitude and learning.

'Then why give the hospital your real name?'

'Because Francis Barr still exists. He has an NHS number. He draws a pension.'

'Does he?' says Harriet, astonished.

'Of course he does—I mean, I do! Good Lord above, Harriet, you of all people should appreciate that I am entitled to some recompense, however meagre, for my years of toil at the chalk-face. Don't *you* have a pension?'

'Yes, of course I do . . . but . . . but . . .' Indelicate to ask: *Then why do you constantly cadge food from us? Why do you need to forage for leftovers in bins? Why do you live in a disused bus shelter, for heaven's sake?* Beside her, she senses Hester itching to ask the same questions. But as women of a certain age and upbringing, of a generation that would no more enquire into the state of someone's finances or the size of their salary than dance naked in the fountains in Trafalgar Square, they refrain from further probing. And as Finbar's expression signals that no further information will be forthcoming, they have no choice but to accept that their curiosity must for the present remain unsatisfied.

CHAPTER 23

One aspect of their rescue mission has privately been troubling the sisters since they left the hospital; neither has felt moved to share it lest they appear mean-spirited or unkind. It is their responsibility for Finbar's welfare. Discharged into their care, they feel a moral obligation to fulfil their duty, not least because they believe themselves at least in part the authors of his misfortunes. Already Hester has identified which worn sheets she is prepared to sacrifice for his bed and Harriet has run through in her mind's eye a haphazard wardrobe for their unexpected guest fashioned from what remains of Jim's effects. She believes, wrongly, that her sister is unaware of the two carrier bags still stowed in her bottom drawer that contain those shirts and sweaters of her late husband of which, even after all this time, she simply cannot bear to dispose. Periodically, she pulls the bags out and upends them onto her bed, intending this time to be resolute and unsentimental, bid them farewell and take them to the charity shop. But Jim's lingering smell and the memories that flood back every time weaken her resolve. She holds his old blue lamb's wool against her face, tells herself to buck up, and then pushes the bundles back into their hiding places. Did she but know it, Hester keeps one of Gordon's old shirts in her underwear drawer.

There is one other consequence of housing a new guest: as they have only two spare rooms, Ben will have to return home.

The drive back from the cafe is conducted almost in silence. As they reach the outskirts of the village, Finbar starts struggling out of the anorak in the back seat, a task involving considerable contortions as he remains confined by his seatbelt. Hester turns around.

'What on earth are you doing, Finbar?'

'Divesting myself of this embarrassment.' He tries to yank his arm out of one sleeve. 'Who knows who might be about? I should be a laughing-stock.'

'Finbar,' says Hester, 'I don't think Daria or Ben will be remotely interested in what you're wearing.'

'Whoa! Whoa!' shouts Finbar, causing Harriet to swerve in fright.

A lorry coming the other way beeps angrily.

'What on earth—?'

'Stop! Stop! You almost drove straight past.'

Harriet pulls in to the kerb and yanks on the handbrake.

'Would you be so good as to let me out, Hester?' Finbar asks. 'I can walk back.'

The penny drops. The sisters turn. Behind the car and across the road is the bus shelter.

'No, Finbar,' protests Harriet, chagrined to realise they had omitted to extend a proper invitation. 'You're coming home with us.'

'Absolutely,' says Hester.

'But that's my home!' says Finbar, pointing back up the road. 'I'm most grateful for your kindness, but—'

'Now, Finbar, please don't be stubborn. There's no way we can let you stay there.' Harriet switches off the engine and turn around to face the old man. 'You've just been released from hospital, it's the middle of winter, and we promised that woman we'd take care of—'

'Harriet, Hester,' says Finbar firmly, 'you are women *sans pareil*. There are few others, if any, that I hold in such high regard. You are kind—yes, you can be a little overbearing at times (especially you, Hester, as I'm sure you're only too aware)—but your every thought is guided by decency and compassion.'

Both women wriggle uncomfortably, confronting their duplicity.

'But I am master of my own fate. I have no desire to appear ungrateful, but I insist—and will brook no argument—that I be permitted to return to my quarters.'

Having resigned themselves to the prospect of entertaining in their home a stranger to soap and water and a guest undoubtedly disruptive, demanding and of unsurpassed prolixity, the sisters now salve their consciences by bending every fibre to persuade Finbar to change his mind. Deprived of their looming martyrdom, and not a little ashamed of their lack of charity,

Hester and Harriet redouble their efforts to assure Finbar that nothing would delight them more than to welcome him into their home, that his stay would be without limit (Hester thinks Harriet has gone way over the top on that one) and that they will be unable to live with themselves should he decline their offer.

But decline it he continues to do and finally, defeated, Hester climbs out of the car and helps him onto the pavement. With some distaste, he hands her the anorak, already impregnated with the faint whiff of his inimitable odour. She holds it between thumb and forefinger, as far away from her own clothes as she can manage without her purpose being too obvious.

'There is one service you might render me,' says Finbar, peering over her shoulder at the shelter. 'I would not be averse to some of your delicious comestibles, the next time you happen to be passing.'

'Of course!' says Hester, weak with relief at their narrow escape and only too delighted at the opportunity to ease her still-pricking conscience. 'I shall set to the minute we get home. Anything in particular?'

'Oh,' says Finbar magnanimously, 'I leave that entirely to you, dear lady. You know my tastes: exacting but catholic.'

Exacting! sniffs Hester inwardly, thinking of his frequent scavenging raids around the village. But she smiles and, with a wave, hurriedly climbs back into the car, tossing the anorak into the back seat. It will need to go straight in the wash.

Harriet watches in the rear-view mirror as Finbar dodges through a gap in the traffic to reach the other side of the road.

'Well,' she says, 'we tried.'

'Couldn't have done more,' agrees Hester.

'I mean,' says Harriet, turning the key in the ignition, 'we couldn't exactly force him, could we?'

Thus comforted, she makes a valiant attempt to find first gear, as a huge tractor lumbers by followed by a significant tailback. There is a sudden blast on a horn that makes them both jump and, seconds later, Finbar's face appears in Harriet's side window, while behind him a passing motorist lowers his nearside window and hurls invective at him, presumably for running out into the road in front of his car. Finbar, oblivious to his narrow escape, is mouthing something and gesturing down the road.

'Hang on! Hang on a minute.' Harriet fumbles to find the window control. As the glass slides down she is rewarded with a lavish blast of Finbar's pungent breath. 'What?' She is imagining some further incursions into his hovel.

'It's him!' yells Finbar, pointing after the tractor. 'Quick! We must follow him.' He yanks open Harriet's door, narrowly missing contact with a passing car. The woman driver looks daggers at them.

'The tractor?' says Harriet, as Finbar takes hold of her elbow, ostensibly to help her out.

'Not the tractor!' retorts Finbar irascibly. 'Do hurry or we'll lose him.'

It takes a good thirty seconds for Finbar to resume his seat and for Harriet to insinuate the little car into the stream of traffic in pursuit of their quarry.

'Recognised the van,' says Finbar triumphantly, fumbling

to fasten his seatbelt. 'Couldn't see the chap, but the van had a dint in the bumper—as, I seem to recall, does your car.'

'It does indeed,' says Hester. 'Harriet had an argument with a concrete post a month or so back.'

'I was wearing my other glasses!' says Harriet hotly. 'Ignore her, Finbar. Go on.'

'And then I saw the number plate and—extraordinary how these things strike you—I remembered—it must be subliminal, mustn't it, because it all happened so quickly—that you could make *syphilitic* from the letters—SYT, you see? No idea about the numbers.'

Harriet bites her tongue with difficulty. 'This is the man who attacked you? You're sure?'

'Yes! Can't you drive any faster? He could be miles away by now.'

The traffic is still crawling along behind the tractor that they can just about see in the distance. From time to time, impatient drivers risk the oncoming traffic and squeeze past. Finbar dodges irritably from side to side in his seat, trying to keep the van in sight as the line of cars weaves around the bends in the road. The tractor breasts the hill in the distance and disappears for several seconds.

'Hurry! Hurry!' yells Finbar. 'Honestly, we'd be quicker walking.'

'I'm going as fast as I can,' snaps Harriet, who hates this sort of stop-start driving that requires all her concentration and plays havoc with her creaky ankles.

'Can't you overtake or something?' fumes Finbar in her ear.

She does not deign to reply.

The tractor comes back into view and, behind it, a logjam of other vehicles. Finbar bangs the back of Harriet's seat with frustration. 'Damnation, now he's disappeared!'

'He must have turned off the road,' says Hester, keeping an anxious eye on the driver. It doesn't do to distract Harriet, especially when the roads are so busy. 'There's a lane off to the right. Single track. We'll try that.'

They inch forward painfully slowly for several minutes, through which Finbar keeps up a constant litany of complaints and exhortations until Hester has to ask him none too politely to shut up. Finally they reach the turning to the lane. Harriet signals and swings across the road in the path of a bus coming the other way; the echo of its furious horn pursues them as they accelerate down the narrow high-hedged byway.

'Harry . . .' murmurs Hester nervously, as they approach a sharp bend. 'Please slow down.' There is no possibility of seeing any approaching traffic in a winding road canopied with low-hanging trees.

Harriet irritably stamps on the brakes, jolting them all forward.

'Steady on!' complains Finbar, easing the seatbelt out of its housing. 'This contraption nearly cut me in two.'

'I thought we were in a hurry.' The effects of Harriet's coffee have worn off, she's regretting not challenging Hester over the flapjack and she thinks the likelihood of catching up with the van after all this time is remote in the extreme.

They reach a T-junction giving on to a slightly bigger road, Hester silently offering up a prayer of thanks that they had encountered no other vehicles in the lane.

Harriet pauses, staring mulishly ahead, awaiting instructions. A motorbike zooms past in front of them, followed more sedately by an Ocado van. Hester and Finbar peer up and down the new road. They make their decisions and voice them simultaneously.

'Left,' says Hester.

'Right,' says Finbar.

CHAPTER 24

Having deposited one extremely disgruntled passenger back at the bus shelter after the abortive car chase, they eventually set off for home. As they pull away, Finbar is still carping about Harriet's driving.

'Really!' she explodes when they are out of earshot. 'Who does he think I am? Stirling Moss? I drove as fast as I could.'

Hester, still thanking her lucky stars that they survived the ordeal in one piece, tries to placate her. 'I thought you did splendidly, Harry, under very difficult circumstances.' Harriet had fumed silently as, at their bidding, she had driven first left for a couple of miles, then retraced their route and searched the road in the opposite direction, until finally they met the back road into Pellington, whereupon the tired and ill-tempered trio agreed to abandon the mission. They had passed innumerable farm gates, a handful of cottages, two grain silos and several enormous barns, but not a single human being and certainly not a mud-spattered black or dark blue van (Finbar isn't quite sure) with a dented rear bumper. Hester knows that much of her sister's uncharacteristic rancour can be attributed to hunger. She'll sort out some lunch the minute they get in and send the boy off to deliver Finbar some provisions. She toys briefly with the idea of a carbonara, discounts it on the grounds of time, and decides to make omelettes instead. Finish up those leftover mushrooms, throw in the remaining ham . . .

'. . . to the police,' Harriet is saying gloomily. 'Or whoever. Personally, I could do with putting my feet up for half an hour.'

'Sorry? What was that about the police? Because of Finbar, you mean?' Hester tries to catch hold of the thread of Harriet's mutterings.

'No!' Harriet sounds tetchier than ever; perhaps it's her blood sugar. 'Daria! I was just saying, we've still her to sort out. It's never-ending!'

⌣⌣⌣

Ben is up when they arrive home, looking greyer than the greyest February day. Hester attributes this to him still being in a sulk from the night before; Harriet knows different but has no intention of enlightening her. He's sitting at the kitchen table, listlessly turning his phone over and over in his hand. Not even Milo's valiant attempts to catch his attention are lifting his mood.

The baby starts grizzling and wriggling in the car seat that Daria has placed on the kitchen floor in the corner while she finishes the ironing. The sisters have given up trying to persuade her not to bother. Harriet gets down on hands and knees to distract him, relieved to note there's no sign of fever on his pale, cool skin. Soon his head nestles deeper into the padding of the car seat; his eyelids flutter. Hester is busy rustling up some lunch. They have agreed in the car that Harriet will be the one to broach the subject of Daria's future.

Taking a deep breath, Harriet levers herself to her feet. 'Daria, we've talked things through, Hester and I, and we've decided the time has come for you to go to the police. We'll take you this afternoon. Straight after lunch. We dare not leave it any longer.'

They are expecting resistance, tears even. But Daria simply pauses in her ironing and then nods solemnly before resuming her task. It's Ben who protests.

'Go to the police? No way! Are you off your rocker?' he shouts, finally roused from his torpor.

'Ben!' growls Hester. 'Enough! Keep out of this. It's none of your—'

'Go to the police and it'll be Daria and Milo in one of them detention places. Or on the next flight out.'

'No, Ben, listen—' starts Daria, putting the iron down.

'You don't know what you're talking about,' Hester barks at Ben. 'Apart from anything else, if it came to it, being in protective custody is probably the safest place for her right now.'

'How'd you work that out? She's got her passport now and that Sampson bloke is off her back—'

'Yes, and someone—probably this Scott creature—is still after her,' shouts Hester before she can stop herself. 'She's still in danger.'

The colour drains from Daria's face. Harriet silently curses her sister.

'Scott is . . . he is . . .?' whispers Daria.

Hester nods, furious with herself. Damn and blast the boy, the cat's well and truly out of the bag now.

'But why?' demands Ben. 'Why's he after Dar?'

'We don't know,' says Hester. 'It's the reason poor old Finbar ended up in hospital, though—well, one of the reasons. We hoped you might have some idea why he's so desperate to find you, Daria.'

'No . . . I . . . Tina, yes, I see this, she is friend, but him . . .' The girl blushes violently, drops her eyes.

'Daria?' Hester's senses are on high alert. She flicks a glance at Harriet, sees that she too has picked up the scent. 'Daria, what is it?'

'The night I leave . . .' Daria stumbles over the words. 'Before, earlier, I hear shouting. Downstairs. I hear my name. Tina is crying, *No, please*. She say Milo's name. Is crying. Scott is . . . he is . . .'—she mimes drinking—'shouting, shouting . . .'

'Shouting what?' says Harriet.

'I do not know. But they shout about me, I think.' She turns dark eyes towards them. 'I do not know why. I go to bed. Then Tina comes to the room when house is quiet . . .'

Harriet decides there's nothing to be gained by keeping Daria in the dark any longer. 'The truth is, we're worried he may be violent. He assaulted Finbar, but we didn't tell you last night about Tina's black eye.' She gestures at her own in case Daria is confused.

Daria's hand flies to her mouth. She spits out a word of unintelligible but unequivocal invective. 'He is animal!'

'Scott?'

'*Tak*. She is afraid of him, Tina, I think. He hit her. Push, hit.' She slaps one hand onto the heel of the other, stinging the air; the women recoil at the violence. 'I never see. But I hear.'

'Did he ever hit you, Daria? Touch you?'

'Me? No. He only . . .' She flaps her hands, trying to summon the word.

'Threatened?' suggests Harriet.

'Threatened, yes. No . . . wrong word. Make worried.'

'And Milo?'

'No, no! With baby, he is . . . okay. Only he doesn't like crying. You think I would stay, he do that?!'

'But you told us—told Ben—that they were both kind to you.'

'Tina, yes, always, very kind. But him, only at first. But then he change, everything change.'

'When?'

'Just before . . .' She looks away, thinking, calculating. She remembers. 'He is angry because I am going outside. A little walk only. The sun is shining. I am wanting to feel it, yes? After so long. Is cold, but . . .' She shrugs. 'I hear voices.'

'Voices? Where?'

Daria shakes her head, waves a hand vaguely. 'Behind trees. I think, we go just a little more, Milo and me. But then Scott see me, he is running, shouting and'—she indicates someone grabbing her arm—'he pull me away. Take me back to house. Very angry.'

'And this was just before Tina drove you away that night?'

Daria nods, face creased with confusion. 'A day, I think, or two.'

The conversation dies as everyone digests the information and its implications.

Harriet is in knots. There's a question she needs to ask. But Hester beats her to it.

'Daria, I'm sorry to ask this, but . . . did you take something when you left? Something that didn't belong to you? From the farm? From Scott and Tina?'

'Oi!' says Ben, indignant on Daria's behalf.

Hester ignores him, keeping her eyes trained on the girl's face.

'You mean . . . do I steal?' The words come out barely above a whisper.

Hester shrugs neutrally.

Daria flushes. 'No! What I am stealing? What I am bringing to your house? Huh? Something hidden? How? I have nothing! Not even for Milo!'

'All right, all right,' soothes Harriet. 'We didn't mean to upset you.'

Ben snorts with derision.

'But, my dear, he's going to great lengths—' Daria frowns, perplexed, so she rephrases. 'He's clearly desperate to find you. He must have a very good reason to be looking for you.'

Daria spreads her hands. 'I don't know! I tell you everything. Only him and Tina I see.'

'In all that time? Really?'

'People come, but always I am sent upstairs. I hear them, but . . .'

'What about outside the house?'

Daria looks askance. 'Outside? No. Like I tell you, only once I am leaving. All the time they are saying, Scott and Tina, stay in house, better no-one know you are here, for my . . . to be safe. You see?'

Very clever, thinks Hester. *Keep the poor child imprisoned while pretending it's for her own good. But then what changed on Christmas Eve?* Catching Harriet's eye she signals: *Let's leave it for now.*

She goes back to the counter and reaches for the carton of eggs. 'Sorry, Daria. We're just trying to—'

'Of course.' Daria comes to her side and empties the water from the iron into the sink. 'I have trust, Hester.'

Humbled, touched, Hester gives the girl's arm a comforting squeeze. 'We're only trying to do what's best for you and Milo.'

'No, you're not,' interrupts Ben angrily, getting up from the table, chair skidding across the tiles. 'You're trying to do what's best for you. The minute things get a bit difficult, you throw them out!'

'We are not throwing them out! How dare you? There's only one person who is going to be thrown out of this house—'

'Hetty!'

'I will not have this . . . child . . . accusing us—'

'I'm not a child!'

'—of not doing our duty by Daria and Milo. Our sole concern is their wellbeing!'

'Yeah, right!'

'Ben dear,' says Harriet, weak with hunger and alarmed at how swiftly the conversation has degenerated into animosity, 'we all know how fond you are of Daria and Milo, but the situation is extremely complicated—no, don't interrupt, just listen for a moment. Your aunt and I have been trying our best to find out what we can do to ensure Daria can stay in England and we think we have the answer.'

Ben's mulishness transmutes into a wary scepticism. 'Yeah?'

Hester, still smarting, snaps, 'I don't see why it's any of his business.'

Harriet keeps her eyes on Ben and continues. 'As we told Daria last night, we've spoken to a lawyer and asked him about her rights, and he has informed us —that she almost certainly has the right to remain in the UK.'

'Oh . . . yeah?' Ben's features start to relax as he digests this. 'Right, well . . .'

'However—'

'Oh God,' Ben groans. 'Here we go.'

'It's complicated. But,' Harriet emphasises firmly, 'on two counts we believe we ought to—indeed, must—go to the authorities and explain about Daria's expired visa. First, because it would look better if she volunteers that information herself, so that the situation can be regularised. And second, because—well, frankly, we're still extremely concerned about her safety. Aren't we, Hetty?' She turns to her still-rankled sister for corroboration.

For a moment it looks as if Hester won't reply, but then she says huffily, 'We are,' all the while skewering Ben with a most thunderous look that falls unnoticed on his averted head.

He, meantime, is starting to regret his presumptions and, worse, presumptuousness. Mottled skin aflame, he shifts uncomfortably from foot to foot, raking the coals of his disgrace for any mitigation. Unable to meet Hester's eyes, he blurts out to Harriet, 'I was only, like, worried, you know?'

'We're all worried, Ben,' she says gently, to be rewarded with a slight, apologetic nod.

He manages to mutter a barely audible, 'Sorry.'

'Well, I'm glad we've cleared that up,' says Harriet robustly, tension trickling away, although her back is aching ferociously. 'How are those omelettes coming, Hetty? I, for one, am starving. Shall we slice some bread?'

Ben, glad to escape Hester's malign force field, rushes over to the bread bin.

Harriet watches Daria cautiously lift a sleeping Milo out of the car seat. 'Are you taking him up for a nap? Okay. I suggest we go into town immediately he wakes.'

Ben, sawing extravagant slices off the loaf, waits until Daria leaves the kitchen, then leans over to Harriet to say quietly, 'I could look after him when you go. You won't want a baby there, will you? Not at a police station.'

'On the contrary,' says Harriet, 'I think having Milo with us would be an excellent gambit. He corroborates Daria's story.'

Hester, whisking the eggs and milk into a froth, nods in agreement.

'Tell you what, then'—Ben plonks the bread onto a plate—'why don't I Google a bit after lunch and see what else I can find out? You know, about immigration and that.'

Even Hester has to admit this is a good idea. She drops a knob of butter into the omelette pan; Ben sidles over cautiously to observe.

'Anything I can do?' He is as eager as a puppy for a treat.

Hetty, pleads Harriet silently, *give the boy a chance. Just this once.*

Hester, almost as if she has read her sister's thoughts, bestows her widest smile on her nephew. 'Indeed there is, Ben.'

'Great!'

'You can make Finbar two rounds of cheese and tomato sandwiches and run them down to him immediately.'

'No, I meant—'

'Quick as you like.'

⌣⌣⌣

Normally, nothing is more likely to engender a sense of well-being and harmony in Hester's breast than the sight of people tucking into well-cooked food, especially if she has been its creator. But here she sits in the warm kitchen, watching everyone greedily devouring her feather-light omelettes, with a distinct feeling of apprehension. Ben had fulfilled his task in double-quick time, reported Finbar to be proper vexed at having to wait so long for so little—'Is this truly the best Hester could manage, boy?'—and jogged back just in time to call Daria down for lunch.

The unease Hester is experiencing centres mainly on their forthcoming trip to the police station, where everything will at a stroke be taken out of their hands (and she remains fearful, pessimist that she is, that they or Henry have overlooked some fundamental flaw that may scupper Daria's chances), but is compounded by anxiety over the sinister Scott's motives. She feels they are blundering about in the dark, ignorant as they are of his intent. As if these two worries were not enough to unsettle her, she is further troubled by an all-pervading sense of guilt at the hope—indeed, likelihood—that within hours this entire affair may be at an end. Sympathetic as she is to the Yushkevich family, eager as she had been to help a mother and child in distress, the past few days have taken their toll. She can barely believe that this whole extraordinary sequence of events only began six days before: it feels as though they have been living in a state of heightened emotion and intermittent fear for weeks. And it is exhausting. Her nights, once hours of blissful unconsciousness, are now peopled with shadowy figures, with blurred faces that resist definition, with shades of nameless dread. Her fall, that inexplicable sensation of something hovering on the margins of her memory begging to be revealed, has spooked her more than she is prepared to admit, even to herself. All she knows is that she badly wants a return to the life that she and Harriet had carved out for them- selves and loved: the comfortable routine, the companionable silences, the familiar sameness of every day unfolding like the last. The house to themselves again.

She knows that, given their guests' various ordeals and suffering—even Ben's familial upheavals—her desire for solitude is selfish. She knows she ought to be ashamed of herself. And she is. But it doesn't stop the thoughts whirling around her mind incessantly, like a washing machine on permanent spin.

Across the table, Harriet is watching her sister. *Why won't she look at me?* she wonders. *She must be as worried as I am*

*about this afternoon. Suppose we've got it all horribly wrong?
Suppose they don't believe us? What if they arrest Daria? And
Peter Sampson? Even—heaven forfend—us? Honest to God, I'm
beginning to wish we'd never stopped at the damned bus shelter!
Someone else was bound to have helped them. Trust us to poke
our noses in. I can't wait for things to get back to normal.* The
import of her ruminations hits her suddenly. Shocked, she
gives herself a metaphorical slap. *Harriet Pearson! Call yourself
a socialist? You are a self-centred, wicked woman! How can
you be so solipsistic? Look at that poor girl, think of that tiny,
defenceless baby upstairs sleeping in a drawer . . .!*

Hungers assuaged, Hester orders everyone out of the kitchen.
They duly disperse: Ben to the computer, Daria for a nap and
Harriet into the sitting room with a cup of tea and, unbe-
known to Hester, a couple of Hobnobs. Hester swiftly stacks
the dirty crockery and cutlery in the dishwasher and then
retrieves Ben's suggestions for the New Year's Eve gathering.
Planning the menu is as good a way as any to keep her most
uncomfortable thoughts at bay. She starts to make a list.

Ten minutes later, she goes to pop her head into the sitting
room but stops in the hall as the familiar trumpet of Harriet's
snores rends the silence. Smiling, she reaches for her coat, hat,
scarf and bag and silently slips out.

CHAPTER 25

'Hello, Molly.'

Molly Wilson spins around from the boot of her sports car, into which she is delving, and straightens up. Swaying slightly on her spiky-heeled boots, she blinks several times before she can focus. 'Oh, hello, er . . .'

Hester helps her out. 'Hester.'

''Course. 'Course it is. Sorry. Terrible memory for . . . how are you anyway?'

Dear God, Hester thinks, *has she driven in this state?* It's a mercy the traffic has thinned considerably since the morning. 'I'm fine,' she says aloud. 'Just doing a bit of . . .' Hester waves a vague hand in the direction of the village store, managing to swallow a reference to Christmas just in time.

Molly just stares, frowning.

Hester plucks a topic from nowhere to break the awkward silence. 'Lucky, aren't we?'

'Lucky?' repeats Molly, baffled.

'I mean, having such a brilliant shop so close to home. Deli counter. Post office. Endangered species.'

'Say that again!'

Hester doubts Molly could.

'Plus'—Molly holds up one chipped scarlet talon rather unsteadily—'drycleaner. Brilliant! On the doorstop—door*step*.' She starts to giggle feebly, loses interest. 'Could never park in town, could you? Right pain in the jacksie, pardon my French. 'Stead, bring it here and Bob's your proverbial. Love it. Don't you?'

Hester, who can't recall having anything dry-cleaned since she retired, murmurs agreement. A sudden *whop-whop* makes them both look skywards as a helicopter passes overhead.

'Noisy bugger,' shouts Molly up at the sky, before turning back to the boot and starting to haul out assorted dresses and jackets, several of which end up on the tarmac. She seems oblivious, indeed catches her heel in one of them, staggering alarmingly as she regains her balance.

'Here, let me.' Hester bends down automatically to retrieve the garments, only to find her wrist grasped fiercely by an outraged Molly, who spits in her face, 'I can manage!'

'Sorry.' Hester rubs her wrist, rattled.

In an instant, Molly's face dissolves, eyes filling. 'God. God. God. I'm so sorry, er ... Don't know what ...' Her eyelashes are clogged with mascara; this close, Hester notices her roots need touching up. She looks terrible, as though she's only just managing to hold everything together.

'It's okay. You sure you wouldn't like me to ...' Hester gestures at the boot's remaining contents: two winter coats and a suede jacket.

Molly's face is still contorted with anguish. 'I didn't mean . . .'

'No, no, forget it. I'll get them.'

'Been on these tablets. Make me a bit . . . sorry. Thanks so much, er . . .'

'Hester.'

'Yeah, that's it.' Molly staggers across the pavement, shoulders the door of the shop open and disappears inside.

Hoicking her bag back onto her shoulder, Hester lifts out the remaining garments, almost dropping a Burberry scarf caught between the coats. She drags it out, noticing the discreet monogram EBW, and hesitates. It's clearly Teddy's and presumably there by accident. Leave it or take it? She opts for the latter—whatever the current state of the Wilson marriage, it's a beautiful scarf and deserves to be looked after. Shoving it on the top of her load just under her chin, she hugs the garments to her chest, anchoring them with her chin, and goes to follow Molly. Slows. Freezes. A door, ajar until now in her mind, swings open. Memory floods back like a returning tide as she inhales again. She rushes through the shop door, dodging in front of another customer with a stammer of apology, flings the clothes onto the counter in front of the astonished owner and bolts.

Molly shouts at her retreating back, 'Thanks, er . . .'

⌣⌣⌣

'Hetty! No!' Harriet's eyes are wide with shock and disbelief. She still looks half asleep, the mug of tea beside her cold and untouched.

'I swear, Harry.' Hester is red-faced and feeling distinctly damp under the armpits after her headlong rush home. 'Come on!' She seizes her sister's elbow and tries to drag her from her chair, which reignites the pain in her shoulder. It outrages her afresh now she knows whom to blame.

'Aftershave?' says Harriet, allowing herself to be pulled to her feet. 'Is that it?'

'Listen,' says Hester with some asperity, 'there was something I've been trying to remember ever since it happened. I couldn't get a hold of it. Now I know why. It wasn't something I'd seen or heard. It was a *smell*. And he's always worn that aftershave. It's unmistakable.'

'Teddy?' Harriet shakes her head. 'Oh, Hetty, I can't believe it.'

'Well, that's a bit rich—you've never had a good word to say for him.'

'No, but . . . attacking you? Teddy Wilson? Breaking in here? He may be a bit fly, but—'

'A bit! Who knows what he's caught up in? Peggy's always saying how close he sails to the wind.'

'But Peggy doesn't like him!'

Hester has managed to get Harriet as far as the hall now. She shoves a coat at her. Instinctively they glance upwards and lower their voices.

'Neither do you,' hisses Hester, 'but now you're defending him!' She begins to manhandle Harriet into the coat.

'I'm simply saying—'

'Listen! You want proof?' Hester starts counting off on her fingers. 'One, all that nonsense at the train station. Two, he tries to send us off to some petrol station miles away to buy himself

317

some time. Three, he rings up that same night—presumably to check how I was or, more likely, to check that I hadn't cottoned on. Four, Peggy says he's been driving around the area aimlessly—'

'New car,' interjects Harriet. 'Just showing off.'

'Five, it was his aftershave on that scarf. That man is involved in this one way or another. Now, are you going to drive me over there or do I have to walk?'

⌣⌣⌣

Harriet is struggling to come to terms with Hester's revelation. Her discombobulation unfortunately manifests itself in her driving; twice Hester has to shout out warnings about other motorists, one attempting to overtake as their car drifts towards the centre line and another pulling out without warning from a row of parked cars. Once again Harriet silently works through Hester's reasoning: it's beginning to hold water, incredible as the initial accusation had seemed. Yes, he had looked shifty each time they'd met; yes, he had seemed unusually interested in Hester's wellbeing; yes, he does have a certain reputation— and then there's his sudden interest in Finbar . . . But what if he simply denies it? Their proof, such as it is, is pure conjecture and rests on something that can't be set down, touched or produced in a court of law: it rests entirely on Hester's sense of smell. Harriet would be the first to agree that it is particularly acute, indeed exceptional; Hester is rarely mistaken when trying to identify herbs and spices in an unfamiliar dish. But aftershave?

'He'll just deny it,' she says to Hester, swerving around an elderly cyclist wobbling up the hill. 'What then?'

'Let's confront him with it first of all,' says Hester, her aching shoulder a reminder of the injury she is convinced Teddy Wilson visited upon her. She glances in the wing mirror to ensure the cyclist is still in one piece.

'But I still don't see—'

'Neither do I. But let's hope we're about to find out.'

Harriet unconsciously touches the brakes as a thought strikes, jerking them both forward. 'You don't think he might be . . .'

'What?' Hester eases out her vice-like seatbelt.

'. . . dangerous?'

'Teddy? Hardly!'

Why not, thinks Harriet, *if he's in cahoots with the likes of Scott or someone of his ilk?* 'And don't forget we still have to take Daria—'

'I know! I know!' They drive the rest of the way in silence.

CHAPTER 26

'Where is he?'

Hester had had no compunction about opening the unlocked front door and stepping into the Wilsons' hall. The tiled floor is littered with what looks at first glance like fragments of paper; bending over to peer more closely, she makes out scraps of fabric, that on even closer inspection prove to be remnants of cashmere with a distinctive checked pattern, meticulously chopped into tiny squares.

Harriet looks puzzled.

'Teddy's scarf.'

'Ah.'

Through the double glass doors giving on to an enormous lounge, they see Molly sprawled on a huge sofa, several bottles and a glass by her side, a pair of dressmaking shears abandoned on the carpet. Mascara is smeared around her eyes and there's a gash of lipstick across her left cheek. She is snoring stertorously, a thin rivulet of saliva snaking its way down her chin onto her blouse. Her left foot still sports a boot, its fellow abandoned in the middle of the hall.

'Molly! Wake up!'

Molly shrinks back into the cushions as the sisters loom over her. She manages to open one cautious eye, then, taking in the two faces glaring down at her, snaps it shut almost immediately. An exasperated Hester yells her name into her ear. Molly flinches, raising a shaking hand to her head.

'Where is Teddy? Where is he?' bellows Hester.

Molly's hand creeps out blindly towards her glass, only for it to be snatched away by Harriet. The hand flails around for a few seconds, then Molly's eyes inch open, finally focus on the distant glass and, realising the intruders' intent, begin to fill with tears. She squints up at her tormentors pathetically.

Harriet holds the Dubonnet just out of reach. 'Where is Teddy?' she enunciates as though to a child.

Molly moans piteously.

'Molly! Concentrate! Tell us where Teddy is and then you can have your drink back.'

Molly struggles up, hand outstretched, head wobbling like a toy dog on the back shelf of a car. 'Dunno. Don't care. Bastard.' She flops back onto the sofa, limp as a rag doll.

'Molly, for heaven's sake. We need to find him—urgently. Where's he gone?'

Molly tries a dismissive flap of her hand, succeeding only in knocking over a pile of glossy magazines on the table beside her. 'I don't know! Out? In bed? With *her*, the little tart?' Presumably she's referring to her husband's latest paramour, although anyone less like a tart than Mrs Vicar—unless she is leading an extremely well-disguised double life and is wont to shed her inhibitions along with her dun-coloured cardigans—is hard to imagine. It is, of course, more than probable, given Mrs Vicar's habitual haunts, that Molly has never laid eyes on her and has assumed her to conform to Teddy's usual conquests: long of leg, generous of bust but often less well-endowed in the brains department.

'No,' says Hester, trying to keep her temper in check. 'His car's in the drive.'

'Oh . . .' says Molly, as though that's the last place she'd expect to find a car. 'What about . . . garage?' Desperately she licks her lips with a tongue that seems to have a life of its own. 'Studi . . .' She has another go. 'Studio?'

'Where's that?' Hester is already striding back into the hall from which innumerable rooms radiate.

'No, no, no . . .' manages Molly, one finger raised in admonition. 'Not house. Garden.' She falls back onto the cushions, exhausted, eyelids fluttering like trapped birds. Harriet settles the glass into her hands to discover that their reluctant hostess yet has sufficient energy to raise it to her lips and upend it. A dribble of viscous liquid like blood meanders down her chin and drips onto her expensive but heavily-creased and, frankly, rather grubby silk shirt. In seconds she's asleep again, snoring lightly, lashes glistening with unshed tears.

Harriet feels an unexpected rush of pity. 'You check the garage,' she says. 'I'll try and locate this studio.' As Hester makes for the front door, Harriet hurries down the hall to the end, through the vast kitchen and out onto the patio through heavy sliding doors. A beautifully-manicured garden stretches into the distance, with clusters of tables and chairs dotted in various shady spots. A water feature tinkles in the centre of the lawn. Beyond the grass, she spies the eaves of a roof through the bare branches and sets off in that direction, cursing the gravel that signals her approach. If Teddy is holed up in there, he'll have plenty of warning. She tries to walk more lightly.

A sudden blast of music—Mahler? she wonders instinctively—makes her jump. At least it masks her footsteps. The music is definitely coming from the building she's spotted. She starts to creep forward again, a reluctant hunter. A hand falls on her shoulder and she stifles a scream.

'Anything?' breathes Hester in her ear. 'Nothing in the garage.'

'Hetty, you fool—you nearly gave me a heart attack!'

'Don't be melodramatic. Is that Mahler?'

'Think so. He must be in there.'

They start to move forward, one tall, one short, both aware of how ridiculous they must look tiptoeing down a gravel path like comedy robbers. The studio comes into view and, through a window, the top of Teddy Wilson's head. They inch forward, Hester inevitably having the more panoramic view.

'Oh God!' she hisses, stopping abruptly and blocking Harriet's progress with her arm.

'What? What?' Harriet cranes her neck but to no avail.

'He's got a gun,' whispers Hester, eyes fixed on the window.

'A gun!' gasps Harriet. 'You don't think . . .?'

Hester raises a finger to her lips and then, without warning, leaps forward, racing the last few steps to the building, wrenching open the door and disappearing inside. There are muffled shouts, the sound of a scuffle, while Harriet stands frozen with indecision on the path. The next instant Hester reappears with something in her hand that she hurls over Harriet's head. It whistles through the undergrowth. A loud bang augments a particularly thunderous section of the Mahler.

The sisters look at one another open-mouthed. Then Harriet gathers her wits and rushes up the path as Hester turns back inside. They fill the doorway, confronting Teddy Wilson, who is on the other side of his desk, struggling to his feet.

'Don't try anything!' Hester's voice has a strangled quality; the gun's discharge has just brought home the danger she was in. Her bruised shoulder throbs from flinging the weapon.

'What the ... what the fuck are you doing?' stammers Teddy, hair wild as they have never seen it, large bags under his eyes. He looks almost as ghastly as his wife.

'Shooting yourself isn't the answer,' barks Hester. 'Thank God we got to you in time.'

Teddy looks at her incredulously. '*Shooting* myself? I was cleaning it. It's my grandfather's old revolver.'

'Cleaning it!' scoffs Hester, regaining control. 'With a bullet in it?'

'Are you out of your tiny mind? It wasn't loaded!'

'Oh?' says Hester, with just a smidgeon less certainty, having just noticed the desk is littered with oily rags, tiny brushes and other cleaning materials. 'Then why did it go off?'

If anything Teddy looks even more astonished. 'It can't have gone off. I don't have any ammunition for it.'

The three of them stand for a moment in mutual confusion.

'Harriet,' says Hester in a studiedly calm tone, all the while keeping her eyes on Teddy, 'would you be good enough to go and have a look?'

Harriet, not altogether sure what she is looking for, backs out of the doorway then stops. 'Hetty . . .'

'Don't worry,' says her sister robustly. 'I'm quite safe.'

Partially reassured, Harriet scoots back down the path in search of the evidence. The gravel path splits in two just out of sight of the studio and she takes the right fork, emerging from the bushes to find a row of neglected cold frames colonised by weeds, the glass streaked with mildew. The one nearest to her sports a broken pane and there, cushioned on a bed of brambles, is an antique revolver, very similar to the old Webley her father kept in his desk drawer. She makes a half-hearted attempt to retrieve it, warily trying to insinuate her hand between the vicious-looking thorns, only to discover her arms are, in any event, too short to safely avoid the jagged spears of the shattered glass. Hurrying back, she finds Teddy and Hester exactly as she left them, Hester combatively guarding the exit and Teddy half sitting, half standing behind his desk. The Mahler surges on.

'Wasn't a bullet,' she pants, squeezing past Hester to switch off the CD player. The sudden silence is a shock. She sinks into an armchair with relief: that blasted corn on her little toe has started up again. 'Cold frame. Gun went through the glass. Just sounded like a shot.'

'I told you,' says Teddy, thumping back into his chair and almost visibly deflating. He looks *terrible*. As waxy as a church candle.

'You're going to tell us a darn sight more before we've finished,' growls Hester, flushing with the embarrassment of having overreacted. She's damned if she'll apologise. After all, if he *had* been intent on . . . 'Let's not waste any time,' she snaps. 'You know perfectly well why we're here.'

Harriet waits for bluster, indignation, accusations of trespass. None is forthcoming. He doesn't even question the accusing finger pointed directly at him. Instead, Teddy Wilson looks swiftly from one sister to another, instantly divining where his best chance of garnering sympathy lies.

'Hester, my dear, I've been a bloody fool.' Even in his misery, he can still deploy his customary—and usually irresistible—look from under lowered lashes. *Please help me*, it says. *You alone understand me.* It has worked, to Harriet's intense irritation and bafflement, times without number on countless women, Hester included, in the past. But today those imploring eyes not only fail to work their magic, they positively enrage both sisters. Four pebbles look back at him. He shrinks back in his chair, muttering feebly, 'A bloody fool.'

Well, thinks Hester, mentally scourging herself, *that makes two of us.* She feels an utter dolt—not just about the business with the revolver but for ever having found this dishevelled, sweaty man in front of her attractive. Her discomfiture is increased by the fact, galling in the extreme, that Harriet's long and unwavering mistrust of the man has been vindicated. 'Is that so?' is all she can muster, given Harriet's ominous silence. But she weights it with as much disdain as she can. It hits the mark. Teddy, face already sheened with sweat, seems to positively run with perspiration as the failure of his usual approach becomes clear. Damp patches bloom under his arms. The studio is fuggy with body odour—not quite up to Finbar levels, but unpleasant nonetheless. She impales him with an unforgiving eye.

'I never meant it to get this far ...' stammers Teddy, mopping at his brow with a soiled handkerchief. He tries another beseeching look.

'What exactly?' The voice of doom is Harriet's.

He waves a helpless hand. 'The girl ... the farm ... you,' he says, tragic face directed at Hester.

'Me?' she says indignantly, as though he is trying to implicate her in his folly.

'I didn't mean to hurt you, Hester. Truly I didn't.'

Does he think using her name will endear him to her? *Think again, buster,* she says inwardly with rising fury, as the last vestiges of affection drain away.

He rushes on. 'All I wanted to do was check out the house. Cottage. Where you live.' He's gabbling now. 'I could have rung ahead. Got someone else to go round. But I didn't.'

Are they supposed to thank him for his consideration?

'Once I realised it was you two after all.'

What is he talking about?

'At the station. All that crap about the baby seat. Should've thought of you two sooner. I mean, who else would be mad enough to get involved?'

Mad? Is he talking about them?

'Trouble was, I didn't know the lie of the land. Never been inside, you see. Your place, I mean. Was looking for evidence. Just needed to make sure. Wasn't going to touch her or hurt

her. Or the baby. Or you. Thought you were going for petrol.
I told you to go for petrol!'

Oh, so it's now their fault!

'I'd be in and out before you ... but you came back too
soon. I pushed the door closed—couldn't let you find me there.
I just wanted to be able to tell Scott I'd found the wretched girl,
so he'd get off my back. It's all his fault really.'

They glare at him as he gapes back at the pair of them for
all the world like a naughty schoolboy. *A big boy did it and ran
away*, thinks Harriet, hard as flint.

'Why is he after her? Scott?'

He looks at first as though he doesn't understand the
question, baulks, rallies. 'Because ... look, I was completely in
the dark at first, I swear it. Didn't know anything about what
he was up to. You must believe me!'

Hester and Harriet exchange exasperated looks. It's like
pulling teeth.

'If Veronica ever found out ... I couldn't bear it.' His eyes
swim. 'Oh God, Veronica. You do know about her?'

Oh, we know all about Veronica, Harriet wants to spit. *Yet
another poor deluded woman taken in by your so-called charm.*

'Yes,' says Hester through pursed lips. 'Of course we do.
Everybody does.'

His eyes widen in surprise.

'Do get on with it. What don't you want her to find out?'

'And as for these illegals ... well, I didn't know, did I? You
think I'd be party to something like that? Me?'

Harriet, never mind Hester, has had quite enough. She
explodes. 'For God's sake, just tell us what the hell has been

going on! Tell us why we found a poor chit of a girl hiding in a bus shelter on Christmas Day with a baby, both at grave risk of hypothermia, and why she's so frightened of this Scott person. Without,' she adds mercilessly, as he opens his mouth, 'any more self-justifying claptrap.' Finally, unnecessarily, she finishes, 'We're fast running out of patience.' She manages not to finish with, *you spineless excuse for a man.*

'Okay, okay.' Cowed. Defeated. 'Right.' He looks at the desk, at his hands, at the walls, anywhere but at them. 'So. A year or so back I leased the farm—you know, on the back road? Place behind the Verndales?—to this pair called Scott and Tina. In a bit of a tight spot. Word gets around. I needed the money. Molly has money but she never lets me—'

'Forget Molly!'

'Yes. Sorry. Right. A few weeks in, Scott asks if he might use the holiday complex. Says he'll pay a bit extra. I thought, well, why not? Things weren't going so brilliantly with the invest-ments—rather overreached myself in the good times, loans being called in and whatnot. You know how it is.' He risks a quick look at their faces; sees they don't know at all. Ploughs on. 'Wasn't going to turn down an extra spot of income. Well . . . more than a spot, if I'm honest. Quite a dollop. Wasn't going to argue though, was I? Didn't ask any questions. Can see there's activity, you know, just driving by from time to time—caravans appearing, a few poly-tunnels, odd bods in the distance, that sort of thing—but couldn't see evidence of much work on the land or any livestock. Still, he paid the rent on time. And I had other things on my plate to worry about. Molly being a right pain in—'

'Never mind Molly!'

'Okay! Well, matters came to a head. Some clients getting a bit . . . awkward, wanting repayments. Some of the people I deal with, they can be a bit . . . well, more than a bit . . . Anyway, I thought, I just need to weather this little storm and it'll come right. Realise a few assets. Decided I had to put the farm on the market. Thought I might be able to reach an accommodation with the tenants—I mean, they didn't look to have done much to the land. I wrote formally and Scott phones straightaway and asks if I could come over for a chat. I thought he wanted to talk timescales. I should have realised. Stupid. Should have been more careful.' He stops for a glug of water. (The sisters assume it's water; it might be vodka or gin.)

'I pitch up. Sorry, old boy, needs must and all that. Can we reach a deal on vacant possession? I mean, it's meant to be a minimum of twelve months' notice, but I thought perhaps a little inducement would do the trick . . . I said, it's not like you've got animals or crops to worry about. He laughed. Crops, he said, 'course I've got crops. I'm a bloody farmer. Come and see.'

Harriet's there ahead of Hester, but only just. 'The holiday complex . . . of course . . .'

He nods miserably. 'Smelt it the second we drew up. Cannabis. Industrial scale. Windows blacked out. Internal tents to concentrate the heat. Huge extractor fans. And these bods feeding, watering, harvesting the stuff, doing God knows what. A production line. Professional. Few more out in the fields—for appearances' sake, I guess. Scott saw the look on my face and said, *You can see why I'm not keen to vacate, Teddy old boy*. Only now he didn't sound so reasonable.'

'Cannabis?' says Hester with a hint of scorn, remembering a few tentative puffs at university that had done absolutely nothing for her—except lend her, or so she had hoped, a spurious coolness among her peers. It hadn't lasted. 'Weed? Not exactly *Breaking Bad*, is it?'

'Hetty! For heaven's sake, don't be flippant. Do you have any idea how strong this stuff is these days? And the money to be made from it? In fact, if you bothered to keep up to speed with these things, there was an article in the paper only last week—'

'All right!' Dear God, spare her one of Harriet's heated disquisitions on the drugs trade. 'I'm sorry. So'—she skewers Teddy with a look once more—'it never crossed your mind just to go straight to the police?'

'The police?! How could I? He had me over a barrel. *You really think they'll believe you knew nothing about it?* he says. *The amount I've been paying you? You're an accessory, Teddy old boy. I go down, so do you.* And then there was Veronica . . .'

'Don't tell me she's involved!' cries Hester.

'Of course she isn't!' snarls Teddy, realising too late that this is an unwise tone to adopt right now. 'I mean,' he says more quietly and deferentially, 'Hester, my dear, I simply couldn't bear to confess to her that I'd allowed myself to get caught up in something so . . .'

'Criminal?' says Harriet acidly.

'Immoral,' finishes Teddy.

If he wriggles once more and tries to evade responsibility, thinks Harriet, *I shall scream.*

'So . . .'

Here it comes again. The hangdog look with knobs on. Does he practise it in front of a mirror? It cuts ice with neither sister.

'What was I supposed to do when the girl disappeared? He made me help him!'

'Teddy,' says Harriet with dangerous calm, 'what we want to know—what we *still* want to know—is why Scott was after her in the first place. What on earth has Daria to do with all this?' *Please don't tell us she's involved . . .*

Teddy shakes his head wearily, all his bombast gone. 'He caught her snooping around the other day. She claimed she was just going for a walk—'

'She was!' exclaims Harriet, unable to stop herself.

Teddy shrugs. 'Whatever. He thought she might have seen something and decided she was more trouble than she was worth. Originally, she was brought in to work on the operation but then, of course, they found out she was pregnant. Tina persuaded him to let her stay and then of course the silly bitch—Tina, I mean—gets all broody and protective of them. So he tells her he's going to move them; next thing he knows they've disappeared. First off, he thought the girl had just scarpered but then Tina . . .' He hesitates; their imaginations fill in the details. 'Well, she . . . spills the beans.' He appeals to them. 'You see his problem? He couldn't risk her getting picked up, could he? He just wanted her out of the way.'

Hester's eyes widen, as do Harriet's, as the same thought strikes them.

'No!' protests Teddy, realising. 'Not like that! Jesus!'

'Well, we don't know, do we? A man like that. So much at stake. We know he can be violent.'

'He was just going to pass her on.' The words slip out, quick, obscene in their matter-of-factness. It takes them both a second or two to rally.

'*Pass her on?* What do you think she is: a parcel? A commodity?'

All that Daria has been through in the past week—the danger, the terror—simply because a lonely young mother, far from home and family, wanted to take her baby out into the winter sunshine for some fresh air . . .

He won't, can't, meet their eyes. Perhaps the heinousness, the monstrousness, of what he has been caught up in has finally hit home. The sisters wait, thunderstruck.

'These people . . .'

'These people?' Harriet hurls back at him. 'These *human beings*!'

'They come here, some of them, inside lorries, no passports, no—'

'And Scott and his like kindly offer them a job? And if they have passports in the first place, presumably he takes them'— she finger-quotes—'for safekeeping.'

Teddy nods miserably. 'I didn't know . . .'

'No.' Harriet is relentless. 'But you suspected. And you did nothing. And you'd have let that girl and her tiny baby be passed on to another . . . another bastard—sorry, Hetty, but what else are they?—for exploitation. Or was it only going to be Daria? Was something else lined up for the baby? New parents, perhaps? No questions asked, just a nice fat wad of cash?'

Outrage, disgust, disbelief fill the air. A muscle twitches in Teddy's cheek.

At length, he raises his despairing eyes to meet theirs. 'It's over, isn't it?'

What is he expecting? Pity? Sympathy?

'It most certainly is,' says Hester firmly. She listens for a second as a now-familiar sound passes over the studio; instinctively they all look up. Stepping back to the threshold, Hester scans the sky to see something high above the trees on course for Peggy's house and beyond. 'Well, all over bar the shouting, I'd say.'

Harriet looks at her, baffled; likewise Teddy. Hester points to the sky. 'Police helicopter.'

'Police?' gasps Teddy, the last remnants of colour draining away. 'What are they—why are they—'

'Thermal imaging,' Hester says with a confidence that suggests to the untutored ear an intimate knowledge of law-enforcement techniques. 'These places pump out huge amounts of heat. Pretty easy to spot from up above apparently. I'd say they're on to your chum, no question. Looks as if it's making straight for the farm.' She steps back into the studio and looks down on a shrunken, broken Teddy. 'My advice? Hand yourself in pretty sharpish, before they turn up on your doorstep.'

Teddy's flickering flame of hope gutters and dies. He nods in utter dejection. 'Oh God. You're right, I have to . . .' His eyes blur with tears.

Harriet, normally given to irrational welling up when someone else cries, finds herself curiously unmoved. If anything, her heart hardens even more. All she can think about is those poor unfortunates trapped in this awful web, exploited, enslaved, in a hostile foreign land; of terrorised Daria and her blameless son. She also spares a passing thought for wrecked Molly Wilson (surely no-one drinks those astonishing quantities of alcohol without some deep unhappiness: does she take refuge in the booze because Teddy is such a beast?) and even for mousy Mrs Vicar, the most recent and unlikely victim of Teddy's lechery, stupidity and greed.

It's almost as if she's articulated her thoughts, for Teddy says simultaneously, voice cracked with emotion, 'And what about Veronica?'

'You should have thought about that before,' snaps Hester the merciless.

'She'll be waiting for me. How can I explain . . .?'

'The longer you delay, the worse it will be for you.'

'Yes, yes . . . I know.' A thought occurs; his face brightens a fraction. 'I don't suppose . . .'

'No!' says Hester. 'Absolutely not!'

Harriet, on the other hand, thinks immediately: *Poor creature, it's not her fault she's fallen in love with a complete bounder. Well,* she corrects herself, *it is in a way, I suppose. But leading such a sheltered life, she won't have known about his reputation* . . . 'Hetty,' she murmurs.

'What?' barks Hester, still riding high on a wave of disgust.

Harriet wavers. This isn't the time to get into an argument with Hester about the innocence or otherwise of the vicar's wife and what consideration, if any, they might owe her. She backs off. 'Er . . . nothing. We ought to get back. See Daria. Reassure her. Take her to the . . .'

'Precisely,' agrees Hester crisply, eyes still firmly fixed on the crumpled form behind the desk. 'And you'—he might have been something she has scraped from the sole of her shoe—'I take it we can trust you to have sufficient conscience and common decency left to do the right thing? Before we speak to the police ourselves?'

Do the right thing! thinks Harriet in alarm. *Good heavens, it sounds like* . . . She remembers the gun. 'Contact the police immediately, she means,' she interjects quickly, for the avoidance of doubt, before hurrying after Hester, who is striding purposefully back towards the house. Faintly in the distance, but long since out of sight, the *whop-whop* of the helicopter disturbs the winter afternoon.

CHAPTER 27

They pull out of the Wilsons' drive in silence. Indeed, they haven't spoken since leaving the studio and retracing their steps into and through the house. Hester had stalked straight past the snoring Molly, still spread-eagled on the sofa, without a glance; Harriet had paused just long enough to check the woman was breathing normally and, for modesty's sake, pulled her ruckled skirt across her exposed and mottled thighs. She can't entirely suppress some pity for her, both for her immediate state and whatever unpleasantness she will endure once the extent of Teddy's crimes is exposed. Vaguely she recalls (or thinks she does) a son away at boarding school and her heart goes out to him too.

They pass Finbar's shelter: he's nowhere to be seen. Books lie in neat piles at one end of the bench. *They must get damp*, thinks Harriet. *He must get damp. His poor old bones!* The sky is now a piercing blue, its earlier clouds chased away by the strengthening wind. She glances over at Hester to remark on the weather and sees her sister plaiting her gloved fingers in agitation. *Oh dear, what's she worrying about now?*

'Did you believe him?' says Hester, face averted. 'Teddy?'

'About what?'

'Zebra crossing,' says Hester automatically.

'There's no-one about!'

'Still. I mean, about him not knowing what Scott was up to.'

'I want to,' says Harriet thoughtfully. 'Not because I hold any brief for Teddy, as you are well aware, but just because it's horrible to think that someone you know, however slightly, is involved in something so … so unspeakable. And I'm not talking about the drugs.'

'No.'

They both shiver at the thought of the men—they assume they're men, hope they are—holed up in some filthy room, locked away without hope, without any future.

'He will go to the police, won't he?' Hester blurts out suddenly. 'I mean, it's all very well issuing ultimatums, but now we know what we know, we really ought to go straight to the police ourselves.'

'We're going to the police anyway—with Daria. All you've done is given him the opportunity to get in ahead of the inevitable. I suppose it just might work in his favour. It would show at least a suspicion of remorse.' Personally, she thinks all it shows is that he's intent on saving his skin, or at least appearing in the best possible light when the sky falls in on his contemptible head.

Hester punches her fist into her hand, angry with the world, but most of all with herself. 'We should have waited to make sure he did it. Oh, damn and blast it! Damn and blast him!'

Harriet brings the car to a juddering halt as they wait to cross the oncoming traffic and turn into their lane. Hester, who knows next to nothing about driving but spends almost every journey with her sister in a state of heightened terror, is sure she ought to apply the handbrake, is about to suggest it, when Harriet continues, in an attempt to divert the conversation, 'The worst of it is, of course, that no matter what happens to Scott and co—not to mention Teddy—those poor people who've been exploited and mistreated will just be shipped back to where they came from. After all they've been thr—'

'Harry!' screeches Hester as Harriet, tired of waiting for the traffic to thin, accelerates suddenly into the tiniest of gaps and hurtles across the road. Hester waits for the inevitable blast of a horn behind them. She is not disappointed.

'Incidentally,' says Harriet coolly, not missing a beat—Hetty is such an old woman!—'how come you knew all about the police using infrared cameras?'

'I read the papers, Harry,' snips Hester, heart fluttering uncomfortably after their close shave. 'One has to keep up with current events, you know.'

'Touché,' Harriet says, laughing.

After a suitable pause, Hester joins in.

⌣⌣⌣

'Where you been?' yells Ben over the banister. 'I've found out all sorts about illegals and that. And what you should've done first off is—'

'In a minute!' Hester calls up. 'We're going to have a quick cup of tea and then take Daria to the police station. Is she awake?'

'Dunno. Been busy. Oh, someone rang.'

'Who?'

'Dunno. Bloke. Didn't leave his name. Just said: *Tell them I've done it.* Least I think that's what he said. He had a cold or whatever. First off, I thought he was blubbing.' Ben's head disappears.

Hester clutches Harriet's arm. 'Oh, thank God. Oh, Harry . . .'

'Hey, hey,' says Harriet, who has been just as worried about their culpability but hasn't wanted to add to Hester's distress. 'There. What did I say? It's done. Now, will you relax?'

'Sorry. Sorry. I just . . .' Hester puts her hand to her forehead. 'I don't think I'm cut out for this sort of thing. Phew. Right. Tea.'

She busies herself with kettle and mugs, while Harriet eases her feet out of her shoes and relieves the pressure on her throbbing corn. She leaves Hester to her own devices for a few minutes, knowing how much she will be regretting her flurry of panic, how much she hates to appear vulnerable.

Hester rattles around the kitchen for a few minutes until, equilibrium restored and eager to put her embarrassment behind her, she checks her watch and says in her normal businesslike voice, 'Actually, given the circs, we should maybe wait half an hour, Harry. We'll catch all the works traffic on the Stote bypass otherwise.' She doubts there will be that many people in at work during the holiday period but is longing for the chance to put her feet up for a few minutes. Running (or more accurately stumbling) back from the shop earlier was not the wisest of moves; her knees are starting to complain. *Must do more exercise*, she thinks, *and frankly it wouldn't do Harry any harm to get fitter. Shift a bit of that flab . . .* She looks over at her sister.

'Harry!

'What?' Harriet guiltily snatches her hand out of the biscuit barrel.

'Honestly!'

Ben ambles in, waving a piece of paper. He reaches automatically for a biscuit.

'Right!' says Hester crossly, grabbing the barrel and closing the lid. 'That's it. This is going away.'

'I've only had one!' complains Ben.

'That's one more than me,' mutters Harriet.

'You want more biscuits, you make them yourselves,' says Hester, shoving the barrel onto the highest shelf in the larder, one she knows Harriet cannot reach easily.

'Okay, I will,' retorts Ben mildly, cramming the entire biscuit into his mouth.

Harriet almost laughs at the look on Hester's face as her bluff is called. She waits for an explosion as her sister searches for a riposte. 'Well, mind you wash everything up afterwards,' is the feeble best she can manage.

'Anyway,' says Ben, thrusting the paper at her, 'I printed it all out. Better read it before you leave.' He goes to take down a mug, remembers something. 'Oh yeah, I forgot—Finbar called round.'

'When?'

''Bout half an hour ago? Proper teed off, he was.'

'With us?' Hester thinks with some shame of the inadequate sandwich she'd sent around; it was childish of her to punish him for his obduracy over coming home with them, especially given her reluctance to accommodate him in the first place.

'Nah. With someone who'd damaged a book or something. In a right huff. I ask you! A book! *Vandals*, he kept saying. *Wait till I get hold of them.* He was wearing some minging kecks, I tell you. Wanted you to give him a lift somewhere. Stomped off when I said you'd gone out.'

Harriet rolls her eyes at Hester: after all they've done for him. 'I hope he's not going to make a habit of this. Expecting us to pick up the pieces after him. Come on, Hetty, finish your tea; I think on second thoughts we should be on our way. I'd rather not be driving back in the dark.'

And if truth be told I'd rather not be driven by you in the dark, now you mention it. Hester is regretting for the hundredth time not learning to drive herself. Journeys with Harriet at night are even more hair-raising than those undertaken by day, given her propensity for leaving her headlights on full beam until being in turn blinded by the flashes of irritated motorists coming towards her.

'Better get a shift on then,' says Ben, peering out into the garden. 'Starting to get dark already.'

Hester swiftly knocks back the remainder of her tea and lurches to her feet. Her knees scream in protest, then her shoulder decides to join in too, albeit in a minor key. Thankfully neither Ben nor Harriet is looking in her direction; the last thing she needs is them fussing about her. A nice long bath when this ordeal is over—correction, a nice long bath with a nice big glass of wine—and she'll be right as rain.

'Nip up and tell Daria we're ready to leave, will you, Ben?' Is it her imagination or is he mumbling something about servants and dying as he slouches out? 'That boy!' she grumbles to Harriet, making for their coats in the hall.

Harriet chooses not to hear. Her stomach is churning with apprehension now they're so close to sealing Daria's fate. The sensible part of her brain knows they're doing the right thing; emotionally, she's worried sick as to what the consequences might be: Daria and Milo spirited away, incarcerated . . . *Stop it! We don't have a choice.*

Ben crashes down the stairs and throws open the sitting-room door. He scans the room, then turns to face his aunts, bewildered. 'I can't find them.'

They're both still shaky, Harriet sitting on the stairs, Hester supporting herself on the newel post. Ben's been around the house again, looked in every room, searched the garden and been outside to check the lane. There's no trace of either of them. Milo's coat is missing from its hook, as is Daria's— strictly Molly's—brown sheepskin. Both of them are trying to push away the possibility that Daria, terrified about their imminent trip to the police, has fled; neither of them wants to put that thought into words. *How could she be so stupid . . .*

'The fridge!' Under Ben and Hester's mystified gaze, Harriet hauls herself up from her seat on the stairs, hurries into the kitchen and tugs the fridge door open. The half-empty bottle of antibiotics is still on the shelf. Is that a good sign? Surely Daria wouldn't leave without it? Unless . . . She tears back into the hall.

'Scott. It's Scott. Got to be.' She grabs Hester's arm, remembers her injury too late, as her sister winces. 'Sorry . . .'

'What?' Hester knows full well what Harriet is thinking, has been thinking it herself for the past few minutes as the only other explanation.

'Scott?' says Ben. 'Bloke from the farm?'

'He wouldn't have told him, would he? Teddy?'

'Teddy?' says Ben, even more lost. 'Bloke with the Jag?'

Harriet rounds on him, desperate. 'Did you hear anything while you were on the computer? A car? Voices? Think!'

Ben shakes his head. 'Had my 'phones on, didn't I? Who's this—'

'Phones?'

'Headphones. Earphones. You know.'

They are consumed with anxiety, terror crawling down their backs. If Scott's got them, who knows where they'll be by now? How panic-stricken Daria must be. If only they hadn't rushed off to confront Teddy. If only they'd gone to the station straight after lunch. If only, if only. Guilt washes over them.

'Police?' Harriet asks Hester, already on her way to the sitting room for the phone.

'Police!' says Ben with undisguised excitement. 'What's going on?'

Hester frets as she hurries after Harriet. 'Tell them to look for a black or dark blue van, very muddy, dented back bumper.

Oh, and the number plate. Tell them about the number plate—what was it?'

'Syphilitic . . . SYT,' says Harriet with instant recall, dialling. She, like Finbar, often plays the number-plate game; it is one of the reasons her driving is so erratic. Her heart is thumping and jumping in her chest. The call is answered on the second ring.

'Emergency—which service do you require?'

The week's events flash through Harriet's mind in a confusion of faces and emotions: Daria shivering in the shelter, cradling her tiny son; Ben truculent on the doorstep; Dick's phlegmy cough; Elizabeth Sampson's shadowed loss-filled eyes; Teddy sweating and blustering . . . it's all come to this.

'Police. Please.'

The front door slams.

'Hello?' cries Daria.

~~~

'Sorry. I am sorry,' says Daria yet again. She cannot understand why Hester and Harriet are so upset. More than upset. Furious, in fact. 'I am not thinking . . .'

'No. Precisely,' says Hester angrily. 'You didn't think at all!' She bangs the kettle onto its base and jabs at the switch.

'Worried us to death!' adds Harriet, who is close to tears. She reaches out to hold Milo's hand; he rewards her with a gummy smile. Her heart turns over.

'What on earth made you go off like that?' demands Ben, who, Daria now sees, is almost as cross as his aunts.

Milo picks up on the atmosphere and starts to snuffle in distress.

'Ssh, shh, little one.' She strokes his fragile skull. 'I am wanting to go for a walk, is all. A walk! Outside! Not to be always in house. Under sky. See birds . . . and . . .' She will not cry. It's not her fault the *babulki* are so . . . not fair.

'And what?'

'I am thinking: if it is not so good for me—when we go to police—perhaps they say, *No, you cannot stay with kind Hester and Harriet, you must come with us.* Perhaps I am lock away. Perhaps they send me back to Belarus. And people say, *This England, what is it like?* And I say, *I do not know! I never see! London I see, yes, of course. But country, no.* So, I think . . .'

'Just in case,' says a chastened Harriet, knowing that most of their anger was founded on fear.

'Just in case,' concurs Daria quietly.

So she had quietly installed Milo in the basket and, creeping away so as not to alert anyone, wheeled the bike down the lane and out into the countryside, breathing in the fresh cold air and pointing out to her son the sights of a wintry English rural scene. And Hester and Harriet, who have never lived under any form of constraint or tyranny (certainly not in the way the Yushkeviches and millions like them have) or had to watch what they say or where they go, accept that only now do they appreciate a little what Daria's life over the past months has been like. And are ashamed and humbled.

'So,' says Daria with a scared little smile, 'now we go?'

'Yes,' says Harriet sadly, 'now we go.'

CHAPTER 28

A police car screams past them, siren blaring, as they enter the outskirts of Stote. Vehicles pull over to allow it passage and it surges ahead. Hester and Harriet exchange a look.

'D'you suppose ...' Hester keeps her voice low; Daria is fussing with Milo in his car seat but Ben never misses a trick.

'Let's hope so,' Harriet whispers back. They both think of Teddy, imagine the shaky hand hovering over the telephone. 'Have you read that?'

Ben's printout lies in Hester's lap. It hasn't made particularly comfortable reading, but she'll not share that with Harry right now. 'Thanks for doing this,' she says to her nephew over her shoulder. 'Very helpful.'

'Yeah?' No mistaking the satisfaction in Ben's voice. 'Quite enjoyed it.'

'Really? Well now, there's a thought. A career in the law.'

'The law—!' begins Ben before cottoning on. 'Oh, yeah, right. Very funny.' He subsides in his seat and turns his attention to Milo.

'But I wanna come in!' Ben protests. 'They might wanna ask me stuff.'

Hester pokes her head back inside the car. 'You are staying here. I told you before we left but you would insist on coming.'

'They're my mates too,' says Ben sulkily. 'It was me she told right at the start, not you!'

Hester slams the door and sets off in pursuit of Harriet and Daria. She catches up with them at the entrance, where Daria is looking up at the large sign apprehensively.

'Come along now,' she says more robustly than she feels. She can see Harriet is wavering; someone has to take control. 'Let's get this over with.'

The station is a hive of activity, people rushing back and forth importantly, a palpable sense of excitement in the air. The desk sergeant, avuncular and portly, lends them a distracted ear through the louvred glass grille as they introduce themselves and begin their story, looking over to a colleague who peers around a door opposite, face split in a grin. 'All right?' He gets the thumbs-up and brings his attention back to them, smiling broadly.

'Sorry, sorry. Got a bit of a . . . situation going on. Now, you were saying . . .' He records names—making rather a meal of Daria's surname—addresses, passport details, tuts at the date on the visa—'dear, oh dearie me'—sighs from time to time, all the while soliciting updates from passing fellow officers with secret signs, winks and discreet nods.

'Quite a mess, isn't it?' he says finally, reviewing his notes. 'And you ladies should've—'

'Yes. We know that now. We came as soon as we could.' The sisters shift uncomfortably like schoolgirls before the head; Daria stands patiently beside them, awaiting her fate. The real possibility of her being taken into custody hits them.

'We'll happily stand surety or whatever's needed,' says Harriet desperately. 'We'll do whatever it—'

The sergeant bats her offer away with an irritable hand.

'Not my call, I'm afraid. Moment you suspected something was up you should've reported it. Still, you're here now.' He regards the trio of adults severely, face softening as his eyes light on the baby. 'He's a proper cutie, isn't he?' He reaches out a sausage finger and Milo grabs it. 'Got a grandson about his age. Bit of a screamer, more's the pity. Still . . .' He disengages his finger from Milo's tenacious grasp and gets back to the matter in hand, consulting a large blue folder beside him on the counter. 'I need to get on to Immigration Enforcement.' Harriet shivers involuntarily. 'But first things first. I may have to ask the young lady to surrender her passport, for obvious reasons.' It's still on the desk where Daria had placed it at the start; his hand closes over it and slides it towards him.

Harriet puts her hand on Daria's shoulder: all those months without it and now it's being taken away again. She whispers a reassurance; Daria nods, watching intently as the sergeant logs the passport and number. He pushes the book over to her to sign.

'Right. Take a seat, would you?' He indicates the hard wooden bench opposite and they troop across to sit in awkward silence, no-one wanting to discuss their business in front of strangers; indeed Hester and Harriet would prefer not to discuss it with Daria either, given the uncertainty. A man in an expensive overcoat leaps up impatiently and approaches the grille.

'At last! Now, about my car—'

'Sorry, sir, one moment. I've a call to make.' The sergeant takes his notes and goes to move away from the counter.

'I've been waiting over an hour already!'

'Sorry about that. I'll see if anyone else is free.' His tone suggests that he won't be rushing to find a substitute. He ambles to the back of the office and picks up a phone, leaving the man fuming. Separated by some distance and a glass screen, Hester and Harriet strain to catch the conversation but hear only the dull rumble of the policeman's voice. From time to time, he glances across at them, then speaks rapidly into the phone, occasionally making a note. Finally, he finishes the call and returns to the grille, beckoning the waiting women over. The man beside them leaps up.

'I've been waiting—'

'You said. I'm just dealing with these ladies—'

'Bloody illegal immigrants! Is this what I pay my—'

'Sir,' says the sergeant with steely emphasis. 'I strongly suggest you sit down and wait as I asked. Now!'

The man looks astonished then furiously retakes his seat.

'Now then,' says the sergeant, lowering his voice so they have to lean forward to catch his words, 'here's the situation.

Like I said, in a case like this, we hand things over to Immigration Enforcement.'

'Sounds rather fierce,' says Harriet, attempting to lighten the mood.

The sergeant fixes her with a stern glare. 'This is a serious matter, madam. Very serious. Particularly nowadays. Now, I've filled them in with all the necessary details, and they may or may not wish to conduct a formal interview in due course. First off, you need to sort out some legal representation as soon as possible and submit an application for permission to stay. Your solicitor will know what's what. The young lady may have to comply with reporting restrictions, but for the moment, provided she stays at this designated address . . .' He looks down. 'The Laurels in Pellington—'

'So'—Hester hardly dares ask—'we can go home? All of us?'

The three adults hold their breath.

The sergeant nods, then gives an understanding smile. 'Oh, right, I'm with you. You thought we might . . .' He nods in Daria and Milo's direction. 'Not where there's kiddies involved. Not as a rule.'

The terrifying spectre of detention recedes. Harriet throws her arms around Daria and squeezes tight.

'And surety?'

'Nope. You've given assurances . . . now you need to get proper advice. Oh, and'—he fishes in his papers and withdraws Daria's passport—'the good news is we don't need to hang on to this after all.' He hands it through the aperture and Daria stretches out a tentative hand. 'Here you go, love. Look after it, won't you?'

The girl takes it, a grateful smile illuminating her face.

Weak with relief, they all three thank him effusively, Daria on the edge of tears.

'About your solicitor—get a specialist,' he says, trying to mask his embarrassment. 'That's my strong advice. Need someone who knows the ropes. Do you have anyone in mind?'

'No, but we know someone who will,' says Hester, thinking of Henry. 'We'll get on to it the minute we get home.'

He scratches what remains of his hair as he consults his notes. 'Okay, then. I dare say we'll see you again soon. Best of luck. You'll get straight on with the application?' The sergeant's natural kindliness resurfaces; he pulls a face at Milo, who gapes comically, his mouth a perfect O.

'You're a lucky lad to have fetched up with these two good Samaritans.'

It's the sisters' turn to be embarrassed. 'Anyone would have done the same,' demurs Harriet.

The sergeant flicks a look over at the man on the bench, now muttering irritably into his phone. 'I wouldn't be too sure.' They share a complicit smile.

The conversation stalls, Hester and Harriet unable to believe they can simply walk out with Daria and Milo and drive home. Except they can't.

The sergeant closes the file, raises his eyebrows. 'Something else?'

'Well,' says Hester with a heavy heart. 'Yes, as a matter of fact, I'm afraid there is . . .'

CHAPTER 29

'Told you he was a tosser,' says Ben triumphantly. 'Didn't I say?'

'You did indeed, Ben,' agrees Harriet. 'Good for you. There's another profession you could consider: detective.'

Ben scowls and forks up the remnants of his risotto. And it really is *his* risotto, for when they had finally set off for home, having given and signed lengthy statements about Teddy and Scott and Tina, and Harriet had suggested that maybe just for once they should get a takeaway and Hester had immediately and surprisingly agreed, it had been Ben who argued and pleaded to be allowed a stab at supper himself. During the long wait in the car outside the police station, he'd amused himself researching recipes on his phone and declared himself all set to try a mushroom risotto.

For once, Hester hadn't argued. Indeed, on their return she had gone off immediately to ring Henry but was unable to reach him. She left a message but, uneasy about finding legal representation in time, had then contacted a local firm of solicitors. They recommended an immigration specialist with whom she had had a brief but reassuring conversation. She had entered the kitchen only to retrieve a really decent bottle of Italian red from their special occasions store, hustled Harriet and Daria into the sitting room, and left Ben to it.

As they had surmised, the jubilance at the station was directly related to the activities at the farm. The detectives to whom they had swiftly been passed on had been understandably cagey, but the women had picked up enough hints to deduce that a successful raid on the cannabis farm had just concluded and that—the best news of all—Scott was in custody and therefore no longer posed any threat to Daria and Milo. When they mentioned Teddy Wilson's name in the course of their narrative, the detectives nodded simultaneously. One said, 'Ah, the famous Mr Wilson,' but no further information was forthcoming as to his whereabouts or indeed any charges he might face. Nothing at all had been said about Tina.

'He'll be for it, though, won't he?' says Ben, unable to let the matter rest. He's simultaneously clearing his plate and using his phone. 'I mean, aiding and abetting and that. Plus duffing you up, Aunt Hester.'

'He didn't duff me up, as you put it,' says Hester stiffly. 'He didn't mean to hurt me.' She's about to remonstrate about the phone and its inappropriateness at the table when Ben continues, 'No, but he, like, broke in. Like, no-one *invited* him, did they? That's gotta be trespassing at least. He's gonna go down, big time, for sure.'

Let's hope there aren't too many Bens on the jury when Teddy appears in court, thinks Harriet. The thought of a trial brings her mind straight back to Daria's interview the following day and all that hangs upon it. *Please God let this solicitor Hetty's found know his stuff.*

'Well,' says Hester acidly, 'nice to see the youth of today keeping an open mind.' She starts to stack the plates. 'That was very good, Ben, if not perhaps quite as *al dente* as a risotto should be.'

'Al what?' He automatically takes the plates from her and heads for the dishwasher.

'Just a little firm to the bite.'

'What, like undercooked?'

'No. More like just cooked. Like sprouts should be: with the tiniest bit of crunch still to them.' Hester in that instant recalls Isabelle's Christmas sprouts, boiled, as Hester and Harriet's father the major would have said, to buggery. Not perhaps something to share with Ben right now. But it reminds her . . .

'It was good of you to cook for us tonight, though, because we're going to be busy tomorrow. We'll need to start at crack of sparrows.'

Ben groans. 'How early?'

'Oh, I don't know. Ten at the latest.' She doesn't want to get up any earlier than she has to either and yet, despite everything, she's quite looking forward to a day in the kitchen; a day of concentrating on the simple pleasure of preparing food for others to enjoy. 'I've made a list and your aunt's going to nip to the supermarket for us first thing. Then she'll take Daria and Milo into town to meet the solicitor.' They'd agreed it would be better for Harriet to accompany Daria alone; no need to go mob-handed. 'So I suggest we all have a quiet evening and get an early night.'

Harriet catches Ben's eye and gives him an admonitory look; he flushes beetroot and looks away. No danger of him sneaking off tonight.

⌣⌣⌣

'I don't mind admitting,' says Hester half an hour later from her armchair, having changed into her dressing gown preparatory to taking her bath only to discover that Daria has beaten her to it, 'that I seriously thought this afternoon that he was going to haul them away. Shove them in some cell and we'd never see them again. Didn't you?'

Her voice sounds oddly quavery. Harriet looks over: surely she isn't *crying*? She feels herself well up in sympathy. 'Oh, Hetty!'

'I know, I know,' sniffs Hester. She heels a tear away. 'I have absolutely had it with excitement. I'm so bushwhacked I can't even be bothered to knit. I'll be out for the count before my head hits the pillow. Here'—Hester waggles the bottle in Harriet's direction—'help me finish this last drop.'

Harriet shakes her head; Hester swiftly upends the dregs into her own glass.

'What a week!' says Harriet. 'Just think: if we hadn't stopped on Christmas morning—'

'Hmm.'

They contemplate what might have been. The joists above their heads creak as Daria pads across the landing from the bathroom. Shortly afterwards and very faintly, they hear her crooning a lullaby.

'We'll have to find a way to tell George and Isabelle,' says Harriet into her glass. She tips the last of her wine into her mouth.

'Edited highlights,' says Hester, draining her own glass. 'There's some aspects better left undisclosed.'

'Oh, heavens, yes,' says Harriet, reminded of creeping back home with Ben in the early hours, 'absolutely. Edited highlights only.'

The phone rings.

'That's probably them now.' Hester waits for Harriet to get up, conscious of her nagging knees. 'Be careful what you say.'

'Of course I will,' says Harriet rather shortly. Why is it always her that has to answer the phone in the evening?

'Hello?'

'Might I speak to Mrs Greene or Mrs Pearson?'

'Mrs Pearson speaking.'

Hester, by now on her feet, looks over with mild curiosity; it's clearly not George or Isabelle. She cocks an eyebrow.

Harriet, listening intently for a few seconds, looks back at her, aghast.

'Er . . . yes . . . of course . . . well, I suppose so . . . we'll come immediately.' She points at the phone, brow creased with incredulity and mouths at Hester, 'Police.'

'They've changed their minds?!' cries Hester, appalled by the careless cruelty.

'Yes, yes, thank you, Sergeant. We'll be with you in half an hour or so.'

Harriet replaces the phone in its cradle.

'For God's sake,' says Hester. 'It's beyond cruel! It's inhuman! That poor girl.'

'No, it's nothing to do with Daria,' says Harriet. 'It's Finbar.'

***

Hester is incandescent. She is tired, achy and itching for a fight.

'Did they say *why* he was at the station?'

'No,' says Harriet, eyes glued to the road. She wishes she'd listened to the optician on her last visit and splashed out on that special coating to improve night driving. She's also hoping she's not over the limit. 'He just said that our brother had asked them to ring us.'

'Our brother! This has gone far enough. Getting him released from hospital was one thing, but a police station! God knows what people must think when they see us walk in. Compared to Finbar, I mean.'

Hester is currently sporting a pair of broken-down brogues, some polyester trousers so ancient that when bought they had been sold as slacks, one of Gordon's old gardening sweaters over a thick sweatshirt and one of her exquisite hand-knitted cashmere scarves. Her hair looks in need of a good brush. On her lap sits a bulging endlessly-recycled old Woolworths carrier stuffed with assorted menswear in case Finbar is yet again in need of replacement clothing. On top is a hastily-assembled picnic of cold meats, cheese and two crusty rolls, plus a slice of Dundee wrapped in silver foil. Harriet, in a tweed skirt, winter boots and her newish wool coat (she can't have had it more than five years), feels positively smart beside her.

They trundle slowly down the approach road to town, hanging back behind a gritting lorry, headlights illuminating the frost sparkling on parked cars and patches of ice that dot the tarmac. The warmish Christmas weather has given way abruptly to an arctic north wind, the temperature on this cloudless night dropping dramatically. Harriet thinks of Finbar in his shelter and shivers. They really will have to take him home with them this time, and given their current domestic arrangements, he'll have to bed down in the sitting room. She decides to postpone that particular conversation with Hester for the moment.

The little car skids slightly as she turns into the police station car park.

'Careful!' cries Hester, as though Harriet is deliberately driving recklessly.

Harriet bites her tongue and steers a careful path between two rows of cars until she spots a sizeable gap into which she manages to insert the car almost parallel to its neighbours on her third attempt.

Finbar is waiting impatiently on the bench opposite the reception desk, still clad, they see to their relief, in the same clothes in which they had last seen him, the only difference being the addition of a considerable quantity of mud on both knees. He hauls himself to his feet and hobbles over to them. '*Deo gratias!* Dear ladies, my saviours!' Turning to the duty sergeant, 'These are my beloved sisters, the paragons of benevolence of whom I spoke, come to rescue me.'

This sergeant, in contrast to his predecessor in the role this afternoon, is lugubrious and almost painfully cadaverous. He is not, unlike his colleague, given to good humour. 'Come to take him home, have you? Give us all a bit of peace.'

Finbar throws his head back haughtily. 'I should never have been brought here in the first place. Had your colleagues not been so intent on behaving in a gung-ho fashion and rampaging about like cowboys, they would have furnished themselves with the facts and allowed me to go about my business unhindered.'

'Take him away, will you?' says the sergeant to the sisters. 'Before I lose my temper and charge him with wasting police time.'

Hester and Harriet each seize an arm and hustle Finbar out.

'Or assault,' yells the sergeant at their backs.

⌣⌣⌣

They bundle Finbar into the car and climb in after him, then twist around to confront him on the back seat. It takes him mere seconds to ferret out the foil parcel; little more for him to wolf down the savouries and set upon the cake. His sour odour soon permeates the cramped space; despite the biting cold, Harriet lets down her window a little.

'Assault?' says Hester, unable to contain her curiosity any longer. 'Did he say assault?'

'Uh-huh,' mumbles Finbar through a mouthful of Dundee.

'You assaulted a policeman?'

He shakes his head violently, so violently that it sets the little car rocking slightly. 'No, no, no, not a policeman. The villain Scott. This cake is—'

'Scott?!'

Finbar fastidiously wipes his mouth and dusts down his beard with his kitchen-roll napkin.

'Finbar! How? Where?'

He busies himself folding his detritus away in the sheet of tinfoil. 'All shall be revealed.' He hands the package of rubbish to Hester, who is too astonished to do anything but take it. Both women sigh in mutual exasperation and Harriet reaches for the car keys.

'Let's get going,' she says. 'I can't feel my toes.'

'Are you cold?' asks Finbar, seemingly genuinely surprised. 'Really? I was just reflecting on what a beautiful night it is. Crisp, bright—'

'It's freezing,' barks Hester, thrusting her gloved hands deep into her lap. 'And while you might be happy to enjoy the wonders of the night sky, we would like to be home in the warm, thank you very much. So kindly explain why, yet again, we've been dragged out of the house—in the middle of the night, this time—to rescue you.'

Finbar harrumphs, muttering something indecipherable behind her, as Harriet gingerly manoeuvres the car out of its parking space and inches towards the exit. She recalls the mechanic doing her last MOT warning her that her front tyres were in imminent need of replacement. That would be about seven months ago.

'What did you say?' demands Hester testily.

'I was about to apologise,' says Finbar, aggrieved. 'I am only too aware what a liability you consider me.'

If this is designed to elicit sympathy, it falls on deaf ears. Far from offering Finbar a roof over his head, at the moment

Harriet would like nothing more than to turf him out of the car and leave him to walk the ten miles or so back to Pellington in the dark.

'However,' he continues, 'I do think a little understanding might not go amiss, since not only do I hold the key to the rogueries of the past few days, but I also helped bring the chief malefactor to justice.' He finishes on a note of defiance and satisfaction, unaware how very thin is the ice on which he currently skates.

Harriet tears her squinting eyes away from the road long enough to glance up into the mirror and observe the old man preening himself. Beside her, she senses Hester gearing up for a verbal flaying should Finbar not spill his intriguing beans forthwith. Unwilling to endure verbal fisticuffs at this hour, she says swiftly, 'Finbar, we're both very tired. Please just get on with it.'

'Without any flourishes, digressions or Latin mottos, ideally,' adds Hester crisply.

Harriet swallows a snigger.

There is a lengthy pause, the clearing of a throat, and eventually a clearly huffy Finbar starts to tell his tale.

'When you deposited me back at my lodgings, I was, I will not lie, disappointed that due to a combination of heavy traffic and—forgive me, Harriet, but the truth is not always kind—your frankly slipshod driving'—Hester puts a restraining hand on Harriet's arm and squeezes—'we had failed to track the van down. I am not a man given to grudges, but in truth, I was still incensed about the attack. My ire reached fresh heights when I discovered that the hooligan (whom I subsequently learnt was this Scott creature) had visited violence not only upon my person, he had also desecrated one of my most precious possessions. My first edition of *Life on the Mississippi*, one of the finest—'

'You have a Twain first edition?' gasps Harriet, in spite of her resolution not to interrupt.

'Indeed I do. In very good condition. Or, rather, in very good condition until that vandal tossed it to the floor, presumably trod on it and broke its spine.'

'Oh, Finbar!' The sisters, both bibliophiles, feel his pain.

'Quite so. Bruises will heal but books . . .' He shakes his head sadly. 'One can patch, one can mend, but the damage is done. Such was my despair, I resolved to drown my bitterness in a small libation, so I repaired immediately to the pub. The landlord there, Vince, is always good enough to install me in a private corner so that I am not disturbed.'

And so the other drinkers are not felled by the pong, thinks Hester.

'He asked me if I had been away. I decided not to mention my sojourn under the care—hah! I should have been better treated in a *kennel*!—of Sister Brice. One never knows who might be listening and it never does to appear vulnerable. I gave him to understand I had been on the road. Whereupon he told me that someone had been asking after me.' A pregnant pause. 'A chap in a battered old van. *Aha*, I thought, *my attacker, checking that I'm still breathing, presumably.*' A bark of laughter that dwindles into a cough. 'Imagine! He must have supposed he'd killed me off.'

Or he wanted to finish you off, thinks Harriet. It's starting to snow lightly: huge flakes drift daintily down on the road, dissolving instantly. She switches on the windscreen wipers and for a moment the outside world is obscured by a smear of snow; with the next swipe of the blade, the road ahead emerges once more, flakes dancing in the headlights. Harriet changes down a gear, the engine whining like a whipped dog, and creeps along even more slowly.

'Could have been anyone,' says Hester dismissively. 'How do you know it was your assailant? Did this Vince have a name?'

'No, says Finbar, 'but Bert Egham—keeps chickens down the bottom of the hill and plays the occasional game of dominos with me in the beer garden in the summer months—overheard our conversation and chipped in: *Oh, Scott Wilkes you mean?* I said, *I believe he drives a van with a registration starting SYT,* and he said, *I know, I sold it to him last year.'*

'My God,' says Harriet excitedly. She's just noticed one of the wipers has a split in it: fortunately it's the left one, because it's leaving in its wake an arc of slush that severely affects visibility on that side.

His audience now thoroughly hooked, Finbar forges on. 'So I quizzed him about this friend of his. *No friend of mine,* says he. *Right miserable bugger, tried to beat me down on price but I wouldn't budge. He paid what I was asking in the end but not without a great deal of fuss and swearing. Lives at Parson's Farm,* he said, *up on the back road. Why is he looking for you?* I muttered some nonsense about having a bit of business to transact and made my farewells. But Bert followed me out. Asked if I was intending to pay a call. Possibly, I said. He wished me good luck, warning me they didn't like visitors up there, especially on foot. That's when I decided to call on you for assistance. Only to find, of course, that you were out. Shopping, I assume, or on some other—'

'We were not shopping!' explodes Hester. 'While you were guzzling alcohol, we were—'

'Hetty, let him finish!'

Hester crumples grumpily back into her seat.

Finbar has the grace to look contrite. 'A thousand apologies. I had not meant to imply your pursuits were limited to the trivialities of the less worthy of your sex. Whatever your errand, I found my plans thwarted. I was not, however, prepared to await your return. My choler had, if anything, increased in the time it took me to reach your house. I recalled all his crimes: the repeated intrusions, the physical attack, his hounding of that poor girl and her babe, his mistreatment of my trusty trolley and then, the final outrage, my violated book. I determined that he should pay for his temerity. Who knew what further villainies he might perpetrate if left unchecked? I resolved to find and confront him, regardless of Bert's warning. But how?'

'Exactly,' says Hester, the account and, with it, explanations once more slipping away like water through a sieve. 'How?'

Finbar permits himself a smug smile. 'My dear Hester, there are few rights of way, lanes or byways around here with which I am unacquainted. I recalled that a path, somewhat overgrown and untended, runs up towards the rear of Parson's Farm behind Handfast House, home to the redoubtable Lady Parvenu.'

The sisters enjoy a private smile at his nickname for Peggy Verndale.

'When that absurd holiday complex was under construction, I often used to wander up there to observe progress: I've shared many a tea with brickies and the like up there. Fine men. Salt of the earth.'

Hester cuts short his encomium to the horny-handed sons of toil. 'And? Do stop getting sidetracked!'

Finbar sniffs. 'And I set off posthaste. Across the fields, my journey repeatedly hampered by locked gates and barbed wire: all totally illegal. They are obstructing public footpaths! I've a good mind to report it to the parish council. I couldn't help thinking someone was going to extraordinary lengths to repel visitors. Anyway, I decided to cut up through the old complex and approach the farmhouse from the rear. There's a goodly distance between the complex and the main house, but I remembered a line of trees that I thought would give cover as well as allow me to check out the lie of the land. And then the wind changed direction.' He pauses.

The women wait.

The pause lengthens.

As usual, it's Hester who cracks first. 'The wind? What about the wind?'

If Harriet thought Finbar looked smug earlier, his face glimpsed in the mirror this time is the epitome of vainglory.

'The answer, as the song has it, was blowing in the wind,' he says gleefully.

'Of course!' says the crossword solver.

'Of course what?' cries Hester.

'You smelt it,' says Harriet over her shoulder to Finbar.

'Indeed I did. One sniff was all it took. One is not the

housemaster of teenage boys for a decade or more without recognising the smell of cannabis. Not to mention one's own youthful peccadilloes. Faint initially, I grant you, but unmistakable. And then, as if to confirm my suspicions, the deus ex machina, one might almost say, high above—'

'The helicopter!' says Hester. She is almost beside herself, caught up in the narrative. 'What did you do then?'

'Just so. The helicopter. And I thought, *They're on to it!* Now all the obstacles in my path made sense. I crept further up towards the complex to see if anyone was about. Almost immediately, a couple of chaps, very thin and ragged, emerged into the open and started pointing up at the sky where the helicopter was circling. I could have simply slipped away and let the law takes its course, but I confess I was curious. I elected to sit tight and observe from afar. But suddenly the van careered into the yard and out leapt none other than the loathsome Scott, presumably hotfooting it from the farmhouse. He started shouting the odds and laying about these benighted wretches who had now been joined by three or four others. He was trying to force them into the back of the van. I thought, *Well, he's outnumbered, surely they'll fight back.* But they didn't. They just cowered and let him push and punch and kick them. I could not stand idly by. I tore up the hill and into the yard—'

'Oh, Finbar!' cries Hester, hand to her mouth. Harriet is sorely tempted to pull up at the side of the road to hear the denouement; she's finding it increasingly difficult to steer a steady course while this gripping adventure unfolds. Stoically if unsteadily, she keeps driving.

'I was beyond fear, Hester! *Vengeance is mine*, I cried. I had, admittedly, the advantage of surprise. He left off his onslaught and turned to confront me. Now I may be slight, ladies, but I am fast. He never knew what hit him. True, he may have been somewhat distracted by the cacophonous noise overhead and the sirens approaching from every direction, but I am proud to report that I had sufficient time to land a mighty left hook— did I ever mention I used to box when a boy?—before the yard filled with noise and commotion, and order fled as the massed ranks of our local and county constabulary descended. I swear I have never seen so many police cars! It was most exhilarating. *There he lies*, I cried, *the villain of the piece!* as he writhed pathetically on the cobbles. They seized him immediately.'

'And you?'

Finbar's expression of triumph is replaced in an instant with one of outrage. 'Far from being lauded as the hero, I was rounded up! It seems that, in all the kerfuffle, the police assumed I was merely one of the villain's peons who had escaped bondage and attacked his tormentor. Although why, in the name of all the gods, they couldn't immediately see that I was of another order altogether is beyond me.'

It isn't beyond Hester and Harriet.

'I found myself corralled with half a dozen or so of these unfortunates, whom the police discovered had been kept in the most appalling squalor in one room. Foreigners, I gather. Certainly it was hard to establish their mother tongue. Or tongues, I should say. In addition, they were plainly terrified of the men in uniform. I attempted to explain I was not of their number but there was such a brouhaha that I could not make myself heard or understood. I was herded into a van and disgorged at the station. Despite my most vociferous protests, it was a good hour or so before I eventually secured a hearing with one of the many officers milling about—I must say, they complain about the reduction in police numbers, but if my experience is anything to go by we have a positive embarrassment of—'

'Red light, Harry!' shouts Hester. They screech to an abrupt and slippery halt.

'Well!' says Harriet into the stunned silence when she recovers her breath. Whether she is referring to her precipitous stop or Finbar's perils is unclear.

'What larks, as my old pater used to say,' chuckles the aged warrior from the back. 'Most satisfactory. By the way, perhaps I should explain why I was obliged to employ the fraternal ruse again back at the station. One sniff of my housing arrangements, and the boys in blue would have been on to Social Services in a flash. You've no idea how much of my life is spent ducking and diving and dodging these wretched do-gooders. A man of my age! Thank heavens for people such as your good selves, living and letting live. I knew I could rely on you in an emergency.'

They trickle past the first houses in the village; the lights of the Glass & Cask appear in the distance. 'Just drop me at the pub, would you, Harriet, my dear?'

'But, Finbar, it's snowing! We can't allow you—'

'A few flakes. Honestly, a mere sprinkling!'

'Finbar,' says Harriet firmly, 'I'm afraid I must insist—'

'No, my dear, I must insist. I know you have my best interests at heart. Or think you do. I am more grateful to you than

I can possibly express for feeding me, but I remain in grave need of watering. I fancy I've earned myself a wee dram after my recent travails.'

Harriet reluctantly dribbles to a halt.

'Now. Might I trouble you to let me out, Hester?'

Hester and Harriet exchange a look: what can they do? Hester extracts herself from the passenger seat and tips it forward to allow Finbar to climb out. He doffs an imaginary hat as she eases herself carefully back into the car.

'I promise, dear ladies both, that I shall only ever in extremis claim kinship with you. However, I am truly grateful for your forbearance and kindness. Adieu.' He pushes the door shut and, with a nimbleness that belies his age, flits across the road.

The sisters watch him disappear into the pub, swallowed up by noise and jollity. Outside in the dark and still-smelly car, faces lit only by the dashboard lights, they sigh in unison with a mix of weariness and disconcerting regret.

'Harry,' says an exhausted and emotional Hester, 'I don't care if a tiny kitten, an abandoned puppy or even a naked newborn baby is lying helpless in the middle of the road—just drive around it and take us home, will you please?'

CHAPTER 30

31 DECEMBER

'All a bit of a letdown in the end,' says Ben, piping the last helpings of cream cheese and chives into Roquefort pastry flutes, under Hester's beady-eyed supervision. 'I mean, no high-speed chases. Or gun battles. Or a siege. A siege would have been cool.'

It's all these wretched video games, thinks Hester testily. *Nothing seems real to them.*

'A siege would not have been cool, Ben. It was all quite exciting enough for me, thank you very much,' she says sharply. Her muscles are still aching ferociously from yesterday's tensions and exertions. Her almost-run back from the shop obviously awoke some long-dormant parts of her anatomy which are still protesting vociferously despite her eventual lengthy soak in the bath last night and a long and oddly dreamless sleep.

She checks her watch. Harriet and Daria have been gone for over three hours.

'Anyway, it's not over yet. Never mind the farm, we've got far more important things to worry about right now.'

'I think everything'll be fine, I do,' says Ben, with the insouciance of youth, his cavalier attitude at odds with the care with which he is coaxing the last few gobbets out of the piping bag. 'I mean, you're in the clear now, n'cha, having made Dar turn herself in.'

'We did not make—!'

'No, well, you know what I mean.'

'She went of her own volition!' Privately, aside from the immediate worries about today's outcome for Daria, Hester is still troubled by one of the fruits of Ben's internet searching: while apparently it isn't an offence not to report an illegal migrant in the country, it most certainly is an offence to harbour one or otherwise help them. She thinks she and Harriet are guilty on both those counts. She had snatched a few minutes with Harriet before she and Daria left for their interview to rehearse their story. *Oh dear, now it sounds as if we were colluding and trying to cover things up. No, the best thing to do in this, as in every situation, is what I know Harry will do: simply tell the truth. After all, we did everything from the very best motives.*

'Ben, you might want to check the quiches?'

'I'm on it,' says Ben, revelling in his responsibilities.

'Just jiggle them gently.'

'Yeah, yeah, I know.' Ben, his back to his tutor, smiles gleefully. He's really getting the hang of this cooking lark. 'No, so, the way I see it, you're in the clear, Dar's gonna be okay 'cos of Sampson being a Brit and Milo is well safe on account of his dad. Peachy.'

'Let's hope you're right,' says Harriet, coming in on the tail end of the conversation. She looks washed out, eyes dark with fatigue.

Hester instinctively looks over her shoulder into the empty hall. Her heart skips a beat.

'Oh no,' says Harriet, realising instantly what Hester is seeking, 'She's just gone straight upstairs. He needed changing. Everything's okay. In fact, it's fine.'

Hester shepherds her sister into a chair, reaches for the kettle. Ben stands frozen by the oven, awaiting news.

'It's ... phew ...' Harriet exhales abruptly as the tension starts to ease. The drive back on roads now awash with melted snow had not been easy, not least because Daria, confused by the welter of information with which they had been bombarded—much of it in complex legalese—had repeatedly sought clarification of what had happened. Even Harriet, who had paid close attention and taken copious notes, is not sure she's grasped all the nuances. 'It's ... complicated, to say the least. The solicitor will make an application on their behalf for permission to stay. Then the immigration people or whoever check everything out, and once they're satisfied, she'll be given leave to remain in due course.'

'In due course? What's that mean?' demands Ben. 'How long?'

Harriet shrugs. 'I don't know. Anywhere between two and six months apparently. While they're processing her application, she's not allowed to work. She has to report to the police in person once a week.'

'And then she's okay to stay?'

'As long as she remains Milo's carer. That lasts for two and half years.'

'Then what?'

'She applies for a renewal. Up to ten years and then she'd be granted indefinite leave to remain.'

'Ten years!'

'Mmm. I know.'

'But she could work once she's got this permission to stay?' Hester can't help leaping ahead, thinking of sharing the house for months to come. She's not quite sure how she feels about that.

Harriet nods half-heartedly. 'I suppose so. I've given them Peter Sampson's details and phoned him to let him know they'll be in touch. Never mind the DNA evidence, they'll apparently want proof that he means to have an ongoing relationship with his son. We didn't even get into whether the Sampsons bear any responsibility for her visa violation. I was hoping her involvement with Scott and Tina might count in her favour, but the solicitor says it's not relevant to her application. I imagine the police will want to interview us all again about the farm at some stage.'

Ben takes a tray of mini cheese quiches from the oven and brings them over for Hester's inspection. She nods approvingly and consults the list in her lap. 'Those rolls should've proved by now.'

'On my way.' He nips off upstairs to the airing cupboard.

There's a sense of anticlimax, of relief tempered with a sense of a story far from over.

Hester thumps a mug of tea down in front of Harriet. 'Listen, do you want us to cancel tonight? You look all in.'

Harriet considers the offer briefly. 'No, bless you. I'll have a nap this afternoon: that'll sort me out. Besides, I think it's about time we let our hair down. Might help take our minds off things. And look at all this food!' She eyes the quiches. 'Shouldn't someone test those?'

Hester slides one onto a plate.

'Goodness me.' Harriet reaches for it before her sister can change her mind. 'What's come over you?'

'I've given up. You're a lost cause,' says Hester affectionately. She watches Harriet eating. 'Okay?'

'More than okay. Delicious.'

Hester smiles wryly. 'Ben.' She rolls her eyes.

'Even the pastry?' Hester is notoriously sniffy about other people's pastry.

'Even the pastry.'

Harriet mumbles through her mouthful, 'I can feel my arteries furring up by the second.'

'Jolly good. Now tell me: this solicitor, he's all right, is he? Knows what he's doing?'

'Apart from the fact he looks about fourteen, yes, he seems to know his stuff. He's seeing whether Daria should apply for asylum, too, in view of what's happening in Belarus—with Artem and her dad, as well as her own situation. So that might help.'

Nodding, Hester sits and reaches for the list, but Harriet can see her mind is elsewhere. 'What?'

Hester sighs. 'I know you'll say I'm an idiot, but I can't stop thinking about Teddy . . .'

'Why? Hetty, he deserves everything that's coming to him. Turning a blind eye doesn't make him innocent. Don't you dare start defending him!'

'Of course I'm not going to defend him!' She can't rid herself of the sense of shame for ever having a soft spot for him. *Thank God no-one ever knew*, she reflects. She says heatedly, 'What Teddy Wilson did was morally repugnant and wholly indefensible. I'm just thinking he's going to have a terrible time of it inside.'

Harriet's heart is unmoved. Molly she can feel pity for, not least for the taint that will undoubtedly, if unfairly, forever attach to her; Mrs Vicar, certainly; but Teddy . . .

'Well you just remember what a terrible time Daria would have had if she'd been locked up in a detention centre. That ought to put Teddy Wilson's fate into perspective. He brought it on himself, Hetty! Assuming he doesn't find a hotshot lawyer to get him off on some weaselly technicality. It's that Tina I feel for, if anyone,' she says.

'I know, poor woman. I'm not saying she's blameless, but that husband of hers . . . Put yourself in her position.'

'I'd rather not,' says Harriet with a shudder. 'Isn't there a defence of marital coercion or something?'

'Hey, hey, look who's awake!' says Ben, returning not with the rolls but with Milo.

The baby, yawning luxuriously, hair ruffled from his sleep, looks calmly around the kitchen as though the events of the past week had never happened.

What resilience! thinks Hester grudgingly, stifling a groan as she tries to get comfortable in her chair. 'Don't you dare say a word to your parents about any of this,' she had warned Ben when he rang home to finalise arrangements for the evening. 'We'll tell them everything in our own good time—including about Daria and Milo.' She and Harriet are still wrestling with the uncomfortable truth that they've deceived George and Isabelle, knowingly and deliberately; they cannot for the moment fathom a way to put a decent complexion on their behaviour. Were they to hear about recent events too soon, their cousins would undoubtedly start fussing and attempting to take the New Year's Eve catering arrangements out of Hester's hands. That she cannot and will not countenance.

Harriet takes Milo from Ben and dandles him. He gurgles.

'Oh, Dar's trying to ring Polina again,' says Ben. 'See if there's any news. I said you wouldn't mind.'

'Mmm,' says Harriet, rapidly swallowing an uncomfortably hot crust from one of the quiches that just happened to come away in her hand while Hester was occupied with her list.

'I expect the police'll want to question me too,' says Ben confidently. 'I'm what they call a material witness.'

Harriet suppresses a smile. 'To what?'

Ben, who has moved on to rolling out thinly-sliced bread for the smoked salmon pinwheels, looks over to where Milo is gleefully grabbing a handful of Harriet's hair and waves a vague hand, 'You know, everything. I been in on it from the off.' He reflects for a moment. 'It is quite exciting, though, whatever Aunt Hester says. You know, big drugs haul, police all over the shop, them poor buggers being locked away out of sight—and all under our noses!'

Certainly under Peggy Verndale's nose, thinks Harriet, remembering Peggy's strident complaints. *She's going to be so furious when she gets wind of what was really happening the other side of her fence* . . . To her nephew Harriet says grimly,

'Not so exciting, Ben, if other criminals find out what's going on and try to muscle in, as they undoubtedly would. Then innocent people get caught up in it. It's not glamorous: it destroys families and communities. Not to mention the havoc drugs wreak on users.'

'Weed?' he says mockingly. 'Come on.'

'Even cannabis,' interjects Hester, forestalling her sister's reply, 'the strength they grow it these days. So while you may have found the past week exciting, I, for one, have had enough excitement to last me a lifetime.'

He shuttles uncomfortably. 'Yeah, okay, fair dos.' He makes himself busy.

The slightly hostile silence is broken by feet running lightly down the stairs. Seconds later Daria bounds into the room, face alight. 'Wonderful! Wonderful news. Artem is coming! To England! It will all be all right. It is exciting, no?'

It takes several minutes for Daria to calm down sufficiently to convey the details of her brother's impending arrival, news of such momentousness it has entirely displaced her remaining anxiety about her status and the hurdles ahead. Artem, it seems, at least in his adoring sister's eyes, will make everything okay. Polina had begun asking around for news of Artem immediately after she and Daria had last spoken, and by chance she had run into a mutual acquaintance the following day. He thought he had heard that Artem was in Lida or Hrodna and he had a number for a contact . . . who passed on a message to . . . someone who had seen Artem a few weeks before and . . . the story, long, convoluted and not helped by Daria's excited machine-gun delivery, culminates in the news that, by methods Daria does not fully understand, Artem has somehow acquired a visa and is even now en route for London.

Oh God, thinks Hester, hating herself.

Here we go again . . . thinks Harriet, berating herself.

'So,' Daria says, beaming, 'please to tell Peter Sampson in case Artem call there and please to ring the . . . that place in London where I am going when I arrive . . .'

'Advice centre?' suggests Harriet.

'*Tak*. Thank you! Oh, I am so happy! I will see Artem, Milo will see uncle. And I will hear'—her face falls for a moment—'about Tata. Soon. Soon.' She drops a kiss on Milo's forehead. 'Uncle Artem is here soon, *soneyka*! He will be loving you!'

Hester and Harriet exchange a look: *Let's hope so*. One of them has to ask.

'Daria, Artem will be here *legally*, won't he?'

Daria, flushing, looks affronted. 'Of course legal! He has visa. He is professor!'

Hester forbears to point out that Daria herself had had a visa when she first arrived . . .

It is left to Harriet to frame the next delicate topic. 'Would you like him to stay for a little while?' Heart sinking, she hopes the emphasis on *little* isn't too obvious.

'Stay? In England? For sure.'

Is she being deliberately obtuse?

'No, we mean here, in this house.'

Daria's eyes widen with delight. 'Artem here? You allow? Oh, Hester, Harriet, you are saint, both. So kind. Kind to me, to Milo, to Artem.' Her eyes glitter. 'How we thank you? Always, you are in our hearts. God is blessing you.'

'Well,' says Hester gruffly. 'I don't know about that.' She musters a smile. 'Looks like we'll just about have time to change the sheets on your bed, Ben, before our next guest—'

'I do it!' cries Daria. 'I do it right now!' She tears upstairs.

And that, it seems, is that.

Hester, urgently in need of some distraction and not trusting herself to speak, reaches over to the table for a bowl and sets about shelling the quails' eggs.

'I can do that!' says Ben.

'There's a knack to it,' she says, carefully rolling the tiny egg on the arm of her chair and teasing the shell off in one long coil. Ben watches admiringly.

'Show us, will you?'

She does, watching him as he tries to master the technique: the first couple he tries emerge a little battered and squashed but he perseveres and soon acquires the knack, grinning at her happily. He's not such a bad lad underneath all that bluster. And he certainly has a light touch with pastry. As long as she's able to push their most recent bombshell to the back of her mind and keep busy, she finds herself quite looking forward to tonight's little gathering. One thing's for sure: George and Isabelle's other guests are in for a treat. The food is going to be superb. She and Ben exchange a smug look and work on.

Harriet, like her sister, in need of some activity and loath to confront the thought of yet more domestic disruption just now, offers her assistance.

Ben waits for Hester to respond and find Harriet some occupation, but she seems lost in thought, so he indicates the pile of washing-up by the sink. 'You could load the dishwasher and make a start on the stuff that wants doing by hand if you like.' He points at a perilous tower of bakeware, trying to keep a straight face as Harriet, who has not expected anyone to take her up on her offer, blenches. Reluctantly she reaches for an apron.

The phone rings.

'I'll get it!' she cries gratefully, and flees.

❧

Harriet finally manages to finish the call. She has to give Peggy her due: she is unrivalled in her ability to sniff out trouble. How does she do it?

'Local news this morning. On the TV. Didn't you see it? Oh, and Facebook,' she says airily, when quizzed. 'Your nephew— Ben, is it?—he's been posting all manner of stuff about all these shenanigans. Cannabis! You might have told me—'

'You're on Facebook?'

'No, of course I'm not on Facebook, Harriet. Why would I be on Facebook? One of my grandsons is and he texted me. Really!' She inhales angrily. 'You see! You wouldn't be told. I said there was something going on up at that place. And didn't I say that Teddy Wilson would have his nose in it? I've an unerring instinct for these things. Still—fancy! Teddy Wilson! Who would have believed it? Well, I would, obviously, I've never pretended otherwise. I always thought there was something not quite pukka about him. I mean, it was Teddy, wasn't it? I know they haven't released any names but that's what everyone's saying. A little birdie told me you had to go down to the station too . . .'

'Peggy, we didn't have to—' How on earth did she get hold of that?

'And I heard there was a young woman and a baby with you. Is that true? I said, *Young woman? Baby? I can't think who that might be.*' Thankfully Peggy swerves on to another track. 'And I said to Ronald: *There you are, you see? Pooh-poohing my suspicions and telling me I was imagining things. Just because you've no sense of smell . . .* And do you know what he said? *Well, why didn't you report it?* And I said, *I didn't know it was cannabis, did I?* How was I supposed to know that? Would you have known, Harriet?' She doesn't wait for a reply. 'Exactly! Of course you wouldn't. People like us don't know about things like that, do we? Thank heavens. But Teddy Wilson!' Harriet imagines her licking her lips. 'So, was he there, at the station?'

'Peggy, I really can't—'

'No, of course you can't say, I understand that. But what exactly was going on up there? Still, that poor woman!'

As Peggy draws breath, Harriet slips in, 'Who are we talking about? Molly or Mrs Vicar?'

'Well, both, Harriet! Do you think perhaps Molly always knew he was a wrong 'un and that's why she drank? I wouldn't be surprised. Imagine, living with the knowledge that your husband was . . . whatever he is! I mean, it would turn anyone to drink!'

'She should have just dobbed him in, then, shouldn't she?' says Harriet. 'Assuming that is, that she knew.'

Veering like a weathercock, Peggy says indignantly, 'Dobbed! *Dobbed?* I'm surprised at you, Harriet, using a word like that. How vulgar. And betray her own husband! I should think not! What a thing to suggest.'

'Well, he betrayed her often enough, by all accounts.'

Peggy huffs and puffs at the other end, unsure where her sympathies should lie. She opts to change tack. 'Never mind Molly,' she says, dismissing her without a qualm, 'Virginia's life is hardly going to be a picnic after this, is it?'

'Virginia? Who on earth is Virginia?'

'The vicar's wife! For heaven's sake, Harriet—keep up!'

'I think you'll find it's—'

'Virginia,' insists Peggy. There is a small pause. 'Or is it Veronica? Well, whatever . . . she's going to have a rough ride, isn't she? I heard there were already reporters camped outside the flat this morning.'

'Perhaps she could sell her story—make a fortune,' says Harriet mischievously. 'The sums they offer are astronomical.'

'Really? How do you know?'

'Oh . . . you know what they're like. Pay the earth for inside information.'

'Inside . . . Good Lord!' says Peggy, almost slavering. 'You know something, don't you? About what's been going on? Harriet! Come on, do tell, your secret's safe with me. Are you and Hester selling your story? You're not, are you? Really?'

Harriet smiles at herself in the hall mirror. She lets the silence stretch, confident Peggy will break first. She does.

'You never are!' Peggy is almost beside herself. 'You want to be very careful, Harriet; they twist things, the media. I've read about it. Still, mind you get your hair done first. They're bound to want a picture. You want to look your best.'

'Good point,' says Harriet. 'Sorry, Peggy, but I really must go.'

'Yes, yes, of course. Well, keep me posted, won't you? Do you know which paper yet? Will it be on the television?'

'Bye, Peggy. Thanks for calling.'

'Ooh, Harriet, before you go—you might want to suggest Hester doesn't wear that brown paisley of hers. It's awfully draining. Don't say I said it though.'

As she finishes the call, Harriet realises Peggy hadn't returned to the topic of Daria and Milo. Riled though she is at Ben's incontinence on social media, she's grateful that at least he's had the nous not to spill the beans about their other guests: the least said about them until their status is clearer, the better. Besides, Peggy is sure to find out all about them soon enough.

Not to mention the next imminent arrival.

'Peggy says not to wear your brown paisley when we're on the news,' Harriet reports when she returns to the kitchen.

'You going on the telly?' says Ben excitedly.

Hester is rolling brandy snaps around a wooden spoon and listening to Radio 4 with half an ear. 'Yes, Ben, and they're making a film about us. Steven Spielberg's popping round for a chat this afternoon.'

'Very funny.'

Under cover of *Moneybox Live*, Harriet sidles around to Ben's side and murmurs, 'By the way, Ben, I understand you've been pasting stuff on Facebook . . .'

'Posting. It's posting. Yeah?' He flashes a glance at Hester, who is apparently caught up in the latest pensions advice.

'Well, you be careful—you don't want to prejudice the prosecution.'

'Prejudice the . . . serious? Will it?'

Harriet realises to her dismay that Ben thinks this is rather an alluring prospect.

'And your parents might get to hear about it.'

That does the trick. Ben's face falls, appalled. 'Jeez . . .'

'Exactly. So schtum from now on, okay?' Ben nods and Harriet raises her voice to make herself heard over the interviewer. 'I must say, this all looks gorgeous. Any more samples going?'

Before Hester can reply, Ben slips two canapés onto a plate and presents it to Harriet with a bow. 'Compliments of the house, madam,' he says.

'We're supposed to be on diets,' tuts Hester, reverting to form.

Harriet steps out of range before Hester can whip the plate away and pops one of the canapés into her mouth.

'Just when I thought you'd stopped all that nonsense!' she says, as the flavours flood her mouth. 'Anyway, you might be on a diet, but recent events suggest life's too short to worry about my cholesterol. Oh my goodness, these are magnificent, Ben!'

'I know. Phat or what? So I've had an idea. I'm thinking of starting a blog. About food and that. With pictures.'

'A blog?' says Hester suspiciously.

Harriet regards her nephew with fondness and admiration. 'That's brilliant. But I've had a thought, Ben, about your A-levels and so forth. Something occurs to me . . .'

Ben gives her an artful grin. 'Yeah. Me too.'

385

CHAPTER 31

23 APRIL

Firelight dances on the ceiling of the sitting room at The Laurels. Hester is poring over a complicated pattern for a multi-coloured cardigan for Milo, muttering irritably to herself as she unpicks a row. This is the fourth item she's knitted for him in as many months; Harriet has never known her so busy. It's typical April weather: after a glorious morning of dazzling sunshine and the promise of spring, sudden squalls swept in mid-afternoon and have continued with varying intensity ever since. Harriet, sitting opposite her sister, listens to a fresh volley of rain on the window, and snuggles deeper into her chair. A fire, at the end of April! And some fools still dispute the existence of global warming . . . She returns to her book of *Guardian* crosswords and the labyrinthine thought processes of the much-lamented Araucaria. In his nineties, he was still capable of foxing the most devoted solver. She rereads the same clue for the hundredth time.

'Oh! I've just remembered,' she says a few minutes later. 'Bumped into Peggy in the Co-op. She says Mrs Vicar's gone back to the rectory.'

'What as?'

Harriet gives her sister a withering look. 'As Mrs Vicar, of course. He's taken her back, apparently.'

They both contemplate a life of perpetual atonement and shiver.

Hester reaches for her glass. 'What time are we expecting Daria tomorrow?' She means Milo, of course: while she is very fond of his mother, it's Milo's bright eyes that light up her own.

'I said to come round for coffee. About ten.'

'Any news?'

'He's got another tooth.'

'I meant . . .'

'I know.'

Three months—nearly four—and they are no nearer to knowing whether Daria will be allowed to stay. Her solicitor is confident she has a solid case: Milo was born in England, his father is English, and Peter Sampson is supporting Daria's application. The Sampsons have been down to visit Milo three times now and have introduced him to his half-sister; each visit has been a little less awkward, although Elizabeth's face continues to betray her sorrow for her lost son. To watch her cradling Milo is heart-rending. Each time they come, Harriet and Hester pray she will announce her pregnancy. They—and she—are still waiting.

'And Artem?' They both smile involuntarily.

Ah, Artem! If it had taken them a few days to take Daria to their bosoms (Milo had been firmly ensconced there from the start), their fondness for her older brother had been instantaneous and mutual. Daria's adoration might have worked to his disadvantage—who could possibly live up to such a billing?—but everything she had said about him had proved true. Bearlike, courteous, gentle and hard-working, they had been utterly captivated by him from the moment he appeared diffidently at their door three days after New Year, drawn face dissolving into such a look of love at the sight of Daria that they had had to look away. His English is excellent but for the occasional confusion: 'It's *A Clockwork Orange*, Artem, not *Chocolate* . . . Yes, you're right, there is a Chocolate Orange, but that's not a film . . .' His usual response to these corrections is a huge guffaw of delight, laughter being his default response to most upsets.

True, there had been a very sticky moment when Milo was first introduced to his uncle and his paternity explained: Hester and Harriet had swiftly stepped in to tell the tale, as Daria shrank back, shielding Milo from Artem's initial anger. He had listened, silent and glowering, to their narrative, betraying no hint of his inner turmoil. Finally, after the full extent of his sister's ordeal since her arrival in England had been related, he had thanked them humbly and taken Daria's hand. 'You have been blessed that these two ladies found you and protected you. I was wrong to be angry. I am proud of you and of my little nephew.' And Daria had thrown herself into her brother's arms, a bemused Milo between them, while Hester and Harriet wiped away surreptitious tears.

Now Artem seems as much as part of their family as Daria and Milo, supporting his sister in her growing autonomy, doting on Milo, and ever careful not to exploit Hester and Harriet's goodwill, adeptly treading the delicate line between dependence and distance. Even Peggy Verndale is charmed by him, simpering whenever they meet. Only Ben treats him with wariness, sniping occasionally about his aunts' supposed favouritism and once, watching brother and sister setting off for a walk, whispering something disparaging about 'spongers' in Milo's ear, unaware that Harriet was within earshot. She had rounded on him, appalled at his attitude, berating him for bigotry, ignorance and spite until, shamed, he had mumbled a surly apology. 'Don't apologise to me! It's Artem you should say sorry to. I'm disappointed in you, Ben, I really am.'

'Jealous,' Hester had observed later.

'Jealous? He can't possibly entertain—'

'Can't he? You've seen the way he always takes her side. I think he fancies himself her knight errant.'

'He wouldn't even know what that meant! Besides, he's fifteen!'

'So?'

Now Harriet watches the frequent exchanges between Ben and Daria with new eyes and realises that Hester is probably right: while Daria treats him indulgently, as she might a younger sibling, he clearly hopes for something more from their relationship. With relief, she sees that his designs have not gone unnoticed by Artem. He'll make sure nothing untoward happens. Besides, the agonies of adolescence require that one should get one's heart broken or at least slightly battered on more than one occasion.

Now she says, 'He's down in London again.'

Artem travels to the capital at least once a week, tirelessly campaigning and soliciting support for Belarusian democracy. Within days of his arrival, he had consulted Daria's solicitor and, on his advice, applied for asylum.

'No news on their father?'

'I assume not. They'd have told us, I'm sure. Artem was speaking to Amnesty International again this week.'

'That's got to help his case, though. Horrible thing to say, but it's proof how bad things are there.'

'I suppose so.'

Harriet puts aside the crossword, hoists herself to her feet and pads through to the kitchen. She listens carefully to make sure Hester hasn't followed her and then reaches for an old sweet tin. Three of Ben's latest experiments—tiny mushroom puffs—nestle inside. *They'll only go stale*, thinks Harriet as she crams one into her mouth, relishing the creamy filling and hint of tarragon.

'Harry!'

Harriet almost drops the tin as Hester snatches it from her. She must have a sixth sense: nearly every time Harriet tries to sneak herself a little treat, she is found out. It makes her feel about five years old.

'I was saving those for Finbar!'

Finbar, thinks Harriet darkly, *does very well out of us. Very well indeed. Anyone would suppose he was the valued patron of a fine-dining establishment, not a freeloading vagrant who lives in a bus shelter and is given preference over me . . .*

'Honestly,' Hester is now grumbling, shoving the tin back on the shelf, 'you can't be trusted. Here am I trying to feed you healthily and you stuff yourself behind my back and undo all my good work.' She sniffs. 'It's not as though *I* don't cook you nice meals.'

'You do, you do,' agrees Harriet placatingly. 'But we have to encourage Ben, don't we? I'm his taster in chief.'

'Indeed you are,' says Hester acerbically. 'Never knowingly underfed.'

'You're not . . .' A thought has crept into Harriet's head.

'Not what?'

'Nothing.' Harriet decides not to voice it.

'No. What?' Hester's head goes back pugnaciously.

'It's just . . . well, you've been the tiniest bit short-tempered recently. I wondered—'

'Short-tempered!' snaps Hester. 'I have not been short-tempered! Well, if I have, is it surprising, after all that's gone on recently? Endless visits to and from the police, pestered for weeks by wretched reporters, all the anxiety over Daria and Artem, finding them somewhere halfway decent to live, the trial hanging over our heads—'

'Do you miss them?'

'Who?' Hester knows perfectly well to whom her sister refers. 'Of course not. They needed a place of their own.'

The village had rallied round magnificently after the terrible events at the farm came to light, appalled that anything so horrendous should have been going on under their unsuspecting noses. One of the wealthier residents had provided a small cottage, rent-free, which the authorities had granted brother and sister leave to reside in while their applications were in progress. Artem, unable to take a job while his application for asylum was under consideration, was offered countless odd jobs, receiving payment in food and fuel. No-one is quite sure if this is strictly legal; no-one is minded to investigate too deeply.

'Is it Ben?' asks Harriet gently.

'What about Ben?'

'I mean, we haven't seen that much of him recently. Except when he drops by with things for us to try. Me to try, I mean . . . I thought you might be missing him.' She waits for Hester to explode.

'Missing him! Making a mess of my kitchen . . . throwing flour all over the shop . . .' She stops, mouth pursed.

Harriet puts a hand on her arm. 'Hetty, he'd never have done it without you. You know that.'

'Of course he would.'

'No. You gave him the encouragement he needed, showed him he was good at something. You did that.'

Hester shrugs. 'I just let him experiment . . .'

'Exactly. It was you who persuaded George and Isabelle that an academic route wasn't necessarily for him. Look how happy he is now with their new kitchen. Look how happy George and Isabelle are too, now that Ben does most of the cooking. That's all down to you.'

'Well,' Hester can't help pointing out as she struggles to maintain her customary composure, 'you say it's not academic, cooking, but let me tell you, there's a lot of science involved. He's going to have his work cut out, that young man. Up at dawn, punishing hours . . . he needn't think he's going to swan in and start cooking all the fancy stuff from the off. I've been checking out these courses he's considering . . .'

'Have you?' says Harriet innocently, knowing full well her sister, aside from following Ben's increasingly popular blog, has been assiduously researching his options for months. The prospectuses dropping on the mat at regular intervals have rather given the game away, not to mention the hours she's spent on the computer.

Hester gives her sister an appraising look. They know each other too well: it's hard for either of them to hoodwink the other. 'Any of that Sancerre left?'

Harriet opens the fridge. 'A couple of glasses.' She smiles and makes for the sitting room with the bottle. 'I've been thinking . . . we really ought to sort out our holiday. You know how quickly that hotel gets booked up. And we do like our usual rooms.' She pours the wine and settles back in her chair. 'Hetty?'

Hester slowly returns and stands in front of the fire, watching the flames. She seems lost in thought.

'Hetty?'

'Mmm?'

'The Scillies? Should we book?'

Hester eases herself back into her armchair and reaches for her knitting, then stops. 'We'll have to check the dates with the police. There's the trial and everything.'

'They said not before the autumn at the earliest. Inspector Parton thought it mightn't be until November. Chances are they won't need us anyway.'

'Right.' Hester is staring into the fire again. A log disintegrates in a small cloud of ash. She leans forward and absent-mindedly prods it with the poker.

Harriet examines her sister's averted face, anxiety stealing over her. Hester looks troubled. Has their ordeal taken more of a toll on her than Harriet realised? Perhaps she's frightened to leave their home, feels safer in familiar surroundings? Perhaps the memories of that extraordinary week, the dangers they faced, both real and imagined, have eroded her self-confidence ... She regrets now so readily pooh-poohing the counselling they had been offered. People react in many different ways to stress. She ought to have been more attuned to Hester's moods, kept a closer eye on her. Maybe she should offer her a way out ... 'On second thoughts, I suppose Daria might need us. Or Artem. We don't want to be out of contact if something crops up.'

'Out of contact?' exclaims Hester. 'We're only talking about the Scilly Isles, Harry, not the back of beyond!'

'All the same . . .'

Harriet sits back, momentarily defeated. Something's not right, that's for sure. She just wishes she could fathom what it is. Goodness knows if anywhere is safe and familiar, it's the Scillies . . .

'Harry?' says Hester, breaking into her thoughts. 'Are you all right?'

'Me? Fine. Are you?'

Hester laughs. Is it a genuine laugh or the tiniest bit forced? Harriet can't be sure. 'Couldn't be better.'

'But . . . you're not keen on having a holiday?'

'Of course I am,' says Hester heartily. 'I think a holiday's a splendid idea.'

'You do?' *What a relief.*

'Absolutely.'

'So . . . shall I book?'

Hester hesitates. *Oh dear,* she thinks, *I do hope Harry won't be too disappointed.* 'Not the Scillies, again, though, eh?'

Aha, thinks Harriet, *so I was right . . .*

'I just wondered,' says Hester, eyes fixed firmly on the glowing logs, 'whether this year we mightn't try somewhere a little more exciting . . .'

ACKNOWLEDGEMENTS

My dear friend and nagger-in-chief Ann Stutz, without whom this novel would never have seen the light of day. My agent Jane Gregory and in-house editor Stephanie Glencross at Gregory & Co, my Australian editors at Allen & Unwin, Annette Barlow and Michelle Swainson, and Clare Drysdale and Sam Redman in London for their enthusiasm, support and wise words. The teaching staff on the MA in Creative Writing at Nottingham Trent University, particularly Sarah Jackson and the late Graham Joyce for encouragement and advice. Galina Palyvian, Translator, Russian Translation Service, United Nations; the Immigration Advice Service (London); and Yvonne Coen QC: all misinterpretations and errors of language and law are my own. Lastly, my husband and two sons for their unflagging encouragement and love.

ABOUT THE AUTHOR

Hilary Spiers writes plays, novels and short stories. She enjoys giving a voice to ordinary women in sometimes extraordinary circumstances. Born in London, she now lives in the finest stone town in England.